SPELLS *for* LOST THINGS

ALSO BY
JENNA EVANS WELCH

Love & Gelato

Love & Luck

Love & Olives

SPELLS
FOR LOST
THINGS

∞ JENNA EVANS WELCH ∞

SIMON & SCHUSTER BFYR

New York London Toronto Sydney New Delhi

SIMON & SCHUSTER BFYR

An imprint of Simon & Schuster Children's Publishing Division
1230 Avenue of the Americas, New York, New York 10020

This book is a work of fiction. Any references to historical events,
real people, or real places are used fictitiously. Other names, characters, places,
and events are products of the author's imagination, and any resemblance to
actual events or places or persons, living or dead, is entirely coincidental.

SIMON & SCHUSTER BOOKS FOR YOUNG READERS
and related marks are trademarks of Simon & Schuster, Inc.
For information about special discounts for bulk purchases, please contact Simon & Schuster
Special Sales at 1-866-506-1949 or business@simonandschuster.com.
The Simon & Schuster Speakers Bureau can bring authors to your live event.
For more information or to book an event, contact the Simon & Schuster Speakers
Bureau at 1-866-248-3049 or visit our website at www.simonspeakers.com.
Interior design by Tom Daly
The text of this book was set in Adobe Caslon Pro.
The illustrations for this book were rendered digitally.
Manufactured in the United States of America
First Edition
2 4 6 8 10 9 7 5 3 1
Library of Congress Cataloging-in-Publication Data
Names: Welch, Jenna Evans, author.
Title: Spells for lost things / Jenna Welch.
Description: First edition. | New York City : Simon & Schuster Books for Young Readers,
[2022] | Audience: Ages 12 up. | Audience: Grades 7-9. | Summary: Willow and Mason,
two teens who are unceremoniously dragged to Salem, Massachusetts for the summer,
meet and help each other figure out their places in the world.
Identifiers: LCCN 2022021167 (print) | LCCN 2022021168 (ebook) |
ISBN 9781534448872 (hardcover) | ISBN 9781534448896 (ebook)
Subjects: CYAC: Friendship—Fiction. | Foster home care—Fiction. | Mothers and daughters—
Fiction. | Mothers and sons—Fiction. | Salem (Mass.)—Fiction. | LCGFT: Novels.
Classification: LCC PZ7.1.W435 Sp 2022 (print) | LCC PZ7.1.W435 (ebook) | DDC
[Fic]—dc23
LC record available at https://lccn.loc.gov/2022021167
LC ebook record available at https://lccn.loc.gov/2022021168

For my mother,
a kitchen witch
who has always been
a bit
Magic

SPELLS *FOR* LOST THINGS

Prologue

Willow

FERNWEH (noun): A German word that means "farsickness," best understood as the opposite of homesickness. A longing for far-off places, in particular those you haven't seen yet. In my case, a chronic, all-consuming, near-debilitating condition causing frequent feelings of panic, claustrophobia, and general distress. Alleviated only by actual travel and obsessive travel research, or by hanging out in my bedroom, which is basically a large travel collage.

See also: *wanderlust*, although much more intense.

See also: *Willow Haverford* (me).

See also: *excellent way to ignore the fact that although I definitely have a place to live, I most definitely do not have a place where I belong. It turns out that home and belonging aren't necessarily the same thing.*

Mason

ASTROPHILE (noun): An individual who is excessively fond of (possibly obsessed with) the study of stars and other celestial phenomena occurring outside of the earth's atmosphere. Typically an amateur, the astrophile may employ tools such as an observation notebook (logbook containing records of night-sky observations), binoculars, and, if they're lucky, a telescope. Not to be confused with an astrologer, a person who uses the stars to tell the future and is the exact opposite of what I do.

See also: *stargazer*, which is what my foster care worker wrongly called me at my last placement meeting. I don't gaze. I study. I sketch. I take notes.

See also: *Mason Greer* (me).

See also: *excellent distraction from the fact that I have zero control over my life here on planet Earth and that the one person I truly belong with has been out of my reach since I was barely a preteen.*

Willow

The day I finish high school, I'm packing everything I care about, boarding a plane to London, and never looking back.

Unless, of course, I decide to start out in Prague. Or Rome. Or Dubai. I hear Edinburgh is deliciously moody in the summertime, and the powdery white beaches of Mykonos are capable of dissolving every worry you've ever had. Lucky for me, the destination isn't really the game changer here—what's important is the *plan*. The moment the final bell rings on my final day at my LA prep school, I'll walk (okay, *sprint*) out the door, fly down all thirty steps, launch myself into a cab, and head straight to the airport for my international flight to Istanbul.

Or Tokyo.

Possibly Sydney?

The important part is that I'm gone. Out of here and away from everything, my before life simply one of my many stops on my journey as a globetrotter.

My wanderlust started with my trip to Paris the summer between ninth and tenth grade. The official reason for my visit was to keep my cousin Beatrice company while her dad worked on a new film project and her mom taught summer classes. The real reason was my insides had been torn in two.

Six months before, on my last day of Christmas break, my parents had taken me to our favorite Chinese restaurant, a dim little spot with greasy menus and the best sweet and sour pork in Brooklyn. The server had just brought our drink orders when my mom said quietly, "We have something we need to tell you." I looked up and noticed the way they were leaning away from each other, and I knew.

Families splitting are like earthquakes. Yes, they are happening every day all over the world, but that doesn't make them any less shocking when they happen to you.

It took less than a month for my parents to divide our life up, and a little under five months for the divorce to be finalized. As far as I could tell, they didn't fight against or for each other; they simply ended, their marriage dissolving as easily as a sugar cube in hot tea, a part of me dissolving with it.

I think the aspect that stunned me most was how quickly my mom and dad moved into their post-divorce lives. It was like they had both been building up energy for years, ready for the moment when they could take off down the runway. My mom's luxury event–planning company suddenly became an enormous success that eventually resulted in her taking on a new business partner named Drew and relocating to Los Angeles, taking me (reluctantly) with her. I thought when we moved to LA that Mom and I would find a groove, start living out our mother-daughter dreams together, but all that seemed to happen was she got busier and busier.

Back home in Brooklyn, my dad started dating Chloe, a graphic designer he'd worked with for a few years. They were engaged and pregnant with triplets (yes, triplets) within ten months.

I'd like to say I handled all of this with grace, but the fact is, ages fourteen and fifteen were not my finest moments.

I yelled. I threw things. One night I went out with friends and didn't come home until four in the morning. Worst of all, I stopped caring about *everything*. My parents' divorce felt physical, like a giant, hungry monster had taken up residence in center of my chest, devouring everything that used to make me happy. I had a hard time eating, thinking, staying interested in anything, really. My grades dipped, and I stopped calling friends on weekends, or playing tennis, or combing through thrift shops on my way home from school. I felt lost and disoriented, shuffling from home to home, neither of them feeling *right*.

Like with most problems, Paris was the answer.

It was my mom's idea that I go stay with my (sort-of) cousin Beatrice. Our dads are technically ex-stepbrothers, but I'm claiming her because not only is she my best friend, she's easily my most favorite person on earth. Part of it is her exceptionally fantastic worldliness: she's lived in five countries, and when you ask her how many languages she's fluent in, she shrugs and says something impossibly cool like, *Depends on what your definition of fluent is.* She knows how to navigate the Métro, how to order café crème at tiny Parisian cafes, how to talk intimidating-looking bouncers into letting you into clubs, and how to pair ratty sneakers with rumpled dresses and still manage to look *très chic.* Even her name is glossy and beautiful-sounding, pronounced *Bay-uh-treece*, or *Bay-uh*, for short.

I, on the other hand, was an absolute disaster in Paris. I asked for ice in my soda and kept forgetting to say *"Bonjour!"* when I walked into shops. I got off on the wrong Métro stop at least once a day, and smiled at people for no good reason. One day while Bea was busy at an appointment, I showed up at the Louvre without a prior reservation (*mon Dieu!*).

What I'm trying to say is, I had never felt so out of place. And I *loved every minute of it*.

Ever since our final family dinner at the Chinese restaurant, I'd been stumbling around in a kind of stupor, wondering desperately if I'd ever feel like I fit in anywhere ever again. At my mom's, I was one more detail to manage in her overly busy life. In my dad's burgeoning new family, I was literally in the way.

But in Paris? I reveled in my displacement. I was a misfit on *purpose*. I showed up with no idea who I was, and the City of Lights said, *No problem. We've been welcoming random American weirdos for decades now. Have you checked out the Quartier Latin?* Pas de problème! *I'll give you directions.*

When I say I dove into everything Paris had to offer, what I mean is I ran to the deep end and cannonballed in. During the day, I devoured the city, a reluctant Bea in tow. I dragged her to sprawling parks and gardens, museums, cluttered book stalls by the Seine, towering cathedrals, and every sunny café I could find. At night we went out with her friends to clubs and cinemas and delightfully smoky cafes. I loved every day of that trip so much that at night when I had the covers pulled up under my chin, I had to put my hand to my chest to be sure that my heart hadn't fallen out of my body. And it wasn't only the twisty roads and twinkly bridges and heavenly smelling crepe stands that captured me. No. In every single one of those adventures, I saw something life-changing.

Possibility.

More specifically, the possibility of one day *feeling at home again*. I'd boarded the plane to visit Bea's family feeling about as rooted as a tumbleweed, but in the unfamiliar streets of Paris, the ground had steadied under my feet. So what if I barely saw my mom anymore, and even when I did, she still felt a million miles away? So what if my dad's new family had filled up our old apartment, my bedroom now a nursery, every square inch crammed with unfamiliar things? So what if I no longer belonged anywhere? So what? There was an entire world out there.

As Saint Augustine of Hippo said: *The world is a book, and those who do not travel only read one page.* Well, I'm going to read every page I can. One of those pages is going to tell me the answer to where I belong. My home is out there.

All I have to do is find it.

Mason

Back in the Middle Ages, people believed that the stars governed our lives. They thought that the planets controlled our destinies, caused illnesses, managed our luck, all of it. Some people still believe it. My mom was one of those people; probably still is. She read her horoscope religiously, and even when things were going really badly for us, she always thought that our luck was about to change, which didn't make sense, because our life was basically a rotating dumpster fire of broken relationships and lost jobs. It wasn't the stars controlling our lives; it was her addiction.

On the days when she was around and lucid enough to be out of bed, she checked her horoscope first thing and she'd call me over to read me mine. Her zodiac sign was Pisces, which she said was the reason for her always being so overly trusting and attention-seeking. I had my own theories, but I knew enough to not share those with her. I'm a Sagittarius, which she said makes me naturally idealistic, and my ruling planet is Jupiter, which means I'm lucky.

Again, no comment from me.

Our horoscopes always said vague things that could apply to

anyone, things like *Ambition can be a strong force for good, but be sure to keep it in check* or *Your physical surroundings have a powerful effect on your well-being*, but my mom treated them like powerful directives from the Universe, a love letter sent directly to her. After she finished reading, we'd spend twenty minutes straightening whatever apartment we were crashing in, or trying to figure out how ambition was leading her off-course, before she'd get a phone call from a boyfriend or a dealer, sometimes both, and she'd close herself back in her room.

One morning I woke up to her shaking my shoulder. It was early, which meant she hadn't ever gone to bed, and her eyes were wide and too bright. "Mason, read this," she said, shoving her phone into my hand. Her web browser was opened to her favorite site, My Horoscope Daily, and she'd pulled up the Capricorn page. The webpage was glowing purple in my half-dark bedroom, and I had to rub my eyes a few times for the words to become clear. *Signs come in threes. Watch for them.*

She leaned in closer. "You see? All we need to do is keep our eyes open. We'll see the signs. Three of them."

I had no idea what she was talking about, so I mumbled a "Cool, Mom," assuming she'd forget all about it, but the three thing stuck. From then on, everywhere we went she looked for three. We chose motel rooms based on whether or not the room number was divisible by three, she turned down streets with threes, she listened for three birdcalls before leaving the house in the morning, every time we went to the grocery store for toothpaste or boxes of cereal, she made sure she bought three of them. One summer we moved to Maine because three people had mentioned it in the course of a month.

The problem was that I had never seen anything that looked legitimately like a sign, let alone three.

The last time she talked to me about signs was at a supervised visit at a park in Boston. I'd been in and out of foster care for four years by then, and my mom looked worse than I'd ever seen her. She was painfully thin, and I could tell she was having a hard time sitting still on the bench. I knew she was itching for a cigarette and I wished they'd let her go have one. She kept calling me "baby" and trying to smooth my hair, which I hated, and she kept telling me she was getting her life back together, that it was going to be me and her soon. She'd dropped out of a bunch of rehab programs already and I knew the state wouldn't let me go back with her unless she got sober for at least a year and had her own apartment. I remember being annoyed with everything that day—my mom, the system, how long all of this was taking, even the dumb jokes she kept telling me that were making me laugh. How was it possible to be so frustrated with someone and still love them so much?

When our time was up, my mom cupped her hand under my chin and smiled at me, and maybe it's just my brain trying to make our last moment together pleasant, but I like to think we had a nice moment. She'd said, "Remember, baby, we belong together. It will all work out for us. Keep watching for the signs; they'll come in threes." And then she walked to her car, her hand already reaching into her back pocket for a pack of cigarettes, her long black hair streaked orange with bleach. As she opened the car door, I caught sight of her tattoo, a pink pearl and shell she'd gotten in honor of her absolute favorite thing: mermaids.

Of course, I had no idea that this would be the last time I'd see her for years, but looking back at what I wrote in my star log that night, I wonder if I at least suspected it.

> *June 5. Too much light pollution to see anything but*
> *Sirius A.*
>
> > *A star went missing yesterday. It was in a galaxy*
> > *seventy-five million light-years away, and definitely*

*memorable—giant, hot, and crystal blue. Scientists
have been watching it for decades now, but recently
someone went to look for it and it had vanished.*

*But giant stars don't quietly vanish. They explode
themselves into massive supernovas that outshine
everything around them until they collapse into a black
hole. The bigger the star, the bigger the show. No one
would have missed this one exploding.*

*There are some theories—maybe it dimmed slowly
and then some space dust hid it from view? Or maybe
it wasn't a star at all but light coming from another
supernova? I can't stop thinking about it. Stars this big
and bright don't simply disappear.*

That was the last time I saw her. After years of incarcerations and
rehabs and homelessness, she suddenly went dark, vanished into the
atmosphere without a trace. But that's not how giant stars work, and
unlike the crystal-blue star, she left instructions. *Remember, baby, we
belong together. It will all work out for us. Keep watching for the signs;
they'll come in threes.* That's the thing I hang on to. One day we'll be
back together and my life will make sense again.

Until then, I keep my eyes on the stars.

Willow

I don't mean to be dramatic, but me floating facedown on a half-deflated pool float shaped like a piece of pizza feels like an apt representation of my current mental state.

Dramatic? Unmoored? A tiny bit ridiculous?

Yes, yes, and definitely yes.

I roll over onto my back—an act that takes considerable effort due to the deflated-pizza situation—and stare up into the sunshine. LA is not cooperating with this moment of angst. If anything, it's more beautiful than normal. The sky is almost hyperpigmented blue, and my mom's new fountain bubbles cheerfully from the lawn. I can hear her speaking to her team through the open window, and her voice is its usual calm timbre, which is one of her superpowers. Mary Haverford never breaks under pressure.

Except for last night? Our conversation had definitely cracked her otherwise impenetrable surface, and I'm still trying to figure out why.

It had all been going so well. I had my entire speech prepared. Even Bea said it was flawless. All I had to do was explain to my mom the many reasons why it would be a great idea to move in with Bea to complete my senior year at the international school where her dad teaches film part-time. The reasons were as follows: cultural experience, relatively affordable (because I have a built-in host family plus a tuition discount from Bea's dad, it would actually cost *less* than my LA prep school), time with family, and an interesting experience to write about in college essays.

I thought I was batting a thousand.

It's hard to pinpoint exactly when it went completely off the rails. Was it when I uttered the words "senior year abroad"? Or was it "leaving home early"? Because she'd looked stunned. Stricken, almost. And then hurt. That was the part that surprised me the most, because I honestly thought she'd be relieved. With me in Paris, she could focus 100 percent of her time on her work as opposed to her regular 99 percent.

My mom and her business partner, Drew, have their entire staff assembled in our dining room for a meeting, and her voice floats from the open window. "A strong contingency plan is crucial for this event. There are a lot of moving parts, and I can't risk damaging this relationship."

She clearly isn't worried about damaging *our* relationship. Why had my mom looked so petrified when I told her my idea? Is it because me going to Paris wasn't her idea, and therefore she can't micromanage it?

I look longingly toward the pool chair where my phone is perched. I want to talk all this through with Bea, but she is in an intensive ballet program this summer, practicing her arabesques and fouetté turns while being yelled at by a variety of terrifying ballet headmistresses. That means it will probably be another hour before I can expect to hear from her, and I am literally counting down the seconds.

Bea will know what to do. She always does. My pizza float bumps up against the wall and I push off with my feet, launching myself into the deep end. If I'm going to feel this adrift, I may as well be this adrift.

Mom's voice again. ". . . we have to leave absolutely nothing to chance. . . ."

I sigh and flop forward onto the pizza slice so my arms and legs can drag in the water. This is the problem. My mom has no tolerance for leaving things to chance, whereas I am in a constant state of wanting to take chances.

Last night had only highlighted the realization that had been creeping up on me for the past year or so. My mom and I are so different, we may as well be existing on separate continents, and no matter how much I want to pretend that isn't painful, it is. A part of me had thought that once we arrived in LA, we'd build a mother-daughter relationship like the one Bea has with her mom, but two years in I only feel farther from her.

Maybe that's part of my wanderlust. Once I'm out in the world, there will be a physical reason for the distance between my mom and me. Maybe then it won't hurt so much?

"WILLLLLOOOOOOOOWWWW!"

I hear them before I see them. The back door of the house flies open and Drew's son, Noah, and an unidentified number of Noah's preteen friends all sprint out onto the pool deck. Ever since Mom installed the pool, Noah and his friends have been a permanent fixture in my life. They are obnoxious, loud, and wherever they go, the heady scent of Axe body spray follows.

I don't even have time to take cover.

The boys catapult into the pool, and I immediately lose custody of the pizza float, which—okay. Fine. But before I can fully recover, one of them starts shooting me with a Super Soaker, and another does a backflip off the diving board, somehow managing to land directly on top of my head while another attempts to swipe my sunglasses.

"Argggh—Noah, call off your goons!" I yell, then I swim for my life, making my way to the side where my phone rests, and send a text to Bea as I pull myself out of the water. SOS.

Noah swims up next to me, churning his legs to keep his head above water. "Willow, did you get my text about going out with me on Friday?" He grins, showing off a glistening mouth of braces, and the hooligans closest to him break out into a series of hoots. I have to give him props for his bravery. And persistence. This is the third time he's asked me out this month.

I sigh and set down my phone. "Noah, I'd be happy to go to the movie with you but not *on a date*. You're twelve."

Two soggy eyebrows go up, and he does his best to give me a suave look. "Thirteen next summer. You're only three years older than me."

You have to admire that kind of misplaced confidence. He goes to the same prep school as me, which means Drew is paying an astonishing amount of money for these lackluster math skills.

"You're twelve and I'll be seventeen in three weeks. We're five years apart." I try to keep my voice gentle—because rejection sucks no matter how old you are—but I'm beginning to lose patience.

"So I'll take that as a maybe," Noah says, flashing me a shiny braces-laden smile.

"You'll take that as a no," I say sternly. "You're too young. Besides, I don't even date people *my* age."

He tilts his head to the side, smacking his left ear. "Why not?"

Because high school relationships are stupid, limiting, and distracting. Because I don't believe in the whole Cinderella thing. Because why would I spend my time falling for someone when I plan to take off the moment I can?

I point to the deep end of the pool. "Could you look for my earring at the bottom? I think it fell off earlier."

He takes the bait, splashing me in his rush. I throw a towel around myself and sink back into the lawn chair, settling my sunglasses over my eyes. The sun beats down on me as Mom's words from last night pound my brain. *Willow, now is not the time for travel. It's time to get ready for college. Have you read through the college prep books I left on your dresser?*

I did read the books. The problem is that none of them have any tips for what to do if the mere thought of one more year of awkward silences between you and your mother makes you feel like you're sitting in the center of a hornet's nest.

The situation got so critical that I made the desperate move of texting my dad for backup. But all he responded with was a heart emoji and a quick Talk soon.

Not holding my breath on that one. Although my dad is the one much more likely to be up for me taking the unconventional route, at the moment he is also up to his literal eyeballs in toddlers. Any offspring that is not attempting to swallow small objects at all hours of the day naturally gets pushed to the bottom of the list, and even when he does remember to call me, he's so exhausted, he can barely form full sentences. Which I get. People obviously have lives.

My phone begins to ring, snapping me back to the pool, where the boys now appear to be engaging in ritualistic hazing. When I see the name on the screen, I sigh in relief. *Finally.* I hit answer on the video call. "Night, Bea."

"Morning, Willow," she says. As transcontinental best friends, it's our customary greeting. She's sitting on the balcony of her family's apartment. Behind her is the city spread out so dark and glittery, it makes the edges of my heart ache.

For a moment I consider *not* telling her, but of course Bea, being Bea, immediately homes in on my actual mood. "What's wrong with your face?" she demands.

"Nothing is wrong with my face," I say, doing my best to not be offended. Bea can be very blunt. "This is the way it looks. How was ballet?"

"Willow, something's wrong," she insists. "Your eyes are squinty and you're fake smiling. What is it? Is your dad not answering your calls again?"

This is literally the only thing I can't stand about Bea. Anytime I try to hide The Feelings, she insists on dragging The Feelings out. My dad and his family are spending a month in Australia visiting Chloe's grandmother, who is not doing very well. No, I was not invited. Yes, that's completely fine. I mean, yes, I was supposed to spend most of my summer with them, and Melbourne is high on my list, but those tickets were expensive.

I shrug, trying my best to look nonchalant. "I haven't been able to talk to him in like a week, but that's because the time change threw them off. The real problem is that I'm being hit on by prepubescent boys." Noah has given up on my nonexistent earring and is now attempting a backflip off the diving board.

Her right eyebrow manages to climb a fraction or two higher. "Willow?"

I exhale. "Fine. Mom and I talked last night. About our idea."

"Ahh!" She lets out a little scream, then gets closer to the screen, her face a bright, beaming circle as she bounces excitedly. "*La vache!* Last night was the *night*, wasn't it? No wonder you're acting so coy with me, I forgot to ask how it went. What did she think? Did she think our idea was brilliant?"

I grip the phone a little tighter. "Well . . . that's one way to put it."

Bea completely misses my tone, taking off at a full gallop. "Mom and I have it all worked out. We'll share a room, and you can drive to school with us. I leave school early every day for ballet, but you can take the bus home. You can spend Christmas with us, or maybe we'll all go to spend time with your dad—"

"Bea," I say, but she doesn't notice. Once Bea gets going, momentum seems to take over.

"Applications are due in only a week, but if you need more time, my mom can get the principal to make an exception. You'll need an essay and to send your transcript. Do you think you should come a week or two before? And are you okay with sharing a bedroom with me?"

My stomach is cannonballing like the preteens in the pool because Bea sounds as excited as I was and now I have to tell her the terrible news. "Bea!" My tone finally catches her attention. I take a deep breath. "Bea, she won't let me go."

Her mouth opens slightly. "What?"

"My mom said no." My words hang heavy in the humid air.

"But why would she say no? It's all planned. We've arranged everything." When she's impatient, her French accent gets a bit stronger.

My stomach is churning. I pull my knees into my chest, try to breathe. "She said I need to be focusing on college."

"But . . . what does that have to do with anything? You can focus on college here."

I hug my knees in tighter. "That's what I told her."

"And?" Bea says.

My miserable face must say it all.

"*Merde*," she whispers. Her brows furrow, and we're silent for a moment. "Do you want my mom to call yours? She might be able to give her another perspective. She *loves* it when her students have experience in other countries."

Bea's mom is a writing teacher at a small university in Paris, so in theory she might be of help, but after the force—nay, intensity—of my mom's reaction last night, I know for a fact it will do nothing. My best option is to appeal to my dad, but how am I going to do that when I can't even get him to call me back?

Before I can stop it, my eyes prickle with tears, which Bea of course notices. "Willow, it will be okay. Really. Maybe . . ."

Her expression falls and I'm instantly flooded with guilt. I hate the idea of my bad mood transferring to her, so I quickly shift gears. "Enough about me. How's Julia?"

Julia is Bea's on-again-off-again girlfriend, and I can typically count on bringing her up to wipe out whatever other topic I'm attempting to avoid. But not today.

"Willow, you can talk to me about tough things too, you know," she says, her eyes big and insistent. "You don't always have to pretend that everything is fine. I'm *here* for you."

A puddle has formed around me, a slight breeze cooling my skin. Part of me wants to tell Bea the real reason I want to leave home early is the woman currently discussing the likelihood of rain at the charity event she's hosting: "We'll need all tents on hand. Plan B has to be flawless."

Bea is watching me carefully now. "Willow . . . is there something else? Are you okay?"

As usual, she's seen right to my center, and my throat goes tight. But explaining the giant mess that is my head to anyone, even Bea, feels impossible. I shut my eyes behind my sunglasses again and an image emerges of our old Brooklyn apartment, my mom, my dad, and me squished in the tiny breakfast nook arguing over Scrabble. The truth is, I haven't felt grounded or settled or at home since the day my mom and I moved out. Which is ridiculous. I have a perfectly lovely home. Two of them. But I miss feeling *at* home.

I've tried to explain my need to travel to Bea, but every time I do, my words fall flat. I've read so many articles and blog posts by other people who experience intense wanderlust, the constant feeling of the world tugging them by the arm. But sometimes I wonder if what I'm feeling is in a different category entirely. It feels less like a desire than a need. Like if I don't get out there and find my place, I'm going to drift out into nothingness, attached to no one and nothing. My breathing starts to quicken and I feel the rush of anxiety pressing down on me. I have to redirect myself. And Bea.

"I'm just really eager to get started traveling," I mumble. It's true, even if it isn't the full truth. "Let's talk later. I'm going to go run on my mom's treadmill." I'm already on my feet, itching to get my body moving. If I sit here with my thoughts for one more minute, I'm going to explode, and I definitely don't want to take out my anxiety on Bea.

"Willow . . . ," Bea says, disapproval etched on her forehead.

"Excuse me, Willow?" The voice comes from directly above me, and I startle, blinking into the sun. It's my mom's assistant, Phoebe, a relatively new recruit handled to hire the burgeoning social media side of Mary Haverford Events. Like most of my mom's employees, she's adopted my mother's daily uniform of crisp white blouse, tailored pants, and minimal jewelry. My mother doesn't just hire employees, she hires devotees. "Can I talk to you for a minute?" Her voice has an air of urgency that makes my heart sink.

This is another part of my LA life I'd love to leave behind. I am regularly summoned.

"Got to run, Bea. Talk to you soon?"

"Very soon." Bea gives me one last concerned look before blowing a kiss and hanging up.

I make my way to my feet. I'm still dripping, my arms and legs lined with goose bumps. "Hi, Phoebe. What's up?" I ask, doing my best to hide the fact that I'm speaking around a lump in my throat.

"So sorry to interrupt you, Willow, but we just finished our staff meeting, and your mom would like a word. Inside." She hesitates. "And, ah, it needs to happen *right away*."

The last two words are heavy with meaning. Of course. My mom probably wants to follow up on last night's conversation. A stupidly optimistic part of me had hoped that she'd let things go, let the issue marinate a bit before we dished it up again. But my mom is not one to let things go. She is ferocious and relentless and very, very in charge. In the words of her favorite poem, my mother *never* goes gentle into that good night.

She probably wants to make sure I'm not getting any more wild ideas.

Phoebe is blinking more than her usual amount. "Are you okay, Willow?"

My vision is tunneling again, anxiety filtering through my body at full speed. I'm a balloon. I'm a tumbleweed, uprooted and ready to go flying into the unknown. Luckily, I have a trick for this.

I don't even have to look through my travel magazines anymore. All I have to do is focus, and there they are: postcards from my future. I see bright city streets and tiny fishing villages, cloud-shrouded mountains and peaceful beaches, all places my feet have never touched but that I know anyway. Those images feel engraved on my soul, my heart a blank passport book anxious to be filled. The desire to get out there and see it all is so visceral, I can practically hear it rushing in my ears.

Go go go.

Soon. All I have to do is survive one more year as an island, and then no one can stop me.

"Willow?" Phoebe prompts again. Her smile is brittle. She's worried about disappointing my mom. "You okay?"

I take a deep breath and attempt a smile. "Completely okay. Thanks for asking."

Mason

In the late 1600s Salem, Massachusetts, was the trial site of nineteen innocent people who were found guilty of witchcraft and sentenced to death, which I assume is the reason I am being driven there in a golden Toyota Corolla listening to slow jams of the early 2000s while hitting every single red light in the Greater Boston area.

To die. Or at least to suffer greatly.

My new foster care worker's name is either Kate or Kaitlin, I can't remember which, and I can't figure that out without asking her or looking at her I.D. badge, which is always settled directly between her boobs, thereby making the whole thing more awkward than it needs to be. She's youngish, probably in her late twenties, so still carrying a bit of hope, but she's overworked because they all are. And watching her slowly wilt over the past few months while the Morgans get qualified to become foster parents has been stupidly depressing. It's like the plants my mom used to bring home from the grocery store. She'd walk in carrying a brand-new one, its leaves springy and youthful, and then she'd put it in the corner of the house and maybe water it for the first week, and then after that I'd watch it die a slow, colorless death.

That's what Kate/Kaitlin is like. My mom's dying houseplants. That's what the foster care system does to people, and she's only made it through one year. I'm an eleven-year veteran.

"How's the music?" Kate/Kaitlin asks. "Is it okay?"

It is decidedly *not* okay, but I give a noncommittal nod. I've been pretending to read my dog-eared copy of *Astrophysics for People in a Hurry* even though I practically have it memorized and staring down at the page makes me carsick. I clutch my star log in my other hand. I've lost so many things moving around in foster care that it's made me paranoid. I keep it with me basically all the time, and whenever I travel, it isn't good enough to have it in my backpack or bag; I have to have it physically in my hands.

She sighs. "Sorry about the traffic. And the heat. I meant to leave earlier, but paperwork at the group home took longer than I thought, and now I think my air-conditioning needs to be looked at. I had a rough time with it yesterday too."

It's only eighty-five degrees, but the humidity is making sweat pool up on my back and under my armpits. I'm damp and sticky and mad as hell, but that isn't Kate/Kaitlin's fault. She's only doing her job.

"Don't worry about it," I say, trying to sound less miserable than I am, because, honestly, she's the one who's truly suffering. She's dressed up in white blouse and heavy-looking slacks, and her makeup is literally melting off her face, leaving dark streaks under her eyes. Kate/Kaitlin fiddles valiantly with her AC before giving up, then we both sit back and sweat.

"Have you ever visited Salem?" she asks.

I have a very vague memory of my mom bringing me here once, probably on one of our drive-in-piss-everyone-off-and-leave sort of visits, but I have zero memories of our time here, and besides, there's a very good chance that if I bring up my mom again, my throat is going to close up. "I don't think so."

She straightens slightly. "You know, it's pretty incredible how this has all worked out. I am really excited about this placement. And *Salem, Massachusetts.* That's interesting, isn't it? Do you like history?"

Does anyone *really* like history? I am obviously affected by history, my entire life shaped by the choices my parents made and the choices their parents made and all that. But I'm trying to staunch the rush of anxiety that I know is coming, so I blurt out a quick "Sure. Salem witch trials, so interesting."

Her chin swivels slightly toward me, her eyebrows shooting up cartoon high. "Right? The thing that I find so fascinating is that there were no witches in the late sixteen hundreds; those poor people were executed for no reason. They were mostly marginalized people being blamed for things people didn't understand. But today, Salem is full of modern-day witches. I'm sure Emma will tell you more. She's really involved with the local historical societies. She even leads tours at one of the museums."

Emma.

Do not freak out, I order my brain, but the anxiety bypasses my brain, hitting my bloodstream instead. Emma Morgan. A person I have only a vague memory of ever meeting but who has suddenly materialized in my life in a very big way.

A part of me had hoped I might recognize her, but as soon as I saw her, that had fallen away immediately. She was a stranger, just like everybody else. I didn't even remember that she was Mexican American.

She and Simon came to the group home a few times to meet me, but I was out with friends and only met them during the placement meeting. Emma was quiet and direct, but not particularly warm. I didn't know what to think. I turn my gaze out the window and am met with an ugly strip mall, cars honking at each other in the parking lot. I shift uncomfortably, trying to keep my heart rate even as I mentally recite the few facts I know. *Simon and Emma are my new foster parents. They have four daughters. They became foster parents specifically for me.*

"Yeah, you told me about her job," I mumble.

"And they're a blended family. Their oldest is from Simon's first marriage; the youngest three they had together." She says "blended" like it's something delicious, an ice cream sundae or a chocolate-covered caramel. She clearly thinks this is the ticket to me fitting in. "Simon is so excited to have another guy around the house."

She's told me this already—Simon told me too—and hearing it again isn't making me feel any less stressed. Who has four kids? In my experience, most people aren't even all that great at taking care of one. And what does it mean to have another guy around the house? Is he going to expect me to know how to talk about sports? Cars? I literally have zero experience with either. "Ah," I manage. Part of me is now wishing I had been around to meet the girls when the Morgans tried to visit. Four new people is going to be a lot.

Kate/Kaitlin was clearly hoping for a more enthusiastic answer, because she nods, then slumps back against her chair, and we go back to silent sweating.

We hit Salem proper, and the more I see, the more nervous I get. Salem is technically a suburb of Boston, but it somehow feels completely different. Yes, it's New England, with cobblestone and a Dunkin' Donuts lurking on every other street corner, and I'm sure there are people arguing passionately about who makes the best roast beef sandwiches like there are everywhere in the Boston area. But Salem has its own unique vibe. It obviously takes its history very, very seriously, because it's summer and there are signs of witches everywhere—witch shops, witch signs, witches on the police cars; even the high school's mascot is a witch. If it's like this now, what will Halloween be like?

Kate/Kaitlin is having a hard time navigating, and as the car slows, my head begins to detach the way it does whenever I'm nervous. Before long, it's like I'm watching myself in this little car, shallow breath, sweating more than is strictly necessary. *Why am I this nervous?* I've done this so many times before, you'd think I'd be used to it. My mom and I moved constantly, but I was with her, and even during the really hard times she managed to make it magical—and no matter where we were, we found a rooftop to climb out on so we could study constellations.

In foster homes I'm expected to fit into an already established environment, and every home is completely different. At least with my mom I knew what to expect.

Kate/Kaitlin must notice I'm deep in thought, because she rallies again. "Isn't it incredible that Emma is someone you already know? It really is so rare to find a placement like this. And how incredible is it that they became foster parents specifically for *you*?"

Calling my new foster mom "someone I already know" is a stretch. Before the placement meeting I did know Emma's name, but only because my mom talked about her off and on like someone I should know for most of my childhood. They grew up together in South Boston and, according to my mom, they had once been very close. My mom had probably imploded their relationship by showing up high or asking for money, because that's the way all of my mom's relationships end, which makes me wonder—why was Emma so adamant about connecting with me now?

"Mmm," I manage. No one would mistake my voice for enthusiasm, but at least I don't sound like I am being roasted on a spit, which is what it feels like, flames of anxiety licking at my stomach and rib cage. And then the car is slowing, pulling up to a curb, and it's all I can do to look up, acknowledge that we're here.

"Does that say 'Skerry'? Okay, yes. I think this is it," Kate/Kaitlin says, flipping on her turn signal. "Most of these big houses are divided into condos. Theirs is the bottom right, I believe."

I force my face upward, my dread turning to impending doom. The house is covered in bright white siding with a cherry red door, and window boxes host trailing green plants. The wooden porch is covered in an indeterminate number of bikes, scooters, and Rollerblades, and a few stray sneakers and sandals. My anxiety is stoked even higher at the visible representation of all the kids who live in that house. They already have four kids. Why on earth did they want to take on one more?

"Look at all that," Kate/Kaitlin says with a cheery sigh. "I know that will be very different for you, especially coming from a group home, but a home is so much better than a group home, and they worked so hard to be licensed." She drums her fingers on the steering wheel for a moment, then looks at me. I can tell immediately that this is going to be a Serious Conversation. "Look, Mason. This is a sort of atypical placement. The Morgans really want you to have the choice on whether or not you stay. But you'll be aging out in a few years. I really think that the Morgans are a good fit for you. They can help you figure out college, school; all of it. You should really try to make this work. This is a place you can truly be at home, Mason. No more of the running away or staying out late, okay? It's up to you."

My fists tighten. I can't help it. Not only is this random new place most definitely not my home; my real home is a person who I haven't been able to see in years. And now I'm thinking about my mom, really thinking about her, and like always, once I start, I can't stop. It's a rupture in a dam, and once it starts, it only gets worse. *This isn't home. I'm supposed to be with my mom.* That single, driving fact swirls through my head, pulses through my veins. Also, I've been in three other homes and none of them ended up working out long-term.

What would make me believe this one will be successful?

"Mason?" Kate/Kaitlin asks. "It's up to you. You get that, right? It's up to you."

"Yeah," I say, but what little gravity I have, I'm losing quickly, blood rushing in my ears, my vision tilting, because when has *anything* ever been up to me? I rake my hair back, try to breathe. I should be used to this lack of gravity. I haven't been on stable ground since my mom lost custody of me. Seven years is a long time for anything, let alone not touching Earth.

Willow

I wouldn't say I *stall* making my way into the house, but it's safe to say I take my sweet time.

My mom's house is what Bea's mom calls *le moderne*, big, open floor plan, lots of glass and steel, a color scheme that ranges from white to light gray, and smoothly poured concrete floors that—despite their built-in heating system—never quite seem to warm up. My mom put a huge amount of work into her new house, and objectively, it's gorgeous. The only real issue for me is that besides my bedroom, it feels like I'm wandering around in a stranger's house. Two years into living here and I still feel like I'm waiting to go home.

As I pass through the hallway, I do my best to avert my eyes from the article my mom recently had framed and hung near the entryway. Last December, my mom won a Businessperson of the Year Award from a big event-planning magazine, and they'd done a shoot in our house, which is where she does most of her planning. I'd been moved when she'd asked me to be a part of it, but then during the shoot, the photographer had positioned us in the kitchen and told us to "Just do whatever normal mother-daughter things you do, maybe bring up some inside jokes?" and we both sort of stood there like paper dolls until he took pity on us and started directing the shot.

It was brutal.

The end results were nice; my mom and I look almost awkwardly similar in our magazine clothes, but every time I look at it, I have a sinking feeling in the pit of my stomach. The photo shoot had made it hard to ignore the giant, growing chasm that existed between my mom and me because the photographer had named it. *Just do whatever normal mother-daughter things you do.* And those things had turned out to be . . . awkward conversation. Weird silence.

People sometimes ask me if I'm excited about my mother's success, and while I'm proud of her, it doesn't feel like it has much to do with me. If anything, it makes me feel like I'm observing her from afar. We no longer exist in the same sphere.

As I make my way through the living room, my eye snags on a pop of color in the sea of normal neutrals. Now I'm *definitely* stalling, but I make my way over to inspect. A wide-mouthed mason jar is perched on the edge of mom's glass coffee table, and it is stuffed with bloodred flowers intermingled with sprigs of something green. I lean in to take a look, instantly recognizing the flowers' cup-shaped blossoms. Poppies. I know because my mom brought in ten different types for a California poppy–themed wedding last summer. But these poppies look nothing like the pristine flowers my mom typically flies in. These ones are wilted and a bit messy, with stems of all different lengths and a few missing petals. And the green is an herb—rosemary? I lean in for a smell and get a quick whiff halfway between pine and mint. Definitely rosemary. I recognize it from my dad's cooking. Who made this?

And then I realize something else that makes me look up uneasily: the silence. An hour ago, when I made my sad exodus to the pool, the house was full of my mom and Drew's staff, busy preparing for their upcoming event. Napkins, color swatches, and half a dozen sample bouquets were laid out on the dining room table, which is now . . . empty. Where is everyone?

"Mom?" I call into the emptiness.

I make my way into the foyer. The house is pin-neat and quiet as a tomb. Even the pile of designer shoes by the door is gone. The only sounds are the muffled noises coming from Noah's crew.

And then I hear another noise, like the tiny scrabblings of a hamster or squirrel. Is that . . . sniffling? Is someone here *crying*?

"Mom?" I call out into the quiet. My voice wavers a bit.

"In here." Her reply is immediate, her voice coming from her private office area, but the sound is off somehow. Muffled. My heart breaks into a jog along with my feet.

My mom's office might be the nicest room in the entire nice house, and according to the magazine photographer, it's definitely the most photogenic. She has a large marble-topped desk, a perfectly aged leather chair, and the exact right amount of knickknacks arranged just so. On the wall across from her desk are her mood boards— six framed spaces that contain ideas for her upcoming projects with fabrics, color swatches, scribbled words, etc. And standing soldier-straight on the custom shelving she had made specifically for them are her binders. The spines are written on in her careful handwriting, and they're placed in chronological order of the date of each event, their insides obsessively documented accounts of every detail that went into each event. If you want to know how many spoons were present at the Berlusconi/Bridget wedding, all you have to do is open the binder.

The binders calm my racing heart, and I look around the room for a moment, reassuring myself of its normalcy.

And in many cases, everything is normal. My mom is sitting straight-backed at her desk, looking like she always does—auburn hair smooth around her shoulders, crisp white blouse, minimal makeup and jewelry. But in some other, indistinguishable way, she looks different. Altered somehow.

"Mom?" I say.

Her eyes don't quite meet mine. "Come in, Willow. Will you please close the door?"

I do it, but this feels off too. I'm not sure I've ever seen the doors to her office closed. There are usually too many people around for that.

"Go ahead and sit," she says.

I get a bit closer and realize with a start that her mascara is smeared around her eyes in little half-moons. It makes my heart pick up speed, a little at first, then a lot. This can't be right. My mother doesn't cry. In her own words, she lacks the necessary ducts. Even on the day she moved out of our Brooklyn apartment and I caught her giving it one last long look, her eyes were completely dry.

Something is wrong. And I don't mean wrong like she just lost a big vendor or a bride canceled a million-dollar wedding. Wrong like *the world has fallen apart and will never, ever be the same.*

All thoughts of our fight fly from my mind, replaced instantly with panic. "Mom? What happened? Is someone hurt?" Suddenly I think of my dad and the triplets, and my chest seizes. They're all right, aren't they? They have to be.

She gestures to the seat across from hers, and I notice a torn envelope and several sheets of paper spread out on the desk in front of her. The letter has been flipped upside down, and a now-broken wax seal—the exact color of the mason jar poppies—graces the top and bottom of the sheet. Seeing the deep red color twice startles me, and for a moment I'm distracted. I squint, trying to make out the letter on the seal. Is that a fancy *P*? My mother notices me looking and quickly sweeps it aside.

"Willow, I need to tell you something. I just found out that ... well ..."
She takes a breath, then lets out the rest of it in a rush. "Willow, it's my sister.
She died earlier this year, and I'm only finding out about it now."

Then she finally looks me in the eye and waits.

So you know when things hit you in waves? That's what
happens here. First, there's the fact that there's a death. Absolute
calamity.

And it's in the family. Double calamity.

But then there are the important facts that absolutely do not,
cannot connect, most notably the fact that *my mother does not have a
sister*.

I hold up one finger. "Sorry. Did you just say your *sister*
unexpectedly passed away?" As if heretofore unknown sisters could
pass away in any other way but unexpectedly. I have a weird urge to
laugh but manage to keep it in check.

Her shoulders fall slightly, so slightly that maybe I imagined it.
"Yes. My twin passed away unexpectedly in February, but the estate
wasn't able to find me until now. I haven't been in touch with her for
a number of years."

My twin?

Do I maybe not know an alternate meaning for the word "twin"?
No, I obviously know what a twin is. I must have misheard, because if
she had a twin sister, if I had an aunt, I'd know about that, wouldn't I?
This is obviously a joke. Except ... does my mother joke?

No, she does not. In *my* words, she lacks the necessary humor bone.

Which means my mother has a twin. Or *did* have a twin. My
heart is picking up speed again. And now I'm running my eyes over
my steady mom, her perfect style, her carefully controlled expression,
and a tiny door is swinging open, one marked *Do You Actually Know
This Person?* I mean, I've always felt about a million miles away from

her, but this is something entirely different. This is next level.

"What . . . I . . . ?" I take a deep breath but only manage another *"What?"*

My shock gives her enough time to pull herself back together. She smooths her hair, then glides back in her chair. "The estate is right outside of Boston. In . . . Salem, Massachusetts." And the firm way she says it, it's almost like a dare.

"Salem?" A flood of images rushes my brain, most of which I'm sure came from movies. Puritans wearing black hats with buckles. Witches riding on broomsticks with black cats. Also, that movie with the three witches, one of whom rides a vacuum cleaner. *Hocus Pocus?* She can't mean that Salem, can she?

I shake my head slightly. "Salem . . . like, where the witches were?"

She hesitates. "There were no actual witches during the Salem witch trials."

Really? I raise my eyebrows at her, and she must realize how irrelevant that information is because she reddens slightly, then pushes back from her desk, rising to her feet. "I'm so sorry to involve you, but I don't have a lot of options. The estate is . . . large. And I can't ask any of my staff to help me settle it because my past is sort of, ah"—she glances at the closed door—"something I'd like to keep in the past. I know I can trust you to keep it all secret."

Now I am genuinely dumbfounded.

My mother has a past? I mean, obviously she does. But a *Past*, capital *P*. Something she has been hiding from me, and from the looks of things, from everyone else as well. She lied to her *staff* about it. Questions are layering on top of each other, forming a tiny volcano in my chest. I genuinely have no idea where to begin.

And then her words play back to me. Wait. Is she asking me for my help?

And I hate that I feel this—a tiny rush of happiness. Is my mom inviting me in to . . . whatever this is? "Me?" I manage.

"I'd really appreciate you coming with me," she blurts out. "I'm not sure what needs to be done, exactly, but this is obviously a very nuanced situation, and I could use some, ah, assistance."

I see something brand-new in her face. Worry? Vulnerability? My mom needs me. I have no idea what to do with that realization. It fills up my chest, making me feel bigger and smaller at the same time. My mom can handle everything, but now she needs me? My eyes are drawn to her hands again. They're shaking. Ever so slightly, but that is a definite quiver.

This is not a drill.

She lost her sister. My heart swells up even more. I have never seen her shaken. *Ever.* And now she's asking me for support in the weirdest, most formal way.

"Of course I'll come with you," I blurt out.

She relaxes slightly, her shoulders sagging for a moment. "Thank you, Pillow."

She says the last part so quietly, I almost miss it. Pillow was my childhood nickname, and it rushes me back to Brooklyn, to our apartment before Chloe and the kids, before LA and Mary Haverford Events. Before I felt like I had to make an appointment to talk to either of my parents. Suddenly I'm enmeshed in weekend trips to farmers markets, museums, libraries, a whole other life—a whole other reality, when I knew who I was. Where I belonged. A lump forms in my throat, and for a moment, my body remembers what life felt like before they split. Yes, there were problems, but at least I knew my place in the world. At least when someone asked me where I was from, I didn't hesitate to give an answer.

A shimmery cord, thin as a spider's web, stretches out between us, and suddenly I'm desperate to keep it there. I take a deep breath. "How did your sister die?"

She hesitates. "Cancer. Complications from her treatment. I didn't know—" Her voice breaks slightly, and she quickly reaches for her throat. "Sorry. I didn't know she was sick."

I'm hit with a heavy wave of sadness, and I'm not sure if it's for my mom or for this person I've never met. "That's awful," I say, my voice coming out quiet.

She nods a tiny nod, more of a dip of her chin. "Phoebe has already booked our flights. We leave for the airport in an hour. Thank you so much, Willow." Then she stands, sweeping the letter into her hand as she heads for the door.

"It's nothing," I say, but that isn't true. My mom is the most organized, detail oriented, careful person on the planet, so the fact that she's been hiding something as big as a twin is most certainly a *something*.

My mom has always been a giant mystery to me, and for the first time I'm realizing there's a legitimate reason for that.

4

Mason

The Morgans' house is close to a large grassy park bordered by enormous old houses, and looking out over it makes my stomach tighten. Everywhere I look, there are families walking together: grandparents pushing strollers, dads with kids on their shoulders, teenagers walking with their parents, and big, goofy dogs on leashes. This is the kind of place where people grow up in generations, where you know exactly where you'll sit at Thanksgiving dinner and who will be in the audience on graduation day. In other words, it's the type of place where someone like me does not belong. Every part of me wants to turn and run.

"Mason, are you ready?" Kate/Kaitlin says in a voice that lets me know she's asked at least one time before. Why do they ask these questions as though my response matters in any capacity? I am clearly not ready, but since when has that ever meant anything? My gaze must tell her what I'm thinking, because she gives me a tight smile. "I'll pop the trunk."

Kate/Kaitlin continues talking, but I have no idea what she's saying as I shrug on my backpack, tuck my book under my arm, hoist my bag onto my shoulder. My duffel bag containing all my worldly possessions is pitifully small, but it still feels like I'm carrying a ton of bricks as I make my way around the millions of tipped-over bikes and tricycles and snarled-up Rollerblades, my feet heavy as lead.

No part of me wants to walk into the Morgans' house, say the things I'm going to have to say, do the things they expect me to do. Inside could be a house made to look like a skate park, surround-sound systems everywhere, a butler whose main job is to serve me Dr Pepper and Oreos every time I ring a crystal bell, and still I would not want to walk into that house. I can't start over again. Not here. Not with someone who knows my mom.

The Morgans' doorway is tucked under the eaves of the porch, and when we reach it, I grind to a halt because *balloons*. And streamers crisscrossing across the door like lasers in a spy movie. And . . . please, no. Is that confetti on the ground?

It's definitely confetti. Of the rainbow variety.

My body slows down even more, and I'm barely moving forward. I catch sight of my reflection in the front window and feel a stab of dismay. As usual, I look all wrong. Too tall, too sullen, too something. My shoulder-length hair has been giving me a lot of problems lately, and it looks more tangled than usual. I rake it again, but only manage to make it worse. Maybe if I stand up straight? I attempt it but immediately hunch again.

I do my best to keep moving. Maybe the decorations aren't for me? Maybe someone in this enormous household is celebrating a birthday? But then I look up into the window and see an extensively glittered sign that reads WELCOME, MASON, and that hope goes up in a puff of smoke. I know that foster families are advised to keep things low-key, make transitions as natural as possible. Did the Morgans not get that memo?

Then a terrible thought hits me. Are the Morgans one of those families who take in kids because they want to look good? If so, maybe the banner is more for the neighbors than it is for me and would be better off saying something like:

WELCOME TO OUR HOME, POOR, PITIFUL FOSTER CHILD!!
(NEIGHBORS: SEE WHAT GENEROUS PEOPLE WE ARE???)

Kate/Kaitlin should be at least as horrified by the decorations as
I am, but instead she is shining like a supernova. Either that or she's
glittering with sweat. "Oh, wow! What a welcome! I told you the girls
are excited to meet you, Mason."

She reaches up to knock, and even before I can start to panic, the
sticky door swings open to reveal Emma. She's dressed a lot more
casually than she was at our meeting, and she looks more tired, too,
wearing flip-flops and an oversize T-shirt with a pair of denim shorts.
She's short and slim with smooth black bangs and brown skin, but at
the meeting, she was wearing clothes that had covered her tattoos. A
row of oranges and orange blossoms winds its way up her left arm,
and a colorful sugar skull takes up most of her right thigh. There's
even a purple hummingbird peeking out of her left shoe.

Emma pushes the screen door open. "Hi." She's looking past Kate/
Kaitlin at me, and she doesn't smile, so I don't smile either. Instead
I sort of nod and shuffle my feet. Her eyes travel up my full height.
I brace myself for the question that every six-foot-three teenager
with limbs like a daddy longlegs endures: *Do you play basketball?
No? Maybe you should.* Every new school I've ever been to, a coach
spots me slouching through the halls and thinks I'm going to be their
new golden ticket to a winning season. Luckily, all it takes is thirty
seconds of watching me gangly and uncoordinated on the court for
their dreams to be dashed. People act like I'm wasting a precious
national resource: *How dare you be tall for no good reason.*

But Emma doesn't say anything about my height. She's doing a
different kind of inventory. Tallying me up, finding the sum, exactly
like she did at the meeting. And I have no idea what she thinks of

her assessment. What is she trying to figure out? Also, I have literally never seen such big eyes before. I feel Little Red Riding Hood looking at the wolf. *What big eyes you have!*

"Mrs. Morgan, so great to see you again!" Kate/Kaitlin chirps. "I'm sorry we're so late."

"You can call me Emma. And you aren't late," Emma says, her gaze still on me. Several piercings line both her ears, and she has a tiny gold nose stud. "How was the car ride?" There's a hint of my mom's accent in her voice, a slight softening of the *R* in "car" that makes my breath hitch. *How was the cah ride?*

The wave of missing hits me so hard, I have to look down at my feet to make sure they're still connected to the porch. She probably calls drinking fountains "bubblas" and the remote control the "clicka," just like my mom does.

"The ride was okay," I manage, and Emma nods, like that's what she expected me to say. Her eyes travel to my book tucked under my arm, and then back to mine, and now I'm battling with some serious self-doubt. Is she having second thoughts?

This place is emotional quicksand.

Kate/Kaitlin shifts uncomfortably. "Not a bad drive at all. My goodness, Salem is charming. These old houses! And these decorations are fun. What a welcome." Up close, the banner is even worse than I thought. It has been painted with a bunch of silver stars that vaguely resemble the Big Dipper constellation, which lets me know that Kate/Kaitlin has told them that I'm into astronomy. I hate that there is a little folder of knowledge about me that gets passed around to every adult that interacts with me. It makes them think they know who I am, when actually they know nothing.

"The girls made it," Emma says. She's still staring at me. It makes me want to sprint back to the hot car.

"Is he here? Is Mason here?" A man's excited voice booms through the entryway, and Emma scoots over to make room for Simon. He is white, clean-cut with medium-blond hair, a slight sunburn, and seriously muscular calves. His T-shirt has a picture of a witch in running shoes and the words *Banks Realty Wicked Half Marathon* in red. Everything about him screams "wholesome." His smile is so big, it nearly tips me backward. He extends his hand. "Mason! So good to finally meet you. How was your trip?"

Boston to Salem isn't exactly what I'd call a "trip," but I'm not going to correct him.

"Fine. Thanks." I'm standing an awkwardly long distance away, so I take a few awkwardly long steps forward to meet his hand, and my duffel bag falls and hits me on the back of my legs. Simon shakes Kate/Kaitlin's hand also, then turns back to me. "Mason, I said this last time too, but you look like your mother. Exactly like her, doesn't he, Emma?"

"Exactly like Naomi." Emma says my mom's name quietly, and it splits me down the middle. It's been so long since I've heard anyone say it. For a moment, I hold on to it. I've always loved my mom's name. Naomi sounds like a name for a sophisticated art exec, someone with a portfolio and a briefcase who answers e-mails at all hours and goes to wine tastings on the weekends. Not someone who has been in and out of rehab programs and jail and shitty basement apartments and all the other places she's been for the past eleven years. Naomi is the name of someone who is going to take charge of her life. It's one of the reasons I know everything is going to be okay.

"Thank you," I say awkwardly, even though I'm not sure if it counts as a compliment. People who knew my mom when she was young always make a point of saying how pretty she was, but they say it in the "used to be" kind of way. She was tall, like me, and in her high school photos she has thick dark hair and rosy cheeks. Her lifestyle had been hard on in her a lot of ways, and sometimes I think the pretty got all used up. Maybe that will get better once we're back together?

Kate/Kaitlin is now giving off the approximate wattage of a supernova. I can see what she'll write in her notes about today's placement. *Instant connection. Great placement.* "Now, remind me, Emma, you and Mason's mom were best friends?" She says it innocently, like she doesn't know the answer.

"More like sisters," Emma says, and I can't help but look at her suspiciously. So where was she when my mom was homeless? Where was she the first time my mom almost overdosed and had to be in the hospital for three weeks? Emma looks right at me, like she knows what I'm thinking. And it unnerves me because I know rationally that Emma can't actually read my mind, but also, can she read my mind? Her eyes are huge and dark and honestly creep me out.

I blink, and Emma blinks back. A conversation is happening between us, only I can't tell what it is. I look away but can't seem to find anything to focus my eyes on.

Kate/Kaitlin is still droning on and on, her voice a honey bee in the heat. "And isn't it nice that you all have all summer to get to know each other? Give Mason some time to settle in before he starts senior year. I can't tell you how perfect this all is."

Perfect for whom? Simon nods enthusiastically, but Emma and I are both silent and weird and I don't know what to do with the vibe going on right now. Usually foster moms are gushing over you at this point, showing you to your room, forcing drinks and snacks on you. Emma looks like she's waiting for me to take the lead, only I don't know how to. She may be small enough to fit in my pocket, but I'm technically still the kid here, even if I feel exactly three hundred years old.

"We're really happy to have him, aren't we, Emma?" Simon

reaches for my bag and hoists it onto his shoulder. "Now, what are we doing still outside? It's hotter than Satan's mixtape out here."

Simon herds us in, and Kate/Kaitlin hustles after him. There's an awkward split second when I don't know if I should go first or let Emma go first, but she gestures for me to step ahead of her, and I do, quickly, careful not to brush against her. Inside the house is an explosion of objects, the entryway full of hooks and baskets overflowing with jackets and soccer cleats and glittery jelly shoes. From the door I can see into the kitchen, and several boxes of cereal stand open on the table, intermingled with colorful ponies and snarly haired Barbies. Even without visual proof, it's evident that a lot of people live here, and immediately I have that disembodied feeling again—this house, this family, has layers and history that have nothing to do with me. I'm an outsider. An interloper. Like I *always* am. My mom having a historical tie to Emma doesn't change that. If anything, it makes it worse.

As we move toward the stairway, Emma says in a low voice, "I'm sorry about all this."

My eyes shoot to her. I met her three minutes ago, and she's already apologizing for not being in my mom's life? Does she think that's enough of an apology? But she's pointing back toward the front door, at the banner and balloons. "The decorations." She meets my eyes again. "Also, I'm very sorry for what is about to happen."

"What's about to happen?" I ask, but I'm distracted because I notice something that makes my pulse shift sharply to my temples. Emma has a small pink seashell tattooed on her inner right wrist. Exactly the same as my mom's.

"FIRE IN THE HOLE!" The jubilant voice comes from the top of the stairs, and suddenly I'm being assailed by colorful orbs—dozens of colorful orbs—that pour from the ceiling while tiny voices cheer and yell. I stumble backward, trying to dodge whatever is happening; my brain can't seem to recognize what they are.

Emma's hand is suddenly on my arm. "Balloon drop," she says.

Balloons. The colorful orbs are balloons. What is wrong with me? My heart is racing so fast, I may as well be sprinting.

"Release the stars!" a girl's voice yells. Before I can react, gold star-shaped confetti rains down on me, coating my hair and T-shirt. Suddenly the ground is unsteady beneath me, the Morgans' glittery celebration swaying in my peripheral vision. There are so many stars.

Don't throw up. Don't throw up.

Kate/Kaitlin claps her hands. "How fun!"

"You okay?" Emma asks. She reaches out to grab my arm, and when I look down, there's her tattoo again. I give up on trying to pretend this is a normal foster care placement. This is absolutely nothing like my other foster homes. Blood is rushing to my head, my pulse throbbing. I step away from her, stumbling over balloons as I attempt to brush stars from my hair and body.

"Fine," I mumble. I just need to get my bearings.

"Come on down, girls!" Simon yells. "Nova. You too. Don't disappear on us."

I thought I'd already hit maximum sensory overload, but as the girls tumble down the stairs, I hit it for sure. *Knowing* there are four of them is very different than *experiencing* the four of them. They're a herd. A gaggle. And so noisy. A couple dozen elbows and knees and lots and lots and lots of hair clatter down, and it takes my eyes a minute to process that they all are, in fact, separate, not just one cluster.

Once they get to the bottom, they stop and stare en masse, and I stare back because I can't help it. It's clear where the divide in their "blended" family is. The oldest is several heads taller than the others, with white-blond hair and long skinny legs, and the younger three are carbon copies of Emma: huge dark eyes, brown skin, and black hair with straight bangs. I should say hi, but my throat unfortunately has all the moisture of Mars, and no words are coming out. My mind begins churning out facts the way it does whenever I'm nervous. *Neutron stars can spin at a rate of six hundred rotations a second. There are one hundred thousand million stars in the Milky Way. Footprints on the moon will be there for a hundred million years.*

"Girls?" Simon prompts.

There's a chorus of *Hi, Mason*s. Blondie is maybe twelve or thirteen, wearing a tennis skirt and a faded tank top along with a serious scowl that lets me know exactly how pleased she is to meet me. The next oldest is probably in second or third grade, her hair pulled back into a ponytail, most of her front teeth missing. Then there are the two little ones. I haven't spent nearly enough time around little kids to know how old they might be, but the youngest looks barely past baby age and is clutching a faded pink blanket.

"Nova, Hazel, Zoe, and Audrey." Emma introduces them slowly, but their names flow through my brain like water through a sieve. I've got to get better at names. The three youngest smile. The oldest scowls even harder at the floor.

"I'm Mason," I say awkwardly, because awkward is my default, and they obviously already know my name. They painted it in glitter letters, although I'm guessing from the scowl on Blondie's face that she had nothing to do with it. I tug at the ends of my hair. I desperately need a brush.

"Why did no one tell us you have *girl* hair?" the second to youngest blurts out. "And why don't you have a family anymore?"

"Zoe!" Simon says. "Long hair isn't only for girls; you know that. And your other questions I'll talk to you about later." He turns to me, shrugging apologetically. "I'm sorry, Mason."

"It's okay," I mumble, but my vision is starting to get spotty. It takes everything in my power to not mess with my hair again.

Kate/Kaitlin chuckles nervously behind me. "Kids! So precocious."

"We made your sign," the second to oldest says. "Nova didn't want to. She had to stop listening to her music and she was soooo mad—"

"Hazel!" Nova and Simon say at the exact same moment. Nova's neck is turning splotchy.

"Oh. Sorry about that, I guess," I say pathetically, but I'm starting to lose whatever ground I've reclaimed since Operation Balloon/Confetti Drop. Panic is prickling the back of my neck and my body is involuntarily leaning toward the door.

"It's not your fault," Nova says in a way that makes it clear it is my fault. She doesn't make eye contact, which is fine by me. I want to be here exactly as much as she wants me to be here.

Simon's voice manages to become even more boisterous. "Girls, what did we talk about this morning? About making our new family member feel welcome?"

"Nova has to share a room with us now because Mason is a boy, so he needs his own," Second to Youngest says quickly. "And Mason can't live with his mom because of the bad drugs. But she's a good person who has had a hard life."

We all freeze. Simon and Kate/Kaitlin simultaneously choke on something. Nova doesn't look up, but I see her eyes widen, and the rest of the girls stare at me with their giant bug eyes.

Suddenly Emma's cool hand is on my arm again. "Girls, we'll let Mason decide how much he wants to talk about his mom. Right now we need to focus on helping him feel comfortable, and I think Mason could use some time to settle in and rest. Why don't you all go to the backyard to play for a while? Mason, your room is upstairs, second door to the left. Think you can find it okay?"

I'm still seeing through the waves, but the floor steadies under my feet. "Yes," I say quickly. All I want is to be alone in a room right now.

"Oh . . ." Kate/Kaitlin hesitates, then motions vaguely toward her clipboard. "That isn't typically how placements work. I'd like to spend some time doing an icebreaker activity—"

"You're welcome to stay, but we've come up with our own plan for that. Dinner, games, and a bike ride. I just wanted to give Mason a moment to settle in."

Emma's voice has authority. She is someone who is used to people listening to what she has to say.

"I suppose that will be all right," Kate/Kaitlin says after a moment, and I can't help but feel a tiny bit of grudging admiration for Emma. Usually the Kate/Kaitlins can't be swayed. She continues, "Emma, I'd love to spend some time speaking with you about placement details. Mason, is there anything you need from me right now?"

A letter or a phone call from my mom. A home. A completely different life. But that isn't something you can ask a sweaty social worker for. Besides, she will probably spend an hour or two with Emma before driving back to Boston. I shake my head.

"All right, then." Kate/Kaitlin's face goes supernova again, and she lowers her voice meaningfully. "Welcome *home*, Mason."

It is easily the stupidest thing she's ever said to me. Emma's forehead creases, and I may be imagining it, but she's looking at Kate/Kaitlin like she's having the exact same thought. Even so, I'm feeling panicked at the thought of Kate/Kaitlin leaving. Once she leaves, this will all be very real.

"Upstairs," Emma says, pointing at the staircase. "Second door on the left. We're having pizza delivered tonight. I'll knock when it gets here."

Before anyone can change their minds, I launch myself at the stairs, star-flecked balloons kicking up under my feet. Step one, make it up to my room. Step two, figure out a way to get out of here.

5

Willow

Salem has a city ordinance that requires all visitors to race through it at roughly the speed of a flying broomstick, or at least that is one explanation for what is going on with my mother right now. She is normally a fast walker, but today she's making her regular walk look like a leisurely Sunday stroll. Clearly, she has a mission. Not that she's telling me what said mission is, because apparently I don't need any information besides the basics. *My sister has passed away. We're going to settle the estate. My plan is to be there less than twenty-four hours.*

By the time we were packed and ready, my mom had completely pulled herself back together. She hasn't said a single extraneous word to me since the morning in her office, and that includes the six hours we just spent on the plane together. I'm used to her either being in her head or on her phone all the time, but today her inattention feels downright maddening. That tiny wobble of emotion I saw back in her office is long gone, and that tiny thread that had stretched out between us has snapped clean.

Sometimes I think my relationship with my mom would be easier if I didn't occasionally feel close to her. She's like a queen in a castle—interesting, beautiful, generous, but also heavily guarded by a moat, drawbridge, and fire-breathing dragon. Every once in a while I get a glimpse of her, but for the most part I'm on the outside wondering what I did to get banished. Honestly, I think that's the part that has made me believe all of this mystery-twin business. If anyone was going to have a treasure trove of secrets, it's her.

Now she's running ahead of me, looking polished, composed, and mildly annoyed, while I run after her, confused, messy, out of breath. In other words, the world has realigned itself.

We're headed to a meeting of some sort. That's all I know.

My phone dings, and I pause for a moment to read the latest installment from Bea, who hasn't stopped texting me since I told her the news. You are 100% positive your mom never mentioned the fact that she had a twin?

As though I could possibly forget something like that. I text back. 1000000000% positive.

I also have a new text from my dad. Sorry we still haven't connected, kiddo. Time change is a big deal with the kids, just got them down. Talk later?

A sigh escapes me. If I were stranded at sea and sent my dad an SOS, it would probably still take him two to three business days to respond. I know it isn't that he doesn't care; it's that his capacity always seems to be completely maxed. It's been forty-eight hours since I sent my *help, please* text, and I'm losing all faith in him coming to my aid. I honestly shouldn't have been surprised that he canceled my visit this summer.

Does he even care that we're missing our summer together? Or is he relieved to have one less thing to worry about?

I swallow back hurt. Thinking this way isn't helping. He's out of the country for the summer because he has to be. And it's not like my visits with him have been all that amazing. I love my monstrous half siblings, but if I'm honest, our visits are really difficult. Not only am I in a constant state of giving someone a piggyback ride; it's oddly disorienting watching this new family burrow into my old family's apartment. I get that that old family is gone, but watching it be erased in a physical sense feels . . .

I look up just in time to see my mom disappear into a crowd of pedestrians, not bothering to check that I'm still behind her. "Mom! Wait," I yell, but she keeps going.

I have no choice but to break into a run to catch up, which is no easy feat as the air is so thick and muggy, it's like inhaling pea soup. I can feel my hair frizzing out of my ponytail, but if I stop to tighten it, I'm almost positive my mom will disappear and I'll be lost forever.

Not that being lost in Salem sounds terrible. Even at breakneck speed, Salem is setting my traveler's heart aflutter. The street we're running down is paved in uneven red brick and it's lined with old-looking buildings, their shuttered windows crammed with fascinating-looking items. CRYSTALS, TAROT CARDS, SPELL KITS, reads one store window. Maybe I could stop for one quick moment . . . except when I look up, the top of my mom's auburn hair is now a full four buildings away, and she's showing no signs of stopping.

My phone chimes again. **And she's never mentioned Salem?**

Never. I'm more than positive on that. Even the magazine spread we were in last summer had talked about where she's from: *Hailing from the iconic Martha's Vineyard, Mary learned her art organically, as an apprentice at her own mother's table.*

And yet when I glance forward, my mom is careening up the street like she's walked it a thousand times before. She definitely knows this place. Did she spend time here with her sister?

She reaches the end of the pedestrian section of the street and a stoplight forces her to pause. I break into a run, finally gaining some ground on her. "Where are we going?" I ask, out of breath.

"Elizabeth," she says, her eyes on her phone.

"And . . . who is Elizabeth?" I wheeze. Another sister? At this point, I wouldn't be all that surprised.

The light changes, and instead of answering, she charges across, bringing us to a small corner park, where I find myself face-to-face with someone I actually do recognize. It's Samantha Stephens, the character from the old sitcom *Bewitched*. She's sitting on a broom in front of a crescent moon, one copper arm raised in a jaunty wave, her hair carefully flipped out. A small plaque is engraved with the actress's name. ELIZABETH MONTGOMERY.

Elizabeth is a location, not a person.

I double over, resting my hands on my knees as I catch my breath. "Who . . . are we . . . meeting?" I wheeze.

Mom is scanning the crowd of pedestrians so intensely, it's possible she's checking for an assassin. "Probate lawyer. She should be here any minute." Her intense cycling routine means she isn't even out of breath.

"What's . . . a probate . . . lawyer?"

She's about to answer when a faint voice, carried over the sound of traffic and pedestrians, comes from across the intersection. "ROSEMARY. ROSEMARY BELL. ROSE! MAAAAAAARRYY!"

My mother looks up sharply, her face going pale. "Oh no," she whispers.

Her panicked tone sends shivers down my spine. "What is it? Mom?" I resist the urge to jostle her. She's as frozen as Elizabeth, and looking in the same direction, which I would find funny if it weren't so unnerving.

"ROSE-MARY. ROSEMARY BELL." The voice is slowly increasing in volume, my mother's face going more and more rigid with each syllable. "ROOOOOSSSEEEMARRRY. OH MY GODDESS, THERE SHE IS."

My mom's eyes are now wide with alarm and she lets out a string of choice words under her breath that I have never heard her say. She is actually quite magnificent at swearing.

"This can't be happening," she says.

The source of the noise isn't hard to locate. It's coming from two elderly women who are holding up traffic as they cross the four-lane street. One is wearing a gauzy lavender shawl covered in sparkles, a lock of her long, snow-white hair dyed lavender to match. The other is wearing a bright red muumuu and thick glasses, her hair a wild mess of wiry gray curls. Despite the fact that they are roughly between the ages of eighty and eight hundred, and the muumuu-wearing one is pushing a tennis-ball-bedecked walker, they're moving like twin freight trains. A car beeps impatiently, and the lavender-haired one flips the car off before restarting her shuffle.

A laugh rises up over my anxiety. "Who is that?"

The muumuu one catches sight of my mom and starts waving her arms in the air. "ROSEMARY."

She is definitely looking at my mom. Confusion floods me. "Are they yelling at you?"

My mom grabs my arm, her voice suddenly urgent. "Willow, I need you to go back to the hotel. Now. I'll explain—"

Frustration replaces my confusion, and I shake off her clawlike grip. "Mom, no. I'm not going back to the hotel."

The women hit the sidewalk, and suddenly the lavender-haired one spots me. Her mouth drops open. "My goddess. She brought the DAUGHTER."

That's when they really start moving.

It's more of an attack than an embrace. I am overtaken by the muumuu-wearing one, who pulls me into a shockingly tight hug, her arms pillow soft.

"You're here! Oh my dear, you're here!" she says into my ear.

"Ma'am?" I wheeze. Along with being alarmingly robust, the woman smells strongly of cinnamon, and if it weren't for the fact that she isn't my grandmother, this might be one of the best grandmotherly hugs in existence. Over Muumuu's shoulder I see my mom has been overtaken by Lavender, who is hugging my mom with the same ferocity.

"Excuse me," I try again. I attempt to unlock the woman's arms. No luck.

"I knew it would work. I knew Rosemary would come back. If only it could have been sooner!" Muumuu pulls back and studies my face. Her face is sweet and wrinkly, like a baked apple, and that with her cinnamon scent makes her seem like comfort food personified. Despite the obvious misunderstanding, I feel a tiny flicker of warmth in what Bea loves to refer to as my cold dead heart.

I carefully disentangle myself. "Hi there. I'm so sorry, but I think there must be a misunderstanding. Neither of us is named Rosemary."

She gives a gaspy little laugh. "I *knew* the letter would work. Violet said I may as well try to make a storm cloud take back its raindrops, but I sprinkled the letter with cinnamon and left it out overnight in the moonlight. Of course it worked!"

Moonlight? Cinnamon? Confusion is pinging through me, but her face is so happy that all I can do is smile.

"That's . . . great," I manage.

"Poppy Bell, I never said any such thing and you know it," the other woman, who is apparently named Violet, says, giving us a little scowl. Poppy Bell. A fittingly adorable name for an adorable woman. I want to follow her back her to whatever fairy-tale story she came from.

Poppy grabs my hands, her face crinkling into a smile, then she points a finger at my heart. "You know when you're truly missing something? When your life isn't complete without it? You feel it in here, and you'd do anything to find the thing you're looking for?" She jabs her finger in the direction of my heart, and all of a sudden I'm flooded with emotion because yes, I do know that feeling. But why does she know I feel that way?

"Yes?"

She smiles, her grip tightening. "That's how it was looking for you two. And, oh, you wouldn't believe the things we've tried. Magic circles, incantations, candle magic, runes . . ."

"Don't forget the spell work!" Violet says. She's finally released my mom, who is so pale, I can see her freckles through her makeup. "You wouldn't believe the number of spells we've performed."

It all finally clicks. Spells? Magic circles? Incantations?

Ohhhhhh. I spin to take a look at the bronzed witch statue, tourists posing in front of it. One tourist is wearing a black witch's hat, and she clambers onto the back of the crescent moon, moving her arm to look like Elizabeth. It all clicks into place. These women are *actors*. Rosemary is probably the name of a famous historical figure from ye olde days of Salem, and these two with their weird outfits and overly loud voices are roping us into a street production or local tour. It's a tourist gag.

I look around and catch a few amused looks from spectators. Suspicion confirmed. This probably happens every hour on the hour to some unsuspecting tourist. And I'm clearly a step or two ahead of my mom, because she looks, as Bea would say—a wee bit *stupefait*.

"Oh, I get it," I say loudly. "You're witches, right?"

Poppy breaks out into a wide smile. "Well, *obviously*, dear. We're Bells, aren't we? All the Bell women are witchy, although I'm sure you would agree all women have a bit of witch in them. It's our birthright!"

My mom makes a gargled noise, and Poppy winks at me mischievously.

Definitely actors. I'm going to write the best entry about this in my travel journal. "So nice to meet you," I say, moving into a loud stage voice of my own. "Unfortunately, we have a meeting right now that we need to get to. Mom?"

But my mom isn't looking at me. Instead, she seems to be slowly hyperventilating, her chest heaving. Is she okay? "Mom?"

"Rosemary, breathe!" Violet says sternly. She claps my mom on the back, which actually seems to work. Now my mom has a pink circle on each cheek.

Poppy clasps one of my hands to her heart, recapturing my attention. "She'll be all right. Such a shock, being here! Your mother was hardly a girl when we saw her last. Oh, she gave us a start, disappearing into the night like that!"

They are not giving up. "Mom, should we go?" I ask, but her eyes dart away from mine.

Poppy grips my hand tighter. "We tried to contact her for years. *Years.* Bell women have always been excellent at disappearing. Of course, Rosemary excelled at it, the way she excels at everything. If I didn't know any better, I'd say she'd dropped off the edge of the world. I know she had her reasons, but couldn't she have sent one measly postcard? A quick phone call on Beltane or Yule?"

Violet joins in, her eyes on my mother. "Oh, you were so tricky. If it weren't for that magazine article, I don't know if we ever would have found you!"

Wait.

Wait, wait, wait.

My pulse flickers slightly. They aren't talking about the magazine article, are they? The one framed in our entryway? I mean, they can't be, because they obviously don't know us. They aren't even calling my mom by the right name. Still, I can't ignore the tension spiraling through my chest. I spin to look at my mom. I don't know which looks tighter, her shoulders or her face.

"Poppy had a hunch you would be in the entertaining business, and of course you're right at the tip top of that industry, aren't you?" Violet says. "Oh, those flower chandeliers! They were stunning."

"That's why I sent the poppies and rosemary!" Poppy says. "It cost a fortune to airmail them to you, but I knew you needed flowers from the Bell garden. Flowers have always spoken to you."

Poppy sent the poppy-and-rosemary bouquet. To my mother. Rosemary.

It's the last piece I need.

Shock and understanding explode in my chest. I swivel over to look at my mom. Her face is inscrutable, but she's biting her lower lip. These women not only know my mother, they know her by a different name. That's why she tried to send me back to the hotel, so I wouldn't unravel more of her secret.

My heart thuds so loudly, I'm pretty sure everyone hears it. I spin toward my mom. "Mom," I say urgently. The people who were watching have gone back to their regular lives. This is not a tourist gimmick or impromptu performance. These people are somehow a part of my mom's life. My mom's name is—or was—Rosemary. I have an entire family history I know *nothing* about.

And I can't get her to look at me. "Mom," I say more forcefully.

"Willow, I can explain," she says. Her hands flutter to her purse, then to her blouse and back again. She *still* isn't looking at me. She waves one arm at me, like I'm a crumb that needs to be brushed away. "Later."

Seriously?

Confusion and upset are bubbling in my chest, making it hard to think straight, but this hand movement sends me straight to rage. Does she really think she can make me wait on this? Is my mom seriously shutting me out right now?

Of course she is. Shutting me out is at the top of her list of considerable talents. The sun is much too hot, and I'm suddenly unclear about how I'm managing to breathe in the humidity. It is absolutely suffocating.

Well, this time, I'm not standing for it.

"You need to tell me *now*," I say. "Who are Poppy and Violet, and why are they calling you Rosemary?" My voice is hard, steely, and it catches both of us off guard. In truth, I sound exactly like her. Poppy and Violet exchange a quick glance.

Mom's cheeks are bright red, a mirror replica of mine, I'm sure. "Willow, these are . . ." She exhales. "These are my great-aunts. They helped raise my sister and me. Along with my aunt Daisy."

"Oh, we shouldn't get *that* much credit," Poppy says. "It was our angel Daisy who did most of the raising while we were off doing who knows what. My, she was a force! So creative! So generous! She never met a project she wasn't up to. Not that you girls were a project. You were her truest gift."

And yet I have never heard of this person?

My mom slides her eyes to me guiltily. "And . . . my name used to be Rosemary. But obviously I shortened it. To Mary. My sister's name was Sage."

I'm not sure why this final detail hits me so hard, but suddenly I'm the one about to hyperventilate. "Rosemary and Sage?" I sputter, and my mom flinches.

"Dahlia, your grandmother, named them for magic. Rosemary

for wisdom, Sage for luck. Goddess knows she needed both," Violet says, sighing.

Daisy. Poppy. Lily. Dahlia. Rosemary. Sage. And me. *Willow.* It's a garden I didn't know I was a part of.

Something big explodes in my center, sending splinters from my heart to the rest of my body. Even though it's familiar, it takes me a moment to recognize it. *Betrayal.* Yet another thing my mom hasn't told me about herself. Yet another wall that I felt but couldn't see. Maddeningly, tears well up in my eyes. But this feels like the last straw.

I look up at my mom, and her gray eyes meet mine. All the new information is hot and bubbly in my chest. "Why didn't you tell me?" I say slowly. *"Why?"*

"Tell you what, dear?" Poppy says curiously.

"Willow, we'll talk later," my mom says firmly, but her eyes are darting from me to the aunts, and she starts fidgeting with her earrings, which is downright un-*Mom* of her. Whatever she has to say, she doesn't want to say it. And that thought manages to make the fire in my chest grow even larger.

"Mom, you need to tell me. The *truth.*" My words rush out from somewhere deep inside of me, and she can't ignore the intensity in my voice. No one can. Even the tourist in the witch hat looks at me in alarm, then slides off the crescent moon.

"Oh dear," Poppy says. She hooks her arm through mine. "The truth sets us free, doesn't it, dear? I suggest we continue, or"—her eyes sparkle—"*begin* this conversation at the house. No time to lose. Let's fly, my pretties!"

6

Mason

Someone is watching me. I know it the way you know when it's about to storm—the air feels charged, electric, and my muscles are tense, ready to burst into action, carry me from harm. I hope I'm wrong, but when I roll over in my twin bed, I'm met by two sets of enormous brown eyes hovering mere inches from mine, and my body reacts like it got struck by lightning.

"What the f—" I start, but luckily my brain catches up and I swallow down the rest of the word, my heart hammering against my rib cage. It is not a pair of highly trained assassins. It's the girls, the youngest two, Zoe and Audrey, whose names I remember only because Emma silently slipped me a paper listing the girls' names and ages after dinner yesterday, when I mixed up the youngest two for the thirtieth time. Names are an ongoing issue. It's like my brain decided that after so many schools and homes, it's useless to remember that the next-door neighbor's name is Henry, or that my homeroom desk mate's name is Ella, because Henry and Ella will probably be irrelevant to my life in less than six months, and why bother encoding stuff like that?

I sag back onto my bed, trying to even out my breathing. I've always had a hair-trigger response to stress or danger, but my heart seems to be beating even harder than normal.

"Hi, Mason," Zoe says. They're wearing matching Disney Princess nightgowns, and Audrey has made an attempt at bright red lipstick. The effect is a bit more slasher movie–esque than I'm up for at the moment.

"Hi, guys." I rub my eyes aggressively. I was dreaming about something in outer space, a deep, empty void that was oddly enjoyable, but daylight has landed me squarely back in reality, and I can't say I'm terribly happy about it.

I yawn, hoping they'll take the hint and scamper off, but when I remove my hands, the girls are still staring, wide-eyed.

"Um? You can draw in your notebook?" Audrey says, pointing to where I've left my star log on the nightstand. My heart rate quickens again, my eyes darting over to it. I've had kids weaponize it before, stealing it or trying to read it to get a reaction out of me, and I have to remind myself that Audrey and Zoe are little girls. They aren't after my notebook. I scoop it up just in case anyway.

"I mostly write," I say.

"Let me see it," Zoe says firmly, and I reluctantly pass it to her. I don't think she can read, which makes this mostly safe, but it's still hard to have it out of my control.

She begins flipping through the pages, her brows furrowed, while Audrey stares at me with owl eyes. After a few painful few moments, she passes it back, disinterested. "Okay," she says.

I still can't get over the sheer number of girls. There are girls on the stairs, in the kitchen, and occasionally in my bedroom, where none of them are supposed to go. The second night, there was a girl literally swinging from the banister until Emma came home and yelled at her, and then there was no TV for that girl that night. And even though names have been a struggle, they've distinguished themselves pretty quickly.

Nova is a dark storm cloud of pure teen angst, and her headphones appear to be surgically attached to her head. Hazel wears glasses and is in a constant state of making things. Zoe is the most extroverted extrovert to ever extrovert, and Audrey is the littlest one. She almost never says anything, but when she does, it's always a question in a tiny high voice and it always begins with "Um?"

"Do you guys need something?" I ask weakly.

"Um?" Audrey says. "You can . . . eat bwekfast?"

Zoe shoos her away. "Mason, we have an important question." Maple syrup is dribbled down her nightgown, and when she leans in, I get a big whiff of it. "Why did your mom have to go to jail?"

The final fragments of my dream void. "What?" I choke.

"Did she rob a bank? That's what Hazel told me. Or maybe . . ." She pauses, making sure I'm listening. "Maybe . . . she murdered someone." Zoe claps her hands together, clearly thrilled with the possibility of the latter. Audrey is looking at me with wide, terrified eyes. I've literally never seen eyes as big as on these girls. They're like anime characters.

Also, I am not explaining that the reason my mother went to jail was for possession with intent to sell. Absolutely not. I take a deep breath. "She didn't murder anyone. But she did make a mistake. Actually . . . a lot of mistakes." Dozens of them? Hundreds of them? That's honestly a more accurate depiction. I'm not even completely sure what the last straw charge *was*, although I do know the judge tried to give her more chances because of me. "But it was a long time ago. She's not in jail anymore."

After I entered foster care, my mom and I had regular visits for years until her drug use got in the way, and then it was phone calls only, but even that became more and more sporadic until one day, they stopped completely. Since then, any information about her has been spotty. I know that about a year ago, she was in a rehab program, but after that she went dark, and my foster care workers told me they'd lost contact with her, which probably means she's using again.

Zoe nods knowingly. "Because of the bad drugs? Mom said sometimes you get . . . addictionized, and then you can't worry about anything else, even sometimes your kiddos."

Audrey looks at me mournfully, and stars explode behind my eyes. I do not deserve this. No one does.

I look up at the ceiling, where someone has affixed glow-in-the-dark stars, definitely for my benefit. Besides the confetti, they're the only stars I've managed to see since I arrived, a fact that makes me antsy. I typically rely on the stars to anchor myself. Without them, I'm even less grounded than usual. "If you want to know more, you can ask your mom and dad and they can tell you."

Zoe's face falls in disappointment. "No, they won't. I already asked, and they said we'd talk about it later. And don't tell them I asked you because they told me I'd be in big trouble if I did. Big. Also, Saturday cinnamon rolls are ready. Dad says you should come downstairs."

Audrey nods solemnly. "*Um.* You can eat cimmum rolls?"

"Let's go." Zoe grabs her hand and they leave, Audrey casting one last furtive glance at me. "He isn't going to tell us anything anyway."

The second they close the door, I fall backward and stare up at the ceiling. This has easily been the longest few days of my entire life.

To be fair, the problem is less with the Morgans themselves than it is with the fact that there are things that remind me of my mom *everywhere*. When I first saw Emma's pearl tattoo, I thought it might have been a nod to my mom's obsession with mermaids, but unfortunately, Emma seems to share the same mermaid-hoarding instincts. The shower curtain is printed with turquoise-finned mermaids, and next to the garage door is a sign featuring a mermaid brandishing a triton and the words MERMAID PARKING.

I get that to most people mermaids are not that big of a deal, but to me, they're big fat emotion bombs. For as long as I can remember, my mom has been obsessed with mermaids. Movies, T-shirts, books, paintings, costumes; all of it. Once we even drove over a hundred miles to see an underwater mermaid exhibit in a small town in Florida.

Emma's tattoo is the worst of it, though. Every time I see it, it's like my brain thinks we've caught a glimpse of my mom, and then suddenly I'm keyed up, heart racing, breath shallow. Luckily, Emma and her tattoo haven't been all that hard to avoid.

Emma is busy, the entire household is, and most of our communication feels perfunctory and half of it comes via notes that she slips under my door. *New blue towels in the bathroom are yours. Spaghetti at six. If you need anything from the grocery store (shampoo? socks?), you can write it on the list on the fridge.*

Her notes are oddly disappointing, because obviously I don't want to spend a bunch of time with her, but if she was going to go to all this work to become certified to foster me, shouldn't she at least be attempting to talk to me? The only real conversation we've had was the first night, when she brought me pizza and told me straight up what Kate/Kaitlin had told her during their "chat." *I know you've run away in the past, and I'm sure you've had your reasons for it. We want you to feel like you can start over here, and the only way we can work through this is mutual trust. We trust you, and we want you to feel that we do. Communication is our main goal right now.*

So Emma clearly thinks of me as a runaway, which honestly isn't accurate, because it had more to do with the circumstances than it did with me. My first foster home was okay, but the couple unexpectedly had to move out of state to care for an ill family relative. My second foster home was great at giving me space. So good at it, in fact, that my case worker decided it was no longer a good fit. Fortunately or unfortunately, by the time I was moved out of that home I'd gotten used to being completely independent, a trait that my new foster family interpreted as defiance. They kept giving me harsher and harsher rules until it really was defiance, and the only way to get any breathing room was to escape. I kept finding other places to be—with friends, wandering the streets, and one night, after a bad fight with my foster father, I went and stayed in a youth shelter. Eventually the placement broke down and I ended up in a group home, which is when I first heard about the Morgans, who apparently worked hard to get licensed for foster care. But if that's the case, then why aren't we talking much at all? Yesterday I wrote *deodorant* on Emma's grocery list, and that was only because I was in desperate need. Emma had written *What kind?* next to it, and I'd written *Any kind*, because I don't actually know what kind I like; I've always used whatever was available. I wished I could write *T-shirts*, because mine are all way overdue for a refresh, and *pack of blue pens*, because blue is my preferred star log color, but *deodorant* was all I could muster.

I've been in worse foster homes, but never any this awkward. What am I even doing here?

I roll out of bed, wincing slightly. Like everything in my room, the mattress is brand new, and it's a little bit stiff and plasticky-smelling. Everything else in the room appears to be new too. Along with my bed, there's a white five-drawer dresser, a nightstand, and a dark blue rug that is so new, it hasn't quite unrolled at the edges yet. Honestly, it's disorienting. I've never really had anything all that new, plus, I keep running into remnants of the room's previous residents, like the Minnie Mouse Band-Aid I found stuck to the inside of the closet door or the sprinkling of glitter on the windowsill.

I take my time pulling on a T-shirt and a pair of shorts as I think over my objective for the day. So far, I've got: *Avoid Emma and her tattoo. Read astrophysics books. Try not to freak out.*

Full day here.

Most importantly, I've got to figure out how to get unsupervised access to the computer. Simon told me I'm fine to use it anytime, but the Morgans' family computer is right off the dining room, in full view of everyone, and someone always seems to be either using it or hovering nearby. I can't have anyone see that I'm looking for my mom.

I grab my notebook from my nightstand and read over the single idea I have written down for escaping the Morgan household. *Option one: Tell Kate/Kaitlin this isn't working and ask to go back to the group home.* Technically I can call and tell my foster care worker that at any point, but that doesn't mean that anything is going to happen. Kate/Kaitlin was beyond thrilled about me being here. All she'll do is tell me to give it more time. Besides, do I want to go back to the group home?

Thinking about it brings a wave of memories of standardized pillows and loud dining rooms. A quick tightening in my chest gives me a good answer. I don't actually want to be anywhere except with my mom, which I guess is the entire point, so what's the difference if I stay here?

I mentally add to my list. *Option two: Run away again and try to find my mom while on the run.* This is fantasy. I don't even have a good starting point for finding her.

Option three: Tell caseworker and/or Emma that I really need to make contact with my mom and tell them to do whatever they have to in order to reestablish contact. That one's even more hopeless-sounding, because I have asked. Dozens of times. But lately all I've gotten are variations of *I'm sorry, but she has to be willing to accept help.*

That's the thing people always get wrong about her. If my mom could get better on her own, she would. They're the ones who aren't trying hard enough.

Also, they clearly have no idea what it feels like to be separated from the one person you're meant to be with. It's like I'm walking around without one of my vital organs.

If I had any idea where my mom was, I'd leave immediately. Mom and I always figured things out together, and even when she couldn't take care of me, at least I was there to take care of her. Not that I need anyone to take care of me. Like a lot of kids in foster care, I've had to grow up fast. That's why she needs me—I'm strong enough for both of us. I glance at the sky through my bedroom window. *Send me one measly sign, and I'll find you.*

Simon's voice comes up the stairs, breaking me out of my reverie. "Mason? Breakfast time."

Breakfast is apparently a requirement at this house. I grab my notebook and astrophysics book, then stand at the door for several moments, willing myself to open it. Might as well get this over with.

The hallway and stairs are a land mine of Barbies and plastic baby dolls, and I move slowly, trying not to step on anything whose head could pop off. I've made my way toward the entryway when I spot Nova.

Seeing Nova outside of her bedroom is like catching sight of a rare bird. She's sitting on the couch with her feet propped up on the coffee table, a center-less cinnamon roll perched next to her, her giant headphones secured firmly to her head. As usual, seeing her angry silhouette makes me feel protective—I don't understand Nova, but I do understand how angry she is. I spend a lot of time in that space too.

"Hey, Nova," I say.

I can tell she's heard me by the way her shoulders tense, but she doesn't turn around. According to Zoe, Nova normally lives with her mom in Worcester, with every other weekend here in Salem, but this summer her mom is traveling a lot for work, so she's spending the entire summer with her dad. I think it's a genuine toss-up for who wants to be here least. If there was any possibility of it, I'd say we should form an alliance. As it is, I'm lucky if I'll get her to ever make eye contact with me. I don't try again.

In the kitchen, Simon is standing in front of the stove, wearing running clothes, sneakers, and an apron. He's beaming, his energy radiating off the walls. "Good morning, Mason! Cinnamon roll? I make them every Saturday, always with a twist. This week is maple-flavored dough with crumbled bacon on top. Want to give it a try?"

I'm not much of a breakfast eater, and the thought of eating frosting this early makes me slightly queasy, but I'm not quite sure how to tell him that. Also, fancy cinnamon rolls are a whole lot better than some of the breakfasts I've been forced to eat. "Thanks," I mumble.

He slides the plate to me, and objectively this is a great-looking cinnamon roll, but it takes all my willpower to manage a small bite.

The flavors are okay together, the crunchy bacon balancing out the sweetness of the frosting, but it's still more than I can handle. Simon is waiting for my reaction. "Nice, right?"

I force myself to swallow against a wave of nausea. "Really nice."

He takes a triumphant sip of coffee. As usual, he looks luminescent, practically humming with energy. There are few people in this world who need coffee less than Simon does. "I told the girls to knock quietly. Did they do an okay job?"

"Yeah." I'm starting to worry the Morgans think I only know a handful of words. *Yep. Nope. Yeah. Okay.* But I can't seem to muster up more than that, especially not with Simon. He's open and friendly, and while I get why that's great in theory, it feels a bit intimidating in practice. He's invited me to exactly ninety outings since I arrived, all of which involve me engaging in some sort of physical coordination. Also, what the hell is pickleball?

The back door opens, and Emma's voice makes my spine straighten. "Simon?"

"In here. Mason's eating breakfast."

Emma steps in, bringing a rush of summer humidity with her. She's wearing her flip-flops again and yet another oversize T-shirt. Her wardrobe doesn't seem to have a lot of range, which normally is something I can respect, but I hate that all those T-shirts show her wrist. "Morning, guys," she says, setting down a bunch of plastic grocery bags. I see my requested deodorant sticking out of the top and a wave of dread passes over me for the interaction that is going to have to happen for me to acquire said sad stick of deodorant. I hate this place with the heat of Venus and Mercury put together.

"Cinnamon roll?" Simon asks her.

She shudders slightly. "Way too early for that. Is there any coffee?"

Simon gestures to the counter, where a fresh pot is brewing. It looks like actual heaven. Before I can stop myself, I blurt out, "Can I have some?" They both turn and look at me, probably stunned to hear me utter a full sentence.

"Oh . . . I don't think kids are supposed to—" Simon starts.

"Black or with cream and sugar?" Emma interrupts, glancing at my barely touched cinnamon roll.

"Cream," I say. She fills me an enormous cup, then grabs a carton of half-and-half from the fridge and sets it in front of me. As soon as Simon turns his back, she casually whisks away my plate of sugary horror and sets it in the sink.

My cheeks feel hot. I don't want to have to deal with a wink or smile or something, but luckily she doesn't do that. She's focusing on her own cup, so I turn all my focus on mine, enjoying the feeling of the hot cup almost burning my fingertips. My group home didn't allow coffee, and I didn't realize how badly I missed it. My mom let me drink coffee from the time I was little, and even though it made me pull faces, I loved the dark, bitter taste. The Morgans have much nicer coffee than I'm used to, and I inhale, letting the smooth, rich flavor fill my mouth. Sitting here feels like a tiny moment with my mom.

Emma pours her own cup and then settles with her back against the counter. There's a long pause, and suddenly I feel hopeful. Maybe now is a good time use the computer? Before I can head for the dining room, Simon raises his spatula and punctuates the air with it, giving Emma a meaningful look.

"Oh, right! Mason, I need to check on a few of my listed properties this morning, and I could really use your help. Will you come with me? It could be a good chance to see the town." He beams at me, and my restful moment pops like a soap bubble.

Subtle. So very subtle.

I know this tactic. I've said no to his earlier suggestions of pickleball and bike rides and one-on-one basketball, so now we're moving on to *I could really use your help*. Honestly, it's a good tactic, because what am I going to say? *Sorry, I have to sit in my room all day again?*

"Um . . ." My heart thuds helplessly.

Emma shifts her cup to the other hand, and I see the flash of pink on her inner wrist. I don't want to go anywhere with Simon, but if I'm honest, the walls of that bedroom are starting to close in on me, and anything is better than being in the same room with Emma and her tattoo. "Yeah. Okay."

Simon lights up by several watts. "How are you on a bike?"

I try to remember the last time I rode a bike but come up blank. I know I've ridden one, but I can't remember where. Was it my first foster home? "Okay," I say again.

His smile could power a small island.

7

Willow

Let's fly, my pretties.

And fly we do.

Not on broomsticks or anything, although at this point I wouldn't be surprised if my mom whipped out a black cloak and matching black hat and zipped into the sky. Instead, we take off as though attempting to break a land record, Violet and my mom whispering furtively ahead of us while Poppy and I bring up the rear. I'm not sure if Poppy has been assigned the job of distracting me, but she's giving it her all.

"Witchy Goodness," Poppy says, clanking her walker toward a small storefront. "Do me a favor and don't buy a single thing from that place. You didn't hear it from me, but they get their spells from the *Internet*." She sighs heavily, her eyes wide behind her glasses. "Witches these days. You know how they are."

I do not in fact know how they are, but I'm too busy trying to eavesdrop on my mom and Violet's conversation to say so.

My mom seems to be trying to give away Sage's house. "I'll sign it over to you *today*. Think, you could use it for your shop and your meetings—"

"Impossible!" Violet says. "She left it for you."

"A bed-and-breakfast," my mom continues, her voice climbing in desperation. "You could even sell it yourselves."

"*Impossible*," Violet repeats.

Definitely the house. Why is she so desperate to get rid of it? I take up a half gallop to try to hear more, and Poppy shuffles along beside me, surprisingly fast with her walker. "Dark Moon Magic! If you need a banishing spell, that's your place. Although I'd stay away from anything curse-related. *Obviously*."

"Mmm," I manage, giving the shop a quick glance. The windows are lined with crystals and candles, and a small card table has been set up with a sign that says BESPOKE TAROT/ORACLE READINGS. APPOINTMENT ONLY.

My mom says something under her breath to Violet, and Violet throws her arms in the air. "Nonsense! You read Poppy's letter, didn't you? It was all part of Sage's plan."

What plan? I'm so eager to hear what they're saying that I get too close and accidentally step on the back of my mom's shoe. My mom shoots a glance at me, and I slow down, doing my best to look interested in what Poppy is saying.

Violet is now waving her arms around. ". . . all over the house. She spent months preparing—"

"Not so loud," my mom says, and Violet drops her voice. Frustration bubbles in my chest. How am I going to figure out what is going on?

Poppy's voice climbs a few decibels. "If you want a custom spell, you go to Marigold. She's been doing it for over fifty years. You'll love Marigold. She was out late last night salsa dancing, which is why she didn't get the chance to come meet you. But you'll see her soon enough."

Mom is now leaning into Violet, whispering intensely. I give up. "Who's Marigold?"

"Our other sister," Poppy says. "She's the baby of the family. Eighty-three and exactly as rambunctious as you'd imagine."

My expression must show her exactly what I think of an eighty-three-year-old being called the baby because her face erupts into a thousand wrinkles. "You'll love her." She points to another shop. "Now, while you're here you must stop at Helga's. We kicked her out of the coven years ago for hexing a new initiate, can't tolerate dark magic, particularly against the newbies, but her fudge is divine!"

Helga's Witchy Delights is a small sweet shop painted bright purple with swirly script in the windows advertising confections. "Okay, that is pretty cute," I admit.

"Your aunt Sage loved it there," says Poppy, her eyes shining kindly. "Her favorite was the butterscotch fudge."

I try the name on in my mind. *Aunt Sage.* Can I call her that if I'll never meet her? "What was she like?" I ask.

"Divine. Complicated. A typical Bell woman." She shrugs, her wrinkly smile back in place. I look up at my mom. I'm not sure that she's divine, but she is definitely complicated.

Violet's voice has risen again. "It won't take long. All you have to do is read, and—"

Mom gives up on whispering. "Absolutely not," she snaps, and I'm a tiny bit relieved to hear her regular voice. "The only reason we're here is to handle the estate. Once that's finished, we're leaving. And there will be no more discussion of this. None."

Her voice is icy and final, and it makes my heart freeze. Ah. There's the mom I know and love. But instead of looking freaked out like most people are when my mom goes into assertive mode, the aunts exchange a bemused smile, which, according to my mom's reddening face, does not go over well.

"Whatever you say, Rosey Posey," Poppy sings. "Let's get to the house."

We turn off Essex into a quiet neighborhood that takes New

England charm very, very seriously. Tall, rectangular houses are pressed tightly against the redbrick sidewalks, their exteriors coated in thick layers of paint. Window boxes burst with bright flowers, and shiny brass knockers gleam from every door.

The aunts take a sharp turn past a brownstone church, and I'm about to ask how much farther we have to go when suddenly they all stop walking so abruptly that I plow straight into the back of Aunt Violet.

"Welcome to the Bell family home!" Poppy says. She's pointing upward, and when I follow her outstretched finger . . .

The entire world stops.

We're standing in front of what I can only describe as the warmest, most exceptionally charming house I have ever seen. It is very New England, two stories high, red brick, old and grand but somehow still cozy, with neat rows of windows, a generous coating of ivy, and a brick walkway leading up to a cobalt-blue door. But it's the gardens that really solidify the magic. Deep flower beds overflow with luscious greenery, punctuated by bursts of flowers of all different heights and colors. An arched trellis drips with purple-blue morning glories, and pink climbing roses reach over the waist-high fence. Three magnolia trees stand under a window, their pink cup-shaped petals open to the sun.

Love at first sight apparently applies to houses, and I am experiencing it in real time. I inhale, drawing in the scent of a thousand flowers. I exhale, and a weight seems to leave my body. It reminds me of the sensation I had when Bea took me to see the Eiffel Tower for the first time—a creeping assurance that my feet were always meant to stand in this exact spot.

"This is it?" I whisper. I can't tear my eyes from it.

Poppy links arms with me. "You can feel it, can't you, dear?"

She doesn't have to explain what she means because I *am* feeling it. It's a settling, peaceful feeling. Like my feet are suddenly more connected to the earth, and I can let my shoulders unwind. It takes longer than it should for me to recognize the feeling.

Home. This place feels like *home*.

I glance over to see my mom staring up at the house too, her face solemn. "You really grew up here?" My voice is accusing. Disbelieving. I have a million other questions, such as *Who would ever leave this place?* and *Why do you look like you want to go sprinting up the street?* but I figure I'll start with the obvious.

Violet pipes up. "This house has been in the family for generations. It was Daisy's when the girls were young, and then after she died, it sat empty for years. Sage really had her work cut out for her."

Violet claps her hands together. "Rosemary, you're going to be so delighted! Oh, the improvements! Sage was *maniacal* in getting the details right. Can you believe she restored the gardens? Daisy always said she wanted to do this very thing, and now Sage has done it. They're exactly like the house's earliest photographs."

My mom doesn't seem to be aware that anyone is here except her. She isn't moving, but somehow she's . . . wilting. Shrinking. Falling back into herself. What is going on with her? Then I follow her gaze and realize she isn't looking at the house at all. She's looking up at the house next door.

"Rosemary?" Poppy says.

She inhales sharply. "The end. How was the end?"

For a moment I don't understand what she means, but then I realize she's talking about Sage. My heart thuds, hard.

"Death is death, dear," Poppy says softly. "But she was at peace. Especially because of the house. It's her apology. Wait until you see."

Curiosity splinters through me. How can a house be an apology? And what was she apologizing for? I turn to look at it again, wishing someone would explain it to me. My mom suddenly looks exhausted, her eyes rimmed red.

"Do you smell those?" Violet says, pointing to a nearby rosebush. The blossoms are as wide as a diner coffee mug, and as I turn to them I'm suddenly aware of a smell reminiscent of brewing tea.

"They're called tea roses," Violet says. "These bushes are a hundred and eighty years old, planted by the infamous Lily."

Another flower.

"Who's Lily?" My gaze is still on my mom. She's collecting herself, and watching it makes my heart feel like an orange gone soft. I'm not used to her being vulnerable.

"Your ancestor," Poppy says. "This is her father." She points to a post where a shiny gold plaque has been affixed:

BUILT FOR

FREDERICK BELL

SPICE MERCHANT

1893

HISTORICAL SALEM, INC.

"Salem was quite the bustling port back in its heyday," Violet says. "He sailed all over the world. It's his name on the house, but if you ask me, our family's story truly began with Lily Bell."

She says Lily's name in a tone close to reverence, and I feel something unspool inside of me. Excitement, yes. But also longing. I'm so eager to understand where my mom came from that I feel physically hungry. "Why? What was special about her?"

"Well, she's the reason we're all named after growing things, for one," Poppy says. "Five generations of women named after beautiful things from this very garden. Now, let's go inside, and we'll tell you *all* about her."

It's all the encouragement I need. I bound for the door, my heart as light as my feet. If the house is this beautiful on the outside, I can't even imagine what it must be like on the inside. I've only made it partially up the walkway when my mom's voice comes from behind me.

"Willow, *stop*. We won't be going inside."

I spin back around, my heart falling. She can't be serious, can she? It literally feels like a magnet is pulling me toward that door.

My mom looks smaller under the shadow of the house, her stark outfit contrasting sharply against the sprays of flowers swaying behind her. But her face is hard. Determined.

"But, Mom . . ." I trail off. I have no words to tell her how badly I want to go into the house right now, and more than that, I can't fathom how she isn't bounding after me. Are we not looking at the same house?

"We're staying on Essex," Mom says, turning to the aunts. "I'm only here to handle the legal aspects. We won't be spending time here."

Violet claps her hands together. "Nonsense. You brought Willow for a reason, and we all know it. You need to complete Sage's plan."

Excitement zings through me. "What plan?"

"There is no *plan*," my mom says loudly. "And we will not be staying in the house. Also, unless the two of you change your minds about assuming ownership, I'll be putting it on the market right away."

Her words hit me square in the chest. "Mom!"

"Think of Willow," Violet says. Rather than panicked, she and Poppy look slightly bemused. My mother sighs as though this is all annoying, but her body is tense, shoulders creeping toward her ears. "I am thinking of Willow. This is the way I've decided to manage it. Plus, I only have a short amount of time before we need to get back to LA."

She can't possibly be thinking of me. She won't even *look* at me. "But, Mom, I really, really want to see it. It would mean a lot."

My words seem to bounce off the wall surrounding her; she doesn't even acknowledge them.

"She wanted you and your daughter to spend your time in Salem in the *house*," Violet insists. "It was in her will. She specified that you spend the summer here."

Now my mom's voice is getting desperate. "I can sign the paperwork over to you this week. Like I said before, you could use it for whatever you want, your coven meetings, a bed-and-breakfast. anything."

The aunts gaze at her adoringly. "Aren't you precious. Our Rosemary, always thinking she's in charge. You must be so *tired*. The house will be a wonderful place for you two to rest."

My mom's fists clench at her sides. "I've already told you. My daughter will have nothing to do with . . ." She hesitates, then continues, her voice firm. "Nothing to do with the . . . *estate*."

"Nothing to do with it?" Violet repeats. Her face breaks out into a smile, which creates at least a thousand more wrinkles in her perfectly wrinkled face. "My dear girl. Did you really think you could outrun your history? It will follow you everywhere." She looks pointedly at me. "It has followed you everywhere."

Um.

Is it just me or are things beginning to feel a *bit* ominous? I edge nervously toward my mom. I need her to start explaining. Now.

"This has nothing to do with her," my mom insists.

"And yet you named her Willow," Violet says. She's traded in her sweet cadence for something stronger, her voice is forceful, unyielding.

They stare each other down in silence and all I can hear is my heart beating hard, filling in the empty space around me. Finally Poppy steps forward, pointing to something over my shoulder. "Look there," she says gently.

I whirl around, and when I see it, my feet nearly lift off the earth.

It's an enormous willow tree. It's old and regal, with long branches that drift gracefully to the ground. Sunlight filters green and gold through its leaves, its trunk beautifully twisted and gnarled. I've looked at pictures of hundreds of willows, and none of them have come even close to this one. She looks like the queen of them all.

Poppy's words come back to me. *Five generations of women named after beautiful things from this very garden.*

I've just found my beautiful thing. This tree is my namesake.

"Mom!" Energy shoots through me, and it takes everything not to dart over to the tree, make sure it's real. Tears prick my eyes, surprising me. It's just a tree. But it's *my* tree. It's proof that at some point my mother named me after an object connected to this place. I'm not sure what that means, particularly because she looks ready to bolt, but it means *something.* I know it does.

"You named me after a tree here?" I whisper.

Her eyes dart away from mine. "Your name has nothing to do with that tree. Or the . . ." She hesitates.

"Tell her, Rosey Posey," Violet says. "A Bell woman has to know her past if she's going to plan her future. Otherwise, she's lost."

The word *lost* hits me like a gong, its impact reverberating through me. I spin on my heel to look at my mom. "Tell me what?"

"No." My mom's voice breaks in, crashing my certainty. "Willow, come on. We're leaving."

"But . . ." My head is throbbing now, my brain desperately trying to untangle what is happening.

"You know that isn't how it works, dear," Poppy says in her gentle voice.

My mom shakes her head, hard. "It's the way it will work for us. Come on, Willow. We're going to the hotel. Aunts, we'll see you later. Tomorrow?"

"Wait!" I say, panicked. My instinct is to grab on to a rosebush or dig my feet into the soil. I can't leave this place, not when I've barely scratched its magical surface.

"Willow, please don't fight me on this," my mom says. Her voice is heavy with sadness, and now I don't know what to do. My mom is clearly in pain. But I can't leave.

Violet seems to sense my dilemma, because she pulls me into a tight hug. "So lovely to meet you, Willow." She squeezes me hard, her voice suddenly in my ear. "Book of Shadows."

Before I can even begin to process what those words could mean, she scurries down the path, Poppy by her side.

"Come to moon circle tomorrow?" Poppy asks my mom.

I don't hear my mom's response. I'm too focused on the key Violet just pressed into my palm.

8

Mason

I may have oversold my ability to ride a bike.

Simon gets me all fitted up on one of the three bikes in the garage, then he spends about thirty minutes adjusting the seat to its maximum height, then hunting through the garage for an extra helmet. By the time we're ready, the girls have all gathered in the garage to watch my grand send-off.

Simon's bike weighs about as much as a paper clip, and the pedals have little domes over the top, which I don't think I've seen before. Isn't the seat supposed to be bigger? Then I remember what the last bike I used looked like. It had a Snoopy basket on the front and red streamers. This realization does not feel promising.

"Ready?" Simon asks.

"Uh-huh," I manage. I need to just get this over with. I aim my front tire toward the driveway, push off with my back leg, and pray for a miracle, which obviously doesn't come. I wobble like a Jell-O mold in an earthquake before crashing to one side and doing a series of hops to keep from toppling over.

"He's really bad!" Zoe yells happily.

"Do you need some training wheels?" Hazel asks. "Zoe's bike has some."

I want to crawl into the recycling bin. "Ha," I say. "I guess it's been a while."

"Girls! Go inside. It takes a minute, plus, we're still in the driveway. Nice and easy, Mason, it'll come back to you," Simon says encouragingly. I can't think of any way out of this, so I hold my breath and try again. This time I make it about six feet before toppling over.

"See!" Simon says. "So much better."

We straggle out of the driveway, and I mostly stay upright, then eventually it does start to come back to me a little bit. I'm not good, but it doesn't feel like I'm going to end up a splat on the concrete either.

"How about a little bike tour of the city?" Simon asks.

Even with the stress of biking, I have to admit that it feels good to get out. Simon takes the lead, which removes some of my anxiety, and we do a loop around the big park, which is paved and a little easier than bumpy brick roads.

"I got a call about a new house earlier today," Simon says over his shoulder. "It's historical, lots of them are, but it sounds like this one could be pretty special. We'll save it for last."

I have no idea what to say to this, so I make a vague "ah" noise, then immediately hate myself for it. Simon must think I have the spine of a jellyfish.

Simon glances back, his pedals spinning beneath him. "Perhaps later we could stop by the high school, see where you'll be starting school in the fall. I even thought we could call around and maybe connect you with other students who will be in your grade?"

Panic bubbles up inside of me, although I manage to keep my gaze pointed forward. I do not want to be connected to a peer through some pity friend date. After years of being around a rotation of adults, I've figured out something crucial: adults go through some state of amnesia that makes them forget what it's like to be a teenager. Otherwise, why would they come up with such horrible suggestions?

"Mmm," I say, narrowly missing a curb.

He swoops in on the silence. "We can do that later. Before we get to the houses I have to check on, I'll just show you around town. Get you oriented. Give you the Salem real-estate pitch."

What I want to say is *No thank you*, but what comes out is "Sure."

It's all the encouragement he needs. He speeds up and I wobble after him, trying to listen but devoting about 90 percent of my attention to not crashing and dying. According to Simon, Salem is technically a suburb of Boston, but it has its own urban, college-town feel with lots of local businesses and plenty of quirky charm to give it its own identity. And even though it has a big tourist draw, most people live here year-round, with the population swelling temporarily near Halloween. The architecture is distinctive, boxy Georgian and Federal designs, which Simon attempts to explain the difference between, all painted in muted colors and pressed tightly together, lining the redbrick sidewalks.

Eventually I start to even out some, and as we wind our way through Salem, he points out everything he thinks I might be interested in. There's the House of the Seven Gables, a dark, spooky-looking house that inspired Nathaniel Hawthorne's novel of the same name; Pickering Wharf, with a walking path that takes you past a restored old ship on your way to the lighthouse; and Burying Point, an old graveyard where several groups of people are picnicking. He shows me the Witch House, where Emma gives tours, and asks if I want to see the new skate park that was put in earlier that year, but I quickly decline the offer. The only thing more pathetic than me on a basketball court is me on a skateboard. I can barely manage the bike.

Eventually he runs out of places to show me and we begin official business. Our first stop is a brown clapboard house near the shore that is currently having its exterior renovated. Simon stops to talk to the men carrying out the job, and I help him plant a FOR SALE sign in the postage stamp of grass out front. The next house is a smaller, newer-looking place, with an ugly stucco exterior and a half-dead lawn, and Simon makes a bunch of calls to some local yard companies to get someone out to treat it. Stops three and four are him checking on the interior, and I jump in to help him with some light yard work, pulling weeds, watering flower beds, that kind of thing. By stop five I'm starting to wonder if we're going to be out here all day. The air is as thick as mashed potatoes, the only relief an occasional breeze that wafts up from the shore. I try not to look at it. Some days the ocean makes me feel better; on others it makes my soul hurt. My mom once told me she must have been a mermaid in a past life. Why else would the ocean feel like home?

"One last stop," Simon says. "This is the one I told you about earlier. I got a call from a potential new client last night who wants to put her house on the market soon. It belonged to a witch."

I think he's joking, but then he turns down a residential street, stopping in front of a large house. Its brick is worn to a mellow red, ivy overtaking its exterior. Sprays of flowers burst out from every corner of the garden and the windows sparkle in the sunlight, and even for someone who doesn't notice houses much, I can't look away from this one. As I climb off the bike, it dawns on me why. This is a *Mom house*. When I was little, we used to get out of the city on drives to look at all the big houses on the coast, and we'd spend hours picking which ones we wanted to live in. Hers were always fancy like this, with big gardens and dozens of windows, flags swaying in the breeze. She'd love a garden like this, especially one so close to the ocean.

I swallow hard, trying to dislodge the memory of my mom, then glance at Simon, who is already heading up the lawn. "What a yard," he says, his voice rising in enthusiasm. "This place will photograph beautifully."

"Did you say a witch lives here?" I ask, stepping over a few downed blossoms.

Simon chuckles. "Word on the street. It's an inheritance situation. In one family for generations, but it sat empty for a really long time. About a year ago, one of the family members showed up and decided to restore it. She really dove in. There was a crew here around the clock for close to six months, and they completely overhauled the place. She was a tarot reader, psychic, something like that, but she passed away shortly after it was finished and left it to her sister, who wants to get it appraised right away. Let's see what we're working with, shall we?"

The door takes a few tries, but as soon as we step in and make our way into the kitchen, I find myself holding my breath because there's this *feeling* that makes you shut up and pay attention.

The house is simple but warm, with soft white walls and honey-colored wooden floors. The only light comes from sunlight filtering in through the windows in thick, lazy beams and there's a gentle coating of dust on everything. Someone has clearly been taking care of the place because potted plants brighten every possible corner, their leaves green and healthy. But it's the peacefulness that gets me. A quiet stillness pervades the house, the world shut out behind the door. I think Simon must be enjoying it too, because for once, he doesn't say anything.

The floor plan is typical, an updated kitchen with wooden countertops and open shelving lined with stacks of white dishes. The kitchen spills into a living room where cozy-looking couches surround a fireplace. Next is the entryway, with a painted staircase, then a reading room with a desk, a large plush chair. The more I look at it, the more I realize it's the careful details that make this house— every single item looks like it was carefully selected. Thickly woven rugs, inviting-looking pillows, clusters of candles, and hanging plant baskets with heart-shaped leaves trailing to the floor. It's magical, relaxing, and minimal in a way that feels intentional, like someone has created a blank canvas for you to make your mark on.

It reminds me of a house my mom and I stayed in for a few months one fall. It belonged to a friend of hers, and while she and her friends partied, I spent most of my time wandering through the house pretending to be a pirate searching for gold. People always thought it was awful that she did drugs in front of me, but honestly it was better when she did it where I could see. That way I knew where she was and what was going on.

"The antiques really make the place, don't they?," Simon finally says, his voice hushed. "Look at that. I'll bet it was once on the front of a ship."

He points to a weathered statue of a woman nearly as tall as I am standing in the corner of the library, and I walk over to take a look. The woman is arched forward slightly, her paint worn down by years, eyes blank, and I realize she had likely started out on the front of a ship. "A figurehead?" I say, the word coming to me.

Simon nods. "Must have belonged to the spice merchant." He points to the stairs. "Want to check out the upper floors? I need to take a look at the furnace."

Almost automatically, my feet carry me toward the gleaming wooden staircase. Upstairs are two bedrooms and a bathroom, and then another staircase leading to another floor of bedrooms. Each bedroom has been carefully furnished and decorated, with plump pillows and woven rugs. The final room on the top floor has a short, slanted roof that I have to duck to enter, but as soon as I step in, I freeze, because . . . *Have I been here before?*

I mean, that's impossible. But have I?

I step in cautiously. This room stands out from the others—it's simpler, but more luxurious-feeling than the rest of the house, possibly because of its rich colors. The wallpaper is a deep, swirling blue patterned to look like waves, and the gleaming gold bed hosts expensive-looking bedding topped with a small mountain of pillows in an array of blues and sea-glass greens. The deep gray rug is thick and extravagant under my feet, and sunlight glows through the pristine windows. The room even smells good—earthy and floral, with a hint of spice, and when I look up at the exposed beams of the ceiling, I realize why. Bundles of dried flowers and herbs are hanging from the beams, their petals and stems reaching delicately toward the ground.

This is easily the best room in the house.

I flip on the light switch, expecting overhead lights to flood the room, but instead, a single light illuminates a small oil painting hung above the bed.

My body recognizes the image before the rest of me does, and I'm jolted forward, my face only inches from the painting by the time my brain catches up. It's a painting of a mermaid, and not an ethereal princess mermaid; the *right* kind of mermaid. Complicated, dark, and a little chaotic. The mermaid is perched on a rock, her dark green fin splayed in front of her. Her hair is long and wild, the ocean painted in intricate gray and blue swirls behind her. The details and style are impeccable, but it's her serious, pointed gaze that sucks me in. She's surrounded by confusion and turmoil, but she's focused on one thing.

What is it?

On a whim, I turn to see where her gaze is pointed, and am

startled to see a wooden ladder propped up against the wall leading to a large glass skylight in the ceiling.

My stomach rolls like the mermaid's ocean. My mom and I were always climbing out on rooftops together to look at stars, and I can't help but wonder if a mermaid is really directing me to a roof? Obviously, I will be going up there.

"Simon?" I call into the hallway. No answer.

The ladder feels unsteady under my weight, and I move slowly, expecting a crash at any moment. At the top, it takes me a few seconds to figure out how to unlatch the window, and swinging it open is all kinds of clumsy, but when I climb through the opening into the quiet, humid air and see what is waiting for me, I nearly lose my grip. Am I hallucinating, or is this real?

It's a mini observatory. A flat, open space about the size of a small bedroom has been gated in, its edges lined with garden boxes. A squishy-looking chair has been pushed into one corner, protected by a cream-colored umbrella, and to the chair's right, as though I've conjured it, a *telescope*.

An actual telescope.

I'm too stunned to move from the ladder. The telescope's lens is pointed up toward where the moon will be when it rises tonight, and I know right away that when I look through the lens, all I will see is clear, unrestricted sky. Below, branches from the tree shroud the rooftop garden from the street and nearby houses. And I feel it, a feeling so unfamiliar, it takes me a moment to recognize it for what it is. *Hope.* My heart is racing now, because, honestly, if someone had wanted to create the perfect place for me, something to make me think of my mom and my life before we were separated, this would be it.

I reach for my back pocket, feeling the wire edge of my notebook.

I could take so many notes here. I could fill entire notebooks with a view like this.

I know what this is. I know it in my bones, my blood, my soul, my heart. It's a sign.

Signs come in threes, Mason. And I just found my first one. My hands are shaking, my legs wobbling harder than they were on the bike. I don't actually believe in signs, do I? Except, a mermaid—the exact kind my mother loved—has pointed to me to what basically amounts to my perfect hideout, complete with a telescope.

What is this?

Fate? a tiny voice whispers. Okay, I can't quite believe it, but I also can't discount it. I can't. Because, what are the chances?

"Mason?" Simon's voice comes from deep inside the house, and I quickly pull the window shut, lowering myself down the ladder. I've just hit the floor when he pokes his head into the room.

"Oh," he says, looking at the room with awe. His eyes graze over the wallpaper, the mermaid, all the dried herbs. "This place is full of surprises. Look how she designed the room around the painting."

I'm almost angry that I didn't notice it for myself. Every color in the painting is reflected in the room's décor.

"It must be special," he says.

You're telling me. My hands are still trembling, so I shove them in my pockets. The mermaid's gaze is boring a hole into the side of my face, but I manage to keep my eyes on Simon.

"I need to take a look at that huge willow tree outside. They're water-seeking, and when they get that big, they can cause problems with everything. Ready to go?"

A stab of panic hits my chest. I can't leave the mermaid and the rooftop. Not yet. But I also can't tell Simon that. "Okay if I use the bathroom first?" I ask.

"Of course." He gestures to his phone. "Emma texted. She was thinking we could all bike to our favorite doughnut shop tonight? I promised the girls we'd go after dinner."

"Sounds great." I can't help my smile, and when Simon sees it, he smiles back. "Thanks for coming with me, Mason. See you downstairs?"

"Yeah." He leaves the room, and I rush the painting again, trying to process this hopeful feeling bubbling up in my chest.

Cautious hope. But hope. And this feels bigger and more awkward and spikier than any of the other feelings I've lugged around up until now. I have been looking for my mom for years and made zero progress. I've asked every adult in my life for help and gotten nowhere.

And now I have this mermaid, pointing me to a space that looks built for me.

No, I have no idea what this means. But what if this is a sign that things are about to change? What if this painting and rooftop are somehow leading me somewhere? It's like I've been summiting, the air thin, each breath a struggle, and all of a sudden there's a clear hit of oxygen.

A clear hit of *hope*.

I can't get ahead of myself.

But *what if?*

9

Willow

I'm feeling so worried and tender and genuinely concerned about my mom, it makes me want to smack her.

What is *wrong* with her?

Yes, she's lost someone important to her, but in my experience of loss, this isn't the way people act. They don't run. And lie. They don't pretend none of it happened.

The aunts take off in one direction, my mom in the other, and it takes me nearly to Essex Street to catch up with her. As we converge with the crowd of pedestrians, I am an absolute cauldron of emotions. I can barely see what is in front of me, because the image of the house feels burned into my retinas. The soft sweeping of the willow branches, those shiny windows, all of those *flowers*. "Mom! We need to talk."

We're walking against foot traffic, and we have to keep dodging groups. We skirt around a sandwich board set outside a shop. UNATTENDED CHILDREN WILL BE GIVEN AN ESPRESSO AND A BOOK OF CURSES.

"Lower your voice, Willow." She doesn't stop, doesn't even look back. And this infuriates me because she doesn't get to shut me out on something this big. Not this time.

I don't lower my voice. "Why do you tell everyone that you grew up in Martha's Vineyard?"

She keeps walking, and for a moment I think she isn't going to answer me, but then her voice floats back to me. "I did live there. For a summer. I lived a lot of places. Motels. An abandoned house. One summer we were homeless and couch surfed for two months."

What?

I grab her hand and plant my feet on the brick road. Force her to stop. "Mom, what are you talking about?"

She stops walking too, and she turns halfway toward me, finally meeting my eyes. "Willow, my mom was . . . not well. When things got too tough, or she found a new boyfriend, she'd drop us off here with Daisy. Sometimes for a night or two, sometimes for months at a time. We never knew when we'd see her again or if she was coming back."

Shock is flooding up through me now, making everything around me almost trancelike. There are obviously things I don't know about my mom, but is it possible I don't know anything about her? "But . . . in the article, you said your mom was a well-known hostess—"

"I lied," she says curtly.

I'm struggling to put the pieces together, remake this woman in front of me. One piece rises to the surface. "You were homeless?"

"Off and on," she says. "Salem was never quite my home, but it was the most home I had." She looks defeated now, her eyes exhausted. It almost hurts to make her keep talking, but I can't help my questions.

"So what happened to your mom?"

She drops her eyes. "The last time I saw her, Sage and I were fourteen. She dropped us off with Daisy, and . . ." Now her eyes are welling up; my hand darts out on its own, grabbing hers again. "We got a call from a police officer in Montana. She and her boyfriend had hit a semi. They were both killed instantly."

"Oh." It's a tiny, crumpled sound. Completely inadequate. *"Mom."* My hand finds its way to my heart like it does whenever something really hurts. By the time my mom was my age, she'd been through so much more than I could even imagine.

She exhales, and for a brief moment we both stand motionless. The sun is setting behind her, and the streets are filling up with pockets of tour groups and crowds coming in and out of bars and restaurants. I have no idea what to say.

She looks more tired than I've ever seen her. I know I can't push anymore, but I can't help this last bit. "And now you've lost your sister. . . ."

Her face contorts with pain, then smooths immediately, the motion so quick, I almost miss it. "Thank you, Willow. But I lost my sister a long time ago." She turns to face me fully. "It has taken me years to move forward. *Years.* I need you to trust me when I say the past needs to remain the past. I'm here to help the aunts settle the estate. We're here to do a job, and that's it. After that, I never want to see this place again. I really don't want you getting mixed up in any of this. Do you understand?"

A lump has risen in my throat, and I struggle to swallow. The door has cracked ever so slightly on my family's past, and now she's asking me to close it back up again. "I understand."

The wall rises back up between us, and this time I don't try to fight it. I may not understand what is going on right now, but I do know one thing: My mom is in a lot of pain.

After the day I've had, the hotel is weirdly normal. Phoebe was obviously trying to impress my mom; it's a boutique hotel decorated in mid-century modern style, with lots of quirky accents like shaggy pillows, peacock-blue sofas, and chandeliers shaped like exploding fireworks. It hosts a rooftop bar (Salem's only!), a small lounge area, and a concierge eager to point us to Salem's best hot spots, a topic my mom shuts down pretty thoroughly.

Phoebe has rented us small adjoining rooms, both with exposed brick walls and views overlooking Essex Street. Once we're inside, my mom hands me her credit card, tells me to order whatever I want for dinner, and then slams the door in my face. Literally.

I flop onto my bed and do a quick review of the past few hours: My mom has inherited a magical-looking house with the best garden I've ever seen. She has two eccentric but very sweet aunts, one of whom has given me access to the house. She had a sister who clearly broke her heart. And she experienced homelessness as a child, her mother in and out of her life.

Out of everything, that's the part I'm having the hardest time with. How is it possible I didn't know something this big about my mother? And if Sage hadn't died and left her this house, would I ever have found out?

The house.

I pull Violet's key from my pocket, testing its weight in my hand. I can't go in there, can I? And had I heard her right? Book of Shadows. What does that even mean?

Before I can google it, I get a text from Bea.

Well??

I text back. My mom GREW UP here. She also has a bunch of aunts who are actual witches. And she won't let me go into the house she inherited, even though it looks incredible.

Bea: Are you joking? I can't tell if you're joking right now. I'll call the moment I can.

Me: Not joking.

Bea: Incroyable! She has always been so secretive.

I look up at my mom's door. This afternoon has only highlighted what I already know: My mom and I have an enormous chasm between us, and I very much doubt that is ever going to change.

Out of desperation, I try my dad. Will he have any of the answers to my questions? But he rejects my call and answers with a text. **Meeting right now, call you later?**

I don't even bother to respond.

I order Thai food and try to watch TV, but the minutes stretch by slowly, and all I can focus on is my mom's closed door. She opened up to me today a tiny bit, and as hard as the things were that she told me, it had felt good to think I was getting even a tiny glimpse into her inner world.

But then she had shut me down so clearly. *I really don't want you getting mixed up in any of this. Do you understand?*

I reach into my pocket and close my hand around the key. Would sneaking into Aunt Sage's house be "getting mixed up" in my mom's story? I mean, yes. Obviously.

But if I don't go, will I ever learn *anything*? And is that fair to me? The aunts must have come to the same conclusion, otherwise, why would one of them have given me the key?

It feels impossible to concentrate on anything except the siren call of Aunt Sage's house. Not only do I want to see what is inside; I'm dying to know what Poppy meant by the house being Sage's apology to my mother.

My mom is in the other room talking to Drew for what feels like hours, and then she finally turns off her lights around nine p.m. I wait another thirty minutes, then knock lightly on her door and peek inside. She's asleep, her usual concoction of sleeping supplements set up on her nightstand. Once she's out, she's *out*.

I don't waste another second.

Outside, Salem is quiet and shimmery at night, the moon shrouded in fog, the air surprisingly chilly after the day's heat. I worry I might have a difficult time finding the house again, but I don't. The same magnet from earlier is pulling me there. I dodge a few night tour groups that are being herded along Essex by lanterns, as well as a few noisy people making their way to and from the open bars. Essex Street, with all of its magical shops, looks a lot more ominous after dark, with only a few upper apartments lit up.

When I finally reach the gate of Aunt Sage's house, I stop, feeling my first hint of trepidation. The houses on either side of Aunt Sage's are dark, but the Bell family house is somehow even darker, a black hole sitting right here in the middle of New England. Even the creeping rosebushes feel ominous under the sliver of moonlight.

I reach into my pocket for the key, then pull out my phone and text Bea. **I'm doing something dumb.**

I start up the walkway but get too nervous to unlock the door and instead attempt to look through the windows. My view is mostly blocked by velvet curtains, and the front door has a stained-glass upper window, but I can't see anything except the edge of a printed rug, and even that tiny glimpse makes my heart skip a beat. Am I really going in? What if Mom catches me?

Before I can talk myself out of it, I push the key into the lock. It slides in easily, turning with a satisfying click, and as the door swings open, I feel equal parts relief and dread.

It's completely dark inside, and I hold my breath as I step in. I feel along the wall for a switch, and when I make contact, an antique chandelier floods the entryway with light and I literally gasp with delight.

It's even better on the inside.

I'm standing at the base of a staircase with a gleaming hardwood banister, two large rooms on either side of me. The entryway is painted a soft white, one wall full of shelves displaying a collection of brightly colored geodes and crystals that glimmer pink and purple. To my left is a library, to my right is a cozy living room, several overstuffed chairs pulled up around an elaborately carved fireplace mantel. Drapey white curtains hang from every window, and candles and plants fill in the spaces in between. It's minimal and magical and so very, very warm.

I slip out of my sandals, letting my toes sink into the plush carpets, then take off, my heart feeling bigger and fuller with each step. The next ten minutes feel like one giant exhale as I tour the main floor. Then I enter the library.

Three of the room's four walls are made of floor-to-ceiling bookcases, a sliding ladder connecting them. Along with books, the shelves are lined with all kinds of interesting items. Maps, cards, thimbles, bells, stones, figurines, sea glass, stacks of vintage postcards. I even find a tiny globe in front of a section made up entirely of travel books. *Peru. Bolivia. China. Australia.*

Did Sage go to all of these places?

As I walk through, I let my hand drag across unfamiliar titles. *Develop Your Psychic Skills. The Door to Chakra Healing. Spirit Guides. Everyday Spells. Witchcraft for All of Us.* One shelf is dedicated entirely to decks of tarot cards. Another is devoted entirely to books about boats and sailing, and on the floor in front of it stands a large, worn-looking statue of a dark-haired woman who seems to be leaning into the wind, the paint of her dress weathered bone white. Every single item feels like it has its own story, and I wish Sage were here to tell them to me.

The longer I look, the more I love it. Sage is a kindred spirit. I can feel it. My dad once said that the best way to understand someone is to look at the things they keep, and I can't imagine anything telling a better story than this house. The space has so much personality, it feels like I'm looking directly at Aunt Sage. She is eclectic, tasteful, adventurous, and interesting, and I'm starting to feel a hollow spot in my throat when I think about the fact that I'll never actually get the chance to know her.

I circle my way back to the living room. This time around I notice that the coffee table holds a single book that has been propped up with candles on either side of it. The cover is light lavender with a baby-pink spine, a small pentagram etched into the center of it. It's clearly loved, whatever it is, with dog-eared edges and several scuffs and bumps.

Maybe it's only the placement, but something about the book feels important. And familiar, almost? And then I see the words scrawled in pen across the top of the cover.

BOOK OF SHADOWS.

My heart leaps. This is what Violet told me to find. I'm nervous to pick up the book, so instead I google the title.

A Book of Shadows is a magical recording of a witch's journey, generally not written for others unless intended as legacy or artifact.

So this is like . . . a magical diary?

My heart flutters. Did it belong to Sage? On a whim, I grab the lighter and quickly light the candle before picking up the book. On the inside cover are five lines:

> ONLY THE INVITED
> WILL EVER READ
> ALL OTHERS
> WILL BE FORCED TO ACCEPT
> THE CONSEQUENCES

Goose bumps ripple up my arms. It appears my aunt Sage had a flair for the dramatic. Part of me wants to start flipping through it, but another, bigger part is holding me back. What are "The Consequences"?

I glance at my phone again. *Generally not written for others unless intended as a legacy.*

Sage may not have exactly given me the journal, but she was my aunt, which makes me her legacy. Even if we never met each other, I am technically her posterity. Would she mind if I looked at her book, or will that subject me to The Consequences?

And then I see it at the bottom. This opening epitaph or whatever it is signed in two swirly signatures. *Rosemary & Sage Bell.*

Seeing those names together takes my breath away. This belonged to my mom too. Now I can't possibly stop myself.

I quickly begin flipping through pages. I'm expecting journal entries, but instead what I find reminds me of a much more colorful version of the old notebooks I toss out at the end of the school year—a bunch of scribbly notes plus drawings and the occasional glued-in item. But most of the book is dedicated to what looks like magical spells. Pages and pages of instructions written out in painstaking detail. Some of them are serious: *Spell for Broken Promises, Spell for Confidence, Spell to Banish Negative Energy.* Others are funny: *Spell to Banish Annoying Lab Partner, Spell to Grow Out Bad Haircut.* They're all handwritten in colorful pens with lots of places crossed out and written over, the margins filled with notes. *Try waxing moon next time. Red and white chime candles for this one. Call in element of fire.* Each spell is marked with either an *R* or an *S*, some both, and on several of Sage's spells I see encouraging notes written in my mom's loopy handwriting. *You've got this! You're the baddest witch in town!* On Sage's *Spell to Pass Geometry Even if Your Teacher Is the Worst,* my mom wrote, *WITCHY SISTERS FOREVER I BELIEVE IN YOU* and affixed several star stickers as well as a handful of loose glitter, which dumps out onto my lap. The book is adorable and magical, and if I thought my heart was hurting before, now it feels like it's swelled to two times its normal size.

It's like meeting an entirely different version of my mom. One who believed in magic, and who had a sister she adored.

Suddenly I realize what the Book of Shadows reminds me of. It's like my mom's event binders, only with glitter.

As I attempt to replace the glitter, I picture my mom from earlier today, her posture razor straight, her mouth set in a firm line, then look back down at the book. Where did this version of my mom go?

And then there's Sage. I can practically feel their friendship soaked into the pages. Was there a betrayal? A fight? It had to have been something big. I flip through the pages, running my finger along the spell names. *Spells for Luck. Friendship Knot Spell. Spell for Getting Rid of an Unwanted Guest.* My finger lands on a section that looks completely different. Dense text that looks like it's been written on a typewriter has been glued across two pages with the words LILY BELL at the top.

Lily. She's the one Violet and Poppy were talking about, the one who planted the tea roses. I pull the book closer to me, squinting at the small writing.

The story began, as many stories do, with a girl who bloomed too big for the space the world had carved out for her. Her name was Cordelia Bell, but everyone called her—

Suddenly a piercing noise rips through the silence, and I jump so high, I send the Book of Shadows flying across the room.

Phone. It's my phone.

I scramble to dig it out of my pocket, my ringtone piercing the air. My heart is pounding, but I feel huge relief when I see that it isn't my mom. I quickly hit answer. "Bea, you scared me," I practically yell into the phone. "I'm clutching my chest and everything."

"I scared *you*?" she demands. "What was that text about? About you doing something stupid."

"I snuck into the house. One of the aunts gave me a key." I have to get down on my hands and knees to retrieve the book from where it slid under the sofa. "And I found this incredible book. It's called a Book of Shadows, and it belonged to my mom and Sage. They practiced witchcraft together."

"Of course you're from a family of witches in Salem," Bea says. "Of *course* you are."

My stomach flutters with excitement. "The book is full of spells, I think—" But then I stop. Dead. Because, was that my imagination, or did I just . . . ? I turn my face slowly up to the ceiling and wait.

A *thud, thud, bump*. My breath hitches.

"Willow, are you there?" Bea says.

"Shh." I strain my ears, but it's hard to hear anything over the pounding of my heart. Blood is rushing to my head. *Am I imagining it?*

And then again, directly above my head, too distinct to be imagined—

Muffled footsteps. My hand flies to my chest, almost like I'm trying to keep my heart from beating out of my chest.

"Bea," I whisper. "Someone's here."

She inhales sharply. "In your aunt's house? Is it one of your mom's aunts?"

My heart is in my throat, but her words calm me down. Of course, it's one of the aunts. They basically invited me over. They're probably waiting upstairs to ambush me with more hugs. "You're right," I say. But then the noise moves to a *thud, thud, thud*. Almost like jumping.

The aunts are energetic, but I'm guessing they don't do a lot of jumping jacks.

"Yeah, I don't think it's them." My heart picks up speed again. "Maybe it's an animal. It sounds like someone is jumping around on the roof. And . . ." Shuffling. A dragging noise. Then quiet. I take a deep breath. "Someone's on the roof."

"Oookay, so you're leaving now," she says.

"No, I'm not," I say. I know I should be feeling scared right now, but instead of bolting, running for my absolute life, I find myself looking up. And then for reasons I don't understand—maybe it's my burning curiosity, maybe it's the powerful-feeling book in my hand, maybe it's the thought that I am the niece of a *witch*—I find my feet guiding me toward the staircase.

"I'm going upstairs to look," I tell Bea. "If you don't hear from me in five minutes, call my mom's cell phone and tell her I'm at Sage's house."

"What? Are you joking? Absolutely not. I order you to—" Bea yells.

"I'll call you back." I turn off my phone and put my foot on the first step.

10

Mason

It's almost ten by the time I make my move.

I've been lying awake since everyone went to bed an hour ago, and I've been counting the minutes, willing the digits on my alarm clock to move faster. After dinner, we rode bikes to Sugar Bean Coffee & Doughnuts, with the girls shouting out helpful tips for my riding while I wobbled dangerously along the edge of the street. The only person who seemed less interested in the outing was Nova, who was forced into a helmet and then emitted a small dark rain cloud that followed her all along the route.

When we got to the shop, I ordered a salted toffee doughnut before joining the several tables the Morgans had claimed against the back wall. And when Emma saw my doughnut, she said, "Too bad it's not a sugared jelly." Which made me choke, because jelly doughnuts from Dunkin' Donuts are my mom's favorite food in the world. She liked to add an extra pack of sugar to the top, which is what made them *sugared* jellies, not just jelly, and of course Emma knows that.

It's a reminder that Emma knows my mom, really knows her. And addiction or not, there is literally no one in the world like my mom. How could Emma have turned her back on her?

For a moment I think I might tell Emma how much I miss my mom, and how much I wish I knew where she was, but as soon as I opened my mouth, the words got all jammed and twisted together, crowding my throat. I know better than to trust adults, least of all this one.

By the time we biked home, I was a total wreck. My jaw hurt from clenching, and my legs were sore from two bike rides in one day. Once we got inside, I made a big show of getting ready for bed, yawning in the hallway. Right before I turned off the light, I realized there was a brand-new book on my bed, the receipt stuck in the front cover. *Letters from an Astrophysicist* by Neil deGrasse Tyson. It's by the same author as the book I was reading on the day I arrived, and I knew right away that it was from Emma. That she noticed what book I had tucked under my arm makes me feel good and weird at the same time. I have no idea what to do with that feeling. It makes me restless, like a kite on the end of a string, and after I turned off the light, the waiting became even harder.

All this is to say, by the time I leave the house, I'm ready to jump out of my skin. I have a few things in my backpack, my astrophysics book, a can of Dr Pepper I took from the fridge, binoculars, and my star log. My shoes are tied, and I'm ready.

I've always been good at sneaking out. It's about timing and confidence. You have to know how to shift your weight, how to climb, when to drop. And then when you're on your way, you have to act like you belong, which is basically the story of my life. Dark clothes are good, sneakers are a must. Windy nights are best, but Salem does what it wants to, so I'm going to have to make do with an airless night.

Being on the second story of a packed residential area isn't ideal, but I know I can make this work. I slide through, careful not to snag my backpack, and glance up at the night sky, and whatever trepidation I'm feeling vanishes into thin air. The sky honestly takes my breath away. The fog that has been clouding up my view since I've arrived is gone, leaving the night sky inky-black, the stars clear points of light, but it's the moon taking center stage. Waxing gibbous surrounded by a giant glow. It makes my fingers itch for my notebook. I want to sketch it, write about the way Mars is twinkling next to it, outshining every star. Most of all, I want to tell my mom everything I've learned. That's part of my reason for the notebook. As soon as we're back together, I'll have a log of everything I've studied during our years apart.

I'm about to climb across the roof, make my way over to the edge, drop to the grass, when I hear a quiet voice that makes every cell in my body freeze. "Em?"

I look down to see one orange-red ember and flinch when the shadow suddenly materializes as Emma. She's sitting in the dark on the back step with a cigarette, so close, she definitely would have seen me. "Out here," she says, and Simon steps out onto the patio.

If I move, they're going to see me, so I stay completely still, hovering like an oversize gargoyle, my breath steady.

"I thought you were done with these," Simon says.

"Very last one," she says, but she lets him take it from her. There's a pause and Emma's head falls to rest on Simon's shoulder. "How do you think he's doing?"

My muscles tense. There is exactly one other "he" in this household.

"I don't know," Simon says. "He still isn't talking much. And he spends so much time in his room. For a minute today, I thought he was opening up . . . and then he left without asking. Were you worried?"

Before I can stop it, annoyance explodes in my brain, my entire body vibrating with it. I hate that two people I barely know are talking about me like this. All I did is go for a walk earlier. I shouldn't have to ask permission to leave the house.

"No." Emma is quiet for a moment. "Naomi needed a lot of time to herself too."

Simon stretches his legs out. "Have you decided when you're going to talk to him?"

Talk to me about what?

"Not yet. I want to make sure he integrates more into the family. I still can't believe the timing. Can you imagine how much this all is?" She exhales, and Simon murmurs something, then they both stand up and go back into the house.

What are they talking about? I force myself to breathe. There's no way of knowing now, and I have to calm down. If I don't, I'll be too loud and angry; I'll make a mistake. I force myself to wait until the count of one hundred, then when I can't wait anymore, I ease myself over the edge of the roof, then run to match my racing pulse. I have never had any control over anything in my life—nothing. Whatever they were talking about, this is another confirmation of that. And I have no intention to integrate into their family, whatever that means. Escaping has never sounded better.

The witch's house is even more beautiful in the moonlight: tall and sweeping, the windows shining in the darkness. But when I look up at it, I suddenly don't think it's a good idea to go into the actual house. That's breaking and entering, isn't it? I want to see the mermaid again, but the roof is what is actually important. Can I climb? I check the windows of the nearby houses, all dark, no one should see me trying to get it. It's risky, but the sky is so perfect for stargazing, I have to at least try.

I quietly make my way through the garden, finding my way to the tree next to the house. The bark is slippery, without enough footholds, and I slip off a few times before noticing the trellis on the side of the house, leading all the way up to the roof. If it could hold me . . .

I try one foot, then the other, and before I know it, I'm climbing into the night, my feet steady, my arms pulling me. As long as I don't look down, I'm fine. When I get to the top, I'm breathing heavily and my backpack feels like it weighs about a million pounds, but I feel lighter than I have in a long time.

The view is even better than I thought it would be. For a moment I stand there, taking it in, then I drag the chair to the edge. I don't even need the telescope yet, that's how clear it is. The sky presses in on me like a warm blanket, the moon settled into a thick orb. I felt completely safe, enclosed and hidden. After a moment I take out my notebook, and for the first time since I arrived in Salem, maybe for the first time in months, I feel my shoulders soften, feel myself relax.

I move to the telescope, pressing my eye to the lens. Instantly, I'm swallowed up in relief. Telescopes are magic. Yes, they let me see things I can't see with my eyes. But more than that, they control. In that tiny circle, everything is contained, on purpose. Nothing is random. I can name it, pinpoint it, identify it. It all makes sense in a way that nothing in my life ever has.

Next I grab my notebook and begin to write. I always write the same basic things in my logbook. Beginning and ending time of my observation session, the date or dates. My location and where I am exactly (I write *WH* for "witch's house"), what the weather and conditions are like. Whether or not there's cloud cover, mist, moonlight, fog, that sort of thing. If I'm using a telescope or binoculars, and if so, what model and magnification. I write down what my target is if I have one. Some nights I have something in mind; other nights I look until something catches my eye. And sometimes I write down a sentence or two about whatever is on my mind.

I adjust the telescope, moving in on my mom's favorite star. The Dog Star. And I don't know if it's the house or the clear night sky, but I keep hearing my mom's voice in my head. *Remember, baby, miracles happen in threes.*

I think about my mom, about how even when I don't want it to, her gravitational pull matters. And that is so unfair. Because some people, like Emma and Simon's kids, get moms they can count on. And some get ones like mine who can't or won't be who their kids need them to be, and where does that leave them? Gravity-less.

The moon is enormous and heavy and oh so solid, and when I hold out my palm, it rests on it, like it's mine for the taking. Maybe that's what makes me do what I do next. I know the universe doesn't care what I think, but I decide to ask it for a favor, just this once. *Please help me figure out what to do.*

I don't know if I'm talking to the Dog Star or my mom or what, but I'm talking to *someone*. The stars twinkle brightly, the planets swirling precisely in their orbits. The universe operates perfectly; would it be too much to ask for this one small thing? "Please send me another sign," I say.

I feel more vulnerable than I have in ages. I feel ridiculous, but also, there's that hope again.

And that's when the window starts to open.

11

Willow

I'm alone on the roof. The nighttime heat envelopes me instantly, and as soon as my eyes adjust, I forget all about looking for the source of the noise, because how is it possible that this house keeps on getting better? I'm looking at an absolutely *magical* rooftop garden. The moon is making everything glow a pearly white, and honestly, I didn't know I needed this space in my life until this very moment. The fence is lined in lights, and a chair has been set up to take in the view of the night sky, and when I turn to look around, absorb the whole scene, I see something that makes adrenaline shoot through my entire body.

There's a ghost on the roof.

A *cute* ghost.

But. A ghost.

He has tangled black hair and a bright white T-shirt and sneakers that are so new, they glow in the darkness. He holds an open notebook in front of him, a pen poised over its pages. He looks as stunned to see me as I am to see him.

I manage not to scream. We stare at each other for a moment, his eyes dark and glittering in the light. My entire body tenses, adrenaline shooting through me, then, in one quick movement, he drops his notebook, sending it tumbling to the ground, then disappears over the side of the railing into the darkness, so silent, it was like he was never there at all.

12

Mason

My head is buried in the stars. All I can think is, *Why am I here?*
Send me a sign. Send me something. I'm thinking so hard that I almost
don't hear the creaking of hinges behind me, almost miss the window
slowly moving open.

For a moment, my brain won't recognize what it's seeing; it's my
body that reacts. I can only see the top half of her, but even so, I
recognize the girl immediately. She has long, wavy red hair pulled
back into a ponytail, and skin so pale, it glows in the moonlight. At
first she's still, and I think she isn't going to see me, but then she turns
around slowly, and when I catch sight of her face, panic shoots down
my arms, pinning me in place. Her gaze is serious and open, her eyes
a question. Even without the stormy sea behind her, I know exactly
who she is.

It's the mermaid.

She's crawled out of the painting, scaled the ladder, followed me
onto the roof. In other words, I asked the universe for a sign, and a
painting *came to life*.

And she's looking right at me.

For one long moment we stare at each other, a current of
electricity running between us. I don't know how it happens, exactly.
I drop everything, and in a move that is half dive, half tumble, I clear

the little fence, slide onto my stomach, lower myself over the side of the house, where my feet magically find the latticework. I somehow make it to the flowery-smelling earth, my feet barely making contact before I move into a dead sprint.

13

Willow

By the time I realize the boy was not a ghost at all but an actual boy, he is long gone and I have missed ten calls from Bea and am in the process of missing another. I fumble to hit answer while simultaneously locking the front door of the house. It is physically painful to leave the magic (pun intended) of Aunt Sage's house behind, but there's no way I'm taking the risk of stumbling upon some other random stranger in the dark. This adventure is over, at least for tonight.

"Willow! You scared the hell out of me!" Bea shrieks into my ear.

"I was right. There was someone on the roof. A boy." I give the front door of Aunt Sage's house a tug, double-checking that it's secure before tucking the key into my pocket and launching myself off the steps.

"There was a *boy on the roof?*" Bea is always calm, but right at this moment she sounds seconds from hyperventilating.

"Yeah, he was really . . ." I'm about to say "cute," because he *was* cute, notably so—big brown eyes and really great hair—but that feels like a weird way to describe an intruder you meet in the night. Particularly to someone whose breath sounds ragged. "He looked close to our age. Do you have your inhaler?"

"Forget about my inhaler. What was intruder boy doing up there?"

"Mason," I say.

"What?"

"His name is Mason. Or at least that's the name on the notebook he dropped." With my non-phone hand, I flip the notebook open to see his name again. *Mason Greer.* But no phone number or address. I flip to a page in the middle and I'm immediately met with rows of careful writing. *Location: Brookline, MA. August 6. Mercury in retrograde. The optical illusion we all love to blame our problems on.*

Suddenly I remember the telescope. Mason wasn't an intruder; he was stargazing. But why was he doing it in Sage's house? Is he connected to Sage somehow? Some sort of cousin or family friend? Had the aunts forgotten to warn him I might show up, so he panicked?

For a moment I'm torn. Should I leave the notebook on the rooftop so he can come back and find it? Or should I keep it to show to the aunts?

I tuck it under my arm. I'm keeping it. If only to have proof that it actually happened.

"What notebook?" Bea asks.

I double-check the door, carefully placing the key in my pocket. "His stargazing notebook. He dropped it when he climbed down the house. I don't know how he did that. The house is three stories high." Of all of it, that may be the part that shocked me most, that he'd somehow managed to climb down the side of the house like a real-life Spider-Man. I can't get his face out of my mind. Freckles, full lower lip, thick eyebrows. It was the kind of face that sticks with you.

Bea exhales noisily into the receiver. "*Mon Dieu!* Willow, that was so idiotic. What if he'd been dangerous?"

The thought had crossed my mind, but the moment the boy's

eyes locked with mine, I'd known immediately he wasn't dangerous, for no other reason than my instincts. His eyes had seemed . . . I don't know. Safe. Which is obviously a stupid thing to think of a stranger you run into in the dark. But if at all possible, he'd been more afraid of me than I'd been of him.

She exhales. "Are you going to tell your mom there was someone on the roof?"

"Well . . ." I now find myself with a moral dilemma. Do I tell my mom someone who was possibly not supposed to be there was there when I was also not supposed to be there? But it didn't seem like he was doing any harm. Also, if I'm honest, he intrigued me. He felt almost familiar somehow. The same way the Book of Shadows had felt familiar, he'd seemed like someone I'd met before.

Speaking of the Book of Shadows . . .

"Oh, that book I mentioned," I say. "It's full of spells. I have to send you a picture of—"

"Are you really changing the subject right now? You heard an intruder and ran toward them while I sat here sweating to death from stress."

"Breathe, Bea," I say. "Back to my family situation. Can you believe my mom had this many secrets?" I continue describing the Book of Shadows to her, my voice rising with excitement. My mom practiced magic. My *mom*. The woman with the twelve blazers and impeccably organized drawers had once written a spell called *Spell to Survive Gym Class* that involved hexing a pair of gym shorts. I still can't believe it.

I'm waiting for her to be shocked, but instead, there's a beat of silence. "Bea, you there?"

She exhales into the receiver. "Well . . . honestly, yes. Your mom seems like the kind of person who would have witches in her family."

"You suspected that my mom comes from a family of witches?"

"No, obviously not. She's just so secretive, you know? Like she's always been friendly enough, but she's so private, it's like you don't actually know her."

I sigh. Bea likes to know everything, so of course she will claim to have known all along my mom had a shady past. "Remember, do *not* tell your parents. And I have to go back there. In daylight. The house felt . . . familiar." "Familiar" isn't the right word. The right word is "grounding," and "homey," and "*right*" in a way I can't quite explain. It almost makes me feel homesick.

"Familiar?"

"Yeah. It felt like . . . I'd been there before."

"Déjà vu?" she suggests.

I shake my head. "Déjà vu" isn't quite right either, because every bit of the house was brand-new to me; it was the feeling that I recognized. Worn-in and sort of ordinary and comfortable. "It felt like . . ." With a start, I realize what it felt like. "It felt like home."

"Home? Like in LA? Or in New York with your dad?"

I know the answer to that. It felt like my *before* home. When I knew where I fit. The thought makes every part of me ache. But I don't want to drag Bea through that, so I shove the thought to the back of my mind.

"I need to figure out who the boy is," I say, pushing my emotions aside. My phone vibrates and I look down to see that my dad is trying to calling. "Bea! It's my dad. I've got to go."

"Call me back." Her voice sounds worried, which, obviously, I hate. Bea has her own problems to deal with. She shouldn't have to deal with mine.

I jog up the street, fumbling to hit answer. "Dad?"

"Hi, Will. Sorry it took me so long to call."

I cast a long look down the street. What if the boy is still here . . . ?

But no. And I'm oddly disappointed by that. I push the boy's face out of my mind—right now I need to focus on my dad.

"How's Australia?" Like usual, I'm relieved to hear his voice. My dad and I have always had an okay relationship, maybe not terribly deep, but that makes sense when we spend so much time away from each other.

"Oh . . . fine. Tired." A kids' TV show blares in the background, and I can hear several tiny voices arguing. "MINE!" June yells.

"How's your week going?"

"Well . . ." Now that he's on the line, I'm not entirely sure where to begin.

"Ollie, give it back," my dad says, his voice muffled. "June? Let go of your brothers."

I close my eyes briefly. Thinking about June, Ollie, and Emmitt's antics is so normal, it makes today's strangeness stand out even more. Typically, I try not to bring my parents into each other's lives, but this time feels important. I could use some support. And judging by the commotion in the background, I probably have about three minutes.

"Dad, what do you know about . . . Mom's family? And childhood?"

"Her childhood?" He sounds distracted again. I'd better move in fast.

"Her mom. And aunts. And, ah . . ." I almost say "sister," but I'm hoping that he'll fill in the blanks on that one.

Another long pause. I think I'm going to have to prompt him again, but he says, "Why do you ask?"

"Mom and I are in Salem. We flew in this morning."

"Salem?" His voice is right up against my ear again. "Hold on, let me get outside." I hear a rustling, then a door open and close. "What are you doing there?"

I want to tell him everything, but suddenly I'm worried that it might be betraying my mom. "She's taking care of some . . . family issues."

A thick, syrupy pause. "What family issues? Does it have something to do with her aunt Daisy?"

He knows about Daisy. I'm so relieved, I let out a nervous laugh. "You've heard of her!"

He hesitates again. "Well . . . yes. She used to visit her when she was young. But it's obviously been years since she passed away. Is she there visiting someone else?"

Used to *visit* her? My heart sinks. My dad clearly does not know the truth either, which means he is likely not going to be much help.

Does he know about her twin? I take a deep breath, anxiety building in my chest, until I'm forced to say it. "We're here to settle Sage's estate."

"Sage?" Long pause. I can feel my heart beating in my ears. Will he know her? "Did she have another aunt? Or cousin or something?"

"No, Sage is her—" I gulp back the end of the sentence. My dad doesn't know who Sage is, meaning my mom really wasn't joking when she said she'd kept her past private. "Um . . ." *I know I can trust you to keep it all secret.* It feels wrong to not tell my dad, but it feels more wrong to betray my mom's trust. My chest ices up, my loneliness rising like the tide.

Once again, I'm a buoy, caught between my parents, the shore a distant memory I may never see again. "A friend of her aunt's," I say quickly.

"Ah." His voice relaxes again. "I didn't realize she still had contact with anyone there. I can't imagine this is easy. Maybe I'll give her a call—"

"No!" I say quickly. "I think it's better if you give her some space.

Plus, she's super stressed with work. I think this came at a bad time. But I'll tell her we spoke."

"All right," he says uncertainly.

I have a huge amount of anxiety surrounding what I'm about to say next, but I need some input from someone who knows her. "Dad . . . do you ever feel like maybe there are things about Mom that you don't know?" As soon as the words are out, I close my eyes, my body tense.

A crash comes on the other side of the line. Now wailing. "Chloe? Can you get . . . ? Thanks." His voice comes back to me. "I know your mother struggles with being open emotionally. Her family is a big part of that. She never told me the full story, and we were together for nearly two decades."

My mom not being open is one of the recurring arguments that had swirled through our Brooklyn apartment for years. I am *not* going down that rabbit hole, not with my dad. "Got it. We'll talk later," I say quickly. "Sounds like the kids need help."

"I'm fine to talk—" But then there's another crash and he sighs. "I'm sorry, Willow. Are you okay?"

For a moment I allow myself to wonder, *am* I okay? But nothing good has ever come of me wondering that, so I force the thought away.

"I'm fine," I say. And I *am* fine. Sort of. I mean, yes, my life sometimes feels like one of those before-and-after home-renovation projects you see on HGTV. There's the before, with the avocado shag carpet and the weird glittery popcorn ceilings, that's me—and then there's the after, which is the new houses and the new jobs and the new families, all tidy and photogenic. And it's okay. It's just that sometimes it's hard to be the only one who misses or who even really seems to remember the before, but things change. I have to change with them.

"I'm fine," I say again, firmly this time.

"You sure?"

I look up at the moon. It's bright white and just shy of full. Suddenly my limbs feel heavy. "I—"

"JUNE, GET DOWN FROM THERE. Okay. Well, let's talk soon. I'll call in a few days?"

"Sure." I'm starting to get that desperate feeling I always get at the end of our phone calls. I want to ask him more questions, like, did he know Mom changed her name? Does he know her story about her hostess mom was a lie? "Hey, Dad—"

But he's already hung up.

A big achy expanse of lonely pools up inside of me. I try to ignore it, the way I usually do, freeze the ocean waves rolling and churning inside of me, but this time it doesn't work. My dad is in Australia with his family. I'm here with my mother, getting a tiny peek at her life while she continues to shut me out. Once again, I don't belong.

Think. I get the feeling that Sage would explain everything, but all I have is my mom, and she's made it very clear that she will not be discussing her past with me. How about the aunts? Will they let me in, or will they honor my mom's wishes?

I stare up. Stars spatter the sky, and the ghostly shadows of the houses around me stand like sentinels. *Where do I go from here?*

If only I could talk to my past mom. The one who decorated things in glitter and wrote magical spells with her twin sister. Would she let me in? What could have possibly happened that was worse than what she already told me about her mother?

And then it hits me. The Book of Shadows. *That's* how I'm going to figure this out. That's why Poppy gave me the key in the first place. To give me a starting point. I'd been reading a story literally titled *Bell Family* when Bea called. The story Violet told me to find.

The story began, as many stories do . . .

Are my answers in there?

A certainty burns through me. Before I can lose my nerve, I rush back into the house.

The story began, as many stories do, with a girl who bloomed too big for the space that the world had carved out for her. Her name was Cordelia Antoinette Bell, but everyone in her coastal New England town called her Lily. No one could remember if the nickname started before or after she planted her first famous garden, but all agreed that the name fit.

   On the outside, Lily was a quiet girl, unremarkable except for her deep red hair, a gift from her Dutch ancestors, but on the inside, Lily's mind blossomed in color. She spent sunrise to sunset working in her garden, and it was said that her poppies were redder than blood and her sweet peas attracted bees from miles away.

   Lily's gardens caught the eye of everyone in the town, including a young witch who lived on the outskirts of their community in a small ramshackle shack. The witch began visiting the girl in her garden day after day, demanding to know what spell Lily used to make her orchids unfurl and her roses bloom. Day after day Lily told the witch there was no spell. She could feel what the plants needed through her hands, and she did what they asked. It was as simple as that.

   You'd think a witch would understand this kind of magic—the kind that comes to you as naturally as a breath. But deep down the witch was like most people—

she didn't trust what she didn't understand, and her resentment grew thick and barbed as stinging nettle.

On the eve of Lily's seventeenth birthday, her parents threw her an elaborate garden party, a debutante ball meant to show off Lily's magical gardens and announce her eligibility to marry. The witch was passing by that night, her basket full of shellfish she'd gathered from the shore, and when she saw Lily dancing in her white dress among all of those beautiful flowers, her jealousy turned to rage. If Lily wouldn't teach the witch her magic, then the witch would make sure she never practiced it again. The witch made her way to the middle of the dance floor, and in front of all the guests, she put a curse on Lily: Lily would never grow another flower for as long as she would live.

The party guests laughed it off, but not Lily. She had seen the look in the witch's eye, and she felt the shift in the ground beneath her feet. What was done was done. Lily went into her house, dusted the earth off her satin shoes, and never touched her beloved garden again.

This was the beginning of the Bell family curse. From that day on, every Bell woman was cursed, their names a reminder of the things Lily had lost.

Or at least that's the way the story goes.

Mason

It's possible I've never messed up anything more than I did last night.

It took me a solid quarter mile of sprinting down Essex Street for my brain to untangle what happened on the roof. She wasn't a painting come to life. She wasn't a mermaid. She was a *person*. A girl with red hair and stormy gray eyes and skin that glowed in the moonlight.

It sounds like I'm describing a magical princess from a fairy tale. She was a genuinely beautiful girl. But that's all she was. A *girl*.

As I reached the Morgans' street, I was hit with the sudden realization that when I asked for a sign, my mother's favorite symbol materialized *out of thin air*. I didn't just see the mermaid painting; I saw the mermaid's doppelgänger appear in front of me. If that isn't a sign, I don't know what is.

And like a dummy, I ran from it.

My mom always told me to watch for signs, but she never told me what to do with one once I saw it. Hopefully the universe is up for second chances.

For some reason, I am supposed to see that girl. She has something to do with why I'm here, I'm sure of it. The problem is I have no idea how to track her down. How does one find a girl who was on the rooftop of a house you were not supposed to be inside in the first place? She'd come from inside the house, which means she had access to it. She's too young to be the owner, but maybe she's related to the owner? Or maybe a house sitter of some sort? Do I ask Simon? Hang out around the house until she comes back? What if someone tells Simon and Emma that I was there?

Now I'm stressed, so I do what I always do when I feel anxiety swirling through me—I reach for my notebook in my back pocket, but—

A cold dread spreads across my chest.

No.

My panicked hand searches frantically through my backpack, fingers hoping to brush against the familiar feel of its worn cover. I dump everything out on my bed. Binoculars, pens, book, soda. Everything but the thing I need most.

The realization hits me so hard, I nearly double over.

I left my notebook on the witch's roof.

A wave of questions is unleashed. What if someone finds it? What if Simon finds it? What if it's *lost*? I'm not remotely ready to deal with the thought of it disappearing, so I focus on what I have to do. It's stupid to go back—my chances of getting caught are too high—but I do it anyway. I run back and scale the dark house as quietly as I can, but when I peek over the top of the rooftop's railing, my worst fears are confirmed.

My notebook is gone.

I spend the night tossing and turning, my stomach in literal knots that last through my few hours of awful sleep. Eventually, I get up and page through the book Emma left for me, but my mind can't focus and I end up getting stuck on a quote by Neil deGrasse Tyson, the words etching themselves onto my brain. *The atoms of our bodies are traceable to stars that manufactured them in their cores and exploded these enriched ingredients across our galaxy, billions of years ago. For this reason, we are biologically connected to every other living thing in the world. We are chemically connected to all molecules on Earth. And we are atomically connected to all atoms in the universe. We are not figuratively, but literally stardust.*

Normally I'd write this in my notebook, but best case it is sitting on a rooftop right now, and that thought sends me spiraling, so I try writing it on my arm. *We are not figuratively, but literally stardust.* I'm pacing, desperately trying to come up with a plan. Right at this moment, with sunlight pooling up on the floorboards, I'm less sure that the girl and the paintings are signs from the universe and surer that I've made a terrible, terrible mistake.

Without my notebook, I'm gravity-less. It's my one true tie to myself.

I've basically turned myself into a black hole, anxiety swallowing every rational thought, when Simon knocks on my door.

"Mason?"

His voice sends an explosion of fear through my body. He's found out already. Someone saw me scale the house. Found the notebook. Part of me wants to dive for my bed and play dead, but he knocks again, then cracks the door open an inch.

"Mason? You awake?"

Word must travel fast in this city. The owners must have called around, filed a police report or something. Maybe it was the girl? The mermaid girl? Did she turn me in? Somehow they traced it back to Simon and me already. How am I going to get out of this? How am I going to explain the fact that I snuck out? I roll over miserably, get to my feet. "I'm awake," I mumble.

"Emma and I wanted to talk to you about something. Do you mind coming downstairs?"

They know. The seriousness of his voice confirms my suspicion. "Be right there," I say, trying to sound as calm as possible, but my heart is pounding, my chest tight.

On the way down, I do my best to breathe deeply and calm my shaking hands. *Okay, Mason. Worst case, they send me away.* In many ways that's actually the best case, because it gets me out of this weird scenario with Emma, but now I have the mermaid to think of. I can't leave before I figure out who she is, and I most definitely can't leave without my notebook.

By the time I reach the landing, I know exactly how it's going to play out. They're going to tell me I've broken the rules and then they'll be monitoring my every move. Yes, I snuck out, but it wasn't for anything bad. I was *stargazing*. No one would have even known if it weren't for the mermaid showing up.

The mermaid.

It all sounds completely crazy in my own head. How am I going to explain it to anyone else?

Downstairs, the kitchen is its usual disarray. Audrey is sitting in the middle of the table, surrounded by a bunch of markers, and Hazel and Zoe are coloring on the floor. Hazel jumps to her feet when she sees me. "Mason! Do you want to play games with us? We can play Uno or Candyland."

Audrey tugs on the hem of my shirt, pointing to the quote I'd scrawled on in my room. "Um. You can write on your arm?"

I'm so anxious, I can barely process what she's asking—if I'm caught, how will I figure out how to see the mermaid again? And I have to find her. I know I'm supposed to. It's a certainty in my gut that I can't really explain in any logical terms. A sign, yes. Fate? Serendipity? The stars aligning? All of the above?

"Hold on a minute, girls," Emma says, walking into the room with a cup of coffee and the container of half-and-half, which she holds out to me. "Coffee?"

Wait. Is this sympathy coffee?

"Yeah. Thanks." My stomach is still in knots, but I manage to take the mug from her and catch the carton of half-and-half she slides my way. The table is littered in all manner of kid clutter— drawings, sticky plates, three stuffed animals, and a pink sparkly shoe. The chaos is only adding to my distress. They must be seriously regretting adding me to the mix.

Simon walks in carrying a plate and quickly takes the seat next to Emma. "Good morning, Mason." He glances at Emma, and she gives him a little nod. "Mason, I wanted to show you this."

He hands me something, and for a moment my brain can't quite register what I'm looking at. It's a glossy brochure with a picture of a boy looking into a telescope. I blink a few times and the title comes into focus. *High School Astrophysics Program, BU.*

"What's this?" My heart is still stuttering.

"BU is Boston University," Emma explains. "A few days ago I ran into an old college friend who told me about a friend of hers who works there. Her name is Professor Ishani Singh and she heads up the astronomy department."

I stare at her. She stares back. How does this fit in with me being caught sneaking out?

"Um . . . ," I manage.

Simon jumps ahead. "I gave her a call. Professor Singh is the head of the entire astronomy undergrad program there. She's really personable and unbelievably smart. I told her about you, and she had some really great ideas for astronomy programs that I think you might be interested in."

Finally it all clicks. This conversation has nothing to do with me sneaking over to the witch's house. I grip the edges of the table. I feel like I've narrowly avoided going over a cliff.

"Oh," I say quickly, and now Emma is studying me. I try not to notice it, but her eyes are so creepily piercing, it's hard not to. Why does it feel like she can see straight into my skull? I quickly bring my coffee cup to my mouth, trying to block her gaze.

Simon bangs his hand on the table, getting revved up in his Simon way. "There's an astronomy program for rising seniors that you could attend in August for high school credit. It's in Boston and—"

I try to focus, I really do, and Simon starts in on this very excited sales-pitchy talk but none of it will stick to my brain, I'm too relieved. No one knows that I was at the witch's house. I haven't lost my chance to get my notebook back and see the mermaid again.

Simon's words pour over me, and I look up to see Emma still staring at me. Studying me. She knows I'm not following what Simon is saying, and she's wondering why.

I quickly swivel my body toward Simon, doing my best to look engaged. Eventually there's a silence that makes me think he's finished. "Interesting," I finally say. "I'll look into it."

He slides the stack of paper toward me. "Do you want to use our computer to look up the program's website? The application deadline is coming up, but I think we can get it in on time, and Dr. Singh thinks you could be a great fit."

The computer. I can ask for space to research the program. I jump to my feet. "Can I have some time now?"

"I'll help you pull up the website and application," Emma says.

"No need," I say, but she gets up anyway, and I follow her to the dining room. She logs in, then types in the website, clicking on a tab marked *New Applications*. Before she's fully out of the way, she pauses and says, "Mason, I think this could be a really good opportunity. I know it can be hard to concentrate on things like this when you have so much going on in your life, but I think you should really consider it."

That sort of snaps me out of the mermaid trance I'm in. Annoyance wells up in me.

She's looking right in my eyes and it's pushing me off-balance, because, really, what does she know about my life? She's here, an adult, in her own home, making her own choices, with her own family. She has no idea what it's like to be me, or how painful it is that I don't actually get to consider things like astronomy camps. Not when my main goal is finding my mom. "I'll think about it," I say quickly, and she gives me a nod and a look that makes me think she's seeing straight though my BS.

"And if this program isn't it, we can always research more," she adds. "There are even a few that are sleepaway camps, two or three weeks. They all looked incredible."

"Cool," I say, but I'm so desperate for her to leave, I'm clenching and unclenching my jaw. This is my first computer access in over a week, and now that it's within reach, I feel like I might explode. She takes the hint and walks out.

I exhale. The keyboard is sticky, like every other surface in the house, and as I scroll down on the website, I find Simon and Emma's friend right away. Professor Singh is young and Indian, with dark brown skin, her black hair swept up into a bun. According to her bio, she studies how galaxies connect with each other via the exchange of energy and matter, and she's used the Hubble Space Telescope to look for hidden matter.

Honestly, this sounds . . . incredible.

Boston University has several world-class telescopes, which is interesting, and even laboratories where they come up with the instrumentation. There are all these photos of students standing together in groups in front of telescopes, grinning, and for one tiny second I allow myself to think about what that would be like—to be around people who used words like "instrumentation," taking notes on things like deep space and matter. But that makes me think about the notes in my notebook, and then it's all I can think about, and now my head is swimming again.

I have to get my notebook back.

After a few minutes, Emma and Simon come in and I make a big deal about how intrigued I am by what I'm reading, which makes Simon smile and Emma stare. I'll take it. With my nerves firing, I push myself up from the computer. "I'm going out for a walk." I watch them exchange a quick glance where Emma seems to be communicating something with her eyeballs, but I don't have even a clue as to how to decipher what that something is.

Simon clears his throat and takes a step toward me. "Hey, Mason, I'm taking Nova to a lunch meeting with a client around noon, then we're going on a trip to Salem Willows. It's a fun hangout in the summertime: arcades, beach, lots to see. I'd love to have you join for both."

Unlike yesterday, this invitation is less of a request and more of a *this is the way it's going to be*. I'm too stressed to refuse, so all I do is nod and agree to meet him outside in twenty minutes. Which I do, but all I'm thinking on our walk is, *Find the girl, find the girl, find the girl.*

But how? I'm obviously going to have to go camp out outside of the house until she shows up again, but how am I going to make that work without alerting Simon to the fact that I'm stalking one of his properties? And what does the girl have to do with the house anyway? Is she related to the woman who owned it? Is that why there's a painting of her in the house?

I'm thinking about this so hard that I nearly trip over Nova as we make our way down Essex. "Watch it!" she shrieks. I don't know if Nova is mad about spending time with her dad, or mad because I'm encroaching on her one-on-one time with him, but she seems extra stormy today. She has also clearly mastered the art of walking and texting, and it's honestly impressive to watch since Essex Street is lined in uneven bricks and packed with people too busy enjoying the weather and all of the weird shops to focus on where they're going. Whatever Nova is doing, she is completely absorbed in it.

I'm not paying much attention to Simon either. I'm studying the hair and faces of every person I pass. At one point I get a glimpse of red hair and my heart speeds up, but when I turn for another look, I see that it's a boy wearing a bright yellow backpack.

Partway down Essex, Simon stops to talk to someone and Nova is forced to look up from her phone. I feel terrible for her. Without her headphones, she's way too exposed and vulnerable-looking. All she has to do is bare her teeth and she's a naked mole rat with anger issues.

The truth is, neither of us are happy about our current living situations. Maybe I could figure out a way to befriend her. My expectations are seriously low on this, but I go for it anyway. "Did your parents name you after the astronomical event?"

"What?"

Nova may be a distant relative of Medusa, as her stare seems capable of turning people to stone. But not me. I've lived with too many other foster kids. On the angry-kids spectrum, Nova barely registers.

I gesture toward the hazy sky. "When stars die, they release a bunch of energy and get really bright for a short period of time. That's called a nova. It means 'new.'"

"You really think they named me for a *dead star*?"

"Why not?" I say.

She goes back to angrily stabbing at her phone, and I go back to hunting through the crowd for the mermaid.

Good talk.

Simon's default reaction to silence is to monologue things. By the time we reach Gulu-Gulu Café, Simon has resorted to reciting all the restaurant's menu items he can remember over the deafening silence happening between us (chocolate orange cannoli waffles! PB&J crepes!), so by the time we get there, I am hungry and actually considering eating breakfast, which might be one of the seven signs of the apocalypse. The café is tucked neatly behind a small park with a statue, and it has a decidedly eclectic vibe, with a gold sign and an enormous dog's face painted in the front window. There's a long wait outside, but Simon's client is already inside, so we make our way in, one after the other, pushing our way through.

"There they are. This way." Simon waves as I duck, narrowly missing being decapitated by a server carrying a tray of mimosas. Simon is heading for the back corner, and when I spot the flash of red, my heart hammers so hard, it nearly splits my chest. It's *her*.

Is it her?

It can't be her. Except, it *is*.

I have the urge to rub my eyes or pinch myself, make sure this is real. And it is real. The mermaid is sitting at the wall side of a booth, her head down as she looks through the menu. The mermaid is right there. *Right there*. While I was busy looking for her, the universe literally delivered her to me.

I'd wondered if maybe the night and my surprise had colored how I saw her, made her fundamentally different somehow, but if anything, she is more mermaid-esque in the daylight. Her hair is big and wavy, attempting to escape from a messy ponytail. And her skin is moon pale, freckles like constellations. Gray eyes and a rumpled T-shirt over shorts, sneakers, a stack of elastics and plastic bracelets on her wrist, and a light blue denim jacket that I'm positive does not come from this decade. All together it works in a way you wouldn't expect. The woman sitting with her has the exact same color of hair but cut into a straight line above her shoulders, her tailored clothing impeccable. They couldn't be more opposite-looking in how they present themselves, but something about the way they hold their shoulders is identical. They look strong, purposeful. If it weren't for the age difference, I'd say they could be twins.

I literally can't breathe right now; too many emotions are vying for my attention. It feels like panic, but it can't be, can it? Because this is *good*. It has to be good. This is the universe reaching down and tapping me on the shoulder. Or maybe slapping me in the face.

My second sign. I force myself to inhale, attempt to calm my pulse like I learned in one of the therapy sessions I had at my group home. If it works, I can't tell. I don't know if I want to laugh or cry right now. Do I introduce myself? Tackle her so we don't get separated again? Okay, I'm obviously not going to tackle her, but what if she disappears again?

My body feels like it's at the starting line of a race, tension and energy building in my muscles. As soon as the starting gun goes off, I'll run to the mermaid. But what will I do once I get to her?

The mermaid is staring down at her phone, and she reaches out for her mug, absentmindedly lifting it to her mouth. What do I do when she sees me? Will she recognize me like I recognize her? Tell

Simon I was at the house last night? What if she blows everything? My mind is scrambling so hard right now. I feel like I'm trying to dismantle a bomb. One wrong move and everyone knows everything.

The mermaid takes another sip. How does she not feel me staring at her?

"Mason, move," Nova says, poking me in the back. I manage to stumble a few steps forward, and this tiny movement, this tiny lessening of distance between me and the mermaid, causes enormous pressure in my head. *What now?* I desperately ask the universe.

"*Mason*," Nova snaps, her voice louder.

And that's what finally does it. The mermaid is mid-drink, but her gaze snaps to mine. For a moment, we lock eyes, hers going wide, and I'm rushed with feelings of connection, understanding, pure perfection. This is magic. This is fate. This is meant to be. She is my sign.

And then my sign sprays a mouthful of coffee across the entire table.

Willow

To be fair, I didn't see Mason right away because I was attempting to caffeinate myself back into existence. My fourteen minutes of sleep last night were not doing my spinning mind any favors.

After the house, slipping back into my hotel room was easy and uneventful. The problem was the story.

The Bell family curse is . . . a lot.

I read it over and over, noticing new details every time. It reads like a fairy tale almost, but the addition of those few details that Violet and Poppy had offered elevated the story beyond make-believe. Lily was a real person, and her tea roses still exist. I can picture her gardening, her back turned to the sun. And we are all named after items in the garden, even if that is news to me.

So that part is true, but what about the rest of it? I mean, a family curse can't be *real*, can it?

A part of me wants to dismiss this weird little story in this weird little book, but I can't, because some part of it feels not quite *true*, exactly, but familiar. Woven into me. Ever since my parents sat me down to tell me that our life together was over, I've felt . . .

Okay, not cursed. But not okay either. But do I really believe in some made-up curse?

A tiny voice inside of me says yes, and the tone is less *I think so* and more *of course you're cursed*, because the truth is I've always felt different, my edges have *never* fit, and a curse that has followed me through my bloodline would do wonders to explain that.

Obviously, it isn't true.

And yet.

When it feels like my brain is going to burst from all of this thinking, I turn to Mason's notebook. If I can't figure out my family, maybe I can figure him out. Why was he at my aunt's house? Does he have anything to do with my family? As I reach for the notebook, I hesitate slightly. This is obviously a *slight* invasion of privacy, but he also invaded the privacy of my aunt's house, which makes this fine. Right?

Before I can stop myself, I lift the cover. And what I see is twisty handwriting with logs and excerpts and what seem like records of stargazing. *New moon, good view of Canis Major.* And *Andromeda Galaxy with binoculars. Easy to find when you star hop from Cassiopeia.*

There are pages and pages of this kind of thing, but as I skim, I realize the entries aren't all about stargazing, and suddenly I feel like I'm stepping somewhere I really don't belong because he's writing about personal things. He's moved a lot. And he's angry and sad and sometimes scared. But the thing that makes me pause is his writing about his mom.

The Earth makes up 0.0003 percent of the solar system. I may not know where my mom is, but at least we're on the same planet. In the context of the universe, that narrows things down quite a bit.

Why doesn't he know where his mom is?

If/when the sun dies, there are some trees that will make it a few decades, but the rest of us will only make it a short amount of time before we all freeze to death. That's how it feels without Mom. I've made it a short amount of time, but I'm running out.

That's when I slam the notebook shut. He may have been trespassing on my aunt's property, but that didn't make it okay to trespass on his grief. Plus, there isn't a single word that makes me think he knows my family. Is it possible our meeting was random?

But now I'm rethinking everything. Fate. Coincidences. My own judgment. Because the boy is suddenly standing directly in front of me, and I just sent a mouthful of coffee halfway across the café. Only a minute ago I was sitting with my mom, trying to come up with a way to bring up the curse, about to blurt out something brilliant like *Heard any curse stories lately?* when I hear his name. *Mason.*

And then I look up, and boom. There he is. The stargazer. Staring at me in total and utter disbelief.

Ditto. Because I'm sure I'm staring at him the exact same way.

Apart from him materializing out of thin air for the second time, the thing that shocks me the most is how tall he is. And how dark and tangled his hair is. His face is somehow even nicer-looking than I remember, with dark, expressive eyes that would leave me speechless even if I hadn't run into him on a rooftop at midnight.

Which I most definitely did.

Lucky for me, as soon as the coffee leaves my mouth, the entire restaurant seems to spring into action, which gives me a few seconds to get my head back on straight. My mom looks at me like I've sprouted a second head but quickly hands me a napkin, and the man Mason is with, a wiry, energetic man in slacks and a checkered shirt, runs over and starts enthusiastically clapping me on the back. A plethora of servers magically appear with cloths, and the entire table next to us begins clucking with concerned comments, including "Is she choking? Is she ill?" A teenage girl standing behind Mason glares at me with unbridled disgust. Is Mason going to tell my mom I was there? I attempt to make eye contact with him, but he's honestly a little bit hard to look at directly because he's just . . .

Again, this is clearly not the most important thing at the moment, but he's extremely nice to look at. He has thick eyebrows, a small scar running through one of them, and his lips are sort of bow-shaped, the bottom one fuller than the top and—

Well. His lips are just really good. Suddenly he blinks and steps backward, like he suddenly remembered his surroundings.

"Willow," my mom says. "Do you need some water?"

"I'm fine, totally fine. I'm sorry, I think I just, ah, aspirated my drink or something." My mom's shoulders relax, and I see the boy mouth my name silently. *Willow.* I don't mind terribly the way it looks on his lips, and that thought nearly makes me choke again.

I have literally never been this instantly attracted to a boy before, and I have to say, the timing on this is extremely inconvenient. Also, I know so much about him. I have literally read several pages of his diary.

"Willow, what . . . ?" my mom says.

"It happens!" one of the cluckers at the next table says sympathetically. "My coffee was too hot too. You poor thing. How embarrassing. How humiliating."

The teenage girl cracks a smile at this, and I realize she's younger than I thought. She and Mason don't seem to have anything in common looks-wise, other than the guarded look they're both exuding.

My eyes go right back to him. He doesn't know what to do any more than I do, but unlike me he seems to have figured out how to wipe all emotion from his face. I do my best to send eye messages. *Do. Not. Tell. Them.* I glance at my mom, then back at him, and shake my head lightly. I'm not sure if he gets it or not.

"Your name's Willow." He takes a few steps forward. "Like the big tree in the witch's backyard?"

Oh no. Anxiety explodes through me, and I do my best to communicate a *stop stop stop*, but his eyes only get brighter. Either he doesn't notice or he doesn't care.

My mom's gaze whips over from where she's mopping up coffee. "You've been to my sister's house?"

My sister. I don't know if I'm ever going to get used to hearing my mother casually say those words.

"We don't mean 'witch' as a derogatory term," Simon says quickly.

"Of course not," my mom says, but her eyes are on Mason.

"Yeah. It's a cool place. I went with Simon." Mason gestures smoothly to the man next to him, then looks at me pointedly. "How about you?" His voice is casual, and relief spirals through me. He isn't going to out me. At least, not on purpose.

"I went yesterday with my mom," I say. "But I didn't get to see inside."

"Excuse me," my mom says. "Do you two know each other?"

"No," Mason says. "I just, ah, thought of the tree in the yard when you said her name. I . . . like the willow."

It's his first stumble, and my mom's eyebrows shoot up like rockets. *I like the willow.* A tiny part of me is hoping he's actually referring to me.

Okay, now I'm getting delusional.

"But you, ah, don't have any connection to it? Outside of . . . ?" My question comes out awkward, and I gesture toward Simon.

Mason shakes his head. "I just went to help out."

Got it. He doesn't know my aunt or anything about the house. So what was he doing there, besides stargazing?

"What an incredible property," Simon says, clapping his hands together. "We had a wonderful tour of it yesterday. And, Mason, I'm glad you brought up the willow, as it was on my list of things to discuss. I'm sure you know all about it, but the roots of willow trees can be so invasive. They just grow and grow—"

"Maybe we should all sit down," my mother says, her voice strained. Mason and I share a quick glance, and I feel my face flush again. He's staring at me like I'm the shiniest object in the night sky.

Yes. I'm definitely getting delusional. The fact that I've read this boy's innermost thoughts is clearly messing with my head.

"Great idea," Simon booms. "And let's redo our introductions, shall we?" He gestures to the kids. "I'm Simon, and this is Nova and Mason. Nova is my daughter. Mason is new to the family."

New to the family? What does that mean? I swing my eyes back to Mason, whose posture is suddenly rigid, defensive.

And then I remember his diary entry. *I may not know where my mom is, but at least we're on the same planet.* His mom is out of the picture for some reason, and this is who he lives with now. Why?

A heaviness fills up my center. I love his name. It makes me think of strong layers of bricks and stone. Someone who has survived a lot. And, yes, I'm projecting a lot onto this tiny moment of staring at his admittedly beautiful face.

"Let's sit, Mason, Nova," Simon says. Mason all but lunges for the seat across from me, with Nova trailing in reluctantly behind him. Simon sits on the far side, across from my mom.

Mason is staring at me. Hard. But even more intense is my mom's gaze on me.

She leans into me and whispers into my ear, "You two have really never met before?" Just *once* I'd like for something to get past her.

"How could I have?" I whisper back. "We've only been here for a few days."

Simon passes out the stack of menus. "Teens, order whatever you want. Here's our server now." I drop my gaze to the menu, but the words are swimming in front of me. I somehow manage to order French toast, and once our server has left, my mom shifts her focus to Simon.

"Shall we get started?" Mom asks. "I'd love to hear your thoughts."

"Absolutely," Simon says, pulling a laptop from his bag and sliding it toward my mom. "I've made a good start on the listing, and I have the contact information of several companies that I think can help you with the estate sale."

His words make my stomach sink—my mom isn't kidding about selling the house. Even though I've only spent a total of forty minutes in the house, I can't stand the thought of it being sold, all those treasures disappearing into other people's homes. I force away the image of all those magical rooms and the ease I'd felt there.

And then I feel Mason's hand on mine. His arm is resting casually on the table, his hand brushing against my wrist like he's testing that I'm real. That tiny touch sets all of my nerve receptors on edge. He has smooth, wide fingernails, and I see a trail of familiar handwriting up his arm and into his sleeve.

I feel like I've just stepped into the center of an electrical storm.

"Please don't tell," I say under my breath as my mom and Simon launch themselves into a deep conversation. I'm not looking at him, and my voice is tiny, but I see him nod out of the corner of my eye.

Relief floods through me, but it's only temporary, as I have about a thousand other things I want to say to him. Also, I hate the fact that Simon and my mom are now discussing "architectural features." She isn't really going to list the house this quickly, is she?

Mason lifts his water glass, covertly blocking his face. His eyes are a deep, dark brown and shiny. "Do you have my notebook?" he whispers.

Guilt rushes through me and I nod. His shoulders relax slightly. "Meet up?" he says.

The thought makes me feel like I've swallowed sparklers. And not just because of how meeting up with him would look to my mom, but because looking at him makes me feel . . .

Okay, this is ridiculous. I'm only reacting this way because I read his notebook. According to what I read last night, he's also sweet and introspective and sort of heartbreaking, but that doesn't negate the fact that he's a complete stranger. Also, I now feel even worse about reading this person's innermost thoughts.

"I'll get it to you," I say quietly. Nova is definitely listening.

He lifts his glass again. "It's you in the painting, isn't it?" His voice is slightly above a whisper this time.

Did I mishear him? "Sorry?"

He lowers the glass slightly, a small smile pulling at his lips. "The *mermaid* painting."

Now he's full-blown smiling, and then I'm blushing again, because honestly it is such a nice smile. Even if I have literally no idea what he's talking about.

Simon is saying a lot of words I don't want to hear, and my attention feels split. *Market value. Historical property listings. Sale prices.*

She can't sell it. She *can't.*

And Mason is looking at me expectantly, his fingers tapping on the table now.

"Did you say 'mermaid painting'?" I think I whisper it, but suddenly I realize my mom and Simon seem to be focused on us now, and I dig my fingers into the booth seat, my whole body tense. Did she hear?

But she's looking at Simon, who is looking at me. "Willow, your mom says this is your first time in Salem. What have you seen so far?"

"Ah . . ." Dragging my eyes away from Mason is difficult. He has so much presence. It's like he's sucking up all the energy in the café. "Not much. I've walked through the city a bit." And by that, I of course mean I raced after my ever-fleeing mom.

He picks up his cup. "What do you think of your aunt's house? Isn't it incredible?"

"Yes!" I blurt out. "Or, at least, what I've seen of it." I glance at my mom, but luckily, she doesn't seem all that interested in my response

"We aren't spending time at the estate," she says smoothly. "Estate." She can't even say "house."

Mason shoots me an inquiring look that is luckily subtle enough to fly under my mom's radar. I shift uneasily in my seat. I meet his eyes and shake my head lightly. *Please keep it together, Mason.* This only makes him smile, and the force of it manages to make my insides glow.

Maybe it's me who needs to keep it together.

"And where are you staying?" Simon asks.

"Hotel Salem," Mom answers. "We'll be here just until I get everything settled. Which should be fast."

She had to add that last part.

Simon sets down his coffee cup, gesturing to me. "Mason here is new to the city as well. He just moved here a week ago. Maybe you two could team up. Go to a movie, or the arcade, or whatever it is you kids do these days. Or hey, you could borrow our bikes and head to Salem Willows. Or . . ." He snaps his fingers. "My wife, Emma, is a tour guide, you could go on one of her historical tours. She makes them really fun. Nova, you could go too."

Nova visibly winces, but Mason straightens up, suddenly looking so much taller. "Sure. Tour, and then we could go . . . out to dinner. Or talk. Or whatever."

My mom's head swivels toward us, and this time her eyes are slightly amused.

Now I'm stuck with a lot of conflicting feelings. I mean, no, I do not hate the idea of spending time with Mason. But can he put a little more effort into not being obvious? No teenager gets this excited for a historical tour. Mom is looking at us with a tiny ghost of a smile that I know has to do with this situation, so now I'm stressed out and embarrassed.

"What a *perfect* idea," Simon booms. "A tour and a talk. What do you want to see? History? Witchcraft? A little of both?"

"History," my mom says quickly.

Simon pulls out his phone. "Great. I'll text Emma. Her company does night tours that are a lot of fun. How about a tour tomorrow?"

Tomorrow? The sparklers are back, but this time I'm not sure if it's excitement or nerves.

My mom's eyes linger on Mason for a moment, then she turns back to Simon. "That's great. You don't think putting the house on the market will take that long, do you?"

Simon sighs. "I wish I could tell you no. But my experience with inheritance situations makes me think it's possible." He nods at her. "But we'll get it taken care of as fast as possible, and I know for a fact that the house will sell in a flash. You don't find that level of restoration almost anywhere these days. It's really a special property. Buyers will start circling it like sharks. Mark my word."

Simon turns to me. "And, Willow, Mason doesn't have a phone yet, hoping to remedy that this weekend, so do you mind if I get your number? That way you and Mason can connect." I manage a nod, and he turns to my mom. "And while they're out, we could meet again, I'll draw up some firmer numbers, pull some comps. We can come up with a sale plan."

Sale plan? My stomach clenches so hard, I'm suddenly nauseated. My mom, on the other hand, looks relieved.

"I'll send you her contact now," she says, pulling out her phone. And I swear, she is holding back a grin when she says it.

I meet Mason's gaze again and my heart jumps back into my throat. This time it's definitely about Mason. I don't know how to describe it exactly, but he feels like a big deal.

16

Mason

Signs come in threes. You'll see, it's all working out for us.

There's so much happy adrenaline rushing through me, I feel like I could take to Essex in my own mini parade, complete with song, choreographed dance, and more balloons and star confetti than the Morgans have ever dreamed of.

Maybe not the choreographed dance part.

But definitely the balloons and confetti part. I'm in a *ridiculously* good mood. The universe has hand-delivered me the mermaid not once but twice. First on a dark rooftop, then in a well-lit café, like it wanted to be doubly sure that I was getting the memo. True, I don't know exactly yet what meeting Willow means, but that will sort of unfurl itself, won't it? My mom never knew what her signs meant right away either. Like once when we came home to three sparrows sitting on our front stoop and two days later she got a new job. I need to have patience. And trust. As long as I figure out how to spend more time with Willow, whatever message the universe is sending my way will make itself clear to me.

I hardly know her, and yet everything about it feels cosmic. Like we were already on this trajectory. The next steps will appear. They have to.

The mere thought of it is filling me up so much, I don't even mind the fact that I get ambushed by three heavily made-up little girls the second I step into the house. Besides, by now I know that escape is inevitable. They're like tiny glittery piranhas.

I'm dragged upstairs to my bedroom, where they've set up a mini salon, complete with vanity, a bunch of makeup, and about twenty bottles of sparkly nail polish. I am treated to something called "fancy eye" by Hazel while Audrey paints green sparkly polish over the top thirds of my fingers and Zoe stabs at my scalp with a fine-tooth comb.

"Wow. Your hair is really hard to brush. And you really needed a makeover," Zoe says authoritatively. "Will someone find me some tweezers? I'm going to pluck May May's eyebrows."

The girls have made a unilateral decision to call me May May, and it isn't the worst thing in the world.

"No, you will not be plucking my eyebrows," I say quickly.

"You're right. We should probably wax," Hazel says.

Hazel leans back to assess her work. If she's putting as much dark purple eye shadow on me as is on her, then I can assume I currently look like I have two black eyes.

"What's the occasion?" I ask.

"Tell him, Zoe," Hazel says.

Zoe clears her throat and Audrey beams at me expectantly. "There is going to be a performance. There will be a stage and a sheet for a curtain. I'm the director and Hazel is the person who makes up the dances, and Audrey will be the set designer." She jabs at my hair. "We are all doing the makeup and costumes."

"Um . . . I can be the *set* designer?" Audrey says.

"Yes. You're doing the background," Zoe says.

Oh no. I do *not* like where this is going. "And who is going to perform in the play?"

"*You*," Hazel says. "You will be our star. We'll teach you to dance and everything."

Hilarious. "No, thanks," I say quickly. "Maybe I can help with audio visual? I'll wear all black and hang out in the background."

"No," Hazel says firmly. "It's about a pirate, so we need a boy. We'll teach you how to dance. Everyone will cheer."

"Girls can be pirates." I'm climbing to my feet. "Besides, I don't think that's a good idea. I'm not much of a performer."

"You have to!" Zoe says. "You're our big *brother*."

That stops me. The girls are staring up at me with collective puppy-dog eyes. The room is at least a thousand degrees. "I'm your *foster* brother. It's different."

They all blink at me. Zoe crosses her arms over her chest, pursing her sparkly pink lips. "I don't understand."

"Me neither," Hazel says. She's dripping green nail polish onto the rug.

"It's okay. Don't worry."

"Girls?" Emma's voice comes from down the hall. For once I'm relieved to hear it.

"We're in Mason's room!" Hazel says.

"What are you doing in Mason's room?" Emma pokes her head around the corner. She's wearing shorts and an old sweatshirt and holding an envelope. When she sees me a quick smile pulls at her face. "Oh, my."

Her smile is getting bigger. I can't stand it. "I guess I needed a makeover. But fancy eye has never really been my thing," I add. "I'm more into smoky eye."

I only know the term "smoky eye" from one of my foster sisters, but it does the trick. Emma's mouth twitches. "Mason, you're a good sport."

"What do you mean fancy eye isn't your thing?" Hazel demands. "Fancy eye is *everything*. And Mom, his hair is so tangly today. Can you fix it?"

Zoe holds the brush up to her mom, and Emma takes it, tucking it into her pocket. "That's enough makeover. It's time for us to go to Salem Willows. Mason, do you want makeup remover?"

I must look confused, because she disappears for a moment, then reappears with bottle of clear liquid and a bunch of cotton pads, then leads me to the bathroom, where we stand side by side in the mirror.

"Apply, then swipe. Like this." She demonstrates on her own makeup-less eyelids, and I watch as my face transforms back to normal. Standing next to Emma in the bathroom might be the most comfortable I've been around her, which isn't saying much, but still. I can see exactly how much taller I am than her, and the mirror removes the need for direct eye contact.

When I'm done cleaning my face, she glances at my hair for a moment. Zoe was right. It's terrible today. I reach up self-consciously, feeling for the tangle that always appears above my left ear.

Growing my hair out is fairly new. I decided to do it two years ago after the visits with my mom stopped, and I decided I wanted a physical reminder of her.

When she wasn't dyeing it, our hair was the exact same color, and she always wore it long, so I decided to do the same. Now every time I look in the mirror I see a hint of her. The problem is the upkeep. I have no idea if this is a normal amount of tangle, and I don't have anyone to ask, so my typical coping method is to give it a few brushes and then call it good.

I start raking at it, trying to get some of it to lie flat. Emma is still watching me, and I'm blushing now. "I know it's bad," I say quickly.

She hesitates briefly. "I was going to say it looks just like Nay Nay's."

I realize with a start she means Naomi. I didn't know she had a nickname for her, and I didn't know the girls were calling me a nickname that was basically the same as my mom's. May May and Nay Nay. My heart starts to skip, my emotions building up, but before I can think of any sort of response, she moves toward the door.

"I'm going to pack up the girls for Salem Willows. See you downstairs?" Then she disappears down the hallway, leaving me with a giant ball of emotions.

Salem Willows turns out to be a small recreation area on the tip of the peninsula that hosts an arcade and a few walk-up restaurants. In the center is a large grassy park full of large white willow trees, and along the water are old houses and a small rocky beach. Scads of kids are jumping through waves, their legs bluish with cold.

I spend the drive getting back to level ground after my interactions with Emma and the girls. The ride is chaotic with the girls fighting over who gets to sit by me, and Simon desperately trying to drag Nova out of the angry cocoon she's built around herself. Simon made her leave her phone at home, which was clearly a travesty.

Eventually we arrive, and everyone piles out and is handed things to carry. I'm assigned the beach umbrella and a nylon net full of beach toys, and the girls are given towels, life jackets, and snacks and we go set up on the beach. We order sugar corn—flavored sweet popcorn—from E.W. Hobbs, then all sit around eating handfuls of it while the girls run screaming into and out of the water.

The willow trees of course make me think of Willow, and as I watch them swaying in the breeze, the last of my uneasiness fades away. Yes, the girls are shrieking, and I'm awkwardly perched on a towel next to Emma and Nova, but right at this moment I'm feeling like anything is possible.

Those signs have to mean I'll see her again, don't they?

Simon walks away and reappears a few minutes later holding an enormous bag of cinnamon popcorn. "Isn't this place great? It was originally a smallpox hospital. They built the park for the patients. Nova, you want to go to the arcade?"

"Not really," she says.

"Aw, come on, Nov. It will be fun." I think she's going to refuse again, but she lets out a little half growl and grudgingly stands up, then the two of them head for the arcade, Nova hanging back a few feet.

Emma passes me the bag of popcorn, her eyes on the girls. "Simon said you might want to go on a Salem tour with his client's daughter? Is that right?"

"Yeah. Her name's Willow." My words come out faster than I can stop them, and instantly I want to take them back. The goal is not to open up to Emma. And besides, I sound like I have a huge crush on Willow, which, okay, maybe in normal circumstances, I would. But that isn't what this is about.

I brace myself, but Emma doesn't smile or wink or do anything embarrassing. Instead she says, "Tell me about her." The full weight of Emma's gaze is overwhelming. Normally she's doing about a thousand things, and having her full attention is like staring into the sun.

Willow.

"Um . . ." *She looks like a mermaid. I think she's a sign from the universe. When I see her I get the feeling I'm going to figure out how to get back to my mom.* I realize how wild that sounds, but also, it's true. "I think she's my age. Her mom inherited the house from her sister. She has red hair." I realize as I'm saying it that this is a pathetic collection of facts. I don't even know where she's from.

Despite my paltry offerings, Emma nods as though the

sunshine in my voice makes perfect sense. "My coworker asked if I'd fill in for her on a ghost tour tomorrow night. I don't typically do the ghost tours, but I'll say yes if it sounds fun to you." She takes out her phone, then pulls up the tour company's website. *Historical Hauntings. An unforgettable night exploring Salem's most famous ghosts.*

The type of tour obviously isn't the point for me, but Historical Hauntings actually does sound fun. I pass the phone back to her. "Simon has her phone number. He said he'd call and arrange it." That part is moderately humiliating, as it feels like I'm being set up on a playdate. I'm obviously willing to deal with that part if it means spending time with her, but it's embarrassing anyway.

Emma's voice is casual. "Your foster care worker says you had to leave your old phone back at the group home. Do you want one?"

For a moment I stare at her.

"Sorry, dumb question. Of course you want a phone," she says.

Excitement rises in my chest, but then I quickly tamp it down. "You don't have to get me one," I say quickly.

"I know," she says. "But friends can make a big difference. Even if she's only here for a little while, it would be good if you were able to contact her. I'll run to the store tomorrow, okay? It will probably be pretty basic, but maybe we can figure out a way for you to get a better phone later down the line. Does that sound okay for now?"

Gratitude is welling up in me, and it's sort of confusing because I don't want to have a lot of good feelings toward Emma, but also she has offered to do several things for me, and all of them mean a lot. She's also pretending not to notice the fact that my eyes are weirdly misty right now.

"Thank you."

"You're worth it," she says, and I'm glad she doesn't look at me.

Suddenly Nova comes storming out of the arcade, headed toward the water, Simon hurrying after her, and Emma sighs.

"What's up with Nova?" I ask. I almost say *Hurricane* Nova but luckily stop myself at the last second.

"She's only with us for the summers. The rest of the time she's in Worcester with her mom. Ever year has been a bit harder to get her to stay. She's getting older, and I know she misses her friends and mom. But Simon looks forward to the time all year."

We turn to look at the two of them. Nova's back is hunched, but Simon is leaning in, trying to get her interested in something. I try to imagine what it would be like to have two homes, one for summer, one for the rest of the time. I'm sure it isn't easy, but the thought of even one stable home sounds both so foreign to me and out-of-this-world incredible.

"I think this summer is all about the pushback," she says quietly. "Letting us know how she feels." Her voice isn't judgmental or upset. She's simply stating facts. I sit with that for a minute. I obviously don't trust Emma—she's part of the same system that has hurt me a million times before—but something about her is intriguing. Which I guess makes sense—she'd been my mom's best friend, hadn't she?

Emma shrugs. "That's my job, though, isn't it? It's kids' jobs to push back and our job to make it safe for them to do it." She says this so naturally, like it's something that everybody knows. Her voice feels genuine, and I get hit with one of those waves like I do sometimes when I miss having a mom. Not even my mom, just *a* mom. What would it be like to have someone to always be there? The pain rises up then, burning like salt water on a wound. I brace myself. I know it won't last forever, but for the moment, it stings like hell.

"The tour tomorrow is going to be great," she says, then she stands up and heads for the water, and I sit for a while, watching the kids diving into the waves over and over, wondering what it would be like to have a parent you could push and push against and never have them break. It sounds imaginary.

17

Willow

"Can you believe it?" my mom says.

"No," I say emphatically. We're racing back down Essex Street, my brunch leftovers dangling from my wrist in a plastic bag. Our meal was so confusing and overwhelming that I could barely eat anything. I have no idea which "it" my mom is referring to, but after everything that has happened over the past twenty-four hours, it's safe to say I can't believe it. I think I'm experiencing emotional whiplash—too many strange things happening at once.

I even have plans with Mason. At least now I can return his notebook to him?

She keeps going. "I was positive we could be out of here in forty-eight hour or less, but Simon thinks it's going to take at least another week to get it all on the market. I have an event next weekend, and my client is going to have an absolute meltdown when she finds out I won't be there for the run-through. Hopefully they can extend our stay at the hotel. We're only booked until tomorrow."

"A week?" I say hopefully. For a moment, Essex's bricks turn to clouds and I am walking on air. If I have another full week here, maybe I'll figure out how to talk to my mom about the curse story. And spend more time at the house. The thought makes my entire body tingle.

My mom's phone chimes and she lifts it to her face, sighing. "There's the aunts again."

"The aunts?" Energy springs through my body, and it takes all of my power not to wrestle the phone from her. "Can I see?"

"I think Poppy learned to text." She reluctantly tilts the screen toward me.

The message says INVITATION FOR WILLOW AND ROSEMARY. MOON CEREMONY AT 8:30, WE WILL SEE YOU THERE and then has about fifty emojis after it, most of them moons, stars, cats, and, confusingly, a clown face. I'm going to assume that last one was an error.

I'm practically bouncing, I'm so excited. "What's a moon ceremony?"

She sighs again, then begins stabbing at the keyboard. "It's for their coven. They gather at full moons and new moons to hold ceremonies."

"A coven?" I demand. "So, what, they gather around a cauldron or something? Cast spells?"

"Who even knows," she says flatly, but she bites her lower lip, and suddenly I remember all of her sparkly writing. *Spell to Pass Chemistry Test. Notice Me Spell.* I've seen her Book of Shadows. It's kind of hilarious that she's pretending to not know what the witches do.

Her phone dings. "Oh, and there's Simon sending the estate company's info." She lifts one eyebrow. "Mason seemed . . . *eager* to spend time with you."

My eyes shoot to hers, but she's back to her phone, a little smile on her face.

I inhale and exhale slowly. I have to stay calm. And casual. "Where do the aunts live?"

She drops her phone into her purse, then heads for the hotel steps. "I don't think it's a good idea. I'm working tonight. I have to do a Zoom meeting for the McArthur wedding—"

"That's fine, I can go on my own!" My voice comes out way too excited, which is a mistake. I mean, yes, unhindered access to the aunts is clearly what I need right now, but my mom can't know that.

Her face swivels toward me suspiciously. "You want to spend time with them on your own?"

"Well . . . yeah." I soften my tone and shrug casually.

"Why?" She's really studying me now, her jaw starting to set in that way it does when she's about to dig her heels in. I have to act like this isn't so big of a deal.

"I mean, why not? We're here, right?" I'm struggling to keep the desperation out of my voice.

We're at the hotel now, and she pulls out her key, fitting it into the lock, and her voice takes on the brassy *I'm in charge* tone I'm more used to.

"Willow, I don't think you spending time alone with them is a good idea. We'll set up lunch with them or—"

I drop the forced nonchalance. If she didn't want me to know about her family, she should have left me at home. "Don't you think it would be good for me to get to know people I'm related to? They're my *family*. I already spend lots of time moving back and forth. Don't you think I deserve to at least know who these humans are?"

I don't bring up the split-families thing often because I know it makes her feel bad that we live so far from my dad and his family and that she has to work so much, but this is an emergency. I have no idea where to go with the curse story, and if she isn't going to be the one to explain this whole bizarre Bell-family dynamic to me, then I'm going to need to see the aunts.

She bites her lower lip, conflicted, but I can see she's relenting a bit. "I don't know, Willow."

"What's the worst that could happen?"

Her eyes dart to mine, sharp and worried. Okay, she obviously thinks a *lot* could happen. Which makes sense if she believes in a family curse. Except she doesn't, right?

She exhales, running her hand through her hair. She's thinking, which means I have a shot. I take it.

"I know they're pretty out there. I would just like to get the chance to know them a bit. Before the house sells. Simon says it will be fast, right? And who knows when we'll be back. If ever."

I can barely force myself to say the part about the house, but it does the trick.

Her shoulders loosen slightly, and she grabs a lock of her hair, pulling down lightly. "You're right. I suppose it can't really hurt. . . ."

She's sort of half talking to herself, which is completely out of character. I jump in before she can change her mind. "Great! What time should I head over there? Do I need to take anything special? And can you give me their address?"

She exhales. "Willow, listen. The aunts . . . they have a lot of ideas about our family's history that aren't accurate, so you can't take them at face value, okay? This town has a way of twisting the truth."

I almost blurt out, *Oh, you mean like the family curse?* but manage to keep it in. Instead, I go for another tactic. "So you're saying that whatever the aunts believe . . . you don't?"

It comes out all kinds of clunky, and my mom narrows her eyes at me. "What are you talking about?" she says.

"Um, like whatever ideas they have about our family's history, they aren't true?"

This is dangerous ground. Her lips are tight now. "I'm saying that time has a way of distorting the truth. There are things that . . ." She exhales. "Sometimes people need something to blame, you know?"

It feels like she's thrown out a tiny trail of breadcrumbs. I desperately want to follow it. "I've asked them not to drag you into any of the family's drama. But if you do hear anything, from other townspeople, whatever, please know it's all stories. Okay?"

She's talking about the curse. Her voice is intense, and my heart is beating in my ears now. "Okay?" she says again.

"Okay," I say quickly.

Her shoulder releases, and she pushes in through the door, making a slight *ahh* noise as she slings her purse on the night table. Then I remember the other thing I need to talk to her about.

"I meant to tell you, I talked to Dad last night." I say this like it's not a big deal, even though I know it is. She didn't tell me *not* to tell my dad, but she didn't tell me I could tell him either. "I told him we were in Salem."

She freezes, then whips around, trying and failing to hide a look of panic. "Right. What did you tell him, exactly?"

"That you inherited some property, and we're here getting it handled."

Her shoulders relax the tiniest bit. "Great. Perfect. It's just that he, ah, doesn't know everything about my time here. No one does, really."

My heart thuds, and I feel myself leaning in hopefully. Because even if she's trying to keep most of it a secret, she has brought me in. For someone as closed off as she is, that's huge. "Because of your falling-out with Sage?" I prompt. Maybe she'll finally open the door to me seeing a bit more.

But of course her face hardens, and she swings it right back shut. "The past is the past, right? There's nothing we can do about it now." She glances at her wrist. "Oh dear, I need to get on a call right now. I'll send you Violet's number, and you can get the details? I'm guessing

I'll be busy most of the day. Let me know if you need anything."Then she bolts for her desk.

That's when I realize something. *Her blouse is untucked.* I realize that sounds silly, but this is my mom, and her daily uniform is never anything but pristine. What's next? Smudged lipstick? A frayed hem?

No wonder she wants to get out of here; it's pretty clear that Salem is bringing up all sorts of things for her, and, yes, I'm dying to know what those things are.

Moon ceremony it is.

I'm too nervous that Simon will be at Aunt Sage's house, so I spend the afternoon flinging myself around Salem in a steadily increasing frenzy of delight. This city is *weird*. Museums range from the serious (Peabody Essex) to the grotesque (Count Orlok's Nightmare Gallery). The witch shops are exactly as quirky and interesting as they seem from the outside, and there are at least thirty restaurants I want to try.

Eventually the cobblestone starts to get to my feet and I head back to the hotel in hopes that my mom will do some more cryptic unveiling of her family's dynamics.

Instead, I find her in full-fledged party-planning mode—Post-it notes taking up most of the wall next to the desk, her headphones engulfing her ears. I keep waiting for a break between meetings, but every time I press my ear to the door, I'm treated to a litany of topics including "event lighting," "guest lists," and something called the "al fresco dining experience."

It's like we aren't in Salem, Massachusetts, with a family curse hanging over our heads and a mysterious aunt who left a book of collected spells that she wrote with my mother.

Let the record show I do not understand my mother.

By 7:55 p.m., I'm a can of rocket fuel. The moon ceremony doesn't start until eight thirty, but if I don't get out of this maddeningly curated hotel, I'm going to explode. Mom is too caught up in her call to talk to me, but when I pass her a note, she scribbles down the aunts' address, *611 Orange Street, look for the white fence*, plus an extra note: *WARNING: Aunt Marigold might be skyclad.*

"Huh?" I say, but she just pulls the phone slightly from her chin, unleashing the tinny sound of someone speaking quickly, and mouths, *Skyclad*, while pointing at her blazer.

No idea. I'm too excited to get going to waste any more time, so I nod like I understand, then head for the door.

Salem is hot and earthy-smelling, even in the evening, and the street has swelled with people who seem exactly as interested in being here as I am, which sets my heart all aflutter.

My phone directs me down by the water, and the farther I get from the city center, the quieter Salem feels. Soon I'm passing rows of large, colorful homes, their window boxes dripping brightly colored flowers. Orange Street is only a block from the water, and when I see the street sign, a thrill moves up my entire body, putting a spring in my step. I am going to a *witches' meeting*. I have to tell Bea. I pull up my phone and find a message waiting from her. As usual, we're on a delay.

ROOFTOP BOY WAS AT LUNCH? I'm not out of class until 10 your time. Call me then?

I answer.

Yes. And I'm on my way to a moon circle with my great-aunts' coven.

Bea: Please tell me you're kidding . . .

I send back every witch-related emoji I can find.

The aunts' house is easy to spot. It's a completely different style from Aunt Sage's, smaller, with a roof that flares out in curved lines. The roof and exterior are all lined in light brown shingles, and light is pouring out of every window. Several large garden boxes sit near the house, with herbs and vegetables growing from them. A sign on the garden gate reads WARNING: WITCH GARDEN. TRESPASSERS WILL BE USED AS INGREDIENTS FOR POTIONS.

I snort, glancing around at the rest of the neighborhood. The aunts apparently have no issues with advertising their witchiness.

I let myself in through the gate. I can hear voices coming from somewhere in the house, lots of laughter, and possibly the crackling of a fire? A few steps up I'm met with another sign: WE ARE THE GRANDDAUGHTERS OF THE WITCHES YOU COULD NOT BURN. And then another: THINGS HAVEN'T BEEN THE SAME SINCE THAT HOUSE FELL ON MY SISTER. And finally, by the door: WITCHES WELCOME, ALL OTHERS MAKE AN APPOINTMENT. And then . . . yes. A pair of stuffed legs encased in black-and-white tights and ruby slippers peeking out from the edge of the porch.

The aunts might be my most favorite humans on earth.

"Is that her?" An unfamiliar voice comes from the open window, piercing the silence. Then the door flies open and I see a flash of wrinkly peachy flesh, a cloud of white hair, and a pair of pink house slippers.

The pink house slippers command a lot of attention, because they happen to be the only things she's wearing. In other words, a very old, very naked lady is standing on the porch, waving frantically at me.

The woman breaks out into an enormous smile, which I'd probably think was adorable if I weren't also dealing with the birthday suit situation. "Willow! My dear!"

"Um . . . ," I squeak. I have absolutely no idea where to look, so I settle on the fake witch legs poking out from under the house. "Are you Aunt Marigold?"

"You bet my sweet ass I am!" she shrieks, and then—to my deep horror—begins shaking said sweet ass in my direction. "My dear, we have waited to meet you for so long!"

"I . . . ah . . ." I look nervously around me. We're on a residential street. Is this okay for her to be running around naked? "I think you've forgotten your . . ."

"Clothes? It's called being skyclad. Nothing between you and the sky, just pure, unadulterated freedom!" She waves her arms in the air and all sorts of bits begin jiggling.

That's what my mom was trying to warn me about. Marigold.

"My goddess, you do look exactly like Sage and Rosemary."

"Marigold! Put some clothes on, for goddess' sake, she's new!" It's Violet, and she appears on the front porch, looking flushed and, to my relief, throws an enormous silk kimono over Marigold, who grudgingly ties the sash. Violet is wearing a long purple dress and dangly moon earrings that reach all the way to her shoulders. "Excuse Marigold. She needs to learn when the proper moment to be skyclad is."

"It's always the proper moment to be skyclad," Marigold says firmly, but she gives me a little wink. Violet gestures to her door, and it makes her moon earrings swing. I suddenly feel stupid for showing up in sneakers and a T-shirt. I didn't even think about what I was wearing, which is sort of normal for me but embarrassing under the circumstances. "Was I supposed to dress up? Or . . ." I gulp, looking toward Marigold. *Not* dress? "I didn't know what to wear. Do I need to wear anything special?"

She shakes her head. "Being a witch is about what happens on the inside. Plenty of witches walking around in sneakers and T-shirts. No pointy hats and black cloaks unless they make you feel powerful."

The aunts hustle me into the house, which is, honestly, like walking into a fairy-tale witch's house. It is so charmingly chaotic that I have to stop for a moment to take it all in. Three rocking chairs have been arranged around the fireplace, with baskets of knitting perched by two of them, a stack of books by the other. The walls are lined with built-in bookcases bursting with books, and the fireplace mantel is decorated in drying herbs. A fluffy cat lies on the rug in front of the fireplace, and he raises one eye sleepily at me before going back to his resting.

Violet leads me into the kitchen, which is a delightful blend of homespun and state of the art. Worn copper pots gleam from hooks on the ceiling above a cast-iron oven range, and a vintage yellow refrigerator sits next to an enormous espresso maker. More herbs are planted in old tomato cans on the windowsill, and several handmade rugs line the floor.

Best of all, as I step into the space, I get a deep whiff of something that sends me hurtling back to my summer with Bea. Poppy is removing a baking tray from the oven, and when I see the round, flaky pastries, I let out a giddy sigh. "You made kouign-amann?"

"For Willow, our guest of honor," she says, sliding the pan onto her stovetop. "My goodness, the French know what they're doing with butter, sugar, and salt, don't they?"

"That's my favorite French pastry!" I say. "I haven't been able to find one in the States anywhere. Did my mom tell you I love them?"

Poppy smiles and shakes her head, and the aunts exchange quick conspiratorial smiles. "No, dear. Just a coincidence." She whisks over to the fridge, producing a pear-shaped glass bottle that I'd recognize anywhere. "And a drink. There's a tradition in witches' gatherings, we serve cakes and ale, which today means basically any food and drink we want."

"Orangina?" I'm basically jumping up and down now. Orangina

is my favorite French soda. Bea introduced me to it at a tiny café in Montmartre, a hilltop neighborhood flooded with tourists and gorgeous views.

Before I can ask how Poppy knows this is my most favorite drink on earth, I'm handed my pastry and soda and then whisked through the house to the back patio.

18

Mason

Once the girls have played in the cold water long enough to turn their limbs sufficiently blue, we reverse the great Morgan migration and pack everything back up and head home. Three neighbor kids are waiting on the porch to play, and their presence makes the sound decibels in the house rise at least a hundred-fold.

I spend the afternoon rattling around my makeup-dusted bedroom trying not to lose my mind. I can't stop thinking about Willow. The tour is still a solid twenty-four hours away, and the fact that I'm not with her makes me antsy, energy pooling in my arms and legs.

I'm just contemplating whether or not it would be creepy if I casually strolled past Willow's hotel, when there's a knock at the door. I assume it's the girls ready to inflict some fresh cosmetic hell upon me, but when I open the door, it's Emma. She's changed out of her beach clothes and is dressed in what I now know are her tour clothes—a blouse tucked into a skirt, ballet flats, huge sunglasses on her head. Something about her is different, though, which sets off my internal scanner right away. I glance at her shoes, her face, and then her hands, and that's when I see it. She has a large shoebox under her arm. Also, she looks nervous.

Instantly, my stomach drops. Why is Emma *nervous*?

She cocks her head. "Okay if I come in? I have something I want to show you. Well, two things."

I step backward, making a little space in my room, and she reaches into her pocket and hands me a smartphone with a red case.

As she hands it to me, I feel a huge mix of feelings welling up. I've had a phone, and once my own laptop, but I've always felt behind compared to my peers because I couldn't afford the *right* phone— the one that would give me access to all the games and streaming services and apps my friends had. And now Emma is handing me that very thing.

"It's a used one. I was planning to buy a flip phone just to get you through the next little bit, but I mentioned to our neighbor that we needed one, and she offered to sell me this one. The number is on the back, and I'll give you the Wi-Fi password. She warned me that the Internet is a little slow."

It could quack like a duck every time I turned it on and I'd still be thrilled. Except, this is too much. Way too much. "I can pay you back," I say quickly.

"It's a gift," she says, and now she's smiling. She's as excited about this as I am. Now I'm conflicted. I want the phone, but I also hate the thought of being indebted to the Morgans. Maybe I'll figure out how to earn money? Even so, I can't help the excitement building in my chest.

Then I remember the second thing.

Suddenly the raggedy-looking orange shoebox comes into focus, and she holds it in front of her.

"What is it?"

She's clutching the shoebox hard, which lets me know this is the thing she's nervous about. I brace myself. Whatever this is, it isn't going to be good. "Last year I was going through some old things at my mom's house—she was getting ready to move, and I found this box I'd forgotten about. It's from high school. Notes I passed with friends, pictures, ticket stubs, that kind of thing." She exhales. "I know you can't store a relationship—a friendship—inside a box, but honestly, I think this is as close as it gets. Everything in here has to do with Naomi."

She pushes the box at me, and I automatically take it, but the moment it's in my palms, I wish I hadn't. It's heavy and smells lightly musty in a way that conjures up old books, but today makes me sick to my stomach. She's giving me a box of my *mom*?

"I haven't told you this quite yet. But your mom . . ." She hesitates, and I realize that her eyes are shiny. I swallow, hard. "I really loved your mom. She was the most important person in the world to me for almost twenty years. I wanted you to see. We were in a play together once. I was terrible, but she was so good. And we played volleyball. She was homecoming royalty our junior year. You can find her in the yearbook. It's all . . ." She exhales. "I thought you might want to see it. Have something to remember her by."

Every hair on my body prickles, my spine suddenly completely straight. Emma is talking like my mom is dead. Like neither of us will ever see her again, and suddenly heat is building in my center, filling me up slowly from my feet to my head until hot pressure builds behind my eyes. "You know she just lost custody of me temporarily, right?" I blurt out. My tone is wrong. I sounds aggressive and angry, which I am—but I typically try to stay away from that. This time I can't. "She isn't dead."

"Of course she isn't." Emma blinks a few times, her lips forming around some new words, but I can't possibly listen to what she has to say. My heart is pounding too hard.

"As soon as she gets clean, I'll be back with her. It takes a while, but she's working on it."

The intensity of my voice fills up the space between us. "Mason, I didn't mean ..."

She raises her arms, and I see a flash of her tattoo. It's like being struck by a small amount of lightning. It pulls the words from my mouth. "Sometimes it takes addicts dozens of times trying before sobriety sticks. Sometimes people get better."

Long pause. The only sound is coming from the girls shouting in the backyard, our eyes fixed on each other. She isn't backing down, and I'm not either, even though my racing pulse wants me to.

"Sometimes they do," she says quietly.

I hate that "sometimes." It's placating and uncertain. It makes my feet leave Earth. My mom is going to conquer her addiction because she has to. We are meant to be together. There's no way she's gone from my life. My mom getting better is not a maybe. It's an eventuality. It's what keeps the stars hanging in the sky. It's what makes the Earth spin. I don't need a box of random high school mementos. I need to get to *her*.

Any good feelings that built up with Emma at Salem Willows are erased. Washed away.

I hold out the box, but she doesn't take it. She doesn't move at all. "Keep it," she says. "In case you change your mind."

I'm not going to change my mind, but the fight is draining out of me. All I want is for her to leave.

"Fine," I manage. Then, as she reaches for the doorknob, a stubborn flicker of hope moves into my field of vision, forcing my words out. "Emma, do you know where she is?"

She pauses and turns back, and I see the answer in her eyes before she says it. "No. I'm sorry, Mason. I lost contact with her at the same time the foster care system did."

Her answer isn't a surprise, but it hits me hard anyway. I wish

I thought she was lying, but her eyes are too clear for that. Emma is a dead end, just like everybody else. Why do I keep doing this to myself?

She nods at me, then walks down the hall, and I force myself to turn around, close the door. The box weighs a thousand emotional pounds, and I have never wanted to hold anything less.

I stumble over to my bed and let it drop onto the comforter, the contents shuffling and jangling inside. It takes me a full minute to work up the courage to open it, and then when I do, I wish I hadn't. It's a field of landmines disguised as ordinary items. Photos, ticket stubs, random bracelets and tubes of ChapStick, a yearbook, even a playbill.

My mom was in a play called *The Importance of Being Earnest*. I scan the cast list and see my mom's name listed as playing Lady Bracknell. Seeing her name in print makes me feel like my head has disconnected from my body. I'm reaching for the yearbook when I find the strips of images of my mom and Emma taken in a photo booth. There are about ten sheets of photos, and a few of them are of random people posing, but they are mostly my mom and Emma. Emma looks pretty close to how she does now, with long hair and minimal makeup. But my mom . . .

My brain doesn't know how to process what I'm looking at. As a teenager she was just as gorgeous as everyone had said—tall with long dark hair and a massive smile that I think I only saw in person a handful of times. She looks like someone with a huge future ahead of her. Someone who was going to do very big things. My hands are shaking now. I *hate* this.

And then I realize why. I don't know the person in the photographs. Pre-addiction Mom is a stranger. She's beautiful and hopeful looking, but she isn't the person who let me sleep on the roof of the car the summer we lived in our car in a national forest, or who I tucked blankets around whenever she passed out on the couch. If high-school Mom walked in the room, she'd have to introduce herself—that's how far she is from the person I know.

This mythical version of her may not have some of her flaws, but she isn't the person I want. I want my *mom*. I can accept who she is, why can't everyone else?

And Emma. My throat tightens again, this time with anger. Emma apparently used to smile all the time. In every single one, she's beaming, usually with her arm thrown around my mom's shoulders. What was her goal with this? To prove she actually had been a good friend to my mom? Because that is obviously not the case. She was clearly only okay with the pre-addict version of my mom, and she hadn't been there when it counted.

Now *I'm* thinking about my mom like she's dead. But she's not. She still has a chance; we still have a chance. We have more than a chance, if the signs are to be believed. Even with those thoughts, dread splays through me, its long tentacles reaching all the way to my fingertips. I grip the box. I'm not interested in my mom's past; I'm interested in her future.

I stand up and shove the shoebox roughly into the top of my closet, doing my best to force it out of my mind as well. My mom, or the universe, or whatever it is, sent me a *sign*, and right now I need to trust that. I don't have time to delve into Emma and my mom's messy past. I need to focus on the future. Right now, my main job is to figure out why Willow showed up when she did. No matter how many times I try to twist it into coincidence, I can't.

I asked for a sign and a mermaid showed up. Everything is going to be fine.

● ● ●

The rest of the night is misery. I feel like a can of soda that's been through a spin cycle and then a round in the dryer, just for kicks. The Morgan household takes at least twice as long as it usually does to wind down. Dinner is pizza that doesn't arrive until seven, and then when it's bedtime, I hear the girls arguing and laughing in the next room for what feels like ages. Finally, I hear Emma leave for her tour, and Simon turns on a golf tournament in the living room.

I spend twenty minutes trying to access Internet from my phone, but like Emma said, it barely works and every click is agonizingly slow. I'm feeling just desperate enough to try the family computer, so I make my way quietly out of my room and downstairs.

As I walk into the dining room, I see Nova slouched in the computer chair. She doesn't hear me come in, so I knock on the entryway and she jumps about two feet before quickly closing the windows on her screen and scraping back in the chair. She stares stubbornly at the floor, her cheeks red.

I study her for a moment, tension thick in the center of the dining room. "Do you need more time? I'm not in a rush."

"You can have it," she mumbles, then shoves past me.

I wait for Nova to stomp out of the room before clicking on the search history. I'm not trying to catch her in anything, but I am genuinely curious. What could she possibly be looking at that would require this much angry energy? I mean, I know what *most* people are looking at when they're sneaking around on the Internet, but I doubt that's what she was looking at in the middle of her family's dining room.

The browser history shows a good twenty websites, and as I scan down the list of all the ones she's been to, my eyebrows go up.

• • •

Why Are Sloths So Slow Plus Ten More Sloth Facts

Hilarious Sloth Memes to Brighten Your Day

This is what Nova the Terrible is reading up on? Sloths?

I click through a few of the fact sites, scanning the lists of facts. *Today's sloths are about the size of a medium-sized dog. But ten thousand years ago, their ancestors, called Megatherium, could grow to be as large as elephants.*

Terrifying.

A typical sloth will fall out of its tree once a week. They can fall ten stories without sustaining significant damage.

Hilarious.

I sit back in my chair. It's like seeing a tiny chink in her armor. Nova likes *sloths*. I click through a few more memes, then double-check that Simon is still watching the game.

And then it's time. I take a deep breath, working up my courage. I've been anxious for solo time with the computer so I can look for my mom, but that doesn't mean I particularly like looking for her. Mom roulette has never been easy.

Here are the rules. Basically, you type her name into as many spots as you can think of, and then try not to succumb to despair when nothing comes up.

I start with her social media sites, which is pointless—she hasn't posted anything on any of them in almost a decade—but at this point it's tradition. Her profile photo is the same across all the platforms—she's standing barefoot on the beach in a pair of cutoff shorts and a Rolling Stones T-shirt. It isn't a great photo; she's squinting, and there's a big glare from the top right corner. You can't even see much of her face because her hair is blowing all over the place, but it's all I have, so I know every square pixel of this photograph. I lean in so close, my nose nearly touches the screen. I wonder for the millionth time who took that photo. Could it have been my father? My mom told me he checked out right after she found out she was pregnant with me, which all but erased him from my radar. If he doesn't want anything to do with me, then I don't want anything to do with him. My mom is the one I care about.

Next, I check the prisons. Federal prisons are fairly straightforward, you just have to search one website and they have all the records for every inmate in the country all the way back to the 1980s. It's the state prisons that throw me because you have to know the name of the facility to search for their status. The only record I've ever found was from when she served time at correctional facility in Suffolk County, and that was five years ago.

Next, I start googling her name plus different states. She loved moving, which means she could be anywhere. *Naomi Greer, Massachusetts. Naomi Greer, New York. Naomi Greer, Maine.*

Nothing, nothing, *nothing*. I give up after about thirty minutes when the dull ache growing in my chest starts to get too heavy. My mother is possibly the only person not on the Internet. But I have to keep trying. I have to.

I close everything out, clearing my and Nova's search histories, then stand up and head for the door, passing by Simon, who is still for once. "I'm going for a walk," I say.

There's a pause and for a moment I think he's going to tell me I can't go, then he turns and smiles, his voice booming. "Of course. Some fresh air, what a great idea. Need some company?" He jumps to his feet, energy coursing through him. Someone should be doing science experiments on this guy.

"No," I say quickly. I don't know if Emma told him about the memorabilia box fiasco, but either way I am in no condition for one of his monologue-style hangouts. He tilts his head, and for a moment I'm nervous that he's going to insist, but then there's an excited burst of applause from the TV and he practically dives for the couch.

I have my hand on the door when my new phone beeps in my pocket and Simon calls, "Mason, that's Willow's number. Her mom texted me. You're on for tomorrow."

19

Willow

As soon as I finish my last heavenly crumb of kouign-amann, Marigold whisks my plate away. Poppy called her the baby of the family, and I get it. Not only does she clearly love attention, she has a shocking amount of energy. She's been hovering around me like a mosquito. "Finally. Now the fun can *really* begin." Her eyes are bright and sparkly, and I feel a twinge of excitement/fear in my chest.

"What fun?"

Marigold raises one eyebrow. "The moon ceremony, of course. Now, out you go."

I'm hustled outside, where I find several cushions positioned around a clay bowl. A small wooden altar has been set up with crystals, bundles of dried herbs, candles, and a deck of cards.

I choose a purple cushion and Poppy hands me a glass jar of water. "Moon water. Drink up!"

I settle myself into the cushion and take a sip of moon water, which turns out to be regular water.

"Good, right?" Poppy asks. "I charged it during that last full moon."

"Delicious," I say, hiding a smile. It's dark and peaceful in the backyard, the moon quiet and unassuming above us. The aunts settle themselves in their cushions, then the three of them close their eyes in unison, taking long, even breaths.

It's so quiet, I don't dare move. Finally, Violet opens her eyes. "I'll open our circle. Goddesses, sisters, witches. We gather under Mother Moon and ask her for insight and clarity. We call in the elements of earth, fire, water, and air, and ask that our circle will be protected."

She pauses a moment, then Marigold pulls out a lighter and lights three candles on the altar. Sitting in the dark with these three women is the best kind of weird, and for a moment I feel my shoulders relax.

Then Violet turns to me. "Now, Willow. You did sneak into the house and find the Book of Shadows, didn't you?"

I nearly choke on my moon water. "Um . . . well, you see, the thing is—"

"Of course she did!" Marigold says. "Bell women have never relied on asking permission. They do what needs to be done! Willow is no exception."

The aunts are like the ultimate hype-women. Excitement bubbles through me, sending my voice bursting out of me. "You're really going to tell me about it?"

Poppy shakes her head. "We promised Rosemary we wouldn't tell Willow about the curse. She made us swear on a witch's honor."

"It was a very reluctant promise," Violet says. "But she's right. We did promise."

All of my excitement is instantly replaced with annoyance. This is my family history too.

"Well, I didn't swear on my witch's honor," Marigold says. "You and Poppy can sit in the corner and listen. I'll do the telling. Besides, Willow already knows. Don't you, Willow?"

All three of them look at me expectantly, and I can't help the smile that escapes me. "Well . . . I read about it in the Book of Shadows—"

"I told you!" Violet says, slamming her hand down on the ground. "I told you she was the one who would get this figured out. All we had to do was give her the key and she'd start the journey on her own. She's plucky, exactly like her mother."

"Don't you mean like Sage?" I ask hopefully, thinking about Sage's perfectly eclectic house.

"No. Like your mother, dear," Poppy says.

My shoulders slump slightly. But almost as quickly, I perk up with excitement. By reading the Book of Shadows, I'd started on a journey?

"But that doesn't mean we are going to shepherd her along," Poppy says. "We promised Rosemary, and I don't take that lightly."

"Poppy," Marigold snaps. "Knowing about the curse is a Bell woman's right. How is she going to navigate the world if she doesn't know what she's up against? Would you like it if you'd been walking around with a malediction hanging over your head you knew nothing about? Look at her. She's bursting with life."

Marigold points at me and I do my best to look both full of life and heavily burdened.

Violet and Poppy exchange a long glance, then seem to reach an accordance.

"Well . . . ," Poppy says. "I suppose if Willow wants to ask us a few questions, we could answer them."

"And perhaps we could give her a tarot reading?" Marigold says. "A reading certainly can't hurt anything."

"Naturally," Violet says. "Go on, Willow. What questions do you have for us?"

They beam at me expectantly, and for a moment I'm too nervous to form any thoughts. Then a million questions spring to mind, and I start with the one that is pressing on me most. I picture my mom's and Sage's handwriting intertwined in their Book of Shadows. "Do you know why my mom left Salem?"

Marigold shakes her head grimly. "She was betrayed."

My heart drops. "By Sage? Because you all seem to be crazy about her." I don't want Sage to have betrayed my mom for a lot of reasons, not the least of which is the fact that I somehow feel like I'm forming a friendship with this person I will never get the chance to meet.

Yes, I realize how delusional that sounds.

"Oh, it wasn't only Sage. Everyone betrayed Rosemary," Poppy says lightly. "We don't blame her one bit for leaving. Not one bit. But I don't blame Sage either. Or their mother, Dahlia. The curse had a strong hold on all of them. Next question."

"But . . . how did Sage betray my mom?" I insist.

The aunts all begin shaking their heads, even Marigold.

"That's a bit we can't get into," Violet says. "Your mother will need to tell you that."

"I always thought it was that boy," Marigold says.

"Marigold!" Poppy says.

Marigold's eyes go wide. "What? It's always a boy, isn't it?"

Shock is rippling through me yet again. "What boy?"

"Never mind," Poppy says. "Next question."

They're all staring at me steely-eyed and I realize it's useless to try to get that story out of them. I may as well try to push a boulder up a mountain. I take a deep breath, doing my best to pivot. "Okay, so I read the story in the Book of Shadows. Is it . . . real? The witch and the garden and all of that?" Skepticism is really showing through in my voice, and I'm alarmed to realize that I sound exactly like my mother.

They all blink at me.

"Well, yes, of course it's true, dear," Poppy says, placing her hand gently on mine. "I'm sure it came as a bit of a surprise, but the Bell women are cursed. All of us."

Her voice is so matter-of-fact, I almost laugh. For being cursed people, they sure are nonchalant about it. "What does a curse . . . look like? And what do you mean when you say it had a strong hold on my mom and grandma?"

Marigold leans forward. "A curse can look different on everyone. Dahlia was always looking for love—that was her curse. Always searching for the next man, or the next audience, and it blinded her to the love that was right in front of her. Your mother . . . Well, sometimes I think it hurt her worst of all. She was so vulnerable."

"My *mom*?" I blurt out. Have they met her? Because trying to imagine my mom as vulnerable in any way is like trying to imagine a giraffe waterskiing. Impossible and slightly comical. I glance between the three of them. They are all looking at me gravely, no hint of *joking*. Then I remember my mom's face when she talked about her mother leaving her in the motel.

My chest suddenly feels heavy. "Okay, why?" I ask slowly.

"Because of her heart," Poppy says, tapping her chest. "As a child she was as big-hearted as they come, and she was always trying to care for everyone. Unfortunately, it's the big-hearted ones who tend to have the greatest risk for heartache. They give it their all, and then the world lets them down in a million tiny ways. Then they build walls. That's why she ran from Salem. She couldn't take it anymore."

"Is that from that heartbreak guidebook you wrote?" Marigold asks Poppy. "When are you writing an updated version, by the way?"

They launch into a new discussion that I can't focus on because my head is spinning. The person they're talking about can't be the same as the one I know. My mom is not vulnerable. "What about Sage? What was her curse?"

Violet sighs. "She had a recklessness. Especially when she was young. Oh, she was a wild thing. Rosemary was always the one looking out for her. Your mother and aunt Sage were as close as two girls could be."

"Those two chickadees were like s'mores and campfires. Avocados and toast. Like cream and coffee," Marigold adds.

"Like two turtledoves," Poppy says. "Wherever one was, the other followed."

The aunts all nod in agreement, then Violet turns to me. "And you, Willow. How has the curse affected you?"

Her gaze is piercing, which sends my heart into a gallop. I'm not cursed. "I don't—it doesn't . . ."

"Think, dear," Poppy says. "Take your time."

It doesn't take long. One glance at the flickering candles and my curse rises to view, sending pools of loneliness washing up over me. It's me as an island, caught between two places. Never quite fitting into either, never quite feeling at home. My curse is that I don't fit.

I open my mouth to explain it, but I can't. It's too painful.

"It's okay," Marigold says. "We all have pain. And that's why you're here. To reverse this."

They must be joking. Only . . . they're not. "I'm sorry, what?"

"Breathe, dear," Poppy says. "You read the curse story in the Book of Shadows, correct? Well, Sage began to suspect that there was more to it than that. All you have to do is follow Sage's trail of letters, and the rest will be clear. You can do that, can't you? Because we certainly believe in you."

They all stare at me, owllike. Incredulousness is swirling through me. Not only do they believe in me, they clearly believe in the curse. I swallow. "Sage left letters?"

"Yes, dear. Starting with the one you found in the Book of

Shadows," Poppy says. "Follow the clues at the bottom of the letters and you'll learn the truth of the curse."

"And once you learn the truth, the truth shall set you free!" Violet booms. "Corny but true."

There's only one problem. Well, there are a lot of problems. But one main one. "But . . . there wasn't a letter in the Book of Shadows."

"Oh, it's there, dear. Tucked into the pages," Poppy says.

I have a sudden image of me throwing the book into the air when Bea called. Had it landed somewhere and I hadn't noticed? "Wait. It's probably still at the house."

Candlelight is bouncing off the aunts' smiles.

"Well, then, I guess we know where you're going next," Marigold says.

Heat rises in my chest and face. "You think I should go back there?"

"We think you should spend as much time as possible there," Violet says.

"But . . ." I think of my mom. Her closed door. Her tense shoulders. This feels like a major betrayal of her, but maybe the aunts are right. How else am I going to get to know Sage except by going to her house and reading her mysterious trail of letters?

This is ridiculous. I need to make sure I'm understanding everything. "So you're saying that Sage wanted to teach my mother more about the family curse, and to do that I'm going to have to find her letters?"

"Precisely," Poppy says. "It's a series of letters, and they're all on the property. She showed us the first letter, but the rest were meant only for your mother. You can imagine it has taken a great deal of restraint to not go over there and try to find them ourselves."

"But . . . why did she set it up like that? Couldn't she just have told my mom?"

The aunts exchange a look as though I have said something very amusing. "Where's the fun in that?" Marigold says.

"You'd have to know them as girls to understand," Violet says. "Those girls were obsessed with finding treasures in the house. It drove poor Daisy crazy. Every time I went over, they'd dug through some random closet and found something new. Back then it was packed to the gills. We used to say it was a Bell family storage locker—I don't think anyone had gotten rid of anything in literal centuries. Antiques everywhere! Plus, the house sat empty for so long, ever since the girls left."

"What do you say, Willow?" Poppy asks quietly. "Are you in?"

I hesitate for a moment, my gaze on a flickering candle. But there's nothing to decide, really. I have to know more about Sage.

"I'm in," I say, and the aunts break out in a series of hoots and cheers.

"Now let's do a tarot reading!" Marigold says, scooping up the deck from the altar. "The girl needs some guidance. Too bad Daisy isn't here. She really knew how to read them, but maybe we can call her in." She shuffles the cards, then places the deck in front of me. "Daisy, this girl needs our help. Now, Willow, pick a card."

I select one from the middle and flip it over. Two of Cups. Immediately, the aunts begin nodding.

"That makes sense," Violet says.

"Daisy strikes again!" Marigold says.

"What does it mean?" I ask, holding it up to the candlelight. The image is of two people on a beach, one is standing barely in the water, passing a cup to a person standing just past the tide.

"You need a helper," Violet says.

I glance up at them. "A helper? Like . . . you guys?"

The aunts all shake their heads no. "It can't be us. We promised your mother," Violet says. She taps the card thoughtfully. "It looks like an equal. Is there anyone, aside from us, who you believe could help you with this quest?"

Great. Now it's evolved to a *quest*.

I do my best to concentrate. "Um . . . My cousin Bea? She lives in France, but I talk to her nonstop—"

Violet shakes her head, then taps the card enthusiastically. "I don't think so. Look at the image again. These people are close."

I lean in to study the image again. One is tall, the other short, and the one in the water has dark hair. Right then, my phone chimes from my backpack, and we all flinch.

"Curses and crystals!" Poppy says. "That scared me. Who is it?"

"Probably my mom." *Ding! Ding! Ding!* My mom, who is apparently sending me a hundred texts. I rifle through my bag, finally finding my phone, and tilt it up to see an unfamiliar number.

Hi Willow, I got a phone

Looking forward to tomorrow, are you good to meet at 7?

This is Mason by the way

I suck in my breath, my heart suddenly thumping.

"Who is it?" Marigold asks, craning her neck over to see.

Maybe we could meet up before?

Or adter

Aftee

AFTER

I'm really good at this

A tiny laugh chokes my throat. "It's . . . a boy I met. On—" I quickly swallow the rest of the words, *On the roof of Aunt Sage's house.* I don't want to get him in trouble by telling them how we met, although I get the feeling the aunts would keep our secret. "He's the real estate agent's . . . nephew." I don't actually know how they're related—nephew feels like a good guess.

"And what is the real estate agent's nephew's name?" asks Violet.

"Mason." Simply saying his name makes me blush. I look down at the card again, and this time I can see it. Dark hair. A slight stoop. The disorienting feeling that I've just stepped out of a dark movie theater into light.

I look up helplessly at the aunts. They're all smiling big, knowing smiles. "What a perfect name," Poppy says. "Strong and reliable. Perfect for a *helper*."

"I don't know if he's it," I say weakly, but then I glance up at the moon and I can't help it. I feel a tiny bit of excitement. What are the chances he'd text me right at this moment?

"Of course he is! And shall we draw up a love astronomy chart?" Marigold asks. "Because I am sensing a match—"

"No!" I nearly fly from my cushion. "Nothing like that. I don't even know him." My phone dings again, this time with the address for where we're meant to meet tomorrow plus a Sorry I'm sending way too many texts. I keep hitting

. . . send by accident. Sorry again

Each text is launching yet another butterfly in my stomach. He has my number and he clearly isn't afraid to use it. This should be annoying, but it isn't. It's ridiculously charming.

Next time I text I promise to send you a normal number of texts

"Well, he is persistent," Marigold says. "I like that quality. You can keep your love games, I like a partner who tells you exactly what they're thinking."

My face is redder than poppies.

"Willow," Violet says firmly. "You need him. Go to the house and find Sage's letter. It will tell you what to do next. And then I want you to bring this Mason to us."

❀ ❀ ❀

The story began, as many stories do, with a girl who bloomed too big for the space that the world had carved out for her.

Lily's father, Frederick, was a spice merchant, a sailor who spent months overseas before docking at their harbor, and he began bringing home packets of seeds for her from faraway lands: poinsettias, African violets, birds of paradise. Whatever Lily planted bloomed, and her ever-changing gardens surprised and delighted the townspeople. As a whole, they were wary of magic, careful not to let it infiltrate their ranks, but surely there was nothing wrong with this kind of enchantment. It was only flowers, after all. And besides, flowers were profitable. Soon her father was importing plants and seeds from all over the world to sell to Lily's many admirers. The townspeople's flowers never seemed to grow the way Lily's had, but they loved to try, and soon the family was one of the richest in town, moving the already-wealthy family to an even larger, grander home, with four fireplaces and a large outdoor area for the Bell family to host their summer garden parties.

The Bells' parties were legendary, an invitation something to brag about, and at some time or another nearly every townsperson was invited. The only exception was a young woman named Thalia Gray. Thalia had grown up working alongside her mother on the outskirts of town in a small cottage that was visited only in secret by those who were desperate for a bone to heal or an argument to mend. The people were careful with the word "witch," it had never served them well, so although they tiptoed around her, crossing the street to the other side when they saw her in town, they called her the town herbalist or, if they were being generous, the town healer. Thalia and her mother's methods worked, but you didn't want to admit it, and besides, she knew the town's secrets. You didn't want someone who knew all your secrets too close.

Lily's success confounded Thalia. While Thalia's and her bottles of tinctures and dried herbs were speculated about, her lifestyle shunned, Lily's magic was prized, enjoyed. More than anything, the witch wanted to belong, to be prized. So day after day, she came to see Lily, stooped over her garden beds, and demanded that she tell her what spell she was using. Day after day Lily told her there was no spell. She could feel what the plants needed through her hands, and she did what they asked. It was as simple as that.

You'd think a witch would understand this kind of magic—the kind that came to you as naturally as a breath. But deep down the witch was like most people—she didn't trust what she didn't understand, and Thalia's anger and resentment grew.

On Lily's seventeenth birthday her parents threw her an elaborate garden party, a debutante ball, meant to announce her eligibility to marry. Thalia was passing by that night, her basket full of shellfish she'd gathered from the shore, and her heart ached as she caught sight of Lily dancing in a white dress among all those beautiful flowers, a suitor whispering in her ear.

It wasn't fair that some were born to be celebrated while others were born to be shunned.

Dropping her basket, Thalia made her way into the garden, then took to the middle of the dance floor. In front of all the guests she put a curse on Lily: Lily would never have the thing she truly desired, not now and not ever, and neither would her daughters.

The party guests laughed it off, but not Lily. She had seen the look in the witch's eye. She knew about magic, and what was done was done.

Lily went into her house, dusted the earth off her satin shoes, and never touched her garden again. She couldn't bear to be where the earth no longer spoke to her. Within the year she was married to a boy from the party, and her once-resplendent garden filled with basil and parsley, practical herbs that could be used to season a dish or calm a fever.

This was the beginning of the Bell family curse. From that day on, every Bell woman would know with a burning intensity the thing they wanted most, but not one of them would ever get it.

Or at least, that's the way the story goes.

Find Thalia.

20

Mason

My texts to Willow are an absolute tragedy.

Once I start sending them, I can't stop, and soon I'm looking at what has to be the most embarrassing line of unanswered texts in history.

If my bizarre behavior didn't scare her off before, this should do the trick.

I force myself to put the phone in my pocket, trying to steady myself by breathing in the night air. The sky is bright from the moon, the air around me like a warm blanket, and I take long steps, matching my breath with my movement.

Without realizing what I'm doing, I head for the witch's house. The neighborhood is extra dark, and all I can hear is a TV playing through a slightly open window. I'm so stuck in my thoughts, my pace going faster and faster, I nearly collide with someone as I round the corner.

"Whoa!" the person says in a surprised, high voice. She drops an armful of things, sending a few papers scattering. I scramble to help her pick them up in the dark, and it isn't until I hand them to her that I realize who it is.

"Oh my gosh," she says. "You are literally everywhere."

Willow.

Willow *again*.

Moonlight has made her completely mermaid again, the resemblance so uncanny, it gives me goose bumps.

We stare at each other in stunned silence, and then she mutters something that sounds like "This is getting ridiculous," but I choose to ignore that, because *mermaid*, and also, *Thanks, Universe. I hear you loud and clear.*

"Willow?" I say, like maybe I don't know it's her. The moonlight is glinting off her hair, and her cheeks are lightly flushed. She's clutching a book against her chest.

I can somehow see her freckles in the dark. Willow must be the only girl in the world who is as beautiful in the dark as she is in the day. How is it possible we're having our third chance run-in? "Were you at the house?" My voice is loud on the quiet street.

She glances toward the house, then back at me, her eyes somehow managing to get even bigger. I step back slightly in an attempt to not fall directly into them.

"Are you following me?"

My enthusiasm drops. She's nervous. That's literally the last thing I want her to feel.

She continues. "Please don't lie, because if you're stalking me . . ."

I put my hands up quickly. "No. This was completely by chance. I needed some air, and I was planning to walk by your aunt's house." I take a deep breath. "Also, I'm sorry about my texts. I was really excited to be talking to you, and they were . . . weird. It's a new phone."

Her shoulders relax and she smiles a little. "It's okay. I thought they were kind of funny."

Now my shoulders relax too. Funny is much better than *stalker*. She points to my arm. "What does that say? I saw it at breakfast."

"Nothing important." I attempt to sort of discreetly tuck my arm behind my back, but she reaches out and grabs it, angling my arm so she can read the quote. This of course sends all sorts of electricity shooting through my body.

"'We are not figuratively, but literally stardust.'" She blinks up at me. Honestly, how do her freckles show up in the dark like this? It's weird, because I get the feeling that if I saw her somewhere random, I might not notice her. But up close . . . "What does that mean?"

I shift backward slightly. She looks like she actually wants to know, and even more surprisingly, I want to tell her. It's been a long time since I've told anyone about what I'm studying. "It's something I read in an astrophysics book. The elements in our bodies were actually formed in stars. Some of our lithium and hydrogen may even have come from the Big Bang."

She blinks up at me and I have no idea if she's thinking that this is interesting or if she's thinking that I'm a nerd. "Really?"

I want to tell her more. Like how connecting that fact feels— that no matter how different we all are, we're technically made from the same *stuff*, but I'm worried I'll sound sappy. Besides, she is definitely made of stardust, and I get the feeling that she has felt right everywhere she has ever been, so all I manage to do is repeat her. "Really."

"Okay," she says quietly. She looks back up at the house; we both do. Then she exhales. "So why were you in my aunt's house that night?"

A fair question. And I need to answer it correctly. Honesty might work.

My heart rate speeds up again. I can do this. "I was on the roof," I correct. "I didn't actually go into the house, except for the day I went with Simon. I came back on my own because, as you've probably already guessed, I'm really into astronomy, and the roof is perfect. There's even a telescope. Plus, I needed some space. I just moved in with Simon's family. And it's . . . ah, hard to be somewhere that you don't feel like is really yours, you know?"

Her eyes flick to mine, then she nods slightly. "Yes. I do know." She says it softly, but I can't ignore the hint of intensity. I feel a surge of hope. Now or never.

"I was also there because . . ." I take a deep breath. I'm so nervous, but this is the moment to take the plunge. I know it is. "Because of the painting."

Her eyes manage to get bigger, and it takes serious effort to not fall directly into them.

"What painting?" Her eyebrows lower. "You keep mentioning that."

I smile at her joke, but then I realize she isn't joking. She's serious. Confusion floods my brain. "The one in the upper bedroom. It's hanging over the bed."

She pulls her ponytail over her shoulder, her eyes studying mine. "I didn't see it."

My stomach plummets. "But . . . it looks exactly like you. You haven't seen it?" Desperation makes the end of my sentence rise. She has to know what the painting is, because if she doesn't, then how does all this connect?

Her expression has turned to confusion, the reality of the situation hitting me like a ton of bricks. *She doesn't know about the painting.* Which means Willow isn't a sign from the universe; she's a girl who simply looks quite a bit like a painting.

Reality sucker punches me, sending me spinning. I am *ridiculous.* Did I really think she'd point me to my mom somehow? I should know better than to do that by now. This isn't the way life works. This isn't the way *my* life works.

Did I really think all it would take for my life to change was a few coincidences? Willow obviously isn't going to lead me to my mom. She isn't even a sign that things are going to get better. She's just a girl. A girl whose eyes are now dark with concern.

"Mason, are you okay?" She takes a step toward me.

"Fine." But I'm not fine. My heart feels like it's turning to liquid, in danger of seeping out of my body onto the pavement. How am I this stupid? It isn't even stupidity, it's desperation. My eyes prick with tears, which is unbelievably embarrassing. "My mom . . . she had this thing about mermaids, and she used to tell me—"

What am I saying? I cut myself off quickly.

Willow is watching me very closely now, and maybe I'm imagining it, but her suspicion is melting into something softer. Concern? Pity? Yeah, I definitely can't do the pity thing. My feet begin backing up. "Sorry to bother you. This was . . ." Stupid? Embarrassing? *Painful*, my brain fills in helpfully. "I'll see you later."

I turn, then immediately begin gaining on the sidewalk, each step bigger than the last. All I can hear is the blood rushing in my ears.

Then I hear her light footsteps behind me, coming at nearly a run. "Mason, what about your mom?"

I speed up, but she speeds up too, then I feel her hand on my back. I manage to slow down, but I can barely look at her. Did I really think this girl was a *sign*? She's beautiful, but she's just a girl. She doesn't hold any more answers than my Internet searches. What was I thinking?

I literally tower over her, but she's looking at me with so much intensity, it makes her seem like she's at least as tall as I am. She's out of breath. "Mason, I still need to give you your notebook."

My notebook. Relief washes over me, so fast and heavy, I nearly crumple. I search her arms, but my star log isn't hidden in the tangle of book and papers.

"Where is it?" My voice is more intense than I mean for it to be.

"At the hotel. I picked it up. When you dropped it. And I, ah . . ." She looks away. "I read some of it. I'm sorry."

She *read* it? My face goes hot, something exploding in my chest. My notebook is private; the thought of someone reading it is basically the equivalent of me walking into a packed train station completely naked. I've written about foster care changes, the times I ran away, nights I stayed up crying. She really picked up my notebook and read it? I study her guilty face for a moment.

"How much?" I manage.

"Not much," she says quickly, but she looks away again in a way that lets me know she's lying. Now her face is red. "I shouldn't have. I'm so sorry. Some of it seemed . . . personal. Once I realized that . . ." She trails off, then takes a deep breath, meeting my eyes.

I have to keep it together.

I stare hard at the ground, trying to retain my gravity. "It's called a star log. I keep track of what I see in the sky. But lately it's also become my everything notebook. And it's really, really important that I get it back."

She takes a deep breath, and I can't read her expression. "If it's okay with you, I'll bring it to you tomorrow. When we go on the tour."

She still wants to go on the tour? After this? I take my own deep breath, attempting to steady myself. When I meet her gaze, her eyes are clear. I hate that she's read my notebook, but she doesn't seem like someone who would use any of it against me. *She's going to give it back.*

She runs her toe along the cement, then looks back toward the house. "So there's a painting that looks like me in there?"

Right. I take a deep breath, the tightness in my chest easing slightly. I even manage to look up a little. "Yeah. She has your hair color, eyes, everything."

She clutches her book more tightly to her chest. "Would you mind showing me?"

The walk to the house is awkward, Willow quiet, and me so self-conscious over the fact that this girl has basically had an unauthorized peek at my soul that I can't remember how to walk like a normal human (do I swing my arms with my legs or opposite my legs?). I spend a few seconds trying to figure out how one climbs up the side of a house without looking like King Kong when Willow produces a key, eliminating the problem. As soon as we step over the threshold, something shifts inside of me.

I think Willow feels it too, because we both pause, taking a breath of the house's air, which smells amazingly of dried herbs and tea leaves, and even though we both feel awkward, being in the house makes everything easier.

"I was just in here," she says. "Right before I saw you. I had to come back to find something I dropped the night I saw you here."

I wait for her to explain, but she bites her lower lip, her eyes darting from mine. "Did you find it?" I finally ask.

A small smile erupts across her face. "Yep."

Again, she doesn't elaborate. Instead, she exhales, spinning like a ballerina to take in the rooms. Here in the house she somehow looks more Willow. Brighter hair, shinier eyes. But more than that, she seems lighter. Freer. Which I recognize, because I'm starting to feel it too. It's the magic of the house. It makes you feel like you're fine exactly how you are, which is not a thing I'm used to.

Willow points up to the chandelier. "We mostly need to keep the lights off. I'm not supposed to be here."

That shouldn't surprise me, but it does. "But it's your house?"

"My mom's." Her jaw tightens, which lets me know there's more to it, but I don't feel like I can ask her. I turn to look at the study, catching a glimpse of all the ship paraphernalia, and my ease grows. "I didn't know about it until recently. Very recently."

"I love this place," I blurt out.

"Me too," she says. And then there's this moment where we smile at each other, and for one tiny second I swear the entire world stands still. "I've never been anywhere like it."

"Same." I point to the study. "Did you know that Frederick Bell made most of his money importing molasses for rum? His first haul made a profit of like seven hundred percent because he was trading directly with the people in China and East India. Salem was ridiculously rich for a couple of decades, and Frederick was one of the people who really capitalized. That's why this house is so nice."

Her eyes are wide with surprise. I know I should probably take it as a warning that I'm about to create a fresh batch of awkward, but the rest comes tumbling out anyway. "Frederick inherited his first ship from his father-in-law, who was one of the very first merchants in Salem. He imported pepper because they used it to make rum, but I read that he imported flowers too, which was way less common. And . . ." Should I tell her this part? I go for it. "I think he's the one who did the mermaid painting upstairs."

Willow's eyes were big before, but now they're enormous. "How did you know all that?" she asks. "Demands" is more like it.

My cheeks start to feel hot. I could go with the truth: *Because I'm obsessed with a painting that looks like you, so I researched everything I could.* But I can't go back to the feeling of despair I had out there on the sidewalk. "Um . . . well, there's a lot of information online about Salem's history as a trading port. And Frederick Bell was easy to look up, especially because he was so prominent. And . . . ah. I sort of like researching?"

This is an understatement, and probably the sort of nerdy detail you aren't supposed to admit to someone you're very attracted to, but not being myself feels pointless at this moment.

She blinks up at me, her eyes widening. "You are the helper," she murmurs. Or at least I think that's what she murmurs.

"Sorry?"

She blinks again, her face flushing as she glances back up at me. "I said you are really helpful." She takes a deep breath and seems to center herself. "Show me the painting?"

21

Willow

I'd found Sage's letter almost immediately. Once I snuck into the house, I saw it peeking out from under the sofa, right next to where I'd thrown the Book of Shadows. If the aunts hadn't told me about it, I wouldn't even have known to look for it. I'd been puzzling over the first clue—*find Thalia*—when Mason and I had almost collided.

And now I'm back in the house with him, staring at a mermaid that he is adamant is my doppelgänger. I'm honestly sort of flattered that Mason thinks I look like her. The problem is, he's wrong.

The painting looks like it belongs in a museum, and I definitely would have noticed it if the first time I came into this room had I not been investigating a noisy intruder, i.e., Mason. The painting is moody and dramatic, encased in a braided gold-flecked frame. And it's large, taking up most of the space over the bed. It's one of those paintings that pulls you in, forcing you to pay attention. The waves are swirling and tempestuous, the mermaid staring like she can see into your soul.

It's honestly very intense. Even more intense, because I can literally feel Mason's enthusiasm for it. He'd been so upset outside, but the second we stepped into the room, he lit up again.

"See?" Mason says, his voice full of excitement.

The mermaid's hair is red, true, but that's where the comparison ends. She has a prominent nose and smooth freckleless skin, and her arms are thin and delicate-looking. But most importantly, the mermaid's expression couldn't be farther from mine. Three seconds into staring at the painting, I know this: the mermaid knows exactly where she belongs. She is wild and confident, and the entire ocean is her home. I'll bet she's never once bobbed around wondering which waves she belongs to, or wondered if another part of the ocean might offer her belonging. She simply *is*.

I don't point out the differences to Mason. He's uber committed to the idea of me looking like the painting. Why?

"What do you think?" Mason asks, and I can tell he's holding back his excitement.

I'm not sure what to think. Honestly, I'm starting to feel a little exhausted from everything that has happened so far tonight: the moon ceremony, the aunts telling me about Sage's plan for my mom, and now Mason. Part of me wants to curl up on the bed below the mermaid and take a good, long nap. "I'm not sure."

Mason points to a small swirl of letters near the bottom. "There's his signature. And look, there's another name too. Maybe a word? I didn't notice it before."

He's standing on the opposite side of the bed, but he leans in close enough that I can smell his slightly sweaty boy smell. He also has a smear of glitter across his right temple that I've been trying not to stare at since I saw him on the street. Every time I see Mason, I struggle with not staring at him. There's something about him that instantly draws you in. He's open and engaging, but I get the feeling he has all these other layers no one can see.

Maybe that's the notebook talking. And yes, I feel terrible about reading it. He clearly had to use a lot of self-control to not panic when I confessed.

For a moment I'm too distracted to focus on what he's pointing at. "Do you think that's like the title or something? It's weird that it's painted into the image. Thalia? Thalio?"

The sounds rearrange themselves a few times in my head before I hear it. My heart thuds in my chest. Did he say "Thalia"? "What? Where?"

"There." He grabs my hand, guiding my finger to the spray of water crashing behind the mermaid, and suddenly I see it. Painted into the white crest of the wave, in teeny, tiny lettering, is the name I read in Sage's letter. *Thalia.*

My heart nearly drops out of my body. "No way. No *way*," I say.

He carefully lets go of my hand, like he's releasing a butterfly. "Does that word mean something to you?"

"She's a person. An important one." I kick off my shoes, then catapult myself onto the bed, stepping over pillows until my nose is only inches from the painting. The name is painted into the white spray above her in an off-white, the letters almost like a crown above her. It would be so easy to miss. If it weren't for Mason, I probably wouldn't have seen it at all.

The letter from Aunt Sage of the curse added a lot of details— but the witch's name had felt like the most important one. Seeing her name in a second place makes it feel a lot more real, but also brings up a lot of questions.

Find Thalia.

I lower my gaze to the mermaid's face. Is this her? And if so, why would Frederick paint her as a mermaid?

"Is she your relative?" he asks.

"No . . ." My hands fumble for the letter, but I manage to stop myself. "We aren't related. But she is, ah, connected to my family."

If "connected" means she cursed my great-great-great-(great?)

grandmother. Not that I'm going to explain that to Mason; he'll think I've lost it. Besides, I'm too busy staring at her. Thalia looks intense. Fin aside, she definitely seems like someone who could get angry enough to create a generational curse.

"Really?" He looks at the painting, then back at me before shrugging. "Okay. I mean, I did read that every redhead in the world is related. You all have a common ancestor." He has one arm up like he's ready to catch me if I topple over, which is honestly a possibility. And yes, it's awkward that I'm up here, but I physically cannot remove myself. Is this my first clue?

"No. She's like . . . a family friend." Not even close.

I squint closer at the painting. This must be Thalia. Except . . . there's obviously no mention of Thalia being a mermaid. Can witches be mermaids? Also, why on earth would Frederick paint a picture of the witch who cursed his daughter? I fumble for the Book of Shadows, knocking Aunt Sage's letter out in the process, and begin to scan through it. *The Bells' parties were legendary, an invitation something to brag about, and at some time or another nearly every townsperson was invited. The only exception was a young woman named Thalia Gray.*

And here she is. My heart begins hammering again.

"What's that?" Mason asks. He's looking curiously at the letter, and I hastily shove it back in my backpack. If Mason is as big of a history buff as he seems to be, he'd probably love this story. But this is all happening so fast, and despite what the aunts said, I still don't know him.

"Um . . . sort of. The thing is, I, ah . . ." I look over, meeting his eyes, and whatever words I was grasping at fly away immediately. I have no idea where to even start.

Well, you see, Mason. My family was cursed by this mermaid.

"Coming up." He kicks off his shoes and climbs onto the bed

next to me, stopping so he can get a closer look. He isn't touching me, but the heat from his body spreads to me, and I'm having a hard time focusing again. "Who's Thalia?"

"She's from a family story. I don't know why she's painted as a mermaid. She's . . ." Am I really going to say it? His eyes are bright on mine. I let the rest out in a tumble. "She's a witch."

I wait for him to laugh, but he doesn't. Instead, his brows furrow, a look of interest spreading across his face. "Like your aunt?"

"Sort of." I catch sight of his hand against the wall. He has very square fingernails, a deep scar on one of his knuckles. They're extremely good hands. I did not actually know that hands could be good. What is it about him? "Well, yes. But this is an older witch, and she sort of . . . didn't like my ancestor."

His eyebrows go up. He's clearly waiting for more. And the aunts said I should ask him to help me, but he's way too close to me, and it's making my tongue and brain refuse to cooperate.

"I could use some air," I say quickly.

He holds my gaze for another moment, then gestures to the ladder. "Rooftop?"

The night is still hot and thick, and I'm feeling even more awkward because moonlight is apparently Mason's place to shine.

Also. He's sparkling. The glitter I noticed in the mermaid's room isn't only on his right temple; it's also in his hair and on his eyelids.

He catches me looking and a cautious smile overtakes his face. "What?"

"You're glittering."

His eyebrows go up. "What?"

"You have . . ." I consider brushing it away, except I'd need to be about twenty inches taller to do that. Also, I'm pretty sure there's an unspoken rule that you aren't supposed to touch strangers' faces. Although, for a stranger, I'm certainly running into him a lot. "I noticed it down on the street. I think it's glitter."

"Oh!" He starts dusting frantically at his hair and face. "I got ambushed by a bunch of little girls. Where is it?"

"Oh, right. I've heard about Salem's little-girl glitter gangs. They sound brutal."

He laughs and I gesture to my right cheek so he knows where to swipe. "Did I get it?"

Not quite, but I like how it looks, so I nod.

"It's Simon and Emma's girls. They have Nova and three little ones. They're sort of . . . a lot." He reaches back and sort of ruffles his hair, an action I've seen him do a few times now.

"My dad has triplets. They just turned two," I offer.

"Whoa. Okay, then, you get it."

I nod again and that's all I can muster. For a moment we sit there awkwardly, then Mason gestures to a chair. "Want to sit?"

We drag the chairs to the edge, then sit with our feet propped up on the banister. The sky is putting on quite the show for us. The moon is a perfect silver, and the dark sky feels close and velvety, pinned up by stars. As soon as Mason looks up his whole energy shifts, and suddenly he's relaxed and alert. "This is great."

"What is?"

"Moon-viewing conditions." He rifles around in his backpack, then produces a pair of binoculars "You must be good luck. The conditions are the clearest I've seen since I got here." He extends the binoculars toward me. "Want to look at the moon?"

I fit the binoculars to my eyes, and suddenly it's like I'm

seeing the moon for the first time. It's rocky and ridged, with deep hollows, the white surface so bright, it's blinding. It feels calming and grounding, and honestly sort of holy.

I lower them and Mason is smiling at me. "Well?"

"I like looking at the line between light and dark," I say.

"That's called the terminator."

"Really?" I lower the binoculars for a moment to look at him.

He's smiling now. "When the moon is full, it's too bright for contrast, so it flattens out all the texture. But right now you can see more of her features."

"What are the features?" I like how he calls the moon a "her."

"Craters, dead volcanos. Mountains. Here, look again."

I point the binoculars back at the moon. "See those big shadowy areas? When people were first looking at them, they thought they were bodies of water, so now we call them 'lunar maria,' which means 'seas of the moon.' They gave them all kinds of weird and interesting names."

I lower my binoculars again. "Like what?"

He starts listing them off. "Lake of Sorrow, Lake of Happiness, Sea of Serenity, Marsh of Decay. We also have Bay of Roughness, Bay of Rainbows, Lake of Dreams, Lake of Fear, Sea of Waves. Then there's my personal favorite: the Sea that Has Become Known."

Once again, I'm semi-stunned by all the knowledge floating around in that head. "How do you remember all of that?"

He smiles, and his body relaxes into the chair. "I've been studying for a long time. My mom and I used to do it together. She worked one summer at this resort in Maine. It had incredible views, and her boyfriend had a telescope he'd let me use." He trails off, and then I'm thinking of all the entries about his mom. I want to ask about her, but that feels way too private. I already know too much.

"So Simon, Emma, Nova, and the other girls. Are they your . . ." I'm trying to ask how he's connected to them, but I'm not sure how to do that without being nosy. *Tell me all your personal family details, stranger.*

His cheek tightens slightly, then he glances out at the sky. "I'm, ah . . ." He takes a deep breath, hesitating, before meeting my eyes resolutely, like he's made a decision. "I'm in foster care. Simon and Emma are my foster parents."

His words hit me hard. His voice is light, but there's a falseness to it that makes me think he's hiding pain, and suddenly I remember all the parts of his star log where he talked about new cities, new homes, more moves. Regret spreads heavily through my chest. I shouldn't have brought it up. I don't know what being in foster care means exactly, but I can only imagine that it must be tough. My problems shrink down until they're microscopic in the moonlight.

"I'm sorry," I say. "Is your mom. . . ."

"Not here," he says quickly. "But it's only temporary."

I'm hunting for any words to match this enormous thing he's told me when Mason suddenly stiffens. He points toward the garden, and when I lean over, I see a flash of movement. It's a person. The figure moves into the light, and when I see the hair color, my heart drop faster than a shooting star. "Mason, *my* mom!" I whisper.

Mason's reflexes are like a cat's. He drops even faster than I do, and the two of us lie flat.

"Why is your mom at the house?" He whispers. His eyes are alert, his body practically vibrating with energy. "I thought she didn't want anything to do with this place."

"She doesn't. That's the whole point." Did she change her mind?

We army crawl together to the railing, then lie on our stomachs, peering over the edge of the enclosed porch. The moon is acting as a spotlight, but even if it weren't, I would recognize my mother's perfect posture in her crisp white blouse anywhere. She lets herself in through the side gate, moonlight gathering on her hair as she makes her way to the back.

"Oh no," I breathe.

"Is she coming inside?" He whispers. "Because I really can't get caught being here."

I really can't get caught being here either. I'm imagining a scenario in which I cling to Mason's shoulders like an extra backpack while he climbs down the side of the house, but luckily my mom bypasses the door, walking sure-footedly toward the back garden.

"What . . ." Mason whispers. I scoot in closer to him, then shimmy as far forward as I can over the ledge. Mom hesitates for a moment, then makes her way to the willow tree. When she gets there, she pauses, looking up at it. For once, the tree is static, its branches still in the windless night.

She's here to look at the tree? My heart is beating so loudly, I'm having a hard time hearing much of anything. She steps under the willow's branches and I lose sight of the top of her head, but then she crouches down, placing her palm on the trunk of the tree.

She stays that way for one, two, three, ten seconds. I'm holding my breath. The sky is completely clear of clouds, the air thick and humid, and all I can hear are insects and the thrumming of my own heart.

What is she doing? Mason is alert next to me, his breathing quiet. Finally, after what feels like hours, my mom slowly drops her hand, then stands. She glances up at the house for one moment, and my heart hammers—can she see us?—then she reaches up, grabbing one of the willow tree's branches and . . . ties it in a knot? Did I see that correctly? A moment later, she leaves through the gate, all traces of her disappearing into the moonlight.

If it weren't for Mason next to me, I might think I'd imagined it. For several moments, neither of us dare move, then I let out a swooping exhale. "She really came to look at the willow tree?"

"No, she came to kneel before the willow tree," Mason says. "And . . . tie a knot in its branches. What was that about? Is she a tree worshipper?"

"Not that I know of." His breath tickles my ear and for one moment I'm aware of how close we are, the sides of our bodies pressed together, his shoulder against mine, his hip pressed against my leg. My nerves buzz together with a light, fluttery feeling that has absolutely nothing to do with what has happened tonight and everything to do with this particular moment.

The aunts said to find a helper. Not a crush.

I roll away quickly, breaking the connection. "Come on, let's go see what she was looking at."

Neither of us is brave enough to turn on any lights, so we creep through the house in darkness, bumping into each other on the stairs and crashing into bookcases and end tables before carefully letting ourselves out into the back. The willow tree looks huge in the darkness, and just as still as it did earlier. I duck under its branches and try to arrange myself in the same position my mom was in.

"See anything?" Mason asks.

"A tree trunk," I say.

"Here." He flips on the light on his phone and holds it over my shoulder as I run my hands along the bark.

I manage to find the knotted branch, and I hold it up for Mason to see.

"Is tying branches into knots a normal activity for her?" He reaches for it too, and our hands brush lightly.

"Not that I know of." I let go of the knot, and then, annoyingly, my eyes sting. I'm exhausted by my mom's secrets. If she would talk to me, it would be so much easier. Why does everything have to be so secretive with her? My body suddenly feels very, very heavy, and I slump against the tree.

"You okay, Willow?" Mason asks.

Fine. I'm fine, like always. But this time the feelings bubble over. "Why won't my mom tell me anything?" My voice comes out spiky and ferocious-sounding, but Mason doesn't look alarmed. He turns off his light, and it's just us in the darkness under the willow branches.

"What do you mean?"

"She acts like Salem means nothing to her. She won't even go inside the house. But then she's out sneaking around the garden at night? I don't get this."

I hug the Book of Shadows to my chest. It suddenly feels like it weighs a million pounds. When I look up, Mason is studying my face in a soft way that makes me want to burst into tears.

He must think I'm a complete disaster. "Sorry, Mason. I didn't mean to unload everything on you."

He steps a little closer, stooping to keep his head out of the branches. "You don't have to be sorry. You can tell me anything you want to."

His eyes are big and sincere, and for a second I consider actually speaking aloud my frustrations with my mom. Not only about how difficult the past few years have been, but about how shut out I feel. I don't tell anyone about those things; why do I want to tell him?

It's probably the influence of the willow tree. Before it can all come spilling out of me, I step out from under a branch.

"I think I'd better go back to my hotel. My mom is going to wonder why I was out so late."

"Okay, I'll walk you," he says quickly.

"No—I think you'd better not. If my mom sees, I wouldn't be able to explain it to her."

He considers this for a moment, then turns to glance back at the house. The dark upper-bedroom window faces the tree exactly and we both stare at it for a moment.

"Okay, then I'll walk you partway." He steps out from under the tree, then extends his hand to me. "Don't trip over the roots."

For a moment, with his hand warm in mine, it feels like maybe everything will be okay. But then I look up at the moon, bright and mysterious, and it makes me think of my mom. Now that I've seen her and her shadows up close, she feels even more distant.

And I'm beginning to think that will never change.

22

Mason

Willow says all of ten words on the way back, and I do my best to give her space, filling in the silence by pointing out Venus and Mars, two bright points masquerading as stars. I'm nowhere near wanting the night to be over, but Willow is obviously struggling with her mom, which is a thing I can understand.

She let me walk her to Essex, and then we parted ways. Watching her disappear down the street was terrifying—like watching a mirage fade into a desert landscape. What if this time she didn't reappear? I had to keep reminding myself that now I had her phone number and that she'd promised to bring my notebook to our ghost tour. Also, not all people disappear.

Of course, thinking of disappearing people sends me spiraling, so once I get back to the Morgans', I sneak back into the dining room and type my mom's name into the search engine. I find one Naomi Greer who is a real estate agent in Kentucky, and an obituary of a Naomi Greer who died at ninety-three in North Carolina. Mom's social media looks exactly the same, but as I scroll through it, I have a new idea. I'll message everyone she's friends with to see if they've heard from her.

I scan through a bunch of profile pictures. She doesn't have a lot of "friends" online, and most of them are as inactive online as she is, but it's worth a try. I pick a handful of the ones who seem most promising and send them all the same message. *Hi, sorry to bother you, but I'm trying to contact Naomi Greer. Do you have any idea how I can find her?*

When I'm done, I sit back in my chair, try to think what my next move is. The Internet obviously isn't working. What I need is someone who knows her. Someone who could give me some kind of clue as to where she could be. There has to be someone who knows where she is. And then I think of it: the playbill from the box Emma gave me.

That thing was full of names. It's very likely that my mom has lost touch with most of the people she grew up with, but what if one of them has heard from her in the last few years? What if one of them is still in her inner circle? She'd always been good at finding people to help us out. I only need one contact.

I do not want to go tromping through Emma's memorabilia, but this is the only new lead I've had in years. What if there's something in there that could help me? These were people who had known her for years, weren't they? Before I can talk myself out of it, I clear my history and head upstairs to find the shoebox in my closet.

The items are exactly as brutal as I remember. There's the shiny version of my mom, healthy and hopeful, posing for photos with people I don't know. I check the back for names but don't find any. I glance through her notes, and her handwriting and the silly bubblegum things she wrote makes my throat ache again. *In chem right now, hate everything except James, who is looking FINE.* And *Meet Cammy and me in the quad? I have something SCANDULOUS to tell you. GET EXCITED!!!*

I wish I knew what said scandalous thing was. And I already have two names. James and Cammy.

212 JENNA EVANS WELCH

I write down their names in my notebook, then keep digging through the shoebox. Anytime I find a name that I think might help, I write it down. Finally, I hit the bottom, where I find a bill-sized envelope. I'm about to toss it back with the rest of the pile when the name on the return address catches my eye. Night Sky House.

Huh.

The envelope has already been ripped open, the letter stuffed back inside, and I carefully remove it.

* * * * *

Night Sky House
Tallahassee, Florida
Dear Ms. Morgan,
Thank you for your recent payment. We have enclosed a receipt for your records.
Sincerely,
David Gonzalez
Director

Of course the "Night Sky" catches my eye. This obviously has nothing to do with Emma and my mom's high school experience—it's dated a little less than a year ago—but I'm curious anyway. Is Emma part of a skygazing community?

I creep silently through the house, pausing on the stairs to make sure the house is completely quiet. One of the girls has a whistly kind of snore, and I can hear the wall clock ticking from the kitchen, but otherwise I'm home free.

At the computer, I open a search window and type in *Night Sky House, Florida*. A website pops up with an orange banner and images of people sitting in a circle, all eyes on one person. *Night Sky Sober Living House. Only in the darkness can stars be seen. Changing lives, one day at a time.*

Sober living?

I'm completely still, but the breath gets knocked out of me anyway. It isn't a stargazing community, it's a place where people can live while they try to get and stay sober. There are several testimonials and a section titled *Resources for Families*. My face flushes as I read through them. Did my mom live here? Is she there now? And why on earth is she in Florida?

I pause on the About page. *We are a facility dedicated to promoting lifelong sobriety for individuals released from recovery centers. We promote life skills, help with job placement, and assist in the creation of better communication and emotional skills. Please see our Results page along with testimonials.*

Does this have to do with my mom? If so, it doesn't fully make sense—why would Emma be paying the bill, and why would my mom be in a recovery center in Florida, of all places? Does Emma have someone else in her life who's an addict? And if it's not about my mom, how did it end up in the shoebox?

My brain is bouncing all over the place, my heart beating so hard, I can hear it in my ears. I have to find out if this is about my mom. I click through to the Contact page and find information about funding and how to apply to the program. Near the bottom I find a contact form with the director's name on it. I'm struggling to keep my breath even.

This is most likely a dead end, a huge dead end, but this is my best shot. I know from past attempts that treatment centers can't give you any information on patients, so I'm going to have to come up with a different approach. I think for a moment, then start typing.

Dear Mr. Gonzalez,
I recently found a wallet belonging to a woman named
Naomi Greer. It had no contact information besides a card
with your facility's name on it. Is Naomi a current employee
or resident, and if not, do you know how I can reach her?
Sincerely,
James Baker

    The fake name seems like a little much, but if my mom is there,
I obviously can't use my own name. Also, if Mr. Gonzalez tries to
search the name, he'll be met with about a thousand James Bakers.
The form asks for an e-mail address and phone number, so I enter
my new number, then pause at the e-mail. "Starboy333" doesn't sound
like a name someone like James Baker would have, so I quickly set up
a new e-mail account, JBaker81, then hit send.

    There. A long shot, but at least I tried.

It takes me several hours to fall asleep because my mind is turning
over every detail of Night Sky House. My mom loved moving around;
she could have ended up in Florida somehow, even though as far as
I know, she has no ties to it. But if she's there, why hasn't Emma
told me? She said that trust is our main goal, didn't she? And what
if that letter has nothing to do with my mom and ended up in there
randomly? What if Emma has a brother or a cousin or someone else
who lives there? It's not like addiction is a rare problem. Before long,
my brain works itself into a knot and I force myself to think about
something different.

    My thoughts land on the situation with Willow, which is a whole
other knot to untangle. I can't figure out what is going on with her.
She is clearly sneaking around the house the same as I was, and her

mom's behavior at the willow tree was beyond bizarre. Also, what was that old book she was carrying around?

And even though she doesn't know anything about the mermaid painting, I still think she's a sign. The part that stresses me out is that when my mom saw signs, they always led her to take some type of action. True, those actions were oftentimes unpredictable, like the time we moved out of an apartment in the middle of the night because she found an empty bird's nest on the walkway. She said it meant it was time for us to leave the nest too. And yes, I'm aware that we might have moved out in the middle of the night for other reasons—such as avoiding the landlord, who I'm sure we owed money to—but at least her signs gave her direction. Am I supposed to be *doing* something? I do know that I want to spend more time with her, but is that enough?

I'm in and out of sleep all night, my brain waking me up every few hours, and I'm relieved when I open my eyes and it's morning. The house is still quiet, so I make my way back down to the computer. I'm about to type in *Night Sky House* again when a voice comes from behind me, startling me so much, I jump from the chair.

"How's it going?"

It's Emma, wearing flip-flops and pajamas, a coffee mug in each hand. For a moment I freeze. Our last interaction was not great, and I know I probably owe her an apology, but the tightening in my chest isn't allowing it, plus, I'm too sleep-deprived to even begin to figure out what that apology should be.

Thank god I hadn't typed in the website yet. "Okay."

Emma crosses the room, handing me a mug. "Have you looked more at the astronomy program?" she asks. "The applications are due next week."

It takes me a few seconds to remember—again—what she's

referring to. I gesture vaguely toward the computer. "I was just about to look at it again. The program."

My voice pitches too high, which is a dead giveaway that I'm lying, but Emma doesn't react. Instead, she sets the coffee on the computer desk, then steps back. It feels like a tiny peace offering, plus, it smells incredible. Not that it erases what she said last night about my mom, but I'm not going to turn down coffee. I reach out and take the cup, trying to focus on the heat rather than the anxiety in my chest.

I hope she'll leave, but instead she settles into one of the dining room chairs. "Audrey was up half the night with a stuffy nose, and I'm so tired, I feel like I'm going to murder someone. Not you," she says quickly. "But someone. How was your walk last night? You were out late."

My back tenses. Am I getting in trouble? But when I turn around her face is smooth and calm. *Keep it simple.* "It was nice."

"Good," she answers. For one hopeful moment I think maybe we're going to sidestep all of yesterday's unpleasantness, sweep it all aside, but then she clears her throat and I know that was wishful thinking. Unless it has to do with my mom, avoidance is not Emma's style. "Mason, I want to talk to you about yesterday."

My throat feels tight. "Okay."

"I'm sorry," she says slowly. "I gave you the box because I wanted you to know that I know your mom. Really know her. And I will always consider Naomi to be one of the most remarkable people I've ever known. She's . . . amazing."

I hear her using the present tense, and for some reason this hurts more, because Emma doesn't actually know my mom. At least, not the mom I know. The person in Emma's photos and the person I love are completely different people. She pauses, giving me the opportunity to respond, but I have too many feelings welling up inside me to even look at her. Part of me is grateful—relieved, even—to hear her say that. But another, louder part is saying the thing I can't say aloud. *Then where were you?*

"Okay," I manage.

"And if you want to talk about her, or yesterday, we can. Anytime. It doesn't have to be today."

She's looking at me with her intense Emma eyes, and there is so much pressure building up inside of me, I might actually combust.

I manage a small noise in my throat, and luckily that seems to fulfill the response requirement. She stands up. "The girls want to take you to Singing Beach in Manchester-by-the-Sea today. Have you been there?"

She's looking slightly away from me now, which is great. My emotions are probably all over my face. I take a quick breath. "No."

"The grains of sand are shaped in a way that they make a squeaking sound when you move your feet across them."

Despite my best intentions, I feel my interest pique. "Really?"

"It's rare. Only a few beaches in the world sing. I thought you might like it," Emma says, a tiny smile on her face.

I quickly look away again. I am very into the idea of seeing something that only exists in a few places, and I kind of hate that she knows that.

Getting to Manchester-by-the-Sea takes twenty minutes. Packing up for it takes two hundred. I know because I am forced to rehearse for most of it.

While Emma and Simon are making peanut butter and honey sandwiches and filling plastic baggies with potato chips and apple slices, the girls insist I begin to learn my choreography for the Pirate

Mason show, which is what they've decided to call it. Emma has apparently told them they will not be buying me tap shoes, so they've decided to change things up from tap dance to ballet, and it is so much more horrible than I could even have imagined. Not only have they planned out the entire one-man show; they expect me to get it right. And there is a lot to learn. Pliés, leaps, and a vast number of twirls. There's even a scene where I'm supposed to dance with a toy shark balanced on my head.

A few times I see Nova smirking at me through the window as I fling myself around the yard, but every time I stop, Hazel begins hurling small objects at me while yelling things like "We aren't leaving until this routine sparkles!" and "It isn't right until we get this right!" which are sayings they learned from a show about dance moms.

The performing arts apparently turn young children into tyrannical monsters. Even Audrey keeps saying, "Um? We can . . . get this right?"

"I need to feel your emotion!" Hazel yells through a megaphone she's made of paper. "You're looking for buried treasure. Show me some feeling! And keep those toes pointed."

They most definitely do not want to feel my emotion. But at least my rigorous rehearsal schedule is sort of keeping my mind off checking my fake e-mail.

I've only checked my new phone nine hundred times.

Finally, Simon appears at the door to ask if I have a bathing suit, which I don't, so he spends a bunch of time going through his to see if he has one that works before ultimately deciding I should have my own, and Emma runs to the store to procure a bunch of swim trunks so I have options. Then it's time for us to drag Nova from her cave. Only, none of the girls can find their towels or swimsuits, and then once they find those things, none of them can find their shoes, and then while they're looking for their shoes, they lose their bathing suits, and Nova retreats to her cave again, and we have to drag her out all over again.

By the time we leave town, it's after two, and I'm getting anxious that we're going to miss the tour tonight. Like a lot of towns in New England, Manchester-by-the-Sea has become an expensive-beach-getaway-type place but has still managed to hang on to some of its original fishing village vibes. The beach itself is crescent-shaped, with white sand and moss-covered rocks, and once we've set up our towels and umbrella and the girls have been lathered up with sunscreen, they take off for the water.

Despite the chaos, it's a nice outing.

The sand actually does sing, and we spend at least the first hour running around trying to get it to make different sounds. Afterward, the girls drag me into a rowdy game of Sea Monster that mainly involves them trying to kick sand in my eyes and/or knock me over. Finally, Emma orders them off me, and I seek refuge in the water, which is so icy cold that only Nova is up for it.

Nova is walking angrily into the surf, her scowl evident even under sunglasses. She looks tiny out here in the water and I realize again how young she is. The expression on her face is particularly angry, and when I turn to see what she's scowling at, my stomach sinks.

It's the Morgans. The late afternoon light is starting to tinge the sand a rosy gold, and Simon is walking up and down the beach, three girls hanging off him. Emma is sprawled out on the sand, a giant sun hat shielding her face, and when Simon gets close to her, he says something that makes her look up and laugh.

They look . . . perfect.

Whole. Complete. Happy.

Without Nova and me there to complicate things, they look like a family from a magazine. And judging from the longing mixing into Nova's usual angry expression, she's thinking the same thing.

I feel a pang of loneliness for her. I'm used to not fitting into families because they've never been mine. But this one *is* Nova's. That must be a special form of miserable.

A rush of protectiveness moves over me. I'm going to get her to talk to me. Even if it's only for a few minutes.

"Nova?" I drag my feet along the ocean bottom, making my way toward her. She's staring out at the horizon, arms crossed over her chest.

"What?" She spits the word.

I take a deep breath, digging through my brain for one of the facts I read in her articles. "Did you know that the oldest sloth in captivity is fifty years old? It's in a zoo in Germany."

Her face whips toward me. I can't read her expression behind her dark sunglasses, but her body is tense.

She doesn't storm away, so I keep going. "They're hard to track, so scientists don't really know how long they live in the wild. But this one is in the *Guinness Book of World Records*. Her name is Paula."

Very, very long silence. The waves are surprisingly strong, and I have to dig my feet into the sand to stay upright.

Then she pushes up her glasses. "Two-toed or three-toed?" I'm startled by the blue-greenness of her eyes. I had no idea they were that color.

I bite back my smile. "Two. And they thought she was a boy for twenty years."

I think she's going to tell me to go away, but instead she folds her arms over her chest. "Oh."

We almost look at each other for a moment. "I didn't know you liked sloths," she finally says.

A wave hits our calves, and the cold water makes us both jump. I take a tiny step toward her. "I think it's funny that their hair is green from all the algae that lives on them. It's almost like they have hair dye. And did you know that they only like to eat the leaves of trees from where they were born? If you take them away from their favorite trees, they can die of starvation. They're like the ultimate picky eaters."

Her eyes are widening with surprise. I wait one beat. Then two. Then it's like a volcano erupts. "They're three times stronger than humans. Did you know that?" She splashes toward me, her voice louder now. "From the time they're born, they can lift their entire bodyweight with one arm. And they're really good swimmers. They're way faster in the water. And their organs are attached to their rib cages so that when they hang upside down, nothing gets smashed. Can you even believe how cool they are?"

Her voice is actually very cute, very high, and excited, and she looks about six inches taller with her back straight, her shoulders unslumped. She looks younger somehow, and freer. It makes me feel the same way, and I can't help the big smile that overtakes my face. She's smiling too, her eyes alert on mine.

This is officially three times more than I've ever heard her say at once. "I can't believe how cool they are. We should find more sloth facts to tell each other."

"Okay," she says, her head bobbing. "I have some books I could loan you. Also, I draw them. Sometimes."

"I'd like to see that." I'm biting the inside of my cheeks to keep from smiling.

"Okay," she says. The tips of her ears are turning pink, which is apparently what happens when Nova is happy. Who knew? "You could put one in your room or something. I mostly keep mine in my notebook so the girls don't mess with them."

"Mason!" I turn to see Emma holding up my phone from the shore. "Willow is texting."

"You'd better answer," Nova says. She's smiling so big, her braces are glinting in the sunlight. "I think she likes you."

23

Willow

My mom's aloofness may be legendary, but here in Salem, I'm witnessing it on a whole new level. It's the next day and I'm marching through Salem, phone pressed to my ear, doing my best to fill Bea in on everything that has happened in the past twenty-four hours. The problem is, she's having a hard time believing any of it—particularly the parts that have to do with Mason—and I'm having a hard time thinking about anything except what happened once I got back to the hotel last night.

My mom is apparently a double black belt in lying.

After I said goodbye to Mason, I'd crept back into the hotel room, trying to imagine what my mom would be doing post–dramatic visit to the willow tree. Sobbing into a fluffy hotel room pillow? Writing her innermost thoughts in a diary? Eating a pint of ice cream while watching reality TV?

I was prepared for nearly anything except for what I actually found her doing—which was sitting at her desk, laptop open, binder spread out in front of her.

She was *working*. Like nothing even happened.

I'd done a quick sweep of her room, ready to spot evidence of the woman kneeling at the willow tree, but everything was exactly the way it was when I left for the moon ceremony. Even her shoes were lined up the same way at the door, which made my entire system flood with frustration. How am I supposed to ever feel close to her when she's this committed to hiding her inner life?

This time, I wasn't having it. I'd flopped onto her bed, aiming pointed questions at her. "So you stayed in working? You didn't go out at all?"

Her shoulders had fallen forward slightly, and for a moment I thought she might confess to something—anything—but then she said, "Phoebe has been looking into how quickly we could manage an estate sale. It shouldn't take long."

Sage's magical rooms had crowded my mind, setting off a typhoon in my chest. The house was the only place I'd felt at home in years now, and she was going to liquidate it? I'd sat up in shock.

"But, Mom . . . don't you think you should take some time to think about it? Or at least . . . go inside? What if there's something you want?" We'd come all this way, hadn't we?

She'd pulled off her glasses, rubbing her eyes wearily. "I can say with absolute confidence that there is nothing in there I want. If I never see Salem again, it will be too soon."

Her voice was strained, but even so, it felt like a tiny glimmer of an opening, so I'd attempted to pry a bit more. "Mom, why do you hate it here so much? Is it because of the aunts? Are you embarrassed that they're witches?"

She'd laughed aloud. "Of course not. Magic and I have always had a complicated relationship, but I think everyone finds it in their own way. I may not believe in spell casting and moon ceremonies like the aunts do, but sometimes I feel like things work out in a way that I can't account for with logic."

That was genuinely surprising, and I'd turned her words over for a moment in my mind. Apparently, she had carried a shard of her teen magic days with her. Then I'd said, "So it isn't the aunts. Or the witchcraft. And you said that you and Sage managed your . . . issues." That part is obviously a lie. If they were truly fine, why hadn't they seen each other in so long? I'd sat up then, projecting my voice clearly. "So . . . what is it?"

Her eyes widened slightly, and she tensed, almost like I'd cornered her. For a second I thought she might actually give me an answer, but then her face settled in a stiff smile. "Home isn't always the place it should be, Willow. I'm glad you've never had that experience."

Her words felt like a slap, and for a moment I was stunned. My home life is obviously miles better than hers ever was, but does she really think mine hasn't been complicated? I've been stretched between two homes and two lives for so long, I've almost forgotten what home feels like. Does she really not see any part of that? The loneliness crept up on me, its tendrils reaching straight for my chest. Why am I so alone in this?

"Mom . . . ," I began, but before I could figure out what I wanted to say, she'd pushed back from the desk, stretching her arms over her head. "I sent your number to Simon earlier. It sounds like Mason really wants to get together tomorrow night. Night, Willow."

And just like that, I was dismissed.

"*Allo?*" Now I hear Bea's voice sing-song over the phone, snapping me back to the present and to her earlier question. "I think you need to start over and tell me one more time," she says. "You ran into him again, what's his name—Star Boy? Completely by coincidence?"

"His name is Mason," I tell her for the ninth time.

"Well, Star Boy certainly seems to be *everywhere*," Bea says.

"This is true." I slow for a moment, remembering the way Mason's face looked when he told me about his mom. I still felt terrible about the way I'd asked him. And then after we'd been interrupted, it hadn't felt right to pick the conversation back up again. Mason's star logs were full of her. Was she still in his life?

My mom showing up had been exceptionally bad timing.

Bea lets out a long, slow exhale. "So your family has believed this old curse story for a long time, but Sage found out it wasn't accurate, so she's telling it to you via a treasure hunt of letters, each of which has a clue leading to the next one?"

Find Thalia. A kaleidescope of butterflies moves through my stomach as I remember standing next to Mason on the bed. Thanks to him I had found her, but I hadn't really looked, had I? "Exactly."

"Ridiculous," she mumbles.

I'm to the end of Essex, and I catch a glimpse of Elizabeth Montgomery and have the urge to wave. "I'm going back to the house. Call you later?"

"*C'est pas possible,*" she says. Piano music strikes up in the background, and a woman's voice calls Beatrice's name. "I think you've lost your mind, *ma belle*, but I love you."

"You too," I say.

I walk as fast as I can the rest of the way to Sage's house, and when I get there I'm hit with how extra magical it is this morning.

The sky is a bright, intense blue, and the flowers are all opened, intent on catching every ray of sunshine. I'm so excited to get inside that I don't see the man standing on the porch until I'm halfway up the walkway, the scent of tea roses filling my nose.

"Hi there," he says in a deep voice.

"Oh!" I can't stop myself in time and my shoe slips, sending me toppling into a flower bed in the process.

"Oh no!" The man rushes over, extending his hand to help me up. I'm covered in dirt.

"I'm sorry, I didn't mean to startle you." He steps back slightly.

The man is Japanese American and probably in his forties, with short dark hair, a plaid shirt, and very cool sneakers.

"It's okay," I say. "Can I help you?"

"I hope so. I mean . . ." He hesitates, shuffling his feet slightly. "I've been trying to get in touch with the owner of the house. Would it be possible for you to pass my information along?" He hands me a card, and when I read it, I freeze. *J. P. Sato, Real Estate Attorney.*

Simon wasn't joking. Word is clearly spreading about Sage's house going on the market. It takes all of my effort not to toss his card into the bushes.

"I'll be in town another week, so the sooner, the better," he says.

"I'll pass it along," I lie, tucking it into my pocket.

"Thanks so much." J.P. heads for the gate, calling, "Enjoy the weather," accompanied by a hand wave back to me. I wait for him to disappear down the street before turning my focus back to my original mission.

The mermaid.

I take the stairs two at a time all the way up to the upper bedroom. When I get there, I stand panting, trying to figure out my next move.

I should probably remove the painting from the wall, but it's enormous and I'm terrified by the thought of dropping and breaking it. Perhaps I can leave it hanging, but sort of move it around?

I run my fingers along the top and sides of the frame, checking for what, I don't know. Maybe there's something behind the painting? The mermaid's intense stare seems to be directly aimed at me now. "Sorry, Thalia," I say. "But you aren't hiding anything, are you?"

I carefully lift the bottom of the painting, gently maneuvering it away from the wall, and suddenly I hear a sliding noise and a tumble of papers falls onto the bed.

I recognize the handwriting before I even bend to pick them up. I've found Sage's next letter.

The story actually began, as many stories do, far, far earlier than most people cared to remember, with another girl. Her name was Sophronia.

Sophronia and her mother, Hanna, lived in a one-room house on the outskirts of town, her father a man who came in and out of her and Hanna's lives as quickly and devastatingly as the unexpected storms that sometimes hit their coastal town.

In between storms, their home was an island, a place of refuge and secret, where a townsperson could knock if a family member had a fever that wouldn't break, or a bone that wouldn't mend, and the old ways came as naturally to Sophronia as they had to Hanna. On full moons Hanna often found Sophronia's bed empty, her daughter standing outside under the moon or at the ocean's hemline, her fingers skating through the water.

Sophronia's mother was not alarmed by any of her daughter's midnight wanderings. What alarmed her was this: Sophronia was undeniably beautiful. Her eyes were dark and bright, her cheeks tinged with pink, and it didn't take long before the rest of town began to take notice. Sophronia's mother warned her to be careful, but Sophronia only laughed. She'd only ever cared about one gaze, and it called to her even more strongly than the waxing tides and rising moons. His name was Frederick Bell.

Frederick was a few years older than Sophronia, artistic and ambitious, with a red beard and a bad habit of not speaking up when he needed to. But Sophronia was in love. She didn't care about the rumors she'd heard of his upcoming nuptials to a girl from a prominent Salem family. Moonlight has a way of illuminating only the things you want to see, and she was happy to see forever in the moon's waning light.

Her mother tried to warn her, tried to tell her what happened when women like them tried to chart their own courses, but Sophronia didn't believe Frederick would betray her, could betray her, right up until the moment that he did.

On the day Frederick married Abigail Archer, Sophronia locked herself in her mother's cabin, away from the water, the town, the moonlight, and in the cabin's harsh candlelight, she was finally able to admit what Hanna already suspected. She was pregnant. Nine months later, Sophronia gave birth to a small strawberry-headed girl who she named Thalia.

Across town, another redheaded baby girl was born just eleven days later, but under such a different set of stars, she may as well have been on the other side of the world. Lily was born into a resplendent house, the family gathered to witness the first birth. Only the baby's father, Frederick, was absent. He was out to sea on his first spice trade, his ship named for the dowry that would be the beginning of his fleet. The Abigail.

Afterward, Abigail sat alone with Lily, promising herself and her new daughter that the sketches she'd found hidden in her husband's study of a young woman with dark eyes and rosy cheeks would never harm them. She knew Frederick didn't love her, but she didn't need love, she needed safety. Life in their New England town had never been easy, even for someone with a comfortable house and a large dowry, and in many ways her life had been similar to Sophronia's. Abigail's father had always had a wandering eye, and behind closed doors, a violent temper, and she'd grown up with her mother whispering in her ear. You must take your power where you can get it. Protect your family's reputation at all costs.

The years progressed, and one chilly autumn evening, Hanna went to sleep and never woke up, leaving Sophronia alone to care for young Thalia in their small cabin on the outskirts of town.

Sophronia knew it cast suspicion on her, the work she did in her small cabin, and she tried to keep Thalia from learning the things that had come so easily to her: potions, spells, how to mix valerian root with honey, words to mend an argument, but Thalia took to it as naturally as breathing. It was in their blood, and she couldn't be stopped from learning.

Sophronia also tried to shield Thalia from the Bell family house, from the luxuries and privileges that in another life, under different stars, could have been hers, but she was unsuccessful at that as well. From the very first moment Lily and Thalia caught glimpses of each other across the town's muddy main street, they were drawn to each other like moths to flames. At primary

school they sat with their red heads bent close together;
at church they held silent conversations across the pews,
needing only their eyes and a few head tilts to tell entire
stories. They loved to walk down the street together,
their arms linked, their step so alike that if anyone had
cared to look for it, they would have seen the truth.

If it had merely been a friendship, perhaps they
could have been kept apart, but sisters, even half sisters,
were different. Their souls had been patterned from
the same materials. No matter how many times they
were warned by their mothers, no matter how they
were coaxed or threatened or punished, whenever one
of them went missing, their mother knew she was with
the other.

Thalia was the one who taught Lily how to grow
her gardens. She showed her how to sift the soil, how to
listen to the plants with her hands, how to ask the seeds
where they wanted to be planted, and the two of them
passed every minute they could together, hands locked
under drooping calla lilies and star-studded jasmine,
fragrant peonies tucked behind their ears.

The friendship frightened Abigail, but it destroyed
Sophronia. She never got used to the sensation of seeing
those two girls together, one in a tattered dress with
bare feet, the other in lace and ribbons. She began
having nightmares and headaches, her feet retracing the
moonlit walks of her youth. Some nights she woke up on
the edge of the ocean, having sleepwalked to the place
where she'd once met Thalia's father. Once she woke on
the Bells' doorstep. The night after Thalia's fourteenth

birthday, Sophronia left their cabin in the darkness of a new moon and never came back. A sailor stopping in at the port would later claim to have seen her walking out into the ocean, her white nightdress spreading out around her in a plume. He'd believed she was a sprite, a water witch. Not a real woman who might need his help. In a moment she was gone.

    Find Abigail.

24

Mason

Please don't bail on me, please don't bail on me, please don't bail on me.

"Mason, do you think we should start without her?" Emma asks in a low voice. The tour group has been waiting for nearly ten minutes and is starting to mutiny, which is only making my steadily rising anxiety worse. She's going to show up, isn't she?

"It's nine minutes past seven," a woman in a Red Sox cap says in a decidedly uncheerful tone.

"One more minute, please. We are missing a guest," Emma says in a voice that says *I realize you're paying me, so I'm being polite, but also I am in charge and you will do what I say.* I guess this is where she learned how to take charge in the many situations I've seen her in—handling groups of unruly tourists on the mean streets of Salem. If I wasn't so stressed out, I'd be impressed.

Willow is coming, right? I double-check the text she sent me while I was at the beach. I could use your help with something. Mind if we talk about it after the tour?

Yes, and absolutely, and also, YES. But what could she possibly use my help with? The thought sends electricity zipping through my body. Whatever it is, I'm in.

I'd shown excellent restraint by responding with a very relaxed-sounding **No problem**. I'd even managed to send it all in one message. But now I'm wondering if she changed her mind. What if she had something come up? Should I text her? And if I start texting her, will I snowball into sending her ninety texts?

Baby steps. Navigating myself around Willow is weirdly difficult.

"Can we give it another few minutes?" I stand on the balls of my feet, scanning the crowds on Essex Street, as though an extra few inches of height will make Willow magically appear.

"Absolutely," Emma says. Red Sox Hat scowls at this, but Emma ignores her. And yes, it's sort of nice to be stood up for.

Right then, I see a flash of red, and then there's Willow sprinting toward us, her ever-present journal tucked under her arm. I'm so relieved, I could melt into the brick road.

"She's here!" I want to punch my fist into the sky, but that seems dramatic, so I settle for bouncing on my toes.

"About time," Red Sox Hat grumbles.

As usual, it's hard to see much of anything besides Willow's hair. It's in its standard ponytail, but more than half of it is falling out in big loose curls that frame her face, and she tugs it to tighten it. Today's outfit is a short, crumpled dress with little blue flowers all over it, plus a pair of white sneakers with shoelaces that are untied. I feel like I could survey a hundred guys and not one of them would list "untied shoes" as something they find attractive, but that's only because they haven't met Willow and her ghostly white legs.

Which I need to stop staring at. "Willow!" My voice is spiked with excitement, which is completely annihilating the laid-back vibe I'm aiming for, but I can't help it. "You made it."

"Sorry, I lost track of time." For some reason I can't possibly guess at, her cheeks turn rose petal pink. She clutches her book to her chest, which makes my heart swoop. She brought my star log, right? I'm missing it so much right now, it's hard to keep still.

"Did you remember . . . ," I whisper, miming writing.

She gives me a knowing nod, gesturing to her backpack. "In here."

Relief floods me. Willow is here, and so is my star log. I can breathe. I want to grab it from her immediately, but I have to play the long game. *Act normal.*

"Willow," Emma says, walking up behind me. "It's so nice to meet you. I'm Emma."

"Nice to meet you too," Willow says. She looks surprised by Emma, her eyes wide as she takes in her tattoos and piercings, but a smile spreads across her face.

"Emma's my foster mom," I add quickly so Emma gets the hint that Willow already knows. I normally don't tell people I'm in foster care. I decided a long time ago that it was easier just to tell them that I was staying with relatives. But with Willow I decided to take the chance—if she's really a sign, then it's probably better that I tell her the truth, and besides, it's possible she already knew from reading through my notebook. It had been exactly as awkward as I'd thought it would be, but at least she hadn't asked a lot of questions. Emma meets my eye calmly, blinking once like, *Understood.* I'm not sure how I feel about communicating via facial expression with Emma, but for once I'm glad for her poker face.

She glances back at Willow. "I hear your mom inherited the Bell family house. So much history there. And those *gardens.*"

Red Sox Hat is now full-on snorting. I know we should be starting the tour, but I appreciate that Emma's taking a moment with Willow.

Willow lights up. "Isn't it amazing? I really, really love the gardens. I recently learned some new things about . . ." She trails off, then glances at me. Her blush is moving down her neck now. "Some family history stuff."

Her text springs to mind. *I could use your help with something. Mind if we talk about it after the tour?* Is that what the "something" is about?

I nod nonchalantly, but I'm suppressing a grin.

"Thank you so much," Willow says.

"Seven twelve," Red Sox Hat announces. "Tour was scheduled for seven sharp."

Emma raises one eyebrow at me, then spins away from us, clapping her hands together. "Love the enthusiasm, *love* the camaraderie, but now it is time to gather within the warm embrace of the friendship circle. I want to impart a few words of introduction." We all shuffle in, Willow squeezing in next to me.

Willow's hair smells faintly floral, and I don't mind the contact terribly, but I do my best to focus on Emma. "My name is Emma Morgan, and while I'm not a Salem native, I am an extremely enthusiastic transplant. I've been leading tours since I was a graduate student at Salem University, which occurred roughly in the Dark Ages. And now some facts about myself you haven't asked for but that I will offer all the same: I listen to murder podcasts to go to sleep, I once got fired from a smoothie shop for not being perky enough, and . . ." She glances at me. "I run the most glitter-infused home on the east shore. I am also, contrary to what you may expect, *terrified* of ghosts, which makes me leading this particular tour all the more ludicrous. I need to warn you, if I see a ghost, I will simply abandon all of you and run. In fact, I may push you out of the way to run. Do not look to me as your protector."

I can't help but laugh, and Emma points a smile in my direction. "So with that caveat, are we ready?"

There's a general mumbling of *ready*s, then Emma turns and begins charging down the street holding an umbrella over her head.

"Do you want to see a ghost?" Willow asks, falling in beside me.

"Absolutely not," I say. "But if I see one, I'll throw you on my back and run, okay?" It's a little out of my comfort zone, but she rewards me with a huge smile. Being with Willow is like holding a sparkler: she's beautiful and exciting, but I'm also hyperaware I might get burned at any moment.

"Do you want your journal now?" she asks.

I cringe slightly that she called it a journal. I mean, yes, I guess that's basically what it is, but the thought of Willow reading my entries is still so painful. "Okay if I get it from you later? I don't want Emma to see."

"Definitely," she says, elbowing me lightly.

"So what did you want to talk to me about?" I ask. She's taking about three steps for every one of mine, and I slow down.

She hesitates, and there's the blush again. I could literally spend all day watching her skin flush that pink color. "Is later okay?"

"Definitely," I repeat, and I can't help the smile overtaking my face. I love the sound of "later." It means there's a future to this.

"Chop, chop, my little onions," Emma calls, her black hair swishing behind her. "There will be no pleasing you until we find a ghost."

"She's funny," Willow says.

Emma actually is funny. And I'm getting the uncomfortable feeling that if I'd met her in the wild, I probably would have liked her a lot. If I'm completely honest, I can see her and my mom being best friends. Emma was probably the grounding force of the relationship, keeping my mom's wild energy in check, while my mom probably kept her from getting too serious. For a moment my throat tightens, but I push the feeling away. Tonight I want to focus on Willow.

We are all herded along until we reach a small enclosure. Twenty stone benches jut out from a low wall bordering a cemetery in a horseshoe shape, each bench engraved with a name and covered in chaotic offerings of tea lights, coins, and handwritten notes.

"Take a moment," Emma says. "This spot is important."

"Salem witch trial victims?" Willow asks, sliding her eyes up at me.

"I think so. Come on, let's look." We trail around with the rest of the tour while Emma waits. The place doesn't feel unwelcoming, exactly, but it does feel heavy, and as I read through the names, the reality of Salem's past solidifies in me in a way it hadn't yet. These were real people. *Bridget Bishop. Sarah Good. Elizabeth Howe.*

Eventually we all meet back up with Emma. "Welcome to the Salem Witch Trials Memorial and Old Burying Point Cemetery. As I am sure you are all aware, Salem has an extremely tragic history. In 1692, twenty innocent people convicted of witchcraft were killed. Nineteen were hanged, one pressed to death, and most of the names connected with these crimes are behind the memorial on these tombstones."

She gestures to the burying ground. Old headstones rise at crooked angles from the grass, many with worn-down etchings. "One of the cemetery's most nefarious occupants is Judge John Hathorne, who is sometimes referred to as 'the hanging judge.' There have been many, many sightings of a dark shadow lurking near his grave, including several instances where it was caught on camera. There have also been sightings of a tall, thin man who wanders through the graves but disappears if you try to look too closely. If he is standing behind me, please do not tell me."

"Yikes," Willow says.

"Now, who is ready to see the most haunted house in Salem? The Joshua Ward House is right this way."

Despite my best efforts, I get completely sucked into the tour, so much so that I *almost* forget that Willow is next to me, her ponytail brushing my arm every so often. Almost. Emma is great at treating the many tragedies in Salem with respect while still keeping things fun, and we stop at a shuttered bookstore, where books are said to fly off shelves, and a restaurant where staff is always waiting with extra silverware on hand because of a fork-stealing ghost. The Joshua Ward House is my personal favorite. It's a large Federal-style building that had once been the home of one of Salem's most notorious witch killers, George Corwin. Emma pulls out an iPad to show an image that had appeared in the background of a guest's photo, and when Willow and I squeeze in for a look, shivers run straight down my back. It's a woman dressed in black, staring intensely through a cloud of black hair.

My mom would love this.

By the time we are close to finishing, Emma has won over the entire group, Red Sox Hat included, and the moon has risen high in the sky. It's a hazy, cloudy night, terrible for stargazing, which is fine because for once I'm more interested in what is happening down here on planet Earth.

Willow is quiet for most of the tour, but she stays close, the ends of her hair brushing my arm as we walk. Once we round the corner back to the spot where we started, she grabs my arm, pulling me to a stop. When I look down, she's holding out my star log.

I grab it quickly, wrapping my fingers tightly around its coiled spine. "Thank you," I say, my voice coming out semi-muffled. Relief is trickling through me, but when I look at Willow, I realize she's blushing again, her eyes darting nervously.

"You okay?" I ask.

She takes a deep breath before meeting my eye. "I was wondering if you'd go somewhere with me. After the tour," she adds.

My heart jumps, and it takes everything in me to answer like a normal human. "No problem."

Her shoulders relax slightly, which is funny because she clearly doesn't realize how much I want to spend time with her. The fact is, Willow could ask me to go cliff diving into a pool of lava and I would still say yes.

25

Willow

The tour is interesting and enjoyable, or at least I'm sure it would be if I had any ability to focus on it. There are two main problems: One, Mason is highly distracting. Even when he's not looking at me, I can feel his attention hyperfocused in my direction. He also keeps brushing his arm against mine, which has the magical effect of turning every nerve in my body into its own tiny bonfire, which is surprisingly not a thing I hate.

And two, I am horrified by the thought of what I'm about to ask Mason to do. The aunts are expecting us tonight, right after the tour, a thought that fills me with horror. What if Marigold is skyclad again? What if they try to do a love astronomy chart, or whatever it was? Will Mason run screaming in the opposite direction?

The problem is, I think the aunts are right: I *do* need him. If he hadn't pointed out Thalia's name in the painting, I doubt I ever would have found it. And even more impressive, he'd guessed at the contents of Sage's second letter when he called Thalia my relative. I am related to Thalia, at least distantly.

Sage's second letter had blown my mind. Not only had the story transformed Thalia from fairy-tale witch to an actual human, I'd been stunned to learn that she and Lily were half sisters.

The clue on the letter said *Find Abigail.* I know from the first letter that Abigail was Lily's mom, and I've been wracking my brain trying to think of anything in the house that could be related to her. Is it another painting? Some other type of object? The aunts had claimed to have no idea where I should look next. Will Mason be able to help me again? If so, it's worth the embarrassment of asking him.

Except now the tour is over, which means I have to *actually* ask him, a fact that makes me want to disappear into one of the spooky cemeteries we toured tonight.

"And that's it," Emma says as we gather in our final friendship circle. "If you loved the tour, my name is Emma. If you didn't, it's Brunhilde. Have a wonderful night, and please enjoy the rest of your time in Salem."

The group begins to disperse and Mason leans in, his eyes eager. As soon as I gave him his notebook, his face settled, a layer of stress evaporating from his body.

"Where to?"

Am I really doing this? Then I remember Sage's handwriting at the bottom of the letter. *Find Abigail.* I will do anything to make that happen. "I have some aunts here. Or maybe they're my great-aunts. Actually, I think they're my *mom*'s great-aunts, which would make them my great-great . . ." I'm so flustered that words are tumbling over each other. Okay, if I can't even explain how the aunts and I are related, how am I going to explain that I'm trying to solve the mystery of a family curse?

I take the plunge. "They want to meet you."

"They do?" His eyebrows knit. "But I thought your aunt was, ah . . ."

Dead. I nearly choke. "Not that aunt. Obviously." I step back slightly, because he smells warm and amazing, and it's distracting, but of course I trip over a curb and he grabs me to steady my arm and then we're right back to where we started. So close to each other. So, so close.

"How do they even know about me?" His eyes are fixed on mine, a tiny smile on his lips.

A ferocious blush passes over my face. "Well . . . because of me. They're helping me figure out a little more about my family and the painting and all that."

"Really?" His eyes are alert, and he reaches up, running his hand through his tangled hair. "They asked me over because they want me to talk about the painting?"

"Yes. Sort of. But I do need to warn you." I take a deep breath. "They're sweet, but they're different. Like really, really different. They're, ah, witches. Like modern-day witches."

He studies me for a long moment, and I'm worried he's going to laugh—or worse, bolt—but then his face relaxes into a smile. "As long as you're there, I'm in."

My blush is approaching wildfire status. He probably doesn't mean it like that, except, when I look up and see the way he's looking at me, I have a strong feeling I might be wrong.

This is really, really not the plan.

"Thanks," I say quickly. "I'll let them know we're on our way."

"Great."

I wait for him to go ask Emma for permission to come with me, but he doesn't move. "Do you need to check in with Emma?"

"Oh." He glances at me in surprise. The thought clearly hadn't occurred to him. "I guess so. Be right back."

While Mason makes his way over to Emma, I take a few deep breaths, trying to bring down the flush in my face. But it only takes a couple of minutes before Emma starts toward me, Mason trailing behind her. "What did you think?" she asks.

Emma is pretty with a distinctly cool vibe, and if it weren't for how short she is, her dark hair and eyes would make me think she's actually related to Mason, not just fostering him.

"I loved it," I say, wracking my brain for some tidbit that wasn't Mason related. "I can't believe how dangerous it was to simply be female in Salem."

"Or middle-aged. Or have too many friends. Or too few friends. Or be different in, you know, *any* way," she adds.

"God forbid anyone be different than you expect them to be," Mason says, and when Emma glances up at him, there's a brief, awkward pause that ends in Mason quickly shifting his gaze down to his sneakers. Forget my mom and me, *this* dynamic looks complicated.

Emma tucks her hands in her pockets. "So, dinner. Do you want suggestions?"

"And maybe a walk?" Mason says. "I haven't been by the water yet." He gives me a quick wink, which makes my insides flutter. Good call. Best to leave *Visit Willow's witch aunts* out of the mix. Too much to explain.

I swallow my nerves. "Suggestions would be great."

Emma nods. "There's a Star Wars–themed pizza place next to the *Bewitched* statue. Lots of weird action figures and funny memorabilia, very kitschy, but you can order by the slice and Simon and I went there about a million times while we were dating. Might be fun to check out."

Wait. Does Emma think this is a date? I haven't been on any yet, but I'm pretty sure that dragging Mason into my family's complicated history does not qualify as one.

Am I really doing this?

"Sounds good," I manage, but now I can't look at Mason. *I can do this. I can bring a cute boy to meet my witch aunts.* Except I'm so nervous that now I'm getting light-headed.

Emma unzips her fanny pack, then holds out a couple of bills to Mason. "Dinner is on me."

He puts his hands up defensively. "Oh, I don't think I should take this—"

"Take it," she says. "You've been helping out a lot. Don't think I haven't seen the hours you put in with the girls every day. And be home by . . . eleven? Midnight?" She smiles at me. "Sorry, I'm not used to setting curfews. What do the kids do these days?"

"Eleven is fine," I say quickly. I check my watch. That gives us over two hours.

"Great. See you back home, Mason." She pushes up the sleeves of her jacket, revealing a pink seashell tattoo, then gives us a little wave as she heads back up Washington Street.

We watch her for a moment in silence, Mason's posture collapsed. Is Mason going to change his mind? Maybe we *should* go for pizza, and I'll tell the aunts Mason didn't want to come. But they were so insistent on him being a part of it. And I am dying to know more about the curse. Seeing Aunt Sage's letter tumble out from behind the painting had been . . . honestly, it had been magic. It made me feel like I was part of the Bell family, like my connection to the women was stronger than the tentative line between my mom and me. I'd do almost anything for another one of those moments. Even ask Mason to help me.

I unzip my backpack, then pull out the Book of Shadows. If I'm going to bring him in on this, I'd better bring him all the way in.

Mason watches Emma disappear around a corner, then turns to me. "Ready?" Then his eyes land on the Book of Shadows.

"Actually," I say, "could you read something first?"

• • •

"I knew it! I knew you were related to the mermaid! Didn't I say you look just like her?"

We're racing toward the aunts' house, and I'm not sure if I'm relieved or overwhelmed by Mason's reaction. The story didn't seem to rattle him at all. He read it once, his head bent studiously over the text, asked a few questions, then read it again. He even seems open to the aunts' theory that discovering the truth may be the ticket to making the curse end.

"Sort of related, right? Because she's my relative's half sister."

Mason doesn't seem interested in semantics. "Remember when I told you that he was a painter? And he imported flowers? I wonder if your aunt and I read the same websites—" He keeps going, but I lose track of his train of thought. Now that he's excited, it's almost impossible to keep up with his long stride. I give up on trying to walk quickly and break into a run.

The aunts' house comes into view and I slow down. The garden is mercifully quiet, and if it weren't for the witchy paraphernalia it would look like every other house.

Except . . . there's a new sign in the window. MARIGOLD'S LOVE SPELLS. APPOINTMENT ONLY.

I hope he'll miss it, but of course he doesn't. Once he checks out the Wicked Witch of the East legs, he looks up at the sign, his face opening in surprise. "Love spells?"

The front door flies open. The first to appear is Marigold, who is, mercifully, wearing her kimono and a pair of high-heeled white booties. Next comes Poppy, then Violet, the three of them crowding in the doorway.

For a moment we all stare at each other.

And then they rush him. "The helper!" Violet shrieks.

"Why didn't the tarot ever send me someone like him when I was a girl?" Marigold says. "Now *this* is a love interest."

I want to dive under the house with the Wicked Witch of the East legs. "Okay, yes. We're friends. Just friends," I say quickly. "Like, we barely know each other."

Mason raises one eyebrow at me, and I feel my face flush. Why can't I stop talking?

"Well, that won't last long," Violet says.

"Now, come inside, I've made you a meal," Poppy says.

The aunts are basically crowd-surfing him into the house. Mason twists back to look at me, his face slightly panicked, a fact I would find funny if it wasn't so horrifying.

"Those lips! That hair!" Marigold is shrieking. "You're like an Old Hollywood movie star!"

I watch helplessly as they drag him through the living room and into the dining room. All I can do is follow.

Inside, the table has been set for two. Mason is clearly trying to take in the whole scenario, but when he sees what is on the plates he freezes. "You're eating fried chicken and waffles?"

"I'm serving fried chicken and waffles," Poppy beams. "It's a new recipe for me, but I just had to make them. And bacon too. Willow, sit!"

Obediently, I take my seat as Poppy whips out her matchbook and lights the candles in the center of the table. Mason hasn't moved. He's still staring at the table with wide eyes.

Then it hits me. These waffles mean something to him, the same way my meal had meant something to me. "Mason, are you okay?"

"I . . ." He takes a deep breath. "My mom worked at this diner in Vermont that served breakfast all day." He looks up to meet my eye. "After she quit, we spent a whole summer trying to duplicate their chicken and waffles. They were always a disaster, but . . ." It may be the candlelight, but Mason's eyes suddenly look very shiny. I feel a tiny tug on my heart. Mason is guarded, but not nearly as guarded as he thinks he is.

"Really? What a coincidence," Poppy says. "Now eat, dear. *Eat.*"

It's all the encouragement he needs. Mason slides into his seat, grabs his fork, and attacks the waffles. It would be disgusting if it weren't kind of endearing. For a moment we all watch him. It's a bit like a nature documentary of a snake eating something whole. It's completely possible he's going to swallow the actual plate. I'm not totally sure where I stand on witchcraft, but Poppy is clearly a kitchen witch.

"Now, I'm assuming our little Willow tree has caught you up to speed," Violet says. "About the Bell family curse?"

"She did," Mason says. "And the letters. I helped her find the first one. I'll help with the others too."

He looks up, catching my eye, and warmth spreads through me. It's nice to have him on my team. "Thanks."

A brief smile slips through his serious expression. "You're welcome."

Violet steps forward. "Now. I'm sure you two will be *plenty* fine on your own, but we've made you a spell kit in case of emergency. We've bundled the supplies and written it all out." She holds up a small package that has been wrapped in brown paper and then tied with a piece of twine that has likely been around since the seventeenth century. They even singed the edges. The aunts really have a flair for the dramatic. Several herbs are tucked into the string, and a small white stone has been attached to it.

"What's in it?" I ask suspiciously. The package is light and smells faintly of herbs.

"A spell for lost things!" Violet says, as though that explains anything. I must look at it suspiciously, because she laughs. "Don't worry, we use everyday items, no need for the eye of a newt or any of those silly things we're always hearing about. Kitchen herbs tend to work the same way they do in cooking. Basil sweetens. Chili might spice things up. If you want something to go away, you might try something like stinging nettle. And if it's love . . ." She trails off, winking at the two of us knowingly.

I'm going to fling myself into their enormous fireplace. I can't even *look* at Mason. "But I'm not a trained witch. How am I supposed to perform a spell?"

Violet shakes her head. "Silly girl. Magic isn't something you learn. It's your birthright! Anyone who tells you that you need special training to perform magic is in it for their own good. Witchcraft is about what is already inside of you. You get to listen to your own inner voice and decide what makes you most powerful."

I want very much to believe that, but right at this moment I'm not sure. I do my best to shake off my misgivings as I zip the spell kit into my backpack. Hopefully we won't have to use it.

"We won't need it for this next letter. It's pretty obvious where the next one is," Mason announces.

I whip around to look at him. His face is serious, even if there's a small amount of maple syrup on his chin. "You know where the next letter is?"

He smiles a little. "Yeah, it's easy, right?"

The aunts are really beaming now. For once they're quiet, but their expressions are a clear *We told you so*. To be fair, they did tell me so, but that doesn't make this scenario any less embarrassing.

I take a breath, steadying my hands on the table. "Um . . . what am I missing?"

Now he looks confused that I'm confused. "We're looking for Abigail, correct? Frederick named his first ship after her."

I'm not sure what that has to do with anything, but Mason is clearly waiting for me to figure it out on my own, so I do my best to scan through the rooms in my mind. The walls had actually been fairly devoid of decoration, besides the mermaid. And I definitely hadn't seen other images of any women's faces. So where were we supposed to look?

"The library?" he says hopefully.

My favorite room in the house. I think of the full shelves and sliding ladder. The sections on travel and tarot and sailing . . .

And then I remember what Sage had written in her letter. Frederick's first ship had been a gift from his father-in-law, named for his new bride. *The Abigail*. That's what the strange half statue was—it was a ship's figurehead. She had probably been on *The Abigail*. Maybe she was Abigail.

"The statue," I manage.

"Bingo," Mason says. "They put them on the front of all the ships for luck."

"Hot *damn*," Violet says. "Mason, you are something. I told you that you needed him, Willow. Didn't I?"

Mason's smile is now bordering on smug, which is a new look for him, but honestly, he deserves it. I knew he was smart from what I'd read in his notebook, but how had his mind worked that quickly? I'd been puzzling over the clue for nearly a full day.

"Is there anything you don't know about my family?" I ask.

He hesitates, then says, "Still figuring you out," and his dark eyes meet mine. The aunts immediately hoot with delight, but even so, pleasure spins slowly through me, fine as cotton candy. He's *flirting* with me, right in front of the aunts, which is embarrassing but also a tiny bit magical. I'm excited to find Sage's next letter, but I might be even more excited to find it with *him*.

"Told you," Marigold says. "Love match in the making, mark my word. . . ."

A tiny noise erupts from my throat, half dismay, half horror.

"Marigold!" Violet says. "We don't tell people who they'll fall for. But he sure is something."

I don't respond because it is suddenly very important that I stuff a bite of waffles into my mouth. She's right. Mason is most definitely *something*. Literally every second I'm with him makes me like him just a tiny bit more.

"You two had better get going," Violet says. "The curse can't wait all day."

> *It was Abigail who knocked on Thalia's cabin door.*
>
> *Abigail had known for years what the townspeople only suspected, and she reasoned that if Thalia was their live-in servant, she could no longer be her daughter's best friend. Her husband could no longer look at the girl with that mixture of regret and sadness, the flames of gossip so close, she could feel their heat. With Thalia under her roof, Abigail would have full control. She made the girl a proposal: If Thalia would be the Bells' servant, she could live in their house. She would no longer be Lily's friend, but she could wait on her, and thus have security and safety.*
>
> *Thalia was frightened and alone, numb with grief, and so she said yes. Of course she did.*
>
> *And so began Thalia's life in the Bell household. For nearly three years, Thalia lived in the uppermost bedroom,*

scrubbing stairways and stoking fires. The room was drafty in the winter, and sweltering in the summer, but Thalia had never known anything different, and besides, she would have lived in far worse conditions to be near her beloved Lily. What did a room matter?

For her part, Lily rebelled at her mother's demands to treat Thalia as a servant, and whenever she could evade her mother's gaze, she worked alongside Thalia. In the evenings she snuck upstairs to Thalia's room, where they spent their time reading aloud and exchanging stories. And Frederick, who had spent the better part of two decades at sea, began spending long stretches of time at home, playing games in the garden with the girls, and taking long walks after dinner. Frederick had been haunted by his decision to abandon Sophronia for so long, it had aged him, turning his beard gray and his back stooped, and now with both girls under his roof, his eyes were calm for the first time in years. He even returned to church, reading his Bible and saying his prayers as devout as any minister, and this concerned Abigail most of all. What if his newfound piety moved him to confess his sin? What if he laid bare the fact that he had had two daughters, both of whom now lived under his roof?

Before long, Frederick began inviting Thalia to ride in the family carriage and insisting that she sit with the family at dinner. When they sat at night to read the family Bible, he occasionally asked Thalia to read aloud his favorite passages from Psalms. "For thou, Lord, art good, and ready to forgive; and plenteous in

mercy unto all them that call upon thee." He took the
girls to the tea-scented wharf to see the many exciting
oddities arriving on ships from faraway places, and
when he learned of Thalia's interest in the natural
world, he made sure she was there to witness every new
animal arrival. On the wharf, she met clever monkeys
and brightly colored parrots. She even felt with her own
hand the thick, wrinkled skin of an elephant, sailed all
the way from India on its way to New York City.

Abigail began to find sketches in Frederick's office
of mermaid girls, their eyes piercing, their hair wild,
and she felt her control slipping from her grasp. The
situation reached a head when Frederick returned
from an overseas trip with two heart-shaped lockets,
an L etched into one, T in the other. The lockets were
a watchman's cry, a warning. Abigail knew then that
the secret would not be contained for long. She couldn't
hear the whispers yet but she could feel them pressing
in around her, and she heard her own mother's voice in
her ear, "Take power where you can get it. Protect your
family's reputation at all costs." She knew she needed
to distinguish the girls from each other, remind her
husband which one was the legitimate daughter. And so
she made a plan.

At the end of summer, when Lily's garden was sure
to be at its fullest, the Bells would host an elaborate
garden party, a celebration of Lily's talents and
an announcement for her eligibility to marry. Her
daughter would be the pinnacle, the center of attention.
In contrast, Thalia would serve the guests with the

other servants. The dynamic would be set, her family safe. All would be well.

Lily met the news of the party with dismay. She had no interest in marriage, now or ever. Ever since Thalia had moved in, Lily had begun dreaming of faraway gardens dripping with blossoms and scents she'd only read about—jasmine and saffron, enormous lotuses blooming in crystal pools in marble palaces. She dreamed of large halls and libraries where she'd learn the names of every plant, studying the way they fit into the world. She had no interest in a life like her mother's, one where her power was gained in meanness and hidden measures. She wanted the world.

Thalia had been born with the world inside of her, so what she wanted was simple: she wanted Lily to be happy.

Over flickering candles and long whispered talks, the girls made their plan. The night of the ball, when the family was occupied with their guests, Lily and Thalia would meet on the beach and then make their way by train to New York City. There they'd find a boarding house, someplace that allowed young women to live alone, and find jobs as governesses or in factories until they'd saved enough money for Lily to find admittance to one of the universities slowly opening their doors to women. They'd figure it out, the two of them, the way they always had.

They locked their intention over the dancing candlelight, pledging their devotion to each other and their plan, and Lily saw in her best friend's eyes a dedication so firm and unwavering, she knew nothing would ever come between them.

Later, after Thalia had betrayed her, Lily would marvel at the way candlelight could hide a person's true feelings. She would wonder how she hadn't seen it, the way her friend's jealousy and resentment had grown in the shadows. Her mistake was in seeing what she wanted to see.

The day of the party, Lily was so nervous she could hardly keep a thought in her head. Walkways were swept, windows scrubbed, the tables laid with exquisite china and delicate porcelain. The gardens, as though sensing the celebration, were particularly resplendent, every flower determined to outshine the next.

Lily's hair was washed and set, her lips rouged, and her temples pressed with rosewater. A few minutes before the ball, Thalia helped her into her new gown, a cream-colored silk trimmed with blond lace and metallic rosettes.

When Abigail caught sight of Lily and Thalia coming down the stairs together, she gasped with delight. Her daughter was so radiant, she completely outshone everyone around her, most notably the girl beside her in the simple wool dress.

Lily began the evening thinking only of Thalia and their plan to escape, but the attention and admiration she received from the townspeople had a dizzying effect. She was used to being admired for her gardens, for the way she made flowers grow, but she'd never been admired for being herself, and the effect was nearly as intoxicating as the bright red poppies blooming along the perimeter of the walkway. As the night proceeded, she found herself checking the clocks less often, her cheeks becoming more flushed. She was so captivating, so in her element, that every young man asked to dance with her, every woman whispered their admiration, and slowly, slowly, she forgot about the plan.

Thalia sat on the beach for hours, watching the tide, checking the moon, listening to the whispering of the stars. By the time she saw the first rays of dawn, she finally felt her heart harden, her love falter. Thalia, who had known deep down for years who her true parentage was, who had lost her mother, who had spent years banished to the upper bedroom of a home she should have lived in in comfort, was being betrayed yet again, and this was the time that broke her.

Thalia snapped.

There were many accounts of what happened next. Some said Thalia appeared in the middle of the Bells' garden as sudden as a storm cloud. Others say the girls met on the walk, and it was only their voices that were overheard. One man even claimed to have seen Thalia standing in the upper bedroom window, her arms held overhead as she uttered the words of the malediction. But everyone remembered the crucial point: Thalia pronounced a curse on Lily, and then disappeared into the night.

For years afterward, the town gleefully told and retold the story of the ungrateful Thalia, who after *being taken in by the Bell family had succumbed to vanity and jealousy. It wasn't anyone's fault, really. That's what happened when you invited a witch into your home.*

The event so upset Lily that she retired from her gardens, leaving her resplendent blooms to be cared for by the servants. She married one of the young men from the party, and she went on to be a productive member of the community. All that remained of her great talent were a few memories, and if it weren't for the names she gave her daughters, it would be as though it had never happened at all.

Once the curse had been planted in the Bell family, it never left. Generation to generation, the Bell women carried it with them. From that night on, every Bell woman would know with a burning intensity the thing they wanted most, and not one of them would get it. It was a pity. But that is what happened when you turned a blind eye to the darkness in someone else.

And Thalia? She was never seen or heard from again.

Find Lily.

26

Mason

Finding Sage's next letter tucked under the figurehead in the library may have been the highlight of my entire life. Willow had stared up at me with an expression that was half *You're my hero* and half *I'm so annoyed you're right, I could smack you*, and then she'd dragged me straight up to the roof for us to read it together.

I can still feel where her fingers closed around my wrist.

As we climbed the ladder, the mermaid's expression seemed a bit more smug than usual. *You see? It's all working out for you.* I still have no idea what Willow's function as a sign is, but I'm all for taking the time to figure that out, especially if it means spending more time with her in the house.

Now we're sitting side by side on the roof, backs against the railing, her hair blowing onto me every time the slightest breeze picks up. I realize this is about as weird of a setup as you can get, but being on this rooftop with Willow, listening to the wind move through the willow tree's branches, is as close to magic as I can imagine. Her face is flushed the slightest shade of pink, and her energy is filling the few inches of space between us.

It's making it hard to focus on the specifics of the letter. I'm assigned the job of lookout, and as she reads aloud, I watch the willow tree. I'm hoping there won't be a repeat visit from Willow's mom.

"Well, that's depressing," Willow says, pushing the letter into my hands. Our fingers touch for one perfect moment, and then she flops back against the railing, her leg brushing against mine as she straightens her knees. Is it just me, or are we now finding ways to touch each other?

"Sisters cursing each other?" I guess.

"Right." She pulls her ponytail forward and starts twisting the ends around her fingers. "I mean, I can understand it. She was jealous because her sister was always the one being celebrated, plus, she'd lost her mom. Also, she was an actual witch, so she used what she had."

"Interesting that your aunts all practice witchcraft," I say. "It makes me think they side more with Thalia."

"Maybe," she says thoughtfully. Another gust of wind sends her hair dancing into my face, and she quickly tucks her hair back, her eyes lingering on my mouth for one quick second.

I mean, that could have been wishful thinking. But ever since we stepped into the house, the energy between us has felt different. Lighter. Easier. More connected. Almost like we've known each other for longer than our handful of haphazard meetups.

Now that I've been here a few times, I can recognize the feeling in the house. It's like the outside world falls away, and I can simply be. I know Willow is feeling it too. Everything about her looks more relaxed, from her rumpled dress to her untied sneakers. I lean in slightly, my shoulder touching hers gently as I gesture to the letter. "I don't buy it."

"Why not?" She doesn't move away. Instead she leans in more, and now her arm is pressing against mine. Is the same electricity phenomena happening to her? *Focus.*

"Because Lily was her sister. And she loved her. They had history. Would Thalia really curse her for eternity because she was enjoying a party?"

"The story doesn't say she cursed her for eternity." Willow's smiling now, her hair back in my face. "And it wasn't about the party. It was about Lily not following through on their plan."

I shake my head again. "I still don't buy it. Something's off."

"Maybe. I guess we need to find the next clue." She points to the bottom of the letter. "Find Lily, aka Cordelia Bell. Any ideas?"

I shrug. "None. I don't think I saw her name in any of my research I did on the house. But I'll look again. And maybe we can search through all the rooms? Maybe there's an actual lily, like the flower, somewhere."

She hesitates for a moment, her eyes locking on mine. "And why were you researching my aunt's house, exactly?"

For a moment I wonder if I should tell her about my mom and the signs, but then I think about what that would actually entail. People never seem to get why I want to be back with my mom so badly—and in some ways, I get it. She's let me down over and over, but that doesn't negate the fact that she's still my mom. Would Willow understand? My stomach rolls. I'm not ready to find out. "Because it's magic here. Every time I'm here, it feels like . . ." I struggle for the word.

"Like you're home?" she asks quietly.

We meet eyes again. "Yeah. Exactly."

She nods. I can't read the emotion on her face, but I can tell that whatever she feels here is important to her. It shifts my attention from myself to her, and suddenly I want more than anything to help her.

"Hey, what if we go do an inventory of the house? I only guessed where tonight's letter was because I'd seen the masthead and the photograph of the ship. Maybe if we walk through the house, we'll see something that makes us think of Lily."

"Good idea. But in a minute? I've had a long couple of days, and it's so nice up here." She sighs, looking down at the garden. "The willow tree looks so pretty at night."

I lean over to take a look. She's right. Moonlight has painted the tree a silvery gray, and the wind has put the entire tree in motion, the leaves and branches swaying gently in the breeze.

"Willow trees must be your thing," I say.

She hesitates. "This will probably sound weird, but I've actually never thought about them all that much. But that one's amazing."

A stronger breeze picks up, and Willow's hair blows into my face, whipping my cheeks and forehead. I pretend to fight it off, and she attempts to cram it back into her ponytail. "You and the tree even have the same hair."

She laughs. "My hair is the worst."

This is obviously not true, and my eyes can't help but linger on her hair. I've never seen red hair quite this color. Up close, I can see copper woven through it. I turn my attention back to the letter anyway. "Okay. So what about you?"

"What about me?" Her eyes are still on the tree, but she's smiling now.

I nudge her knee. "The curse story says that every Bell woman will know what they want. You're a Bell woman. What is the thing you want with a burning intensity?"

Her cheeks turn a subtle shade of cotton-candy pink. "Um . . ."

Don't read into that, Mason, I instruct myself. I'm obviously not her burning desire. Although it obviously wouldn't be the worst thing in the world. "I mean, any secret projects or plans?"

"Besides figuring out my twisted family history?" Her eyes dart up to mine. "I mean, yes. But . . . it's sort of personal."

Hilarious coming from someone who has literally read a book full of my most private thoughts. I pull my notebook out from my back pocket. "Hey, look. You know a lot about me. It's only fair that I know more about you, right?" I'm starting to be more okay with the fact that Willow knows my deepest, darkest secrets. If someone was going to read my star log, Willow wasn't a terrible choice.

"I took you to meet my witch aunts," she says.

"Who were awesome, but I want to know more about *you*."

Her cheeks flush pink again, and for a moment I think she's going to shut me down, but then she nods. "You're right. Fair is fair." She takes a deep breath. "I'm really interested in traveling the world. And by interested, I mean I'm obsessed. My whole bedroom is covered in pictures of places I want to go, and I have a list at home with over a hundred places I plan to visit. It's literally the first thing I think about when I wake up, and the last thing I think about when I go to sleep. But sometimes when I think about it, I feel . . ." She exhales and her shoulders drop. "I get so scared it isn't going to happen."

A tiny plume of surprise rises in my chest, both for what her life goal is and also for her worry. Travel isn't exactly something that is on my radar. I know a lot of people are into it, but I've moved so much that sometimes I think I like the idea of staying still somewhere more than I like the idea of going somewhere new. But according to Willow's intense expression, this is a huge deal to her. Why is she doubting herself? Willow seems like the kind of person who should have limitless confidence. "Where do you want to go? Give me a few examples."

"The Pink City," she says automatically. "It's in India. Its real name is Jaipur, and most of the buildings are a dusty pink color because it's the color of hospitality and in the 1800s the leader painted the entire city in order to welcome a visitor from the British monarchy. It has all these palaces and forts, and there are elephants walking around mixed in with cars, and at night the people fly kites from the rooftops." She sighs, pulling her knees to her chest.

Okay, I can see what she means. That does not sound terrible. "Where else?"

"Cinque Terre. It's on the Italian Riviera and it means 'five hills.' Each hill has a fishing village built into cliffs, with a hiking trail that connects them all."

She looks at me expectantly. I'm enjoying picturing these places with her, but more than that, I'm enjoying watching her face light up in the darkness. "Continue," I say.

"Machu Picchu in Peru, Madagascar, Cambodia, Iceland, Ecuador . . . Want me to keep going?"

"I'd love to go to Iceland. It would be a great place to see the northern lights." My mom and I had seen the northern lights together once. It was when we were living on the resort in Maine. There had been dozens of people partying at our cabin that night, but she came to find me and wrapped me up in a huge blanket and took me out on the porch of the cabin so we could watch together. It makes my throat ache to think about.

Willow pulls her knees in tighter. "I read about a place there called the Five Million Star Hotel. Every room is in a clear bubble so you can look at the stars and northern lights all night."

I feel a tiny ping in my chest. Mom would *love* that. "Seriously?"

"It's on the Golden Circle, which is a route you can drive in Iceland. It's one hundred and eighty-six miles and you can see three of Iceland's most popular natural attractions."

I remember absolutely everything, but her knowing the exact mileage of the route surprises me. "Wow. You weren't joking. You really do know what you're talking about."

Now her smile gets self-conscious, and she looks down at her sneakers. "Sorry. I get a little, ah, excited, when I talk about travel."

I wasn't actually expecting Willow to open up to me, and my body is humming with the happiness of it. "It's cool you know exactly what you want to do."

She shrugs. "I don't have all the details worked out yet. I mean, obviously, I'm going to have to find a job that either allows me to travel or pays me to do it. And I know I want to go to college, so I'm going to have to figure out how that fits in. Right before I came here I was actually trying to talk my mom into letting me spend my senior year abroad. But it didn't go very well." She shakes her head, then looks up at me. "What about you? What's the thing you want with a burning intensity?"

The answer is obvious. *To find my mom.* But I know that isn't the kind of answer she's looking for. She wants me to say something like *Become a skydiving instructor in Australia* or *Start my own tech business and live on the beach.* Things other people our age are interested in. The problem is that I've never really felt like I could relate to most other people our age because they're walking around with no idea of what it's like to be missing something as crucial as their mom. Still, I'm up for trying. I try to imagine what I'd want to do if I had a completely different life, the kind that allowed space for anything.

I stare up at the sky, trying to imagine what alternate-reality Mason would be interested in, and I'm surprised when it appears almost immediately, the thought a dim glimmer in the distance. "I want to discover something in space that one else has. I don't care how small or insignificant. But something new."

I know how true it is the second I say it. Alternate-reality Mason would be an astronomer, but more than that, he'd be a discoverer.

Willow's smile sends warmth tipping through me, and suddenly I'm the one talking way too fast. "Last year some researchers found something that might be the first planet we've seen outside of the Milky Way. It's twenty-three million light-years away, and it looks like it's orbiting two stars. It was a team of like ten people, and I couldn't stop thinking about what it would have been like to be there. I mean, we've been discovering planets outside of the solar system—exoplanets—since the nineties, probably four hundred of them, but they were all in the Milky Way. There's so much more out there, and we're getting so much better at looking. Space is infinite, but when I think about how infinite it really is . . ." I'm getting carried away, my voice punched with enthusiasm, in the same way Willow's was, and I quickly stop myself. "Sorry. I'm a nerd."

She bumps her shoulder into mine. "I read your star log, remember? I already know you're a nerd. And since when has being a nerd ever been bad?"

The reminder that she read my notebook feels like a tiny punch to the gut, but I manage to regain my footing. She isn't weaponizing my notebook. In fact, she gets why it's important to me, because she loves travel the way I love astronomy. Not everyone has something they love so much. Suddenly I'm filled with certainty, not about my mom or me, but about Willow. One day, not too far away, Willow will pack her bag, lace up her shoes, head out, and see all of it.

"You'll do it. Curse or not, I know for a fact that you'll travel the world."

Her smile is brilliant now. "Really? How do you know?"

"It's obvious. Planets orbit the sun, and Willows orbit the Earth."

She's beaming now, and I imagine that smile carrying her through crumbling castles and mountain villages and bright city streets. No matter where I try to picture her, she fits.

"I think you'll accomplish your goal too." She gestures to the sky. "You'll find something new."

It's sweet she thinks that. She has no idea how different our lives are. I shrug. "Yeah, maybe."

"No, really. You're smart and persistent. Why wouldn't you?"

Because I have a completely different life path. Because I have to find my mom. Because dreams like that are for other people. But I don't want to burden her, so I smile. "You handle the Earth, I'll handle the sky."

"Deal." We shake on it, and then for a couple of seconds neither of us lets go. For those seconds my entire world feels right.

Back at the Morgans, I take the porch steps two at a time, then make my way into the dining room, heading for the computer. Before I get to it, a voice comes from the dark living room. "How was it?"

I startle, spinning to find the voice's source. Emma is cocooned on the couch in an enormous fuzzy blanket with only her feet poking out, a closed book resting on the ground next to her.

"Good. Really, really good." I realize I'm smiling again, and I do my best to smooth out my face, but I can tell by her expression that I'm only partially successful.

She sits up. "Did you like the pizza place?"

I stop my *Huh?* in the nick of time. Willow and I were supposedly going out to a Star Wars–themed pizza restaurant. "Delicious. Thanks for the suggestion. Willow ended up paying, so . . ." I reach for the money in my back pocket, but she stops me.

"Keep it. You can use it on your next date."

I know that isn't what my night with Willow was, but the thought sends a ripple through my body anyway. If hanging out on rooftops with Willow was a religion, I'd convert immediately.

Emma stands up now, uncoiling the blanket from around her, and yawns sleepily, and I realize she's been waiting up for me. The thought of it gives me a strange feeling. Parents waiting up for you to get home is the kind of thing you see in families in sitcoms. I'd never pictured it happening to me.

She picks up her book, and I realize it's a new copy of the one I've been carrying around. *Astrophysics for People in a Hurry.* "Wait. You're reading that?" I ask.

She shrugs. "When I saw you carrying it around, I figured it must be good." Confusion settles over me. I'm not sure how to feel about that information. Are we going to talk about the book now like a tiny two-person book club? Is she trying to suck up to me? But the book actually is good, so maybe she was actually interested? She continues. "After the tour, I texted my contact at BU's astronomy department. I told her you're not sure about the high school program, and she suggested you come in for a tour. She said she'd love to show you around the observatory."

"Wait. Really?" I blurt out. I've been trying not to really picture the program, but now I can't help it. I've never been to an actual observatory, and the thought of even getting close to one of those giant telescopes sends heat rising through my body. "I'd love that."

"Thought you might. She also invited us to a meteor-watch party at the end of summer. I can't remember what it's called. The Pers . . . Perse—"

"Perseids," I say. "You can see them in July and August. Some nights you can see more than a hundred meteors an hour. They were the first meteorite shower I saw. The girls would love it."

"Then I'm glad I accepted that invitation too." She gestures to the dining room. "Speaking of the girls, they wrote you a note. I assumed you'd be on the computer again tonight, so I put it on the desk."

My chest freezes. Emma apparently knows about my nocturnal computer habits. I always clear out my search history, but is it possible she knows what I'm doing? I'm about to stutter out some excuse about why I've been staying up half the night on the computer, but before I can come up with anything, she says, "Night, Mason," and disappears down the hallway.

I can't figure her out. Not at all.

On the computer desk I find a large note written in crayon. *MASON DRESS REHERSUL TOMMORW DO NOT BE LATE WE HAVE A COSTUM!!!* Like everything related to the girls, it's covered in glitter, which immediately transfers to my body and I have to spend several minutes trying to pick it off my shirt and jeans.

I do not like the sound of a *DRESS REHERSUL/COSTUM*, but I'm too excited about my night with Willow and my conversation with Emma to worry much. Besides, I'm dying to start researching Willow's ancestor Cordelia.

I pull up the website with Salem's newspaper archives, but as I type *Cordelia Bell* into the search engine, I feel a tug of guilt. This is my time of day when I search for my mom, not the history of random Salem inhabitants. Shouldn't I be using it to its fullest?

Obviously, yes.

My fingers hover over the keyboard.

I stare at the screen for a long time. I need to check to see if any of her social media friends responded. The problem is that tonight felt so *good*. It's been a while since I had fun like that, and the thought of more zero-results pages makes my insides go cold.

I'll see what I can find on Cordelia first.

27

Willow

I have never met anyone even a little bit like Mason.

He's a giant contradiction, pun intended. He's open, outgoing, endearing, his emotions right out on the surface, exactly as the aunts described. But he's also a closed book, the only indication of everything he's been through hanging out in the notebook he keeps jammed in his back pocket. His notebook was filled to the brim with heartache. And I can't stop thinking about him blurting out the thing about his mom and the mermaid. What was the connection?

Beyond that, I don't know that I've ever met anyone as smart as he is. His notebook had given me a bit of a glimpse, but when he recited all the information about Frederick Bell, I realized he seems to store way more in his brain than the typical person.

But most surprising is the way I *feel* around him. On the one hand, it's all blushing and attempting not to say stupid things and trying to decide if I'm looking at him too much. On the other hand, something about him is so *easy*. Like I've known him for so much longer than I actually have. I'm not sure if I've ever felt that before.

I'm not on board with the butterflies filling up my stomach, so as soon as daylight streams full steam through the windows, I roll over to grab my phone and remember yet another fact about Mason. He's a chaotic texter.

I have six text messages from Mason, four from last night and two from this morning.

You awake?

I found something about CB last night, sending link now.

Get it?

There's definitely more to the story.

Want to meet up?

And then one from an hour ago. Now are you awake??

"CB" for Cordelia Bell. I click on the link for a website called Salem Register Newspaper Archives.

Huh.

He's saved a search on "Cordelia Bell" with a date range of 1801 to 1869, and several images of newspaper clippings are pulled up. The printing is a bit blurry and I have to squint, slowly making out the words.

> *$50 REWARD*
>
> *Reward for information concerning whereabouts of*
> *family servant Thalia. Seventeen years old when last*
> *seen, but has been three years. Red hair, fair complexion,*
> *small of stature. Wearing black dress and may be*
> *carrying gold locket. Last seen in Salem, MA, June 4,*
> *1832. C. Bell of Salem offers reward.*

My heart skips. Lily and Thalia are real. I mean, obviously they're real, but seeing their names in newsprint makes them suddenly so much realer. I quickly click on the second image.

> *LOST. Gold locket inscribed with initial "L" and image*
> *of turtledove has been missing three years from June.*
> *May have been sold. Item is precious beyond monetary*
> *value. Any information of its whereabouts will receive*
> *double its worth. C. Bell of Salem, MA, offers reward.*

Lily was looking for Thalia via newspaper? Also, how on earth had Mason found this?

I google *turtledove locket 1830s* because I can't think of what else to do and pull up several pages of antique lockets for sale. I click on one and find a whole page on the history of lockets. Lockets were apparently very in vogue during the Victorian era. They'd been around since Queen Elizabeth I, who wore one carrying a photo of her mother, Anne Boleyn. Queen Victoria, who had been alive when Thalia and Lily were, had carried on the tradition, wearing a necklace containing eight pendants, one for each of her children. When her husband, Prince Albert, died, she'd even worn a mourning locket.

I can't find any with a turtledove etching, but when I google *turtledove meaning*, I find lots of information. Turtledoves are a symbol of love and friendship, and everywhere I read it says that turtledoves appear in a set of two.

If Thalia had cursed her sister, why would Lily have been trying so hard to find her? And why did she care so much about the locket? Had Thalia stolen the locket engraved with Lily's name?

I let out a groan. It's all so confusing. I'm not sure how this information will help us with Sage's directive to *Find Lily*, but I am dying to get back to the house to try.

The door between my and my mom's room is slightly ajar, and I throw off the covers and hurry over. Her room is empty, her laptop and binders missing from the desk. It's slightly alarming to find her gone. Besides her meetings with Simon and her willow tree ritual, she basically hasn't moved from her desk since we got here.

I text Mason. Going back over, can you come meet me?

My phone chimes a moment later, but it's my mom. Awake? I'm posted up working from a coffee shop. I can order you breakfast.

I hesitate for a moment. My mom and I have somehow managed

to see each other even less than we usually do, but I'm too eager to get to Sage's to waste any more time. I do a quick search on my phone of *places to see in Salem*, then respond. **Mason invited me to tour House of Seven Gables with him. That okay with you?**

She responds. **Of course. Enjoy.**

I take the fastest shower possible. Mason or not, the house is calling to me like a siren. Maybe that's why Frederick painted mermaids; everything about Thalia makes you feel like diving in, no concern for safety.

I'm pushing my way through the hotel doors, wet hair still dripping on my shoulders, when I nearly trip over Mason, who is camped out on the steps, a cardboard drink holder and a Dunkin' bag beside him.

"Mason!"

He jumps to his feet. "*Finally.* I thought you were going to sleep all day. I've already had three coffees."

Mason is wearing the same green T-shirt he was wearing the night before, and his hair is mussed to perfection. Which I notice for informational purposes only. "Wait, did you not sleep?"

He shakes his head, grabbing the bag and offering me a jelly doughnut. "Not really. I stayed up most of the night researching. Once I found the newspaper archive, I couldn't stop. I found obituaries, stuff about Frederick's business, I even found an article talking about Lily winning a prize for her gardening. Here, you should put a pack of sugar on your jelly doughnut."

"Willow?" My mom suddenly appears on the steps, causing me to nearly drop the doughnut Mason handed me. She's dressed for the day in her typical outfit, laptop tucked under her arm.

"Mom, I thought you were working at a coffee shop."

She looks tired this morning, her eyes red-rimmed. I think again about her kneeling at the willow tree. Being here is taking a toll on her, that's for sure. "I wanted to catch you before you two go on the tour."

"The ghost tour? We—" Mason starts.

I step on his foot in the most subtle way possible. "We didn't realize it, but House of Seven Gables doesn't open until later."

Mason doesn't miss a beat. "Did you know they added a secret staircase to the house to make it more like the one in Nathaniel Hawthorne's book? It's also the oldest mansion in North America."

Mason, as it turns out, is an excellent person to have in your corner, should you ever have to lie.

"I did know that," my mom says, her tired eyes landing on him. "I've taken that tour a time or two myself. It was a popular field trip choice."

I feel a slight stab in my chest. My mom went to school here. Would I have ever known that if it weren't for Sage leaving her the house?

Mason grabs the bag from his steps. "Would you like a doughnut? I have glazed, chocolate frosted, Boston cream, cinnamon, strawberry, and a bunch of drinks, but I think they've all gone cold. . . ."

"Boston cream, please." He hands her the doughnut, and she takes an enormous bite. I can't remember the last time I saw her eat junk food, and it's a tiny bit shocking to watch. She lets out a little sigh, crumbs on her mouth. "Thank you. This is heaven."

"No problem." Mason turns and smiles at me. "We could walk around first? Go see the *Friendship* on the pier? It's a replica of a ship from the 1700s."

"Sounds great."

My mom has that smile again. Oh well, let her think this is about a crush. I've got bigger things to worry about.

• • •

"How'd you know that fact about the House of the Seven Gables?" Once my mom disappeared into the hotel, we'd started out walking but that had morphed into a full-on run once we'd cleared Essex Street. I don't know who is more excited to see the house again, me or Mason. It's nice to not be alone in this.

"Simon. He took me on a bike tour of Salem." The doughnut bag is banging against his leg, but neither of us slows down. "I can't wait to show you what else I found in the *Salem Register*. I even found an announcement about Lily's party. It was called a 'Victorian garden party.' And did you know Frederick died only a year later? Also, classified ads used to be one of the best ways to track down those who had gone missing. I wonder if Lily posted more in other newspapers?"

His words are swimming over my head. Once again, he's burying me in facts.

"So do you have any ideas about where we'll find the next letter?"

He shrugs. "I feel sort of stumped on this one."

"We'll find it," I say, but I'm not nearly as confident as I sound. The house is large, and we have limited time to search.

The top of the house comes into view, sending sparks of joy through me, but when we get to the gate, we both stumble to a stop.

The house has a new addition. A giant, ugly FOR SALE sign is now planted in the front. We both stare at it in horror.

"Oh no," I manage. My heart is literally sinking into my shoes, the jelly doughnut Mason gave me suddenly heavy in my stomach. I make my way over to the sign, Mason at my heels. WITCHY CITY REAL ESTATE. Simon's name and number are attached to the bottom in a swinging section.

"I hate this so much," Mason says. His shoulders are slumped again, arms crossed tightly.

I'm drifting again, the shore too far from my grasp to reach. I've only spent a few hours in this house, but it already feels like losing a home. How much longer will I have with it now that it's on the market? Will we leave immediately like my mom said?

I have the sudden sharp urge to run up the steps and hurl myself into the home's depths. Maybe if I lock the doors and refuse to come out, my mom will rethink selling the home?

"Hey, who's that?" Mason whispers. He's looking over the top of the rosebushes, and when I follow his gaze my heart manages to sink even lower.

It's the guy who gave me his card. "Hide," I whisper, grabbing Mason's arm.

"Where?" Mason's eyes are big and searching, his body alert, but I'm too busy eyeing the willow tree to explain. If we duck, we could potentially make it across the yard and under the branches without him seeing us.

Too late. He's spotted us and now he's making his way to the gate, his stride long and purposeful. "Good morning! How are you today?"

"Morning," I manage. He's wearing another plaid shirt and the same sneakers. Today he's carrying a briefcase, which I eye warily.

"Willow, who is he?" Mason says in a low voice. He has his arm around my shoulder now, his gaze moving from the man on the walkway to the garden statue at his feet.

I feel a tiny jolt. Mason is figuring out the best way to defend me.

"It's okay," I whisper.

When the man sees the FOR SALE sign, he pauses.

"How can I help you?" Mason says, his arm still firm around me. I don't mind it terribly.

He turns his attention back to us. "Officially on the market, I see. Do you know if the seller is holding any showings?"

So he is a buyer. He must have heard rumors before it was even officially listed. Simon was right, buyers are like sharks. Had he been circling the block since I saw him last, waiting to see if a sign went up?

I bite the inside of my cheek hard. Nothing against this guy, but he can't have my house.

I mean Sage's house.

I mean my *mom's* house.

Mason must feel my shoulders stiffen because he takes the lead. "Not that I know of. But if you have any questions, you can call Simon. He's the real estate agent on the sign."

"Great." The man pulls out his phone and takes a photo of the sign. My anxiety ratchets up a notch. What if he asks if I gave his card to my mom?

Luckily, he doesn't ask. Instead he pushes his hands into his pockets. "Thanks a lot, you two. I hope you enjoy your day."

He turns and saunters back up the sidewalk, taking the final dredges of my hope with him. Simon was right. Sage's house is going to be under contract in no time.

"That's not good," Mason says, echoing my thoughts. He's completely right. That man is going to make an offer on Sage's house, and my mom is going to accept it. He's probably going to do it right away. Which means my window for finishing Sage's treasure hunt has gotten infinitely smaller.

I suddenly need something to prop myself up on. I lean into Mason, glad his arm is still around me. Mason must have the same thought, because he squeezes my shoulder lightly. "Let's find Lily."

• • •

We check the grounds to make sure there are no more real estate investors lurking around the house, then we quietly enter through the front door and begin scouring the house top to bottom. The official plan is to look for anything "Lily-ish." Yes, it's a foolproof plan. No, it does not go well.

Mason and I are quiet, but it's a nice kind of quiet, working side by side as we check every drawer, box, picture, and closet. We're trying to move quickly, but we keep getting sidetracked by what we find. The aunts weren't exaggerating when they said Sage had carefully curated the items in the house. Despite its tidy appearance, the house is full of interesting things—we find an old upright telephone, a yellowed typewriter, a silver tea set, even a collection of black-and-white baseball cards packed neatly into a worn shoebox.

Even with the sense of urgency looming over us, the house is delightful in the morning. Sunlight is filtering gauzy and warm through all the giant windows, and everything has a soft, soothing feeling. It makes me want to curl up on a warm patch of floor and nap.

We're in the study, the *Abigail* masthead giving us judging eyes from the corner, when I begin to lose hope. So far Mason has checked every drawer of the roll-top desk while I move the bookcase ladder around, trying to find anything that could help.

"What if it's something with an actual lily on it?" I ask, pulling a book titled *The Gardener's Year* from the shelf. I thumb through the pages, but all I find is a lot of information on gardening and some baby's breath pressed between the last few pages.

"I feel like that's too obvious," Mason says. He's shuffling through a pile of papers, which he carefully replaces. "Do you think your mom would know how to find this next letter?"

That's the problem. This treasure hunt had been set up with my mom in mind. "Yes, but there's no way I can ask her."

I sit down on the ladder, folding my arms over my chest. I'm doing my best to not think about the fact that I'm going to lose this place soon, but it's pressing in on me, making my chest feel heavy and tight. I've spent only a few hours in this house, and it already feels imprinted on my soul. How can my mom let this place go?

I keep imagining my mom and Sage as children. The aunts said they could spend hours exploring the house, red heads bent together as they found some new treasure. When had that changed, exactly? And why did my mom clam up every time I tried to bring it up?

The aunts' words come back to me. *Those two chickadees were like s'mores and campfires. Avocados and toast. Like cream and coffee.*

It's easy to draw the comparison between my mom and her sister and Thalia and Lily. Two redheads side by side, the rest of the world pushed to the outskirts. Two sisters whose relationship had come to a screeching halt.

My mom still couldn't talk about it. Whatever had happened between her and Sage, losing Sage had clearly been the most painful part of it.

Like two turtledoves. Wherever one was, the other followed.

The idea approaches like a summer storm. Clouds building gently at first, and then before I know it, I'm sopping wet. *Turtledoves.* Could that be it? I drop the gardening book, stumble off the ladder as I scramble for my phone. "I know what we need to look for."

"Um . . . you okay?" Mason asks.

I'm too busy searching to answer.

"What is it?" He hurries to me, peering over my shoulder as I search my phone.

I pull up the photo of the old *Salem Register* article. According to Lily's ad, she was missing a locket with one turtledove on it. But turtledoves don't come on their own. They come in pairs. Both girls had received a locket. Where was Thalia's?

"We need to find the other necklace. Do you think it could be in the mermaid room?"

We stare at each other for a moment, and then we race for the stairs.

And still we must try once more. This time with the truth.

The story ended as it began, with a girl alone on an ocean shore, her destiny rising with the tide. Thalia had always known Lily was her sister, in the same way she knew the moon would empty and fill, but what she didn't know was how far Abigail would go to make sure no one else knew.

Frederick had been unwell for close to a year by then. Doctors had been consulted, and nothing could be done. The night before the debutante ball, Frederick called the girls to his study. There he asked Lily if she might like to attend school. A college in Ohio had begun admitting women, and there was a program devoted to botany. Thalia could travel as Lily's companion, and if she liked, perhaps she could find an area of study to excel in as well.

The sisters stared at each other in disbelief. Lily was ecstatic, her face shining, hair spilling from its twist, and Thalia, always the quieter of the two, could barely contain her laugh. They would no longer have to run away together. Their dreams had been handed to them as easily as the velvet box he handed to them next. Their gift was a set of golden lockets, a turtledove engraved on each. Two sisters, always together.

Lily's locket was a lovely gift, but Thalia's was a declaration. He had not said it in words, but Frederick had declared her his daughter, and with it, offered his acceptance and love. A deep feeling of relief swept over Thalia, and as she placed the locket around her neck, she felt her mother beside her, the words Sophronia had spoken over her nearly every night as a child suddenly in her ear. "All is as it is. So mote it be, today, tonight, under moon, over sea."

After dinner that night, Lily and Thalia met in the garden, their hands clasped in excitement. It was the end of childhood. They could feel it in the way the summer heat lingered in the evening air, in the sway of the willow branches around them. The morning would bring them a new world, but tonight was theirs.

They spent the night in Lily's midnight garden. Moonflowers opened, the bright yellow evening primrose and night blooming jasmine following suit. Even the night scented orchid opened to peek at the moon.

It was Lily who asked to exchange lockets. A few moments before dawn, they stood together under the willow tree, and as Lily placed her locket over her sister's heart, she made a promise. No matter what the future held, they would remain together, their hearts as intertwined as the wisteria that grew along the house. Nothing could come between them, not now, not ever.

Thalia's heart was filled with joy, and as she gazed up into the branches of the willow tree, she caught a glimpse of the future the way she sometimes did. She expected to see Lily among other young women at the school, thick books clutched to her chest, eyes heavy after a night of reading. But what she saw instead was this: a long white dress. Pink-cheeked babies. Years of dusting and soft satin slippers and stacks of teacups and books and letters.

She didn't see flowers, and she didn't see herself.

No matter how hard she looked, it was only Lily in this future. But Thalia kept that to herself. The future has always been malleable, and she didn't want to frighten her sister. Besides, dawn was already on its way, its pink hues lightening even the heaviest thoughts.

The girls stayed up nearly until dawn, and when Abigail found them the next morning in the upper room, they were fast asleep, their red hair tangled together on the pillow, their new lockets clasped around their necks.

That was the moment Abigail made her decision.

It was late in the evening, the garden full of partygoers, when Abigail, holding a valise, ordered Thalia to follow her to the moon-swept beach. They walked in silence, and when they arrived, Abigail told Thalia her options. The valise contained jewelry and money, all items that the town would soon believe Thalia had stolen. A ship sat in the harbor, paused in Salem on its way to England. Its occupants were steadily working, preparing for imminent departure. Thalia could either board the ship tonight and use the items in the valise to create a new life for herself or stay and face imprisonment.

If Thalia left, Lily would be allowed to continue with her gardens and be sent to school. If Thalia stayed, Lily would suffer. Frederick's doctors had told him he would likely not make it to the following summer, and once he was gone, Abigail would take Lily's gardens away and forbid her from attending school. Either way, Abigail would see to it that Thalia never came near her daughter again. The choice was hers.

Thalia listened quietly, and as she looked at the hardness in Abigail's eyes, she knew she was hearing truth. She also knew that Frederick would pass much sooner than everyone suspected. He had one moon cycle, maybe two before he would take his final breath, and Abigail would be the one left with all the control. If she left now, she could at least leave Lily her flowers.

Without saying a word, Thalia reached down and carefully took the valise. It was the only time she saw Abigail smile.

Abigail paid the ship's captain in gold to take the girl as a passenger without leaving a record of where she had gone. No one was meant to hear from her again.

Thalia stepped onto the ship, keeping her back to Salem and Lily. She kept her eyes fixed on the dark ocean ahead, the horizon blurring through her tears, but the moon steady above her. She would do anything to protect her sister. Even leave.

All is as it is. So mote it be, today, tonight, under moon, over sea.

As the ship pulled away from the harbor, Lily felt a shift that stopped her feet on the dance floor. It was as though the world had suddenly tilted on its axis. She went to the kitchen to look for Thalia, but was only met with her mother, who insisted she return to the party.

When the party was over and Thalia was discovered missing, Lily became frantic. By morning, the entire town knew the story. Thalia, the young woman who had been so kindly taken in by the Bells, had succumbed to vanity and jealousy, and then the night of the ball had shown her true colors by stealing from the family and then escaping into the night.

The curse came later.

As Lily became more and more heartsick, her garden fell into ruin, and soon rumors swirled that the young witch had stolen more from the Bells than just their valuables; she had stolen Lily's extraordinary gift. Some said Thalia had left her curse written in soot in front of the family's hearth. Two women claimed to have seen an X drawn in blood across Lily's favorite rosebushes. One man claimed to have seen Thalia standing in the shadows during the party, arms overhead, mumbling a curse as Lily danced.

Sometimes, the truth of a story lies only in how many times it's told, and the Bell family curse took root as quickly and as wildly as the willow tree in Lily's garden. If you were a Bell woman, you were cursed. Even if you claimed not to believe in it, you carried it with you—if only in the curve of your hip or the restlessness in your heart.

But the curse's real tragedy was the effect it had on the relationships between the Bell women. No matter how deeply you loved your sister or mother, aunt or cousin, grandmother or daughter, the curse wound its way in, pulling at the relationship's roots and blotting out the sun. If you were a Bell woman, you expected to lose the one you loved most.

The last story is ours. You know where to find it.

28

Mason

Willow looks like she's had the wind knocked out of her. The letter was in the jewelry box, pressed into its own velvet-lined drawer, the locket's chain carefully wrapped around the sealed letter. After reading the letter, Willow holds the locket for a long time, running her thumb carefully over the engraving of the turtledove before opening it.

"It's empty," she says, passing it over to me.

The locket looks old, tarnished, and slightly dented on one side, but it's still beautiful, and intricate, with its delicate chain and tiny hinges. The turtledove has its wings extended, its beak tilted upward. "I don't think they had time to put a picture in it."

"So this one was Thalia's," Willow says thoughtfully. She takes a deep breath. "Would it be weird if I put it on?"

"I think you have to."

I hand it to her and she attempts to put it on, but after a moment of trying, she looks up, meeting my eye in the mirror. "The clasp is really small. Can you . . . ?" She hands the necklace to me, then turns to look in the mirror, sweeping her hair up off her neck, and I realize what she is asking. She wants me to put the necklace on her. Which is fine. Except I've never put a necklace on anyone before, and I've certainly never put a necklace on someone who looks like Willow.

I can do this.

I step in close, my hands steady as I settle the pendant on her chest and fit the chain around her neck, but then I catch sight of her watching me through her lashes in the mirror, and her skin is hot under my fingers, and suddenly I'm fumbling even worse than she was. How do people do this?

After an embarrassing number of attempts, I manage to get the clasp in place, and then quickly let go. The locket slides into place, framed by her clavicle and bringing out the copper tones in her hair. It looks like it was always meant to be hers.

"Perfect," I manage. We meet eyes in the mirror, and for a moment I feel something—but that's not quite right, because it isn't a something. It's more like the absence of a nothing. The big, empty feeling I walk around with all the time, the deep, dark hole I'm constantly trying not to fall into, is gone. And for a moment I feel okay with being exactly where I am. I'm not with my mom, but I am in a house, with a girl, and her eyes are so pretty in the mirror, it hurts.

Willow drops my gaze. "That story was really hard. I can't get the image of her standing on the beach out of my mind. I can't believe how horrible Abigail was."

"It sounds like she was a survivor. People do really crazy things when they're scared to lose what is important to them." A flood of my own crazy things come to mind. Like the time I ran away in the middle of the night at eleven with no money and no plan. I'd been trying to make it to a Greyhound bus station, walking on a dark country road, when two men with a dark storm cloud hanging over them tried to pick me up. I'd ended up running into the woods and I was lucky they hadn't followed me. I know now how stupid it was—I didn't even know where I was running to, exactly—but at the time, nothing had felt more dangerous than not trying to be with my mom.

Was that how Abigail had felt? Like she might lose her family?

Also, I don't know why I'm relating to Abigail on this. Thalia and Lily's story is so heartbreaking and tragic, it feels impossible to look at it squarely in the face.

"I get what Sage means," Willow says slowly. Her hand is on the locket now. "About female relationships."

"What do you mean?"

She turns around to face me. "My mom and I . . ." Her expression falls. "It isn't great. Like it really isn't great. For a while I thought our relationship was kind of normal. I knew it always hurt, but I thought maybe everyone's did. Then I started watching my friends' relationships with their mothers, and it looked so different. Like maybe they don't always get along, but at least they see each other, you know? With my mom, it's like she's a million miles away at all times, and anytime I take a step toward her, she takes three steps backward."

Willow's words are coming out so slowly and painfully, it makes my chest ache. My mom has a giant rap sheet of issues related to parenting, but I'd always felt close to her. Sometimes I'd felt smothered by her closeness. She was constantly fiddling with my hair, asking me about my day, trying to come up with new and fancy ways of making macaroni and cheese. Even now, she's constantly in my peripheral vision.

"That sounds really painful," I say. I lean in slightly, put my hand on her shoulder, and I feel her muscles loosen.

"Yeah." She's twirling the locket now, her eyes shiny. I look away, giving her a moment. "Sorry," she says.

"Nothing to be sorry about." As I look down at the letter, a thought occurs to me. "Do you think the curse is partly to blame?"

She's swiping her other eye now. "But the curse was made up by Abigail."

"Right, but the letter said that the curse's power comes from believing that you're cursed, right? So what if your mom thinks the curse is real and it makes it hard for her to get close to you because she's so afraid she'll lose you?"

She's quiet for a long moment. "Maybe." She brushes her eyes quickly.

"The problem with that is that in the meantime, while she's trying not to lose you, she is anyway."

"Yeah." Her voice is barely above a whisper. She bobs her head, and we're quiet, but the silence is full. There are so many ways a relationship can go wrong, it's amazing we keep trying at all.

"We should probably go," Willow says, reaching for the locket's clasp. "If that guy who keeps showing up is as eager as he seems, he may want Simon to do a showing right away."

Willow's eyes are still a bit watery, but she looks calmer now.

"You should keep that necklace," I say. "Especially if your mom is planning to sell everything in the house. It's like your souvenir."

"Maybe," she says quietly.

I'm desperate to not leave the house, but more than that, I'm desperate at the thought of no longer being with Willow. "Hey, do you maybe want to hang out a little bit longer?"

"Definitely." She slips the locket under her shirt. "You're right. I'm going to keep this."

We end up at the Star Wars pizza place that Emma told us about, and while we split a pepperoni droid (a small and medium pizza put together to look like BB-8), we discuss our next move.

Willow holds up her phone. "Violet texted back. The aunts have no idea what the last line of Sage's letter is referring to." She sighs, then takes an enormous bite. The pizza has perked her up a lot. If she were something I was observing in the night sky, I would write that fact down for future reference. *When subject appears dim, feed her pizza and she will regain her sparkle.* Not that Willow could lose her sparkle, but I hated seeing her so sad.

"'The last story is ours. You know where to find it,'" I repeat. The tough part about this final clue is that it is so clearly geared toward Willow's mom that I'm afraid we won't be able to find it without her. Not that I want to tell Willow that.

"What if we do a really thorough job of searching the house?" she asks, but she makes a face immediately. "I know it's useless. We already did that."

"I'm honestly more worried about time," I say, making her grimace. The new FOR SALE sign feels like an enormous clock ticking down our time to find the next letter. But we can't have made it this far only to fail—Willow needs to know what happened between her mom and aunt. I, of all people, understand that.

"It says that the next letter is about them." She picks up another piece of pizza, leaving a trail of gooey cheese in her wake. "Meaning it's the most important one."

"She really hasn't told you anything about her and Sage?" Despite the fact that the conversation is revolving about a family curse, sharing a pizza with Willow is oddly normal. Like we've done it a hundred times before.

She shrugs. "Only that they haven't been in touch for a long time. And the aunts said Sage betrayed my mom. But I have no idea what that means."

She has cheese on her chin. Has cheese ever looked cute on a chin?

"Okay, let me see the letter again," I say, wiping my hands on a napkin. I've read the letter maybe eight times now, but perhaps there's something I missed.

She passes it to me, grabbing a napkin for her face. "I'm going for more root beer. Want a refill?"

"Sure, thanks."

While Willow waits at the soda machine, I scan the letter. This one is long and detailed, but besides the last paragraph, everything about this letter is about Thalia and Lily, not Willow's mom and aunt. And the clue is so personal, I doubt that anyone outside of Willow's mom would have any idea what it meant. How are we going to figure this out?

I check my phone and see I have a text from Emma. Still with Willow? My mom asked if we could bring the girls to visit her in Rockport, and Simon has a meeting. Are you ok with an evening on your own? You can invite Willow over.

Emma is seriously desperate for me to have a friend. And obviously I'm thrilled at the thought of a night alone. Yeah, I'll ask her. Having a little breathing room from the family has been good for me. I'd even heard Emma intervene in what sounded like an early-morning rehearsal wake-up call outside my bedroom door.

Willow plops down my drink on the table. "Okay, I have an idea, but I have to warn you it isn't a great idea. You'll probably laugh."

She fidgets with her straw, barely making eye contact. Now I'm all kinds of intrigued. "I won't laugh. What is it?"

"What if . . ." She exhales. "What if we use the spell the aunts gave us?"

"The spell for lost things?" I try hard not to crack a smile, but it happens anyway and Willow folds her arms across her chest defensively.

"I know it sounds ridiculous, but they did tell me I needed a helper, and they were right about that, weren't they? If they hadn't told me to ask you, we wouldn't be sitting here now."

A rush of pleasure fills my center. The way she says it makes me feel like me being here is important to her. I manage to keep my face normal. "I guess so."

"And Sage was a witch, and my mom sort of was too, at least as a teenager. Plus, the aunts are too, so maybe there is something to all this witchcraft stuff. Not to mention, they told me it was best to perform the spell close to a full moon. We're basically there, right?" Now she looks defiant.

I wipe the smile off my face. "I think close enough."

She uncrosses her arms. "So what if we go to the house tonight and try it out, and then . . . I don't know. We can search Sage's house one more time? It could be our last chance."

Casting a spell for help is obviously ridiculous, but there's no way I'm saying no to more time in the house with Willow. Or anywhere, really. "All right. I'm in."

She bites her lower lip, her cheeks still flushed. "I think I need to collect items for it, but it can't be that hard. There are spell shops everywhere. Come with me?"

I don't even bother to answer. We both know I'm going to say yes.

Finding spell supplies is embarrassingly easy in a town like Salem, and once we have everything we need we spend the rest of the day wandering around town. Willow wants to try her aunt's favorite sweet shop, and she devours a mint chip sundae served in a chocolate witch's hat while I drink a soda concoction called Witch's Brew.

At some point you'd think we'd run out of things to talk about, or places to see, or foods to try, but we don't. Willow doesn't ever get tired, and so neither do I. We walk and walk, wandering through neighborhoods and parks and alleyways, going into and out of stores, and peeking in on tourist sights. We stop for popcorn, and more sodas, and several bottles of water, and the entire time we talk.

I find out she's a night owl, she prefers vintage clothes over new clothes (more soul), and she once had a pet hamster named Angel who bit anyone who came near it.

I tell her that I'm an early bird, the only item of clothing I ever loved was a pair of red Converse sneakers that were stolen out of my locker during ninth-grade gym class, and I've never had a pet, but I always thought it would be cool to go to an animal shelter and find a big dog who needed a home.

I find out she wants a tattoo, a tiny airplane leaving a heart-shaped trail of jet fumes in its wake. I somehow end up telling her about my and my mom's favorite landlord, a woman who kept ducks and geese in her yard and would fill up kiddie pools for them to lounge in on hot days.

By the time we stop for dinner at a hot dog walk-up counter, my feet are absolutely demolished, but I feel the best I have in ages. My limbs are relaxed and loose, my face aching from all the smiling. Salem is interesting, but I have the feeling we could tour the waiting room of a dentist's office and still have an amazing time. I don't ever want this day to end.

We decide on a joint alibi and I send a text to Emma. We're going to a movie at Cinema Salem. Should be out around ten

Emma texts me back. Enjoy! Zoe wants me to tell you that tomorrow is opening night, so if you don't come home I'll know why ;)

Even texting Emma feels fine today.

"Okay?" Willow asks.

"Okay." Her hand is swinging by her side, and before I realize what I'm doing, I reach out and take it.

She looks up at me in surprise, then laces her fingers through mine, and we head for the house.

I don't have many days in my life that I'd like to repeat, but I could live in this one forever.

❀ ❀ ❀

SPELL FOR LOST THINGS

By Violet, Marigold, and Poppy Bell

Items needed:

• Paper and pen

• Chime candle, blue or black, with candlestick

• Clay or porcelain bowl

• Dried thyme

• Chalk for drawing circle

Instructions:

Spell best performed during full moon with a partner.

Sit in silence to clear mind, and then draw circle around area for casting spell.

Light candle, and by its light, write down description of every lost thing you can think of. The more lost items you add to list, the more powerful the spell will be.

Read papers aloud, then tear into strips and light them on fire in the bowl.

As the paper burns, recite the following three times:

What was lost, now is found.

Bring it to me, safe and sound.

As I will it, so mote it be.

*When only ashes are left, sprinkle sage over the
candlestick as an offering and then scatter ashes on
earth. Allow candle to burn out on its own.*

29

Willow

My day with Mason was Salem-level magic.

Maybe it's the fact that he doesn't have any connection to the rest of my life, but suddenly it feels radically important that he knows me—really knows me—and a dam bursts inside me, my words flowing out faster than I can stop them. I tell him things I've never even told Bea, about the divorce, how I'd told everyone it came as a surprise but in the split second before they told me I'd known exactly what they were going to say. About my school, where I have friends to sit with and hang out on weekends, but not the kind you expect to keep forever. I tell him about my visits to Dad's, where I stay on a pullout bed in the study across from my old bedroom, which now houses three rambunctious toddlers. I tell him about how my mom always seems to have her mind in two places.

And Mason is more than a good listener; he's a landing space. He absorbs my words, creating a soft cushion for anything I want to tell him. Even better, he opens up to me too. He tells me more about his mom and how he keeps his hair long to remind him of her. He tells me about the first place he can remember living and about a cat that slept at the foot of his bed at one of his foster homes.

We talk so much that when he reaches out to take my hand, it doesn't feel rushed or awkward the way you'd think it would with someone you've only known for a week. It feels like we've been on this trajectory all along, and it's the obvious next step. If he hadn't grabbed my hand I would have grabbed his.

And now we're up on the rooftop sitting in the center of a magic chalk circle, the moon round and mysterious, and somehow giving off more light than it ever has, about to perform a spell that will supposedly help me find a letter that will explain to me how my family's curse affected my mom and her sister.

What is my life?

"I think we're ready," Mason says. We're sitting cross-legged, facing each other, with only a little space between us for the bowl and candle. "All you."

His eyes are doing the smiley thing they do, and a tidal wave of embarrassment crashes over me. I'm having serious second thoughts. "You know, we could not do this. It isn't too late to actually go to a movie."

He leans forward, resting his hands lightly on my knees, and immediately I feel heat climb up my neck. But in a good way. I rest my hands lightly on top of his, allowing the sensation of his skin on mine to crowd out my worries. "Willow," he says sternly.

"Mason."

He squeezes my knees. "Are you kidding me? A group of witches wrote us a personalized spell. We're doing it. But obviously you have to take the lead. You're the one with witches in your family." He leans back, taking his hands with him.

He's right, the aunts wrote the spell for me. I'm not at all sure this is going to do anything, but I'm more than willing to take the chance. Maybe if I don't quite look at Mason, I'll be able to keep it together? I hold up the spell again. "Okay, I guess we start with centering. Close your eyes."

I close my eyes and settle my hands on my knees in the spots where Mason's hands had been. But then I'm thinking about Mason's hands on my legs, and the soundtrack of all the night insects chirping fills my ears. Focusing might be impossible in this situation.

We sit in silence for maybe a minute, and after a while I actually do begin to feel centered. My head is stacked over my spine, and the world outside this circle seems to melt away. I open my eyes and peek at Mason. His eyes are closed, his lips curving up slightly in that way that makes me wonder what it would be like to kiss him. Phenomenal. Magical. Life-changing.

I have to get it together.

"Okay, I think we're ready," I say. His eyes flick open and I light the candle, then carefully tear out two pieces of paper from the blank notebook I bought during our spell-ingredient gathering. "Now we write down things we've lost. Obviously, I'll write about Sage's final last letter, but the spell says to write about as many things as possible."

He taps his pen against his leg. "Like things? People?"

"I think all of it," I say. We're quiet for a moment, both of us hunched over our papers. I write *Sage's letter*, then wait for more ideas. They start small, spanning all different years of my life. *My first denim jacket. The bracelet Chloe gave me before the wedding. Fluff Bunny. Algebra textbook.* But then they start to morph from physical objects to more intangible things. *My home in Brooklyn. Feeling like I belong. My parents' marriage.* When I get to twenty, I stop. That has to be enough.

Mason is scribbling too. The chime candle is burning quickly, and when I realize it's burned nearly halfway, I clear my throat and gesture to it. "We'd better get going."

He nods, recrossing his legs. "Okay, you first."

Mason stares down at the candle flame as I read my list. I don't offer explanations for any of the items, and I feel a new sort of lightness in me as I tear up my list and place it in the bowl. I haven't actually found any of those items, but speaking them aloud makes that fact feel more okay. I want Mason to experience it too. "Your turn."

He takes a deep breath, leaning back slightly. "Mine got sort of, ah, deep."

I gesture to my scraps. "You heard mine, right?"

"Right." He exhales again, meeting my eyes self-consciously. He ruffles his hair quickly. "Okay, fine. Here goes."

Mason's list is similar to mine in that he starts with simple things, slowly building bigger. *Minecraft pillow. Copy of* Children's Atlas of the Universe. *Red Converse.*

When he gets to the last one, he pauses. "Okay, this is the big one."

I lean in slightly, but it's too dark for me to read it.

His hands are shaking lightly, the paper quivering. He takes a deep breath. "My mom."

His eyes shoot up to mine. It has clearly cost him something to say this aloud, and my throat tightens. "Because she lost custody of you," I fill in.

"No, I mean, yes, but it's more than that." He grips his paper tightly, resting his forearms on his legs. "I've actually lost her. Like I don't know where she is."

I look at him in confusion. "What do you mean?"

He shakes his head, making his hair fall into his eyes. "I used to have regular contact with her, but it's been a while now. When I lived with her, we were constantly moving, switching states and jobs, everything. I know she went to jail at some point, and also that she was in a rehab center, but now no one knows. She was also homeless off and on. So I don't know if she's on the streets or safe or what. My foster care worker doesn't know either, so I don't have any way of finding her."

The tightness in my throat intensifies. This is the big secret he's been carrying. I have no words for him, so I reach out and grab his hand, squeezing it tightly. "What about Emma and Simon?"

He shakes his head bitterly. "They don't know either. Emma was friends with my mom, but they haven't spoken in a long time."

We both stare into the candle; the wind is making the flame flicker, and for a moment I'm swallowed up in what this must feel like to Mason. I've lost many things, but not like this. My mom may be distant emotionally, but I always know exactly where to find her. I hold on tightly until Mason releases my hand.

His voice is halting. "I found an address at Emma's house that made me wonder if she might have been in a rehab program in Florida at some point, but I e-mailed them and didn't hear back. I've also been reaching out to people she's friends with on social media. I feel like I've done everything I know how to do. And it still isn't enough. I think it would take actual magic to find her."

I'm not so sure about actual magic, but it seems to be the only thing we have right now. "What's her full name?"

"Naomi Grace Greer."

I tear out another sheet of paper and write her name in big letters. The aunts didn't say I could ask the moon for things, but they did say I could follow my own intuition. I roll the paper up, then light it on fire and look up at the moon. "Please help us find Naomi Grace Greer. Mason needs her."

The paper catches fire quickly and I drop it in the bowl, and we watch the paper darken and curl before letting off white smoke. Our chime candle is nearly out, so I grab a pinch of dried sage and sprinkle it over the candle, making the flame sputter. I read from the spell. "'What was lost, now is found. Bring it to me, safe and sound. As I will it, so mote it be.'"

Mason's head is down, so I can't see his expression, but the words hang suspended between us, the moment full.

I press Thalia's necklace close to my heart as we watch the candle flame work its way to the bottom, finally going out with a little wink and rush of smoke. We sit in silence for a moment, watching the smoke wind its way upward in circular patterns, moonlight forming a puddle around us.

Once the smoke disappears, Mason leans in. "You know what tonight feels like?"

My mind immediately answers for me. *Like watching lightning bugs float in the darkness. Like the moment when the edge of the ocean meets your bare feet. Like that first rumble of thunder from a full sky.* And it isn't because of the spell or the letters or even my aunt's magical house. It's because of Mason.

I look up quickly, searching his eyes for some sign that he's feeling the same thing. But he's looking down at the melted candle wax, his gaze calm. "What?" I manage.

He pauses, then draws his eyes up to mine. "It feels like a beginning."

It takes a moment to sink in, but then my chest is hot, a star growing larger and larger. He means a beginning like us. And this realization is so big and bursting, so completely right, that it completely outshines every other reason I'm here. Whether or not we find the letter, I know for a fact that Mason and I are meant to be on this rooftop right at this moment.

"I know," I say, and then a smile spreads across his face, and neither of us looks away, the moment charged and full.

Mason stands, then puts his hand out and pulls me to my feet.

We're both smiling at each other, the night air pressing us gently toward each other. "Come on. Let's go find the letter."

I follow him, my hand tight in his. The letter suddenly feels very small compared to what is happening between us.

This is happening, isn't it? It's so unexpected and perfect, I almost can't believe it's real. How is it possible I stumble upon a boy on a rooftop one night, and it's *Mason*? Does real life work like this?

We don't make it all that far. Mason climbs down the ladder first, me following, but when he gets to the bottom, I hear him stop, and when I turn to see what he's doing, he's waiting with a hand on either side of the ladder. I lower myself a few more rungs, then turn around, pressing my back into the ladder. Moonlight from the rooftop window is shining down on us like a spotlight, lighting up his face, and for once Mason and I are eye to eye. The mermaid painting is over his shoulder, and even though it's barely an outline in the darkness, suddenly I am very aware of Thalia's ocean.

Neither of us looks away.

It's only a few seconds that we stand there, but it's all it takes for the swirling in my center to rise, the ocean waves to crash in hard. I feel the craggy rock against my skin, salt air whipping through my hair, and an urgency and boldness that is brand-new.

I know what I want. I want Mason.

The first kiss is easy. As soon as I find Mason's mouth in the darkness, he presses into me, my arms making their way around his neck while his encircle my waist. It's the second kiss that builds in heat until Mason is leaning up against me, the ladder hard against my back, and I've lost absolutely every thought except for this. My body was made to melt into his—his back warm under my hands, his mouth soft against mine. Mason is carefully lifting me off the ladder, mouth still on mine, when I hear it.

Deep in the house a door opens, and then a voice. "Willow?"

It's my mom. In the house.

My brain is having a hard time reconciling these two things together.

One minute I'm completely wrapped up in Mason, prepared to spend the absolute rest of my life kissing him, the next I'm in a full-fledged panic, reality hitting me starkly in the darkness.

My mom knows I'm here. And it isn't going to be pretty.

Mason freezes, his hands firm on my waist, his posture hypervigilant. I don't want him to get in trouble. Not when he was helping me.

"Go up on the roof," I say. "I'll keep her busy while you climb down."

For a split second I see him think it over, then he shakes his head calmly. Firmly. "I'm not leaving you here."

"Willow? Mason?" my mom yells. She's on the stairs now.

Too late anyway. I remember the spell on the roof, the circle. Panic courses through me. If she sees it, she'll know exactly what it is, and I'll never spend time here again. "Don't tell her what we were doing."

"Kissing?" I can see his smile in the darkness, and for one moment I completely forget about the impending doom headed toward me in the form of Mary Haverford.

A laugh bursts out of me and I raise my fingers to my lips. Mason's smile grows. "I meant casting spells. But don't tell her that either."

"Or . . . we could run away together?" I know he's joking, but his voice has this perfect vulnerable edge to it, and before I know it, my mind kaleidoscopes me forward into a series of images. Me burrowed in my bed while I talk on the phone to Mason deep into the night. Me visiting Mason on a busy college campus, his sweatshirt tied around my waist. More ladder situations.

For once I can see something concrete in my future that isn't travel. It's him. Mason is going to be part of my future, no matter what is about to happen.

"Mason—" I start, but I don't know how I'm going to tell him that, if I should tell him that, but the words are crowning up in my throat. How do I tell him *Everything in my future feels fuzzy except for you*?

It's way too soon for that. But here's the thing: It wouldn't scare him. I know it wouldn't. Because it's *Mason*.

"It's going to be okay," I finally manage.

"Willow." The door flies open and the room floods with light. For a moment Mason and I blink at each other before turning to look at my mom in the doorway. She is wearing her usual tailored blazer, her hair smooth. When she sees me, her shoulders round forward, her body sagging in relief.

"Mom," I say weakly.

But her relief doesn't last long. Her eyes trail over the room, taking in the bed, the ladder, the rug, before finally landing on the painting. For one moment I wonder if this might be okay, if she's going to be so overwhelmed by the beautiful house that she'll forget about the fact that I'm not supposed to be here, but then she clenches her jaw and whirls on me, sending my hope scattering.

"You *promised*." Her voice is so hard, so betrayed sounding, it sends a shiver down my spine.

Mason is next to me, so close his arm is brushing mine. "It's my fault," he says, but my mom's eyes never leave mine.

"Mom, I know, but the aunts told me about these letters and—"

She cuts me off. "I told you that I needed to keep this chapter in my life closed, and you completely disregarded that." My mom's face is angry, but it's her hurt that is really stabbing me in the chest. She feels like I've betrayed her. Have I betrayed her?

No. This is my story too.

I swallow hard. "Mom, I . . ." I don't know how to finish it. How do I get her to understand how important this place is to me?

She wraps her arms around herself tightly, her gaze firm on mine. "What are you even doing here?"

"We were exploring. It was my idea," Mason says quickly. "I'm really sorry, Ms. Haverford, I wanted to stargaze on the roof—" She turns her blazing gaze on Mason and he quickly closes his mouth.

She turns back to me. "Willow, we're leaving."

"Okay, I'll meet you back at the hotel," I say quickly.

"No, I mean we're leaving Salem. Phoebe booked us a flight for tomorrow morning."

My heart sinks faster than I thought possible. Mason and I exchange a look. He looks resolved, like he knew all along that this is what would happen. But I can't accept that. "Tomorrow? But what about the house?"

She shakes her head. "I got an offer an hour ago. I went to the theater to wait for you to get out so I could tell you the news, but there wasn't a movie playing." She looks around the room now, her eyes pausing on the mermaid.

Panic is building in my body, setting my chest on fire. I can't leave tomorrow. Not before finishing the story. I can't go back to my regular life, the one where I'm trying desperately to find somewhere that I belong. Here in Salem I'm grounded, steady. I'm not going to give that up easily.

Resolve makes me brave. "We need to talk about this. All of this." I spin, gesturing to the room. "I know about the curse."

"The curse." She slumps back against the wall, folding her arms over her chest. "Willow, that 'curse' destroyed my family. I'm not letting it come between us."

"Mom, it's already come between us." How can she not see this? She blinks a few times, and her silence makes me brave enough to push again. "You've been lying to me about your past and our family for years. And its created so much distance." I take a deep breath. "What happened between you and Sage?"

She's silent for a moment, then she straightens, dropping her arms to her side. "Willow, it's in the past. What happened here has nothing to do with you."

It feels like a slap. Tears well up in my eyes. "It has everything to do with me. This is my family history too. I haven't felt home in so long. But ever since I got here . . ." I take a deep breath. "It feels like I found the thing I was missing. Please don't take it away."

Her face is softening, and for a moment I feel hope. "Willow, I'm so sorry. The divorce was so hard, and you were so brave to move and leave everything behind. I've been working so hard to build a new life for you, but I'm afraid I've pushed you out in the process." She walks forward, resting her hands on my shoulders. "We'll work on home. But Salem isn't it, okay?"

"Mom, please." I'm genuinely pleading now. Every part of me is asking her to reach out, to listen to me. "I saw you at the willow tree the other night. I know you're hurting. Please don't shut me out anymore."

She's quiet for a long moment. "Say goodbye to Mason. I'll meet you downstairs."

Mason

After I leave the Bell house, I don't know what to do with myself.

The past few hours have been an enormous swinging pendulum of emotions. Had it all really happened?

I can't believe I told her about my mom. Sitting up there with her on the roof the loss had taken shape in front of me, its dark edges clear and defined. Normally that loss is something I can't share with anyone, but somehow it had all come spilling out to Willow. And now she's leaving. This is why I don't open up to people—they're never in my life long enough for it to matter. But even more importantly, I'm worried about her. Leaving her behind felt completely wrong. Is she going to be okay?

I pace Essex Street for about twenty minutes, too far from the hotel to get Willow into trouble but close enough that I can get to her right away if she needs me. I send her text after text.

Are you okay?

I'm on Essex.

Do you want me to come check on you?

I make my way over to the hotel, but I have no idea which window is hers. My phone dings and I scramble to pull it out of my pocket, but it's only Emma. We're back from my mom's. Headed home?

I obviously can't stay out here all night, but it takes genuine

JENNA EVANS WELCH

effort to start putting space between me and the hotel. **Yeah.**

She responds immediately. **Okay, I'm just getting into bed. Door is unlocked.**

When I get back to the house, every window is dark, and I stumble on the porch steps, making my way inside. I'm not in the mood to do a Mom search, but I force myself to go to the dining room anyway. Maybe it will get my mind off things.

I slide into the chair, my fingers automatically logging into my faux e-mail account. I have to see Willow before she and her mom leave tomorrow. Should I camp out on the steps again? Ask Simon and Emma to intervene? They might if I ask. I'm so deep in thought that it takes me several seconds before I truly see what is on the screen in front of me.

I have one new e-mail. From David Gonzalez.

My hands start trembling as I click on it.

Hello,
Thank you for your e-mail. Due to patient confidentiality, I am unable to assist you.
Best of luck,
      David Gonzalez

Another dead end.

I bang my hands against the computer desk. Why do I ever think anything will work? Why do I think anyone will ever come through for me? Shouldn't I know better by now? No matter what I do, everyone lets me down.

A heavy blend of emotions is filling me up, squeezing out my breath. I force myself to inhale, try to form a coherent string of thoughts. Does this e-mail mean my mom was a patient? Would he have said so if she wasn't? And if Emma was involved in her treatment somehow, then why doesn't she know where my mom is now? Shouldn't she have some kind of information?

I need to start searching, looking for more people to contact, but anger is making my chest tight, rage turning my head fuzzy. Why will no one help me? And more importantly, why will no one help her? My mom can't get better if she doesn't have support, but our lives are absolutely full of red tape. No matter where I go there's another barrier to getting back to my mom. Is that why she's gone dark? Because it feels hopeless to her, too?

But she wouldn't give up on me. I know she wouldn't. And more importantly, I won't give up on her. I pull up her social media profile, start scrolling, flipping through the contact names that are now familiar. Felix Reyes. Chad Baker. Anika Henderson. Someone has to know where my mom is. Could it be one of them? I'm clicking so fast that it takes me several moments to notice that I have a notification for one new message. I click on it quickly, and when I see who it's from, I freeze. *Brody West.* He's one of the strangers I contacted last time around.

I click on the message. Yo, haven't seen your mom in a long time but last time I saw her is at Marcus place in Newark. Ivy Apartments on Franklin. Good luck

I read it once. Then twice. The third time, I realize I'm not breathing.

I search for *Ivy Apartments, Franklin, Newark*, and immediately an apartment complex in New Jersey pops up. I hit Google Images, trying to zoom in, but it's a pretty nondescript building, surrounded by patches of dead lawn. Is my mom here? Why is she in Newark?

Why not? my brain fills in. She moved constantly. And I have no idea who Marcus is—a boyfriend? A dealer?

My hands are no longer trembling, they're shaking. Did the spell for lost things work? And I don't have an apartment number, but the building is close enough. If she's there, I'll find her.

Now my entire body is shaking. I grip the edge of the desk, waves of nausea moving through me as I remind myself that it's *inhale, then exhale. Inhale, then exhale.*

And then I have another terrible thought.

What if she's moved already? We never stayed anywhere long. The longest we ever stayed anywhere was six months. It hits me then, hard. I have to go there. *Now.* Before it's too late.

My hands are still shaking as I check bus schedules, train schedules, prices of cabs. Within a few minutes, I have a plan. I'll take the early train from Salem to Boston, and then board a bus to New York at 6:30 a.m., where I'll transfer to another bus headed to New Jersey. If everything goes right, I'll be in Newark by noon. All together the trip will cost me eighty-seven dollars, which I have, thanks to the money Emma gave me so I could take Willow to the movie, plus money I have left over from the monthly allowance I've been getting from the foster care system since I turned fifteen. My mom's apartment will be a twenty-minute ride from the bus station. And if she isn't at the address . . .

Well, I'll figure it out from there.

This time it isn't running away. Running away means leaving your home, but I'm running *to* my home. It's completely different.

I start by putting my things in my backpack. My notebook and books, every bill and coin I have, my toothbrush, most of my clothes. I even find an old water bottle that I don't think anyone will miss and fill it up just in case. I debate taking the phone and charger, but they'll probably be able to track me with it, and besides, I don't want to take more from the Morgans than I have to.

After that, there's nothing to do but wait.

If I was in NASA preparing for a launch mission I'd be doing final safety checks. But I'm not an astronaut. I'm a seventeen-year-old in what I overheard my first foster mom call "a difficult situation," which is like saying that a goldfish has a water problem. I'm not the problem; everything else is. My life hasn't been difficult; it's been stupid. It hasn't made sense. Until now. So long as I don't think about Willow, I'm fine.

Of course, I don't sleep at all. Instead, I sit propped up on my bed, watching the clock change and listening to the sound of one of the girls snoring in the next room. They are going to be so upset about the play. I know that my running away is going to be hard on the Morgans. The girls will probably be confused and worried, and there will be a lot of questions from the foster care system and Kate/ Kaitlin, but once all of that dies down and I'm officially gone for long enough, I hope that their lives will go back to normal. Nova will even get her room back, and I'm sure the littles will find someone new to cast in their tragedy.

I don't mean to do it, but as I sit there, my brain insists on spitting out memory after memory of my time with the Morgans that no matter how hard I try, I can't quite spin as bad. Simon's endless invitations, all the dance rehearsals, the beach with Nova, Emma slipping me coffee.

In a completely different set of circumstances, the Morgans might have made me a great home. But no matter how many positive things happened, they can't be my home. My mom might be a million things I wish she weren't, but she's my sun. She's what I orbit, what I depend on to be me. Without its star, the Earth would be a lifeless ball of ice and rock. Without my mom, I'm spinning into oblivion.

It's Willow I really can't think about.

Once I leave, I won't be able to contact her. Not only would it put Willow in a bad situation; it's too risky for me and Mom. Because I've been removed from my mom's guardianship, it will actually be illegal for me to be with her, so if anyone finds out where I am, I'll be removed, and I know in my heart that I can't survive that again.

I can contact Willow after I've aged out of foster care. Maybe she'll be traveling, and I can meet her at a train station in Barcelona or on a bridge in Florence. By then, she'll probably have figured out how to keep her shoelaces tied and her hair slightly less wild, but she'll still be the same person, and we'll pick up where we left off. We'll still get our chance.

Or maybe it will be too late. Maybe you'll never see her again.

The thoughts force their way in, and I do my best to shove them back out. Our last day together was perfect. That has to count for something.

I spend a good ten minutes writing and deleting my final text to her. I want to tell her *I'll come back for you*, or at the very least *I'm sorry*, but all of those will alarm her and might tip off my plan. So instead I settle on **Good night, Willow**, which isn't quite goodbye, but it's all I can say and I hope she'll understand.

And then it's 4:45.

I don't think a note is a good idea, so I leave my worn copy of *Astrophysics for Teens*. In the front I write, *For Nova, Hazel, Zoe, and Audrey.* I put on my backpack, look at my tidy bedroom one last time. I'm about to crawl out the window when I suddenly know exactly how to say goodbye to Willow.

I take my star log out of my pocket, scribble an entry in the back, and then write her name on the front cover. WILLOW. Her name looks like it belongs there. I set the notebook carefully on the desk, my fingers lingering on its spine. This notebook has been with me for so long, it's basically part of my soul now. I can't believe I'm even considering this. But leaving it is right. I won't need it anymore, not when I'll actually be with my mom. Besides, me leaving it will let Willow know how much it means to me, and now no matter what, a piece of me will always be with her. Besides, it means I'll have to find her again.

I keep waiting for someone to stop me, but no one even gives me a second glance. Salem is dark and uninterested, and I manage to board the train without any issues. Once I get to Boston, the transfers are confusing and nerve-racking, and at one point I nearly get on a train going an entirely different direction. I think I might relax once I'm on the long train ride, but I'm so anxious that all I can do is watch the scenery rush by me. I'd planned to buy food, but my train tickets cost more than the website said they would, and I need all of the rest of the money for my cab. I sit with a growling stomach, my eyes wide open, trying my hardest not think about what must be going on back in Salem.

Will Willow think that I was lying when I told her that last night felt like a beginning? I meant it, but that was before I knew my life was about to take such a giant turn. Who will realize I'm gone first? Zoe and Audrey? Emma, when she shows up with my coffee? What will Simon think? I've never worried about what will happen when someone realizes I'm missing—at the group home it meant they had to fill out paperwork. But here with the Morgans, it's different. The girls had called me their brother. What were they going to do when I wasn't in my bed?

It's probably the sleep deprivation, but the closer we get to Newark, the more tangled my thoughts become. My emotions get dragged into it too, and soon I'm an absolute ball of stress and nerves.

My chest is tight, and I can barely form a coherent thought.

They'll know I had to do it, won't they?

By the time my train pulls into Newark, I've been awake for twenty-nine hours, but it feels like twenty thousand. I feel fuzzy and hyperalert at the same time. The woman seated across from me is drinking coffee and eating a bagel, both of which I would give my left arm for right now, and my eyes feel red and scratchy, my energy jangly, but I'm here.

I'm here.

I stand before the train fully stops and hurry to the bathroom to splash some water on my face and look in the mirror. My eyes are bloodshot, but they're bright too.

I'm about to see my *mom*. And that's worth every intense feeling racing through my chest right now.

I wait nearly twenty minutes for a cab, and when the driver pulls up he looks at me disapprovingly. I give him the address then try to relax, shutting my eyes when the stress gets too intense. It takes thirty minutes to make our way through traffic, and when the cab driver pulls up to the address, a thread of disappointment moves through me. The apartment building is old with peeling white paint and a parched lawn. The upper apartments have balconies crammed full of rusted barbecues and lawn furniture, and looking at them makes my stomach twist. I've never seen this particular apartment building, but I've known many like it. We lived in so many of them.

"This it?" my cab driver asks gruffly.

"I hope so," I mumble. I hand him most of the rest of my cash and step out, pulling my backpack after me, and the cab drives away immediately. I have twenty-seven dollars left. I try not to think about what it will mean if this isn't where my mom is. She has to be here.

The walk up to the apartment entrance feels about a million miles long, and my legs feel shaky. A dog is barking, and conceptually I know it's hot out, the sun is out and the air is thick with humidity, but I feel cold.

The apartments are a maze of peeling white buildings. A few people have tried to make them look nicer with potted plants and welcome rugs, but most of them have scuffed doors and rotting railings. I see a cat in one window, nearly have a heart attack when a dog lunges at me from behind a screen door.

I have no idea which apartment she's in. Do I start knocking on doors? Stand in the hallway and yell her name? I stop at one door with a ratty Christmas wreath attached to it. A TV blares from inside, a game show or a commercial, something with a man's heavy voice talking about the incredible deal you'll get if you call right away. Before I can lose my nerve, I knock. Then knock again.

Nothing.

The hallway's noises and smells are bringing back memories of things I thought were gone. People pounding on our door in the middle of the night. Being alone for hours with nothing but a bag of popcorn and the TV for company. My mom's eyes closed for hours on end. Acid creeps up the back of my throat, my legs wobbly beneath me.

I knock again.

Finally I hear footsteps, then a chain, and the door flies open to reveal a small old woman with yellowed teeth, her hair tucked under a shower cap. She looks up at me angrily, all but baring her teeth.

"Who are you? What do you want?"

"Sorry. Excuse me. I'm . . ." I shake my head, trying to rearrange my thoughts. "Does Naomi Greer live here?"

"In this apartment? No!" She begins to close the door, but I quickly put my hand out to stop her.

"In this apartment building. She lived here with someone named Marcus, I think. She's tall and she has long black hair. She's . . ." *An addict. Has let me down over and over.*

The woman's scowl deepens. "You can't be here. You can't just be standing around in our halls. I don't know why they let you all be here. I *know* about the drugs."

She thinks I'm an addict. Which means two things: one, she probably does know about my mom, and two, *Mom's still using.* Of course she is, but it hits me hard anyway. What was I expecting? A fairy tale? That I'd find her in this apartment with a steady job and a fridge full of groceries? I shake my head quickly. I can't deal with that now. Once I find her, I'll figure out what to do. "It's not like that. I'm supposed to meet her here, and—"

She points at me. "I'll call the police! Don't think I won't."

I put my hand against the wall, trying to steady myself. "Naomi is my mother. I'm . . ." I take a deep breath. "I'm trying to find her."

Her eyes widen behind her glasses. "God help you," she mutters. "But you can't be standing in the hallway. Get out of here before I call the police." Then she slams the door. My knees give out, and I sink down to a crouch, my heart pounding.

"Mom," I say loudly. The word rips out of me. I'm not calling her, I'm yelling at her. *Mom, why did you do this to me? Why am I standing in this hall? Why can't you get your life together?*

Rage carries me to my feet. I stand up and yell her name again. "Naomi! Naomi Greer!" I walk up and down the halls. *"Naomi."*

It's useless. It has always been useless. I throw my bag to the ground, kick it so hard it flies down the hall. I have to get out of here, before someone calls the police, before the lady comes back out, before I completely lose it and start punching holes in the wall.

I've just picked up my backpack and am rushing down the hall when I hear a door open, and then my name.

"Mason?"

I freeze. The voice is different than I remember. Cracklier. Raspier. But I remember it with every cell in my body. I force myself to turn around. Her hair is cut short, shorter than mine, and she's wearing a faded flowered dress with flip-flops. She looks awful, thin, with sunken eyes and cheekbones, arms and legs skinny as twigs. This woman is a mere shadow of my mom.

But it's *her*.

I can't move. "Mom," I whisper.

Her mouth falls open. "Mase. It's really you." She starts to move toward me, one arm outstretched, but stops herself before she actually touches me. Her eyes are glazed, unfocused, and they sweep up my frame. "I can't believe you're this tall. Jesus, you're an adult."

But I'm not an adult, and I want her to say something more than me being tall. "Mom . . . I found you. Finally." My eyes are getting hot, my voice thick. I can't believe she's here. Right here. After all this time.

I walk toward her, but she takes a step back. "Mason, what are you doing here?"

Her tone makes me freeze again. "What do you mean? I'm here to find you," I say. "Isn't that obvious?"

"How did you find me?" This time her tone is unmistakable. It isn't a happy *I can't believe you found me!* It's a *You weren't supposed to find me.* My mom hasn't only been hiding from the foster care system—she's been hiding from me.

My insides turn to ice. This can't be happening. She must be too surprised, or maybe this is bad timing. All she needs is some time to adjust. "I . . . I found someone online who knew where you were.

I came to find you. I thought you needed me. . . ." I'm light-headed, stars erupting in the corners of my vision.

She falls back against the dirty wall, her gaze on my left shoulder. "You're supposed to be with Emma."

My heart thumps so hard, I'm surprised it doesn't burst out of my chest. "You knew where I was? This whole time?" I manage a shuddery breath. There has to be an explanation for this. Something that will make my mom knowing where I was *okay*. "Mom, I've been looking for you for so long. No one would tell me where you were. Why didn't you contact me?"

She's quiet for a long time. "You need to go back to Salem, okay? Go back with Emma. I need that."

"What?" The ground is tilting out from under me, and my vision blurs. She has to be joking. Why would she say that? "But, Mom, I found you. We can be together now—"

"No. Mase—" She holds up her hand. "I can't. You have to go."

No. No no *no*. I stare at her in disbelief, the seconds passing through me like tiny knives. This can't be happening. This must be a nightmare, or she's high and she doesn't know what she's saying. She doesn't want me to leave. All she needs is time.

I step forward and she instantly recoils. An action I have to ignore if I'm going to remain intact. "Mom, let's go inside and—"

"Mason, *no*. It's better for you to not be with me. I'm trying to give you a chance." Her voice is steadier than I've ever heard it, and the surety of it hurts more than the words.

"Mom, give me a chance now." Hot tears are blinding my eyes. "You don't even have to take care of me. I'm almost seventeen, I can take care of myself. I'll work, and I'll help pay rent and for groceries. You won't have to do anything."

Her eyes are huge, but she isn't looking at me, she's looking down at the dirty linoleum, arms crossed tightly. She begins shaking her head.

"Mom?" My voice sounds strangled, tight. I don't know how to make sense of what is happening right now. I belong with my mom; my mom belongs with me. All these years she's been promising to get clean, to get her life on track so we can be together. What have all these years been for if it wasn't for us to finally be reunited?

"Mason, I can't." Her voice is so quiet, it could be a whisper. "You deserve more." Then before I can say anything else, she walks past me into her apartment, closing the door firmly behind her.

31

Willow

Once we get back to the hotel, I shut myself in my room and I cry for what feels like hours. It's all pretty clear now. My obsession with my family's history, Sage's house, the letters, all of it has been about one thing: my mom.

The Bell family curse is about female relationships breaking apart under forces that hadn't been entirely under their control. And now history is repeating itself. I can't control my mother. Our relationship is broken.

And I'm not even close to being okay with that.

Hours later, I wake to my phone ringing loudly. According to the space around my curtains, it's not quite morning, and it takes me several moments of fumbling to finally locate my blaring phone on my nightstand. But when I see the name on the screen my confusion is replaced with a little rush of pleasure. Mason.

Mason, who I kissed. I can almost feel his lips on mine and for a moment I smile, because last night was so good, so right, how I'd folded into him, how his hands had felt in my hair. Regardless of how terrible the night had ended up, being with Mason had felt exactly right.

"Hi," I say, my voice scratchy with sleep.

"Willow, is Mason with you?" The voice is decidedly not Mason's.

It takes a moment for my brain to figure out who the hyperalert woman's voice belongs to. Emma. Why is Emma calling me on Mason's phone?

"What?" Sleep flies away from me. "No. Why? Is everything okay?"

She exhales into the speaker. "No, it's really not."

"What do you mean?" I lean over to switch on my lamp, but my legs are tangled up in my sheets, and all I manage to do is send an empty cup crashing from my nightstand.

"Willow?" My mom opens our connecting room, flooding my room with light. She's wearing pajamas, but she looks wide-awake, like she hadn't actually been asleep. "Who is it?"

I point to the phone. "Emma."

Mom's eyebrows knit together in concern. "Is everything all right?"

"When did you see him last?" Emma asks in my ear.

My stomach tightens. I don't want to get Mason in trouble for sneaking over to the house with me, but something tells me I need to tell her the truth. People don't call at this hour without a good reason. "Last night. We were . . . together at my aunt's house. And then he said he was going home." My mom crosses the room and sits next to me on the bed.

"Did he tell you anything about running away?"

Her words hit me like a bucket of ice water, and for a moment I'm too stunned to think. I must be misunderstanding somehow. Is she saying that Mason ran away? Because there's absolutely no possible way that can be true. "What are you talking about?" Panic is rising slowly but surely in my throat.

"He took his books and some clothes. He left his phone. And also . . ." Her voice is tight, like she's been crying, and now my throat is closing in on itself. "He left gifts. For the girls and you."

My heart slams against my chest. "That—that can't be true," I stutter. "I'm sure he's just stargazing or something. Have you checked my aunt's house?"

My mom takes the phone from me now, pressing it to her ear. "Emma, this is Mary. What's going on?" She listens for a moment. "Willow and Mason have been spending time at the house together. I think we'd better go over and check it out. Can we meet you there? Okay, see you in a minute."

"Mom, he didn't run away," I say. "He couldn't have."

Her face is lined with worry. She reaches over and clasps my hand tightly for a moment. "You really didn't know? Because I know how important it is to kids to honor each other's trust. But in this case, the right thing to do is tell an adult." She's studying my eyes.

"I really don't know anything." A big, shuddery sob works its way to my throat. "If I did, I would tell you."

She nods, squeezing my hand tighter. "All right. Willow, you're going to be okay. I'm right here with you, and you aren't going to be alone in this."

I notice she doesn't say Mason is going to be okay, or even that the situation will be okay. She says *you* will be okay. My eyes flood with tears, and for a moment I'm drifting again, my body and heart desperate to find something to hold on to. But then my mom squeezes my hand, and my feet find footing again. "Okay."

She stands, taking back her hand and resting it gently on the crown of my head for a moment. "Now let's go help Emma and Simon look for him."

By the time we pull on our clothes and race to Sage's house, dawn has turned the sky a light, happy pink that is completely incongruous with the way I feel. My phone had a single text from Mason. **Good night, Willow.** What does that mean? And why was there only one text? He never sends just one.

My mom and I are silent the entire way, and for once I'm able to match her fast walk without any trouble. Emma and Simon are on the doorstep waiting for us, and I can tell by their heavy expressions that they haven't found Mason inside the house.

"He's not here," Simon says, and my heart falls even further.

I look up at the house, marveling at how normal it seems. How can it look normal when the entire world has fallen apart? "Did you check the roof?"

He nods. "No sign of him."

Emma steps off the porch, her concentration on me. "Willow, things get very dangerous very quickly for kids who run away. I've already called the police and his social worker, and they're on their way. But the longer he's gone, the more dangerous it is. Is there anything you can think of that would help us figure out where he went?"

I wrack my brain, but nothing is coming up. "I don't know," I manage.

"Is it possible he didn't run away?" my mom asks. "Could he be out for a walk or a bike ride or something?"

"He has a history of running away," Simon says.

My face snaps up to his, shock exploding in my chest. "What do you mean?"

Emma exhales. "Mason has had a few difficult placements, and he's run a few times. The foster care system was concerned about us taking him in, but they decided to give it a shot because of the personal connection I had with his mom."

I am spinning out, my head racing in circles. Mason never

mentioned anything about running away; his notebooks didn't talk about it either. "I don't understand," I say.

"Where did he run to before?" my mom asks.

"Friends' houses, youth shelters, parks . . ." Emma says. "Once he made it to a halfway house where his mom had stayed, but she wasn't there anymore."

My stomach lurches, thinking of Mason searching for his mother and not finding her.

Simon adds, "Most kids try to run back home, but Mason doesn't have a home to go back to . . ." He trails off, and now I'm sure we're all thinking the same thing. Mason could be headed *anywhere*, which makes this search so much scarier.

Emma wraps her arms around herself. "We know he came home around eleven, because I heard him come inside. But I don't know how soon he left after that. His window was slightly open, so I think that's how he left."

"That was right after he left the house." I look at my phone. It's almost six, which means about seven hours have passed since I saw him last. How far could he have gone? A line from his star log comes back to me. *The Earth is traveling at thirty kilometers per second.* Very, very far. Especially if he could have radiated out in any direction.

"What were you kids doing at the house?" Emma asks.

All the adults eyes turn to me and my face burns. "We were looking for letters. My aunt . . . she left this trail of letters that we had to follow clues to find. They were all about my family's history. Mason was helping me."

My mom has gone completely still beside me. I'm careful not to look at her. "We couldn't find the last letter, so last night we did a magic spell up on the roof. My great-aunts wrote it for us."

Emma and Simon stare at me in confusion, but my mom's voice comes clear and steady. "What kind of spell?"

"It was called a spell for lost things. We were supposed to make lists of things we'd lost."

"What did he list?" my mom asks.

"Lots of things. Shoes and books and stuff. And then he told me about his mom. He said he didn't know where she was and he'd been trying to find her. He said he was researching jail databases and looking anywhere he could online for information about her. And earlier this week he found an envelope with an address of a rehab facility, so he'd e-mailed the director." My fuzzy brain is piecing it together now. "But he said the director hadn't e-mailed him back."

Emma and Simon exchange a long look.

"Do you know where he is?" I ask, hope pulling up the edges of my voice.

"No. But my guess is that he found her. We'd better do the same. Thank you, Willow." Emma hesitates. "He left something for you."

My spine snaps straight. "What is it?"

She reaches into her bag, and when I see the worn blue cover of Mason's notebook, a giant wave of panic rises up inside of me. WILLOW has been scrawled on the front. He wrote my name on his notebook? I know how important it is to him. Did he really leave it for me?

"Oh," I say, my throat tight. Emma holds the notebook out to me, and I take it, gripping it tightly between my thumbs and fingers.

"What is it?" my mom asks.

I take a deep breath. "It's what he keeps track of his stargazing in. It's really important to him."

"Which means *you* are very important to him," Emma says, her expression unreadable. "I read through it in case it had any clues, but

I didn't find anything. There's an entry about you in the back."

My throat tightens even more. I want to flip it open immediately, but I'm too anxious to do that in front of everyone. "We need to find him."

"We'll find him," Simon says, but Emma's face is telling another story. My throat is aching now. They'll find him, won't they?

"We'll check in," my mom says. "And please let us know if there's anything we can do to help in the meantime."

"We appreciate that, Mary," Simon says, his shoulders sagging. It's alarming to see his energy so dimmed.

Emma pulls me in for a tight, crushing hug, and for a moment I'm too surprised to react, then she releases me and she and Simon sprint for the car, and a moment later they're gunning up the street.

My mom and I stand in the nighttime quiet for a few seconds, the only sound coming from the insects. My brain is an absolute tangle, but when I look up at the dark sky, I know something for sure. The stars existed without Mason and they'll exist after him, but to me, the constellations make zero sense without him. Without Mason they're just a random smattering of stars.

I make my way up the walkway so I can flip through his notebook under the porch light. I find it on the very last page.

> _Things that Willow and the Night Sky Have in Common:_
> _1. Beautiful_
> _2. Unpredictable_
> _3. Makes you glad to be alive._

After I read the entry, I sink down onto the porch, my mom huddling beside me, and I bury my face in my knees, tears finally spilling down my face. Mason is really gone. This entry was goodbye.

I keep going back to the thing he said on the roof. *This feels like a beginning*. Was that all it was, the *feeling* of a beginning? He must have known by then that he'd be leaving, which meant that last night's kiss was goodbye. But that isn't what it felt like, and it isn't what I want. I've known him for such a tiny blip of time, but I feel like there could have been something big between us, and all I want is the chance to figure that out. I want that for us. I want that for *me*. And now it's very possible I'll never even get that chance.

Eventually, I run out of tears, and when I look over at my mom, I'm startled to see that her eyes are as red as mine. "Mom?"

"I'm sorry. It's just . . ." She pulls her knees into her chest. "This is how Sage left."

A tingle runs down my spine, making me sit up straight. "What do you mean?"

She looks back at the house. "The year that Aunt Daisy died was really hard on Sage. It was hard on me too, but Sage couldn't cope at all. I was constantly getting calls to come pick her up from parties and bars. She even got arrested. It wasn't like her, and I was so worried about her. And then the night of Aunt Daisy's wake, she left."

My mind is searching for some way into this. Aunt Sage's house and her letters had given me a glimpse into who she was, and she didn't seem like someone who would abandon her sister. "Why did she leave?"

She shakes her head. "I don't know. All I found was a note that said 'Forgive me.' And that was the last I ever heard of her." She sighs, tapping her feet against the ground. "I spent months trying to find her, but she'd vanished. The Bell family curse in action, I guess."

Shock and sadness are spreading through my chest. "So you lost your aunt and your sister." And now I'm thinking of Sage's letter.

No matter how deeply you loved your sister or mother, aunt or cousin, grandmother or daughter, the curse wound its way in, pulling at the relationship's roots and blotting out the sun. If you were a Bell woman, you expected to lose the one you loved most. The curse may not have been what she thought it was, but it had stripped her of what she loved anyway. She'd been carrying that pain my entire life.

"And my mom. And . . . a relationship too." She glances over at the house next door and I remember what Marigold had said during the moon ceremony. *It's always a boy.* I'm dying to ask her about him, but I'm scared if I interrupt her that she'll lose her momentum.

She sighs again. "Losing Sage was the absolute worst thing that ever happened to me. Harder than the divorce, harder than losing my mom, all of it. I think because I was left with so many questions. It was so painful here, I had to leave. I never thought I'd come back."

I'm holding my breath, my heart heavy. No wonder my mom hated it here so much. It reminded her of all the worst parts of her life.

She leans into me slightly. "Willow, I'm so sorry I didn't tell you before. You were right about me being afraid. Everyone I loved left me at some point, but that wasn't your burden. I'm sorry it affected you so much."

My heart is bursting. And now that she's opened up to me, it's my turn to open up to her.

I take a deep breath. "After the divorce . . . it's like you went dark on me. We used to be so close, but then we moved to LA and it was like you turned into a stranger. And I miss you. I really, really miss you." As soon as I say the words, I feel them, deep down in my chest.

Her eyes are welling up now. "When I got pregnant with you, I was so scared of messing up the way my mother did that I decided I was going to be the perfect mother. I bought all the books and went to all the classes. I was going to get motherhood right. But none of those books tell you that motherhood is one long goodbye. From the moment your child is born, you are preparing them to leave you. It's the entire goal."

She looks up at the house. "Willow, I'm so sorry about our fight back home. When you told me about your idea to spend your senior year in Paris, I panicked. I knew graduation was coming soon, but the thought of it coming a whole year earlier ..." She exhales, and my heart tightens, and suddenly my brain is repatterning every interaction I've had with my mom over the past few years. She's been so distant and worried. Most of all, she's been afraid because she doesn't want me to leave. She really, really doesn't.

She looks up at me. "Tonight might not be the right time, but there's something I wanted to talk to you about. I'm not quite ready for you to leave. Not yet. So last night, after our fight, I called Bea's mom for advice. She knows of a summer program for new high school graduates. It starts in Paris, but they'd take you to nearly a dozen other countries."

Surprise plummets through me, but when I meet her eye, she looks like herself. Determined. Steady. "Really?" I ask cautiously.

"Really. Here, look." She pulls up the website on her phone and hands it to me, and I watch the website's revolving photos in shock for a moment. The Netherlands. Croatia. Poland. Switzerland. Bulgaria. The program is literally called "Find Your Place in the World: A Program for College Freshmen."

"I'd love to send you to that," she says. "It would be a good first step to traveling on your own. And it means I get to keep you for another year."

My heart is overflowing now, and I'm not sure if it's from the surprise or from her saying she wants me home for another year. "Mom, this is ..." I take a deep breath. "I mean, obviously I'll have to get accepted first, but it sounds perfect."

"You'll get accepted. And this program will be only the beginning for you." She has a small smile on her face. "I never tell anyone this, but Daisy taught me to read palms. I saw your future a long time ago."

Surprise sparkles through me. "Really? Are you serious?"

"Let me show you."

I hold out my hand, and she cups it in hers, tracing her finger along the center of my palm. "This big line is your lifeline. Yours is extremely long, which reflects all of the energy and enthusiasm you have for life. That's your Willowness."

Willowness. I feel like I'm glowing from the inside out, tears prickling in my eyes again. "I really like that."

She squeezes my hand slightly. "So does everybody else. Now, see these smaller ones at the bottom that intersect it? Those are your travel lines, and they're the clearest, deepest travel lines I've ever seen. I could see them when you were barely a toddler. They surprised me so much. Those lines mean you'll have lots of opportunities to travel, especially to places very far away from where you were born. They also mean you'll have a lot of travel luck."

My heart feels like it's spiraling, bursting in a million different directions. My mouth hurts from smiling this big. "That's really what it means?"

She gives my hand a little squeeze. "I saw your future in travel a long time ago. That's why I sent you to Paris when Dad and I were divorcing. You were losing so much of your identity, and I wanted you to get a taste of who you were going to become."

I should be out of tears by now, but I flood up again. Not only does she really see me, she's been supporting me too. All along. And with that realization comes another one. I want that big life out there, but also, I want this. Sitting on a porch next to my mother, the distance between us finally beginning to dissolve.

"I miss you already," I blurt out.

She smiles big now. "I've been preemptively missing you since the day you were born. But you'll carry some of me with you. That's what home actually is, right?" She looks up at the house and sighs. "I never actually left this place. Not really. Maybe that's why I was so scared to come back—I'd have to admit that."

I nod, my throat tight, and she leans forward, gently touching the locket around my neck. "Now back to what you said earlier. What letters did Sage leave?" She says "Sage" with a new tone, one with a little less pain.

I take a deep breath. "She figured out the real story behind the Bell family curse. The witch isn't who you think she is, and what happened to Lily is completely different than everyone thought. Sage told the story through a series of letters. They each had a clue leading to the next one."

My mom's eyes are heavy, and for a moment I'm afraid she's going to shut down again. But then she says, "Of course Sage figured it out. She was always magic that way." She wraps her arms around her knees. "Will you show them to me?"

The last story is ours. You know where to find it. I take a deep breath. "Of course. And actually, I need your help finding the last one."

And still, there remains one story to tell.

This story began, as many stories do, with a girl who bloomed too big for the space the world had carved out for her. Her name was Rosemary.

Rosemary and her sister, Sage, were born to a woman with the soul of a dandelion. She blew into and out of their lives, as unpredictably as the Southern winds. One day, their mother brought them to Salem and left them and their suitcase on the doorstep of the home of their aunt Daisy. It was one of the kindest things she ever did for them.

Rosemary and Sage were different from the girls they went to school with. Instead of a mother who baked cupcakes for the class party, they had a mother who would occasionally call from dusty towns they could never remember the names of, and an aunt who could tell them their future by looking into teacups. Other girls had Rollerblades and dolls; Rosemary and Sage had an old house packed full of family heirlooms. Other girls had birthday parties and ballet classes. They had each other and their next-door neighbor Peter, a painfully shy boy who played with the girls when he was feeling brave and left them bundles of flowers under the willow tree when he wasn't.

It was enough.

One night their aunt Daisy told them about the family curse, and although Rosemary laughed it off, it frightened Sage because a part of herself recognized it. Would she become like her mother, intent on looking for love in places where it couldn't be found?

Their mother showed up only a handful more times, looking more spent and weary with each visit, and by the time the girls were teenagers, they had stopped looking for her silhouette in the driveway, and no longer held their breath when the phone rang.

Aunt Daisy fell ill shortly before the girls graduated from high school, and as Daisy drifted away, Sage felt herself coming apart, piece by piece. She discovered that her fears had been founded, her mother's dandelion soul had taken root in her, and before long she was staying out late every night, drinking and partying, leaving Rosemary to care for their dying aunt all that long year.

The night Daisy died, Rosemary sat alone, her calls to Sage unanswered.

Of course, it was Rosemary who planned the wake. It was a beautiful event held in the gardens, and half the town showed up to talk about Daisy and eat the beautiful quiches and salads Rosemary had spent all day preparing. Sage was sticky and uncomfortable in her funeral dress, and as she tried to sneak away from the party, she stumbled upon a scene that stunned her.

Peter was proposing to Rosemary under the willow tree. And Rosemary was saying no.

Sage managed to duck behind some bushes, and as she listened, the truth slowly unfolded.

Rosemary had spent the year caring for her aunt, yes, but she had also spent the year falling in love with Peter. Now Peter wanted her to come with him to school in New York City so they could begin their life together. He'd marry her today or tomorrow or in fifteen years. It didn't matter. And now that Daisy had passed, she was free.

But Daisy wasn't the only reason Rosemary had stayed in Salem. She had stayed for Sage. All Sage had was her, and she would not leave her sister behind. Peter tried to reason with her, and then argued with her that she deserved her own life. Sage could manage her own mistakes, chart her own course. It wasn't up to

Rosemary to save her. Rosemary repeated herself firmly. Quietly. "I will not leave Sage."

As she listened, Sage's heart grew panicked, then ashamed. All this time she had tried to convince herself that her choices were only impacting herself, when really, they had affected her sister as well.

Peter told her he couldn't ask her again. He couldn't bear to say goodbye to her again. If this was no, she needed to mean it. Rosemary told him that her mind was made up. But as Peter walked away from the willow tree, Rosemary reached for one of its branches, carefully tying a knot in its end. It was a willow love spell, one that asked that one day your love would return when the moment was right. Rosemary did not mean it. But she would not abandon her sister.

Sage snuck back to the house and spent the rest of the night pacing. She knew in her heart she could not transform her dandelion soul overnight. It would take years, and miles, plus maturity she did not yet have. She also knew that her sister would be true to her word; she would never leave Sage, even if it meant sacrificing her own desires.

Rosemary would never leave. But Sage could.

Sage left that night when the moon was fullest. She wanted to tell her sister so very many things, but in the end she could only think of two words to write on the note she left under her sister's bedroom door. "Forgive me."

Sage's road was long and winding after that. She saw many places and met many people, but no matter how many years passed, every time she glanced in the mirror, it was her sister's reflection that looked back at *her. Bit by bit, her soul settled, and she found herself longing for her roots.*

Sage made her way back to Salem, but by then, Rosemary had replicated her sister's actions. She'd vanished without a trace. Sage had no way to find her sister, but she knew the power of intention. Maybe if she re-created the magic of their childhood, her sister would return. The home had been abandoned for years by then, and she spent months digging through the treasures that had occupied their youth. As she did, she found clues, pieces of history that led her to the heart of the family curse. It was about estrangement. Separation. The way to end a curse of separation was to reconcile. If two Bell women were able to fight their way back to each other, the curse would be broken.

Sage grew impatient, particularly after her fortieth birthday, when she learned she likely would never have another one. Sage tried again to find her sister, but Rosemary was hidden, and Sage knew she wouldn't be able to find her until the moment was right. The curse would know when it was time to break.

And so she trusted. And she said goodbye. And when she thought there wasn't much more time, she wrote her letters, and spoke her final words into the night sky, certain they would one day find her sister.

All is as it is. So mote it be, today, tonight, under moon, over sea.

Sage

32

Mason

I'm left staring at the scuffed white door, my brain trying to comprehend what has happened. My mother has closed the door on me. This isn't real. She can't mean this.

My heart surges, rages. I knock on the door, quietly, and then louder. "Mom? Mom!" This has to be a mistake. It is a mistake. She doesn't understand the situation somehow. Then I'm hitting the door with both hands. "Mom! Open the door!"

"You!" The door behind me flies open. It's the old woman again and she's holding up her phone. "Get out of here. Now! I'm calling the cops."

I can barely see; my head is buzzing, my limbs shaking, but I can't be found by the police. My heart drags me forward, away from my mom's door, and then suddenly my stomach lurches. I need out. Now.

Somehow I find my way out of the apartment, my chest heaving, tears pouring down my cheeks. I make it to the curb before I throw up.

And then I start to cry, harder than I ever thought I could. I cry for five-year-old me trying to hold my mom's eyes open to show her a picture I'd made, because all I wanted was for her to be proud of me. I cry for seven-year-old me, who went to bed hungry after eating only condiments all day, because those were the only things that were in the house. I cry for nine-year-old me, sitting in the back of a foster care worker's car, watching my mom get farther and farther away in the back window.

But most of all, I cry for today me. The one sitting on this curb.

All this time my mom has been my destination. My end goal. The thing that kept me going was believing that she was looking for me the way I was looking for her. I thought she was fighting for me, but she was hiding. I showed up at her door, and she wouldn't even let me inside.

Maybe there are such things as signs, but if there are, my mom and I aren't the kind of people who receive them. We're the kind of people who struggle and suffer. Why did I think it could be different? I sit on that curb crying until every last tear is used up, and then because I have nowhere else to go, I start to walk. My feet are heavy, my lungs burning from the exhaust and fumes from passing cars. I cross an overpass, then an intersection, making my way into a run-down park. I have maybe seven hours before it's dark, but then what will I do? Walk the streets all night? Try to find a youth shelter or a secluded area in a park? But what if I get robbed or caught by police? And what will I do tomorrow?

I walk for hours, until my feet are sore and I'm forced to stop at a gas station for water. My head is pounding, and I'm so hungry I can't feel it anymore. But I keep going. What else can I do?

I gulp down my water and immediately wish I had more. Eventually I end up at a playground, a young mom is pushing her baby on a swing, and I must look as terrible as I feel, because when we make eye contact, she quickly looks away. I find a graffiti-covered bench to sit on and open my backpack to look at what I have even though I already know. Twenty-four dollars, some clothes, some books, and a few toiletries.

That's it. That's all I have in the world.

I rifle through my items again, my breath getting more and more shallow, when suddenly I spot something at the bottom of my bag. It's the playbill, the one the girls left on the computer desk for me. They must have put it in my backpack. This time I don't worry about the glitter.

The first page lists the girls in their respective roles as director, choreographer, and "costume person." The next page is an illustration of me, which I know because I'm holding a blue notebook, my hair a black scribble. I'm standing in a ship, three yellow stars dotting the space above me, black crayon filling in the rest. A bubble is coming out of my mouth with the words "ARGG MAYTEES!"

The next page is called "Story of Play." The spelling is terrible, the writing slanting all over the place, but I manage to read it. *Mason the pirate is looking for treasure and he gets lost! But he has a boat and he goes on a ride! Come see the amazing story. Mason sees the stars 1 2 3 and he follows them to the treasure! He will dance a lot and maybe do the splits!*

My body has gone completely still. I read the second to last line again. *Mason sees the stars 1 2 3.*

I flip back to the drawing of me to check the stars, and there they are. One. Two. Three. Exactly like my mom said.

And that's when I actually see the signs.

I see the girls forcing me to rehearse. I see Emma sliding me a hot coffee across the kitchen countertop. I see Simon dragging me on bike rides, and Nova standing in the freezing-cold water, her face earnest as she recites facts about sloths.

And most of all, I see Willow sitting across from me on the roof, and me being able to tell her how I actually feel.

My mom was wrong. Signs don't come in threes. They come in tens. Or hundreds. They come in as many as you need. I didn't have to look for the signs; I'd been swimming in them. I'd been *breathing* them.

The mom with the baby is packing her things up, and she pauses, then slowly rolls the stroller over to me. "Hey, are you okay?" She's younger than I thought, with deep brown skin and large glasses. She looks tired but kind. Exactly like Emma.

I swallow, then shake my head. "No. I need some help."

33

Willow

Watching my mom read Sage's final letter nearly undid me.

Once she read the clue in the last letter Mason and I had found, she'd stood up and walked immediately to the willow tree, reaching into a heart-shaped hollow positioned on the far side of the trunk. Apparently, they'd always left their messages to each other there.

Sage's final letter was in a small weatherproof case. She tried to read it aloud to me, but her voice broke partway through, mascara running all over her face, and I ended up reading the rest.

I'm getting more used to seeing my mom cry.

Afterward, we sit for a long time in silence, our backs to the trunk, listening to the swishing wind move through the willow's branches. My mom's hands are planted on the earth, her eyes closed, and I reach my hand over to link pinkies with her. "Are you okay?"

There's a long silence. "I wish . . . I wish I'd known she was looking for me. You would have loved her."

"I do love her," I say, and she tightens her finger in mine.

I have the letter in my lap and I skim through it again. *The way to end a curse of separation was to reconcile. If two Bell women were able to fight their way back to each other, the curse would be broken.*

Understanding lands on me then, as gentle as a dandelion's parachute. My mom and I are Bell women, which means our reconciliation was enough to break the curse. "Did we end it?"

"Yes," she says quietly. "I think we did."

I reach up and place my hand on the heart-shaped locket, and maybe I imagine it, but a gust of wind picks up, rustling the branches around us in what sounds like ocean waves, and suddenly I have a vivid image in my mind. It's the mermaid, free of her rock and fin, walking purposefully toward the shore, where a red-haired girl waits, arms outstretched. *Thank you, Willow.*

Tears prick my eyes again and I squeeze the locket. *Thank you, Thalia.*

We're quiet for another moment, my mom still lost in thought as I read through the letter again. It's hard to reconcile the fact that this is the last letter I'll read from Sage. Part of me wishes I could keep finding hidden glimpses of her forever. I begin the letter again, pausing at the line about their neighbor. *They had each other and their next-door neighbor Peter, a painfully shy boy who played with the girls when he was feeling brave and left them bundles of flowers under the willow tree when he wasn't.*

"So where's Peter?" I ask.

"California, last I checked." She glances at me guiltily. "After the divorce I looked him up."

It's weird to think of my mom stalking an ex-boyfriend online. "Did you contact him?"

"Absolutely not. That is very past history. Plus, I know I hurt him. I hope he's moved on with his life and that he's very happy."

An image of my mom kneeling at the willow tree suddenly springs to me. "Who were you calling that night at the willow tree?"

"What?" She turns to look at me, her eyes wide in surprise.

"Mason and I were here. On the rooftop. The aunts told me what a knot spell is."

"You were watching?" Her voice is aghast, but she exhales and her shoulders drop a few inches. "It was him. Being here stirred up a lot of old feelings. That first person you love . . . They're pretty special, aren't they?"

She meets my eyes steadily and I realize that she means Mason. I'm not sure if I've fallen in love with Mason yet, but I know that given the chance, I will certainly end up there. What if I don't get that chance? And more importantly, is he okay?

Worry filters through me. "They're going to find him, right?"

"I think so." Then my mom is quiet for a moment before saying, "Would you like to do your own willow knot spell? For Mason?"

I look up at the branches. "How?"

"I'll show you." We both get to our feet. "Choose a branch, whichever one calls to you, then I want you to hold it in your hands and close your eyes."

I obey. My branch is green, its leaves sweeping gracefully downward, and it is light and pliable in my hands. I close my eyes.

"Now picture Mason. Really picture him."

That's easy. I picture him up on the rooftop, the way the candlelight had reflected in his eyes. How his hand had felt on mine.

"Now you ask the willow tree for its magic. Tell it what you want, in your mind or out loud. Then you tie a knot in the branch. You want it to be tight enough that it doesn't come undone, but not so tight that you break it."

I close my eyes, feeling the shelter of the willow tree around me. The words come easily. *Willow tree, please keep him safe. And if it's not too much trouble, please bring him back to me.* I open my eyes and tie the knot carefully; it's easier than I thought it would be. I release it, and stand back.

When I look at my mom, her eyes are soft. "This tree has a good track record."

"Yeah?" I say.

She nods. "All those years ago I asked the tree for love, and it sent me you. That's why I named you after it."

A quietness settles around me then. Mason will be okay. He has to be. "I knew it."

"You knew it." She gestures behind her. "Now let's go inside."

We don't say it explicitly, but at some point, Mom and I make the decision to camp out in the house until we hear from the Morgans. To pass the time, my mom shows me the house room by room, telling me stories about each one. I can't stop thinking about Mason, but I find myself swept into her stories anyway. She shows me the room where she and Sage attempted to secretly hatch a nest of abandoned robin's eggs, and another room with a trunk full of old dresses and gloves and hats that they had spent hours dressing up in. She shows me a secret panel in the library that opens to a small cupboard filled with seashells and sea glass, and the peony bushes that she and Sage had built fairy gardens under. We even read through her Book of Shadows, her telling me the stories behind every spell. Her childhood was painful in many ways, but it had also been filled with magic.

Eventually we end up sprawled on the couches in the front room, me on one, her on the other. Light is filtering in through the high windows, and my mom has the Books of Shadows open on her lap. If it weren't for Mason being gone, this would score in the top ten best afternoons of my life.

But Mason is still missing. No part of me can forget that.

"Did Simon text back?" I ask. Every hour or so my mom texts Simon to see if there is any update.

Her voice is regretful. "He says nothing yet." She holds up her phone. "But the aunts texted. They've been performing candle magic for him, and Poppy says they'll be over soon. She said for me to tell you, 'Don't worry, dearie. He's making his way back to you.'"

"I hope so." I collapse, sinking even more deeply into the sofa. I want to believe Poppy, but I can't stop thinking about the thing Emma said earlier, *Every minute matters right now.* The problem is, the clock refuses to stop ticking.

I need to think about something else. Anything else. I shift on the couch, rolling onto my side so I can see my mom's face.

"So what about the house? Did you accept the offer yet?" The question is forced. With Mason still missing, the house-selling feels like barely a blip on the radar.

"Verbally, yes. But I haven't signed anything." She has her arms tucked behind her head and she looks up at the ceiling thoughtfully. "It feels pretty great here, doesn't it?"

A flicker of hope ignites in my center. "Would you ever consider . . . keeping it?"

She's quiet for a long moment. "I'm not sure how that would work. And the offer was good. Really good. Obviously, things will be delayed on Simon's end because of Mason, but I don't want to lose the buyer."

I think of the buyer looking up excitedly at the house and sigh, sinking even deeper. "You won't. Every time I saw him, he was looking at the house like he couldn't wait to get inside."

"Sorry, what?" She gives a little laugh, but her face is confused. "Who are you talking about?"

"The buyer. He kept hanging out around the house and asking me and Mason questions. He even gave me his card. I obviously didn't tell you because I wasn't supposed to be here in the first place." That was only days ago, but it feels like an actual lifetime.

She sits up. "The buyer's a woman, and she's from out of state. She's been looking for a place to turn into a bed-and-breakfast. She's on her way into town to see it tomorrow. Who did you see?"

"Huh?" I sit up too. "There was a guy, we told him to call Simon. His name was . . . Santo? Sato? Something like that."

"Did you say Sato?" Her voice is calm, but something in her tone makes my gaze swivel toward hers.

"Yeah. Everything okay?"

She's leaning forward now. "Do you still have his card?"

"Maybe in my backpack?" My mom follows me to the door where I left it, and then watches me as I dig through the messy contents. I'm expecting her to give me a lecture on keeping things nice, but when I find the card crumpled at the bottom, all she does is grab it from me. I crowd in next to her to look at it. *J. P. Sato, Real Estate Attorney.*

"I was right. His name's Sato," I say.

"He's an attorney," she says quietly. A blush is creeping down her neck, the same as it does mine, and as I watch her, the pieces are suddenly nudged into place.

I point to the card. "The *P* stands for Peter, doesn't it?"

She can't tear her eyes from the card. "Yeah. That's him."

My heart is fluttering like a hummingbird's wings. "Are you going to call him?"

Right then, her phone chimes, making us both jump. She pulls her phone out of her pocket, and as soon as she sees the screen, her eyes go wide with relief. "It's Simon. They found him."

34

Mason

Emma tells me not to move. Not one muscle, not one finger, not one hair.

The mom at the park is named Deja, and after she talks to Emma, she insists on waiting with me. For several hours, we sit on the bench in the shade, eating baby Andre's Cheerios and yogurt bites as the sun slowly begins to shift from the center of the sky. I'm nervous, but settled too. I don't know what's going to happen next, but I do know that waiting here is the right thing to do.

"You don't have to stay the whole time," I tell Deja.

Andre is staring at me with enormous eyes, and she jiggles him on her knee. "Yes, I do," she says. "Because if Andre ever has hard times, I want someone to be there for him too."

That makes my eyes sting a little. "I'm actually a pretty good kid," I say. "Even though I've made some bad decisions."

"I know. I could tell by looking at you. And all good kids make bad decisions sometimes." Andre makes a gurgling noise and she chucks him under his chin. "You hear that Andre? Every one of you."

Emma must speed the entire way, because she makes it in just under three and a half hours. The minivan comes screeching into

SPELLS FOR LOST THINGS

345

the parking lot, and when she sees us she honks twice.

"This must be her," Deja says.

"Yeah." My heart is beating so hard, I can hear it in my ears. Emma throws open the door and jumps out. She's still wearing pajamas, and she doesn't bother to close the car door.

We meet eyes, and I freeze. How am I going to apologize to her? I don't have time to work it out, because Emma comes flying up to me, pulling me into a crushing hug, and knocking all my words out of me. She's crying, her breathing heavy, and for a moment I'm too stunned to react. This was not the reaction I expected.

She steps back. "Mason. I was so worried. I was so worried." Tears are running down her face, and when she looks me in the eyes, I believe her. This person—this stranger, really—does care about me. The thought pierces straight to my heart.

"I'm okay," I manage.

Next she turns to Deja. "Thank you so much. This means a lot to me that you waited."

"Happy to," Deja says. She smiles at me. "Good luck, Mason."

"Thank you," I manage. Deja buckles Andre into his seat, and they wave to me as they stroll away.

Emotions are crowding up in my center, pushing every thought out of my head. I can't stop looking at Emma. Her response to seeing me is actual light-years away from my mom's, and this is the most emotion I've seen in her ever.

I take a deep breath. "Emma . . ."

But she's pushing a folded piece of paper into my hands. "Mason, sit. I need you to read something."

I look down in confusion. "What is it?"

"Just read it," she says, and I plop down onto the bench. The paper is folded in thirds, and when my hands finally manage to open it, I see that it's a letter. The handwriting is shaky, but I know who it belongs to immediately.

Dear Emma,

Once we promised to do anything for each other, and here I am asking for that anything.

Mason is sixteen. I've failed him for all sixteen of those years. I've been trying to get clean for so long, and I no longer think I can do it. He deserves so much more. Will you please consider being Mason's guardian? He's an incredible boy—thoughtful, kind, smart, patient. Everything I wish I was. You'll love him. I've already called his social worker.

You should hear from her soon.

Naomi

P.S. He loves stargazing.

I almost can't finish the letter, my eyes blur up so badly. Everything about this hurts, actual physical pain radiating from my heart into the rest of my body. *She gave up.* Not only that, but she asked Emma to be my guardian. That's why my mom acted that way today, and why the Morgans had showered me in stars the moment I walked into their house. My mom had told them to.

"Why didn't my foster care worker tell me about this?" I ask.

"Because nothing had been confirmed. Your mom sent me this letter six months ago, but they couldn't find her to determine if she actually wanted to terminate her parental rights," Emma says, and I can see in her face how very sorry she is about this. "The timing was a coincidence. Right after you moved in, they called to tell me your mom had come out of the woodwork and made it official. The plan was to let you adjust for another week or so, and then talk about what was going to happen at your next meeting."

Terminated her parental rights. She's really gone.

I'm holding the letter too tightly now, and giant wracking sobs are heaving their way through my body. I've lost my mom twice in one day. No one should have to endure this.

I don't know how long I cry for, but at some point the storm begins to lessen, and then I realize Emma's hand is on my back, moving in slow circles. She isn't saying anything, but I focus on her hand, the way it's keeping me connected to Earth.

Finally, the storm passes. I'm still aching everywhere, my head clasped in my hands, but I'm breathing. I focus on that, trying to focus on my feet on the ground, my elbows on my knees. The worst has happened, but I'm still here.

I've been quiet for a full minute when Emma speaks. "Mason, I'm so sorry. I should have told you right away. Immediately."

She's right, she should have. But she is apologizing, and regardless of what Emma did or did not do, it doesn't undo what my mom has done. "Why did . . ." My voice breaks and I have to pause before I try again. I hold up the letter. "Why did you say yes?"

She doesn't hesitate. "Because your mom was one of the best friends I ever had. There was a point when I had to end our friendship, but I've never stopped caring about her. The last time I saw her, I told her that if she ever needed help paying for her recovery that I would help. I didn't think she'd take me up on it, but then she got into Night Sky. And then a few months after that, she sent me that letter."

She grabs both my hands now, her thumbs hooking around mine. "Mason, I said yes because of her. But now I'm saying yes because of you." I look up, and her eyes are steady. "We want you with us. We want you in our family. We can adopt you, or you can stay in foster care, it doesn't matter. And I'll fight every bit of bureaucracy and red tape there is to make it happen. But we can only do that if you choose us too."

Something is blooming in my center, growing so fast I can hardly process what is happening.

"Mason, I loved your mom. *Love* your mom." She looks up at me, her eyes red again. "And I'm sorry I've been so aloof. I thought I was prepared, but ever since you walked through our door, I've been processing everything that happened between me and your mom, and it's been so much. I didn't want it to affect you, but of course it has." She drops her gaze, wiping her cheeks. "I want a good relationship with you, Mason, and I'm more than ready to do the work. I'll advocate for you, I'll work through whatever we need to. This isn't going to be easy. I know that." She looks back up, her eyes serious. "But I'm in if you're in."

The words are gentle, but their impact reverberates through my entire body. I know from experience that promises aren't always kept. But right at this moment, a person who doesn't have to love me is telling me she'll be here for me. And I believe her.

I don't have to look for the answer, because it starts forming right in front of my eyes, billowing and compressing, heat building until something brand-new is born.

"Should we go home? Figure it out from there?" Emma asks.

Family isn't something everyone has. I know that. I've spent most of my life without it. And I have no idea what this family will look like in the future, but right at this moment, I know it's meant for me.

"Okay." My voice is hoarse.

"Okay," she repeats, and her voice is equal parts relief and happiness. She stands up. "Now, come on, let's go home."

• • •

I expect Emma to drive me straight home, but she doesn't.

First we stop at a diner for burgers and fries, and I do my best to clean up in the bathroom, changing my clothes and splashing water on my face. I have never had a homecoming before, and the thought of seeing all those faces again terrifies me. I also allow myself a split second to think about Willow. I know she'll be home in LA by now, but maybe when I get home I'll call her and explain, and maybe she'll understand. The thought sends panic racing through me.

One thing at a time.

It starts raining about an hour into our drive, and the gentle hum of the radio combined with pattering rain on the windshield creates the best possible lullaby. Emma tells me I should stretch out in the back, and within minutes I'm fast asleep, my face mashed onto a seat belt, my legs curled into me, someone I trust at the wheel. It may be the best sleep I've ever had.

When I wake up, it's dark and my neck is in terrible shape. I sit up, trying to get my bearings. Emma has stopped the car, and I realize with a start that I'm back in Salem, but instead of being at the Morgans' house, we're on Orange Street.

Every window in the house is lit, several with candles in them, and something about it feels festive. Even the flowers seem colorful in the darkness. I think I see a flash of light up on the rooftop, but maybe I'm imagining it. My chest is constricting in on itself, but I feel a tiny bit of hope. "What are we doing here?"

"You want to see Willow, don't you? Or do you want to wait?"

The hope kindles. I do not want to wait. "She's here?"

Emma turns to look at me, then gestures to the door handle like she already knows what I'm going to do. "She's expecting you. Pick you up in twenty minutes? I'll drive up the street and wait for you."

"Sure," I manage.

My legs are tingly, my entire body self-conscious, but I manage to unfold myself from the car, walking on rubbery legs as I make my way up to the door. How am I going to explain to her everything that happened since I saw her last?

I'm partway up the walk, trying not to hyperventilate, when suddenly a window flies open and there's Marigold's smiling face staring down at me. "Yoo-hoo! Mason!"

I stop, surprise rooting my feet to the walkway. What is Marigold doing here? Soon Poppy and Violet join her in the window, and then all three of them are waving frantically at me.

"Welcome home, our boy!" Violet calls.

"Oh, you gave that girl a scare," Poppy says. My chest tightens again. I would have panicked if Willow had disappeared in the night. What am I going to say to her?

"I'm sorry," I manage.

Marigold points enthusiastically downward toward the door. "Well don't tell *us*. Go ahead and knock, Mason. We'll be watching! We told Willow's mother we'd chaperone." The three of them begin cackling, and I feel myself blushing, Willow-style.

I have to do this with an audience? I look back and realize with horror that Emma hasn't even left yet. I'm surrounded.

I somehow manage to make it to the door, but before I can knock, it flies open, sending light pouring out onto the steps. It's Willow, but like a fairy-tale version of Willow. She's barefoot and wearing a coral-pink dress that somehow makes everything about her more her. More freckles, more pinkish tones to her skin, even her eyes are bigger. I know absolutely nothing about dresses, but I know this one is special—it has a heart-shaped neckline and a full skirt that looks like it comes from another era.

But the thing that stops me dead in my tracks is her *hair*.

It's the first time I've seen Willow's hair down, and looking at it makes me feel like the air has been sucked out of me. It's long and shiny and it cascades down in chaotic waves that somehow seem to encapsulate her entire personality while also stealing every coherent thought I've ever had. Even more surprising is what's woven through her hair, a crown made out of a willow branch interlaced with flowers. I have never, in my entire life, seen anything as beautiful as Willow is right now. And now I'm supposed to talk to her?

"Oh—" I stammer. Emma honks once, then pulls away, while I manage a sort of half wave behind my back.

"What did he say?" Poppy says from overhead.

"I think he said 'Oh,'" Violet says. "Not a great opening line."

This is a category one disaster.

Willow takes another step forward, making it easier to see her face. "You're back."

My heart leaps at that, but her voice is wrong. Plus, she isn't smiling. Does she want me to be back? Emma said she was expecting me, so why does she look so unsure?

Mason, say something. I open my mouth, but words refuse to appear. *Say literally anything.*

"You look—" I stammer again. I almost say *You look like the Andromeda Galaxy.* The galaxy is stunning, with a pinkish hue and trillions of stars, but it's too weird of a comparison, and besides, Andromeda doesn't hold a candle to how beautiful Willow is tonight.

She seems to realize I'm not going to finish my sentence, and she drops her gaze. "Thank you." She hesitates. "The aunts made me a crown. It has something from all the women in my family. It's supposed to make me brave." I can see Willow's flush, even in the darkness. Her neck is suddenly pink.

"I . . ." It's all I can manage. I look down, shuffling my feet a little. *You can do this, Mason.*

There's a great cackling from up above. "He's the one who needs the bravery crown! He's tongue-tied."

Kill me now.

Willow steps forward again, craning her neck upward toward the aunts. "Okay, that's enough. You guys said you were going to give me some space."

"Who said that?" Marigold demands. "I paid for a show."

"There's no show," Willow says, flushing an even deeper pink.

"All right, girls, let them have their moment," Violet says, and then the other two are herded away, the window banging shut behind them.

And now it's the two of us. Me sweating profusely while she blushes profusely. This feels classic us.

Not that there is an us. I'm sure I've ruined my chances of that. Except, maybe she's into second chances?

"Sorry about them," Willow says, not quite meeting my eye. "They were very excited about, ah, this," she says, making a sort of sweeping gesture with her hand. She meets my eye for a split second, then looks away again. "And they had this whole plan. Dress included. I guess they had it made when they were teenagers, and they used to fight over who got to wear it. I couldn't talk them out of it."

"I'm glad," I say, which is possibly the greatest understatement of all time. "You look . . ." Finally the word comes to me. "Stunning."

Her shoulders relax. But she's still way too far away. She moves backward onto the steps, putting us at eye level, which makes me think of the ladder kiss. But I can't think about that now. Not when I have so much to say.

Just start.

"I owe you an apology," I say, pressing my words into the darkness.

"Did you know you were leaving? Last night?" Her eyebrows go up slightly, almost like a dare, and my throat goes dry.

"No! Of course not." Her face is wary. Which is fair. "After we did the spell . . . I went home and an e-mail with my mom's address was waiting for me. The spell worked, I guess." My words are tumbling out now. "I thought I had to find my mom. I'd been looking for her for so long, and I thought she needed me. But I was wrong. When I found my mom . . ." The pain rises up again, fresh and searing. Willow's eyes are softening and I look away. If I'm going to get through this, I need to stay focused. "She's still an addict, and she can't . . ." I hesitate. This is the most opening up I've ever done to anyone. Maybe one day I'll tell her all the details, but not today. "She can't take care of me. I called Emma. I waited for her in a park, and she came and found me."

Willow's eyes are steady on mine, and I pause, collecting myself. "Emma asked me tonight. If I want to stay. Permanently." It feels like I'm talking about something made-up. Can permanent even exist for me?

She leans forward slightly. "Like they'd adopt you?"

I shrug. "I'm not sure yet. I'm going to give that some time. But either way, I want to stay with the Morgans. They're the kind of people who will stick with you, you know? I thought I'd try the whole family thing out. Also . . ." This is the hard part. "I want . . . this."

What I'm trying to say is *I want you*, but that feels too big and my mouth can't form the words. Why is asking for what you want so difficult?

She nods, her face serious. "I was really worried. Really, really worried. We all were."

"I'm so sorry." I take a step toward her, but force myself to stop. "And I'm so sorry that I left without telling you why."

"You could have trusted me," she says.

"I know that."

We stare at each other for a few beats. The smell of sweet tea is rising from the garden, and the katydids seem to be singing their hearts out, and for a split second I allow myself to rest in the now. She might say no. But right at this moment there's still a possibility.

Then she says, "My mom might be keeping the house. She's out tonight, meeting up with an old friend, and um . . ." She hesitates. "We talked about spending the rest of the summer here, and maybe even transferring here for my senior year. My mom is considering taking a sabbatical so we can have a lot of quality time together before I leave for college."

My heart jumps. Soars, really. Is she saying what I think she's saying? Theoretically, this is the greatest news ever, but her face doesn't seem to be matching the marching band in my chest. What does her staying in Salem mean for us?

Is there an us? Reality seizes me then. If her body language is any indication, there might not be.

"That's great," I blurt out. It's great on a lot of levels, not the least of which is the fact that Willow is telling me she may be staying in Salem for an extended period of time. Only a day ago I'd known deep down that this was the beginning of something big, but now that I've broken that trust, that future might be over. That thought grows large and expansive, filling up my chest, and if there was ever any doubt about how I feel about her, that doubt is now completely wiped out. I want to be with Willow. Today, and tomorrow, and for as many days as she wants to be with me after that. Maybe even more importantly

I want *us* to start now. Even if it means getting my heart smashed to smithereens, I have to try.

"Willow?" I take a deep breath. "The other night when we were here. When I kissed you, and when I said that it felt like a beginning? I meant that. I really did."

And there it is. My heart.

A noise that sounds suspiciously like a window being stealthily opened comes from above, but Willow's eyes are on me, so I keep going. "I really, really like you." "Like" feels too little, but if she gives me the chance, there will be time for other, bigger words. "I can tell you everything. You're funny and sweet and beautiful. And literally everything is more fun with you."

Her face is still completely blank. Except, is that a tiny hint of a smile? "What's more fun with me?" she asks.

"Exploring Salem, night tours, sneaking into old houses, stargazing . . ." Am I supposed to keep going? *Making out on ladders. Having dinner with old ladies who apparently love spying.* "Casting spells on rooftops. Searching for clues."

Hope is edging its way toward me. Small but insistent. "Every minute with you is magic." It's a Salem thing to say. But I mean it. Magic is when unseen elements come together to form something brand new, and that's exactly what is happening here.

Her smile is brilliant now, which makes me feel like there's a balloon expanding in my chest. "You're not just saying that because we're in Salem, are you?"

I shake my head hard. "You'd be magic anywhere. In fact, you're going to be magic all over the world." I take a deep breath. "Can we start over?"

Her smile is brighter than anything I've seen in the night sky. "I think we just did."

I hurry toward her, ignoring the ecstatic cheers happening above us. And Willow doesn't hesitate for even a single second. She jumps into my arms, and then her mouth is on mine, and what I'm feeling is bigger than anything I've ever experienced. A star exploding. Atoms reversing themselves.

Gravity.

All is as it is. So mote it be,
today, tonight,
under moon, over sea.

Acknowledgments

All my love and gratitude to: Laurie Liss and the team at Sterling Lord, thank you for being so firmly in my corner. Simon & Schuster Books for Young Readers, in particular—Justin Chanda, Kendra Levin, Nicole Ellul (thank you for the past eight years; my stories wouldn't be what they are without you), Chrissy Noh, Nicole Russo, Lisa Moraleda, Morgan York, Sarah Creech, Tom Daly, Jenica Nasworthy, Katherine Devendorf, Lindsey Ferris, Chava Wolin, Sara Berko, Alyza Lui, and Dorothy Gribbin.

For research help: Carter Cesareo, for telling me about Salem. Carolyn Christensen, for her wonderful and witchy insights. Meg Hastings, for telling me about her experience as a foster parent (I'm ready for the squirrels). Sarah Timms Thompson, for teaching me about the world of event planning. Ali Fife, for the spontaneous night of stargazing. Stacy Smith, for the ghost tour. The staff at The Merchant Salem hotel for their insights. The ghost at The Merchant Salem hotel for not letting me see her (yes, I slept with the lights on for three nights). My coven, for casting spells with me over Zoom and for providing a safe space to speak aloud my very biggest hopes and fears. My readers worldwide for making my writing life so much bigger and better than even a big dreamer could have imagined—I care about you so much!

For general love and support: my family, in particular my wonderful siblings and parents. Sam and Nora, I see and love the people you are. And David (always David), you know what you did.

Finally, thank yo u to nine-year-old Jenna. One day your books are going to connect you to so much love.